Celebra

J(

Phenomenally successful author of more than 200 books with sales of over 100 million copies!

Penny Jordan's novels are read and loved by millions of readers all around the word in many different languages. This beautiful collection of six volumes offers a chance to recapture the pleasure of a special selection of her fabulous stories.

As an extra treat, each volume also includes an introductory letter by a different author. Some of the most popular names in romantic fiction share their personal thoughts and memories, which we hope you will enjoy.

Mediterranean
nights

Three classic Penny novels so evocative you can feel the warmth of the hero's homeland and understand the passionate Latin temperament that drives him in everything he does.

**Mills & Boon® proudly presents
a very special tribute**

PENNY
JORDAN
COLLECTION

DESERT NIGHTS
Available in August 2012

WEDDING NIGHTS
Available in September 2012

MEDITERRANEAN NIGHTS
Available in October 2012

CHRISTMAS NIGHTS
Available in November 2012

PASSIONATE NIGHTS
Available in December 2012

SINFUL NIGHTS
Available in January 2013

PENNY JORDAN
COLLECTION

Mediterranean
nights

Published in Great Britain 2012
Mills & Boon, an imprint of Harlequin (UK) Limited,
Eton House, 18-24 Paradise Road, Richmond, Surrey TW9 1SR

MEDITERRANEAN NIGHTS
© Harlequin Enterprises II B.V./S.à.r.l. 2012

The Mistress Purchase © Penny Jordan 2004
The Demetrios Virgin © Penny Jordan 2001
Marco's Convenient Wife © Penny Jordan 2002

ISBN: 978 0 263 90227 3

028-1012

Harlequin (UK) policy is to use papers that are natural, renewable and recyclable products and made from wood grown in sustainable forests. The logging and manufacturing processes conform to the legal environmental regulations of the country of origin.

Printed and bound
by CPI Group (UK) Ltd, Croydon, CR0 4YY

Dear Reader,

Back in the 1980s, I never missed buying the latest Penny Jordan. I read her novels as escapism. She was, indisputably, one of the great Mills & Boon® authors who kindled my own desire to write romance. She had a magical ability to get under the skin of her characters, adding a depth and quality to her stories that few could equal. Her heroines were so real in their thoughts that they often stopped me in my tracks. Sadly, she is gone now—but the legacy of her many books remains.

Lynne Graham

Penny Jordan is one of Mills & Boon's most popular authors. Sadly Penny died from cancer on 31st December 2011, aged sixty-five. She leaves an outstanding legacy, having sold over a hundred million books around the world. She wrote a total of a hundred and eighty-seven novels for Mills & Boon, including the phenomenally successful *A Perfect Family, To Love, Honour & Betray, The Perfect Sinner* and *Power Play*, which hit the *Sunday Times* and *New York Times* bestseller lists. Loved for her distinctive voice, her success was in part because she continually broke boundaries and evolved her writing to keep up with readers' changing tastes. *Publishers Weekly* said about Jordan: 'Women everywhere will find pieces of themselves in Jordan's characters' and this perhaps explains her enduring appeal.

Although Penny was born in Preston, Lancashire, and spent her childhood there, she moved to Cheshire as a teenager and continued to live there for the rest of her life. Following the death of her husband she moved to the small traditional Cheshire market town on which she based her much-loved Crighton books.

Penny was a member and supporter of the Romantic Novelists' Association and the Romance Writers of America—two organisations dedicated to providing support for both published and yet-to-be published authors. Her significant contribution to women's fiction was recognised in 2011, when the Romantic Novelists' Association presented Penny with a Lifetime Achievement Award.

The Mistress Purchase

PENNY JORDAN

PROLOGUE

'EXCUSE me!' Sadie Roberts grimaced as her plea was
ignored and she had to try to wriggle her way past the
small group of men, all hanging fawningly on the every
word of the man who was addressing them. And what a
man, Sadie acknowledged with a small, irritated female
surge of hostile and unwanted but still undeniably fierce
awareness of him. If maleness was an essence, then this
man possessed a potency that made Sadie's sensitive female receptors twitch warily.

He stood a good four inches above the older man who
stood faithfully by his side, and whilst his voice was cool
and low pitched it had a timbre that made Sadie shiver
sensually, as though a soft, scented velvet glove had been
slowly stroked over her bare skin.

Trapped where she was by the sudden surge of people
trying to move down the narrow tented corridor that led
from one part of the trade fair to another, Sadie wobbled
perilously on her unfamiliar high heels—the shoes, like
the heavy make-up, were her cousin Raoul's idea—and
found herself being inexorably pushed closer to the arrogant stranger. So close, in fact, that she could have put
out her hand and touched him. Not that she had any intention or desire to do such a thing. Had she? Wasn't she
secretly thinking…wanting…? Frantically Sadie made a
grab for her reckless thoughts.

He, the man she was tensing her body into denying its
reaction to, had lifted his hand to look at his watch, its
fingers lean, tanned, the nails neatly cut and clean, but

still very masculine. It was a hand that belonged to a man who was fully capable of dealing competently with any number of manual tasks, whilst the suit he was wearing clearly identified that he was equally capable of writing a cheque to pay someone else to do them!

Oh, yes, he would be very good at writing cheques, Sadie decided. He had that kind of arrogance. A wealthy man's arrogance. It was there in the cool look of hauteur he was slanting over her; a slow, thorough visual inspection that was a disturbing combination of sensuality and slicing assessment.

Another rough push as someone else fought their way through the tightly packed crowd almost sent Sadie straight into him, so that their bodies might have meshed in a shared physical exchange that would sting her blood and stop her breath.

What was the matter with her? Why should she feel so alarmed, so unnerved, so…affected by the knowledge that beneath the cool silk mohair of the immaculate suit he was wearing surely lay a body that was all raw masculinity, solid hard muscle and sinew, all…?

Immediately Sadie froze, pushing away her unwanted and disruptive thoughts.

Irritated with herself and her uncontrollable reaction to him, she seized the opportunity provided by the thinning of the crowd and made herself walk away.

Hot-faced, she hurried back down the corridor in search of her cousin Raoul.

'Come here, Sadie, and let the guys get a whiff of our scent.'

Stony-faced, Sadie turned to face her cousin and co-director.

She was still furious with Raoul for the trick he had

pulled on her this morning, in persuading her to wear the perfume house's current scent. This was a scent created in Raoul's father's time—when he had briefly managed the small family-owned business. And even she was more annoyed with herself, for being gullible enough to fall for it. She should have listened to her own instincts and refused to go along with Raoul's plans the moment she had smelled the appalling concoction which was now offending her own olfactory senses! Instead, she had given in to a bout of sentiment and told herself that she wanted to do everything she possibly could to mend the breach in their family!

She had assumed that she was simply going to accompany Raoul to the trade fair. But Raoul had other ideas! The clothes, the make-up and the 'big' hairstyle he had bullied her into were bad enough, and just not 'her' at all, but she had bitten on her lip and given in—in the interests of cousinly harmony. But, oh, how she wished now she had not done so!

For the last few interminable hours she had been subject to a barrage of leering looks, suggestive remarks and totally unwanted physical intimacies from the would-be male buyers Raoul had persisted in inviting to sample the perfume she was wearing on her skin!

She loathed the scent. It was everything that Sadie detested most about modern synthetic-based perfumes, completely lacking in character and subtlety, with no staying power, and thin and cold where a perfume should be rich and warm, lingering on the senses like good chocolate or a lover's caress. And, even worse, this perfume had a brashness about it, a sexuality—there was really no other word—that Sadie personally found so loathsome that she now actually had a nauseating headache from wearing it!

'That's it. I've had enough. I'm going back to the hotel right now!' Sadie told her cousin grimly, as she evaded the unwelcome attentions of the red-faced overweight buyer who had been trying to nuzzle the side of her throat.

'What's wrong?' Raoul demanded, grinning slyly at her.

'What's wrong?' Sadie took a deep breath.

Eighteen months ago, on the death of her much loved maternal grandmother, Sadie had inherited a thirty per cent shareholding in the small prestigious French perfume house of Francine, which had been in her grandmother's family for several generations, along with the secret recipe for what had been the house's most famous scent.

Her awareness of the rift that had existed between her grandmother and her brother, Sadie's great-uncle and Raoul's grandfather, which had caused her grandmother to distance herself from the business and take no part in it, had initially coloured Sadie's reaction to her inheritance. But Raoul, who owned the remaining shares in the business, had invited her to heal the rift which had developed between the two branches of the family during her grandmother's time and not only take her place on the board but also put her skills as a perfumier to good use and work in the business.

But then she'd had no idea just how far from her own idealistic imaginings and dreams Raoul's plans for the business were!

Raoul, with his shrewd business acumen and lack of sentimentality, seemed determined to use every means he could to promote the perfume house, no matter how unsavoury or out of keeping with the house's history and traditions!

'What's wrong?' Sadie repeated furiously, her wide-set topaz eyes appearing pure gold with emotion. 'Do you really need to ask me that, Raoul? Can't you see how this...this publicity gimmick of yours is cheapening not just me but our perfumes as well? Do you really think that what I have just had to endure will encourage women to buy our scent? That by being pawed over by...by—'

'By the world's most influential megastores' perfume buyers?' Raoul cut in, the humour gone from his voice and his face set.

'I don't care what you say, Raoul,' Sadie told him. 'I'm going back to the hotel!'

Without giving him the opportunity to reopen the argument, she spun round on her heel and headed for the exit.

Initially she had been excited at the prospect of this trade fair, especially when Raoul had informed her that it was to be held in Cannes, which was so close to Grasse, where their great-great-grandfather had first begun his perfume business. But now she couldn't wait to get away and return home to her cottage in Pembrokeshire, over-looking the sea—and to her own burgeoning business, involving perfumes she made to order for a small group of discerning clients who came to her by word of mouth.

No, the world of big business most definitely wasn't for her—and as for the way that Raoul had set her up! Angrily Sadie hurried along the poorly lit tented walk-way, too engrossed in her own thoughts to pay any attention to the small group of besuited businessmen hovering by the exit until one of them stepped in front of her, giving her a look of insolent sexual inspection before addressing his colleagues.

'Come over here and check out Raoul's latest offering, guys,' he invited.

Sadie froze, anger, contempt and disgust all burning into one hot golden fireball in her eyes as she flashed a look of fierce hostility at him. The height she had inherited from her father's family enabled her to meet the man's piggy-eyed leer, but a small quiver of female vulnerability still shuddered protestingly through her body.

The other men were surrounding her like a pack of jackals—not capable of hunting down their own prey, she decided, but all too eager to drag down and feed off someone else's. They were like vultures...

One of the men made a sexually abusive comment about her in French, causing Sadie to lock gazes with him in silent contempt. Thanks to her maternal grandmother, her own French was fluent and comprehensive, but there was no way she was going to lower herself to making any kind of response to what she had just overheard.

Instead she stepped sideways and, keeping her head held high, walked past the group of men, mentally promising herself that she would make sure Raoul knew exactly what she thought of him and his promotional ideas when he later returned to their hotel!

She was almost past the men when one of them suddenly reached out and grabbed hold of her arm.

Sadie was wearing a sleeveless black dress, and the sensation of the man's unwanted touch on her bare skin made her shudder and immediately pull herself free. Not only angry now, but also beginning to feel queasily apprehensive, Sadie kept on walking, her gaze resolutely fixed on the exit.

Which was no doubt why she didn't see the other man who suddenly loomed up at the side of her, having either bypassed or emerged from the leering crowd she had just escaped from.

She might not be able to see him, but she was immediately conscious of him, Sadie acknowledged as the felt the restrictive shadow his presence cast over her. And instinctively she knew! A sharp frisson of awareness shuddered through her, causing her to turn slightly towards him, even though she didn't want to. Her recognition of him was immediate—and shocking. His height and the breadth of his shoulders made her catch her breath, and she could sense too the alien and intensely male quality about him that had stopped her in her tracks earlier that day. Now it caused her to sway a little on her high heels as her body registered things about him that broke through her normal reserve.

She turned back sharply, determined to continue her journey. To her shock he lightly tapped her on the shoulder. Immediately Sadie swung round on her heels to confront him, her tawny gaze suddenly hazing as she realised just how far she had to look up before she could look into his eyes.

Just how tall was he? Six-two...six-three...four? He looked as though he might be Greek, Sadie recognised; he had olive skin colouring and the right kind of arrogantly and openly aristocratic good looks—the sculpted cheekbones; the hawk nose, the clean jawline and the thick jet-black hair. But his eyes weren't a warm, rich brown, they were an icy pale green, and he had a lean fitness about him that was possessed by very few Greek men in their early thirties, which Sadie estimated he must be.

Sadie saw him look at her and then frown slightly, leaning closer to her and very deliberately sniffing the air. The disparaging look he gave her made her whole body burn.

'That's an unusual perfume you're wearing. Is it up

for sale as well?' he demanded, in a voice that was pure soft sensuality with an accent that was equally pure Australian.

Sadie had had enough. In fact she'd had more than enough. Jerking back from him, she hissed bitingly, 'How dare you imply that I am for sale? What is it about men like you?'

'Men like me?' His pale green eyes narrowed icily. 'Well, let's put it this way—when it comes to women like you, then men like me tend to be a bit on the fussy side. I like my women like my perfume. Exclusive!'

He broke off suddenly, turning away from Sadie as the older man at his side touched his arm, and murmured something to him whilst looking at Sadie with distaste.

CHAPTER ONE

"Hubble bubble toil and trouble."

Sadie grinned as she met the teasing look her best friend Mary gave her as she stepped into the workroom where Sadie distilled the ingredients of her perfumes.

'Mmm... What a wonderful smell!' Mary exclaimed enthusiastically.

Sadie's smile widened. 'It's a special personal order I'm doing.'

'For someone famous? Who?' Mary pounced.

Sadie shook her head and laughed.

'You know I can't tell you that. It's a matter of client confidentiality.'

'Mmm...well, since the press got wind of the fact that a certain very, very famous singer has asked you to design a special signature scent for her, I can only assume...'

'Don't ask me any more questions about it,' Sadie begged fervently. Her smile changing to a look of concern. No doubt other people in her position would have welcomed the publicity she had received when it had become public knowledge that she had been asked to design the singer's perfume, but Sadie valued her privacy and her anonymity. And besides...

'I take it that you're still going to France?' Mary asked her.

Sadie's frown deepened.

'I don't have any real choice,' she admitted tersely, 'Raoul is making it impossible for me not to go. He's

13

determined to sell the business to this Greek billionaire who wants to add it to his luxury goods consortium...'

'Leoneadis Stapinopolous, you mean?'

'Yes,' Sadie agreed even more shortly. 'Or the Greek Destroyer, as I call him!'

'Destroyer?' Mary shook her head. 'You really don't like him, do you?'

'I certainly don't like what he's planning to do to Francine!' Sadie told her fiercely.

'Well, by all accounts he's a very shrewd operator,' Mary allowed. 'The consortium he heads is worth billions, and since he took on that new designer to redesign the women's wear side of his acquisitions...well, there isn't a woman going who doesn't secretly yearn for a little something with their label on it.'

'No?' Sadie gave her a grim look. 'Well, I certainly don't.' When she saw her friend's face, she protested, 'Mary, he doesn't just want to buy the perfume house, he wants to buy the rights to the perfume my grandmother left to me as well.... Raoul is trying to pressurise me into selling it, but there is no way I am going to. That perfume was designed by my great-grandfather for my great-grandmother. He only allowed a handful of clients to have the perfume. My grandmother left the secret of its make-up to me because she knew that I would protect it! The whole reason she quarrelled with her brother was because he wanted to do exactly what Raoul wants to do now.'

'So don't go to France, then!' Mary told her forthrightly.

'I have to. I own thirty per cent of the business, and there's no way I'm going to let Raoul sell it to this... this...Greek...'

'Sex god?' Mary supplied helpfully, with a gleam in her eyes.

'Sex god?' Sadie queried disapprovingly.

'Haven't you seen his photo in the financial press?'

When Sadie shook her head Mary grinned.

'Wow, is he something else! His great-grandparents were Greek, and they settled in Australia as a young couple.'

'You seem to know a lot about him,' Sadie challenged her.

'Like I just said, he's a very sexy man—and I'm a sexy-man-hungry woman!' Mary grinned. 'Speaking of which, you are crazy, you know, hiding yourself away down here in Pembroke when you could be living the high life in Paris and Cannes—not to mention flying here, there and everywhere mixing powerfully potent perfumes for your celeb clients. How does Raoul feel about your business, by the way?' she asked.

'Francine no longer makes one-off perfumes to order,' Sadie responded, 'so there is no conflict of interest there. But…'

When she paused, Mary urged her to continue. 'But?'

Sadie gave a small sigh.

'Well, Raoul is pressing me to produce a new perfume. The one he tricked me into wearing at the trade fair was one of his late father's ''mistakes''. Grandmère always said her brother did not have a ''nose'', and her nephew seems to lack one also! Now he wants me to create a new perfume for Francine.'

'But you don't want to?' Mary guessed.

Sadie gave an exasperated sigh.

'I do want to. I want to very much. In fact it would be a dream come true for me to create a new Francine perfume. But…' Sadie lifted her hands expressively.

'As you know, my perfumes come from wholly natural materials, and are made in a traditional way, whereas Raoul favours modern procedures and chemically man-ufactured products. And it's not just that! I just hope that I can persuade him not to go ahead with this sale, Mary. Raoul is the majority shareholder, of course, but we are one of the last few remaining traditional perfume houses, and to sell our birthright for—'

'A mess of pottage?' Mary interrupted obligingly, tongue in cheek.

'I just don't want to sell the business to this Greek billionaire, and I have said as much to Raoul.'

'Mmm. All this talk of potions and lotions reminds me—how about mixing up a little something special and man-attracting for me?'

'I make perfume, not magic potions,' Sadie reminded her sternly.

Mary gave her a wicked look.

'Same thing, isn't it?' Her expression changed when she saw how sombre Sadie was looking. 'Something else is worrying you, isn't it?' she guessed.

Sadie frowned.

'Everything is so complicated, Mary. As it stands now Francine is worth very little in financial terms. The busi-ness is almost all dried up, and the staff are mainly free-lancers. In reality all that is left is the name. And it is the name that this Greek Destroyer wants to buy.'

'Just the name?'

'I don't know! Raoul rang me last night and told me that he has informed Leoneadis Stapinopolous that I am working on a new scent, and that my scent and my skills will be part of the deal. I told him that he had no right to say any such thing. I am a minor shareholder in Francine, that is all. I do not work for the house!'

Angrily Sadie paced the floor.

'Raoul accused me of being deliberately difficult and of not realising what a wonderful opportunity this sale is. But an opportunity for what, Mary? Granted, it will give us both a considerable sum of money—especially Raoul, since he is the majority shareholder. But it will destroy the true essence of Francine and I just cannot agree to that. Never mind create a new scent. Raoul is putting so much pressure on me, though…'

She gave Mary a wry smile. 'If I do what Raoul wants me to do I shall be selling my birthright and my creative soul! Raoul reminded me last night that I was very fortunate to have been left the formula for Francine's most famous perfume by my grandmother. In actual fact he made me feel a little bit guilty about it, Mary.'

'Guilty? You? What on earth have you to feel guilty about?' Mary demanded robustly. 'Sadie, I know strictly speaking it is none of my business, but we have been friends for a long time and I just think that you should perhaps be a little bit cautious where your cousin is concerned,' she added forthrightly.

Sadie smiled in pleasure as she stepped into the foyer of her hotel. She had booked it on the recommendation of a client, who had raved about it to her, and now she could see why!

Although its location in Mougins meant that it was some distance away from Grasse, which was where the tall narrow house which was home to both the business headquarters and her cousin Raoul were situated, Sadie did not mind.

The hotel-cum-spa was the kind of place she loved— it was a positive haven of tranquillity and charm, unlike the glitzy Cannes hotels favoured by Raoul, who had been openly angry and bitter when he had told Sadie how much he resented the fact that the Paris premises the family had once owned were no longer in their possession.

'Why the hell did our great-grandfather choose to sell the Paris house and retain the one in Grasse? When I think what that Paris place would have been worth now!'

Sadie had said nothing. Her own grandmother had told her that the elegant family apartment and shop the family had originally owned in the capital had had to be sold in order to pay off her brother's gambling debts, and Sadie had no desire to reopen old family wounds!

She had booked into her hotel for the whole week, having decided to combine her business meeting with Raoul with visits to the flower-growers in the area from whom she sourced some of her supplies of natural ingredients for the perfumes she made.

As she checked in and signed the visitors' book Sadie hid a small smile as she saw the elegant French woman behind the reception desk sniff discreetly in her direction. The perfume Sadie was wearing was unique, and one she had steadfastly refused to supply to anyone else, no matter how much they pleaded with her to do so.

It was based on the original secret recipe her grandmother had left her, but with a subtle addition that was Sadie's own, which lightened its original heaviness just enough to make sure that it wasn't in any way oppressive and at the same time enhanced and echoed the scent of Sadie's own skin. It was Sadie's own favourite creation, her very personal signature scent, and she knew without false vanity that it was a perfume that—if she had wished to—she could have sold over and over again.

In its bottle the perfume always reminded her of her

grandmother; on her own body it was entirely and uniquely her.

The instructions she was given by the hotel receptionist took her to a low complex of rooms separate from the main building, set close to the adjoining spa block.

Her room itself was everything she had hoped it would be—luxuriously comfortable, elegantly simple and totally peaceful and private.

She had just enough time to unpack and change before she had to make her way to Grasse to meet Raoul, so that they could talk through her objections to his plans to sell the business to Leoneadis Stapinopolous—or the Greek Destroyer. Her mouth curled a little disdainfully as she reflected on the billionaire's motives for wanting to acquire Francine.

He would no doubt have seen that several of his competitors in the high-stratosphere business world they all occupied had already recognised the financial advantages that came with marketing a successful perfume—especially in today's climate, when so many women wanted to follow the example of actresses and models who had expressed their preference not for a modern perfume but instead for one of the rare and exclusive signature perfumes of the traditional perfume houses.

Her disdain changed to a frown, and she paused in the act of pulling on a comfortable pair of jeans. Formal business clothes were not really her thing, and after all this was not a formal business meeting, simply a discussion with her cousin and co-shareholder.

Francine had once produced some of the most coveted scents of its time, but Sadie knew that her grandmother's brother—Raoul's grandfather—had sold off the rights to virtually all of those scents, using the money to finance a series of disastrous business ventures and settle his gambling debts.

Today the only scents of any note Francine still produced were an old-fashioned lavender water and a 'gentleman's' pomade—neither of which, in her opinion, did the name of Francine any favours. For Sadie, the fascination and inspiration of working with old scent was in sourcing the necessary raw materials—some of which were no longer available to modern-day perfume makers, for reasons of ecology and for reasons of economy, in that many of those who grew the flowers needed for their work had switched from traditional to modern methods of doing so.

Sadie considered herself very fortunate in having found a family close to Grasse who not only still grew roses and jasmine for the perfume industry in the old-fashioned labour-intensive way, but who also operated their own traditional distillery. The Lafount family produced rose absolute and jasmine absolute of the highest quality, and Sadie knew she was very privileged to be able to buy her raw materials from them.

Both in their seventies now, Pierre Lafount and his brother Henri actually remembered her own grandmother, and delighted Sadie with their stories of how they could remember seeing her when she had visited the growing fields and the distillery with her own father. The Lafount family's rose and jasmine absolutes were highly sought after, and Sadie knew that it was primarily because of their affection for her grandmother that they allowed her to buy from them in such small quantities.

'Virtually all that we produce is pre-sold under contract to certain long-standing customers,' they had told Sadie—from which she had understood that those customers would be the most famous and respected of the established perfume houses. 'But there is a little to spare and we shall make that available to you,' they had added magnanimously

Raoul, typically, had laughed at Sadie for what he called her sentimentality.

'You're crazy,' he had said to her, shaking his head in disbelief. 'Paying heaven alone knows what for their stuff, when it can be manufactured in a lab at a fraction of the cost.'

'But that is the whole point, Raoul,' Sadie had told him dryly. 'The essence of the scents I want to create cannot be manufactured.'

Raoul had shrugged dismissively. 'Who can tell the difference?'

'I can!' Sadie had answered calmly.

And now apparently Raoul wanted to sell Francine to someone who was as ignorant and uncaring of what real scent was all about as he was. Well, not if she had anything to do with it, he wasn't, Sadie decided stubbornly.

As she went to the parking area to collect her hire car Sadie noticed a frenzy of anxious activity surrounding the presence of a huge Mercedes limousine, with its windows blacked out. But she had too much on her mind to do any more than give both the vehicle and its entourage of anxious attendants a wryly amused glance as she skirted past them.

Spring was quite definitely on the way, Sadie acknowledged as she sniffed the air appreciatively. The scent of mimosa was heavenly!

She knew the way to Grasse almost as well as she knew the history of Francine and although modern motorways and roads had altered things since her grandmother's time, Sadie suspected that just from listening over and over again to her description of the place she could almost have found her away around the town blindfold.

Her grandmother's childhood had been in her own words an idyllic and financially cocooned one; her father had adored and spoiled her, but then war had broken out and everything had changed. Sadie's great-grandfather had died and her grandmother had fled to England with the young English major she had fallen in love with.

The quarrel between her grandmother and her great-uncle had led to a rift which had never been healed, and stubbornly her grandmother had refused to return to Grasse. Maybe she never physically went back, but in her memories, her emotions and her heart she had returned over and over again, Sadie acknowledged as she eased her hire car down the narrow maze of streets crowded with historic buildings. Here and there she could see the now disused chimneys of what had once been the town's thriving perfume distilleries.

Other perfume houses had turned their work into a thriving tourist industry, but Francine remained as it had always done. The tall, narrow house guarding the privacy of a cobbled courtyard which lay behind its now slightly shabby façade, the paint flaking off its old-fashioned shutters and off the ancient solid wooden gates, beyond which lay the courtyard and a collection of outbuildings, linked together with covered galleries and walkways, in which Francine perfumes had traditionally been made.

Had *always* been made! Sadie frowned as she swerved expertly across the path of a battered old Citroen, ignoring the infuriated gestures and horn of its irate driver, swinging her hire car neatly into the single available parking space on the piece of empty land across the road from the house.

If Raoul had his way, and Francine was sold to the Greek Destroyer, then the manufacture of its perfumes would be transferred to a modern venue and produced with synthetic materials, its remaining few permanent elderly employees summarily retired and their skills lost.

Hélène, Raoul's ancient and unfriendly housekeeper, opened the door to Sadie's knock, her face set in its normal expression of dour misanthropy.

The few brave beams of sunlight which had managed to force their way through the grimy narrow windows highlighted golden squares of dust on the old-fashioned furniture in the stone-floored entrance hall. It made Sadie's artistic soul ache not just to see the neglect, but also the wasted opportunity to create something beautiful in this old and unloved historic house.

The rear door that opened out into the courtyard was half open, and through it Sadie could see the cobbled yard and hear the tinkle of water falling from a small fountain into the shallow stone basin beneath it. A lavender-flowered wisteria clothed the back wall of the courtyard, and a thin tabby cat lay washing its paws beneath it in a patch of warm sunshine.

Instinctively Sadie hesitated, drawn to the courtyard and its history, the memories it held of her ancestors and their creations. Its air—unlike that of the house, which smelled of dust and neglect—held a heady fusion of everything that Sadie loved best.

Hélène was growing impatient and glowering at her.

Reluctantly Sadie turned away from the courtyard and headed for the stairs that led up to the house's living quarters and Raoul's 'office'.

Hélène, who protected her employer as devotedly as any guard dog, preceded Sadie up the stairs, giving her a final suspicious look before pushing open the door.

Ready for the battle she knew was about to commence, Sadie took a deep breath and stepped firmly into the room, beginning calmly, 'Raoul, I am not—'

Abruptly she stopped in mid-sentence, her eyes widening, betraying her, as shock coursed through her, scattering her carefully assembled thoughts like a small whirlwind.

There, right in front of her, standing framed in the window of Raoul's office, was…was…

CHAPTER TWO

SADIE gulped and struggled to regain her equilibrium and self-control, but those perma frost eyes were trapping her in an invisible web of subtle power.

His gaze made her feel dizzy, disorientated, helplessly enmeshed in sensations and emotions that terrified her into fierce, self-protective and angry hostility. And yet at the same time beneath all those feelings lay another, stronger, and darker one too. A rush of instinctive awareness of her vulnerability towards him as a man who, at the deepest most intense level of herself, she was responsive to.

She could feel her body quickening like mercury just because he was there, her every single sense reacting not just to the sight of him but to everything else as well, including his scent, male, potent and dangerous, prickling her sensitive nose, making her want to both breathe in the essence of him and yet at the same time close herself off from it and from him. Instinctively Sadie tensed against what she was experiencing, her eyes liquid gold with the intensity of her feelings.

She gave a small inward shudder.

'I warned you, didn't I, Leon, that my cousin doesn't exactly present a businesslike image?' Sadie could hear Raoul saying.

Leon? Leoneadis Stapinopolous? The Greek Destroyer? Silver spears of hostility and wariness glinted in the gold of Sadie's gaze as she stared at him.

'Miss Roberts.' A brief inclination of his head, an

Olympian acknowledgement of her presence which matched the unimpressed Australian scorch of his voice.

'Okay, Sadie, now that you're here let's get down to business. Leon doesn't have much time,' Raoul breezed on.

So he had no time and too much money. It was a dangerously volatile combination—much like the man himself, Sadie reflected inwardly. He hadn't, she noticed, made any attempt to shake hands with her, for which she was mightily thankful, as the last thing she wanted or needed right now was any kind of physical contact with him.

He had made no indication of having recognised her from the trade fair. Perhaps he had not done so. Maybe, unlike her, he had not suffered that feral surge of instant recognition. Maybe? There was no maybe about it! He was a man who was armoured against any kind of emotional vulnerability!

As Raoul started to talk expansively about the benefits which would accrue to them all on Leon's acquisition of Francine Sadie had to force herself to focus on what he was saying. Deliberately she started to turn away from Leon to face her cousin, hoping that by doing so she could lessen the almost mesmerising effect Leon's presence was having on her.

She spun round on her heel and a flurry of dust motes danced around her. Out of the corner of her eye she just caught the swift movement Leon made as he stepped towards her, his fingers curling round her upper arm, shackling her. She could feel the pulse throbbing at the base of her throat, driven by the acute intensity of the sensations bombarding her—the cool, steely grip of his hand on her arm, the sleek suppleness of his fingers, hard and strong, the dry, controlled warmth of his flesh, the steadiness of the surge of his blood in his veins as her own pounding heartbeat went wild.

Instinctively Sadie's head snapped round. Her eyes were on a level with his throat. A drenching surge of hot female awareness roared over her, swamping her. She wasn't used to feeling like this, reacting like this, wanting like this, she acknowledged shakily.

Wanting... How could she want him? He was a stranger, her enemy, representative of everything she disliked and despised.

He was leaning towards her, his cold gaze releasing her as his eyelids came down, shuttering his eyes away from her as his head slanted towards her throat.

It was impossible for her to stop the fierce tremor that raced through her as she felt the warmth of his breath against her skin

'Well, at least the scent you are wearing today is a great improvement on whatever it was you were touting at the trade fair.'

His hold on her upper arm slackened the imprisoning bracelet of hard male flesh, his hand sliding smoothly down to her wrist and then holding it whilst the soft pad of his thumb pressed deliberately against her frantically jumping pulse. The shuttered lids lifted. Shockingly, the ice had melted and turned into a shimmering blinding heat that sent her heartbeat into overdrive.

'What is it?'

What was it? Didn't he know? Couldn't he tell?

'It's obviously a very highly marketable scent, and...'

Scent; he was talking about her perfume! *Her* perfume, Sadie reminded herself savagely as she pulled herself free and stepped back from him.

'Pity you didn't choose to wear it at the trade fair. What you did wear—'

'Was Raoul's father's creation and had nothing to do with me,' Sadie snapped sharply, quickly defending her own professional status. 'I didn't even want to wear it!'

'I should hope not,' Leon agreed suavely. 'Not with your reputation.' He gave her a silkily intimidating look. 'One of the reasons we are prepared to pay so generously for Francine is, as I am sure you must know, so that we can secure the combination of its old recipes and your perfumery skills. We want to bring to the market a new perfume under the Francine name which...'

The briskness of his manner snapped Sadie back to reality. This man was her enemy—bent on destroying everything she held dear professionally—and she had better keep that thought right to the forefront of her mind! Accusingly she looked at Raoul.

'Raoul, I think—' she began.

Raoul stopped her, smiling fawningly at the other man. 'Leon, Sadie is as excited about your plans for Francine as I am myself—'

'No, I am not,' Sadie interrupted him sharply. 'You know my views on this subject, Raoul,' she reminded her cousin. 'And you assured me that we would have time to talk in private today, before we met with...with anyone else!'

What was the matter with her? Why was she finding it so hard to so much as say his name without betraying the effect he was having on her?

'Raoul may know your opinions,' Leon cut in smoothly, 'but since I do not, perhaps you would be good enough to run them past me.'

'Sadie—' Raoul began warningly, but Sadie had no intention of listening to him, and refused to be intimidated by the challenge she could see gleaming dangerously in Leon's eyes.

Leon was no longer the man whose presence had swamped her female defences, the man who had somehow reached out to her and touched her senses and her emotions at their most primeval level. Instead he was the man who was threatening everything that mattered most to her. And there was no way that Sadie would break the mental promise she had made to her grandmother that she would cherish and protect the inheritance she had passed on to her in every way that she could.

Turning to confront Leon, Sadie began as calmly as she could. 'I may only be a minority shareholder in the business, but I do own one-third of the shares.'

'And I own two-thirds, 'Raoul reminded her angrily. 'If I want to sell the business to Leon, then as the majority shareholder—'

'The business maybe, Raoul.' Sadie stopped him, her face beginning to turn pink with the force of her emotions. 'But—'

'I am not really interested in which one of you has the majority shareholding in the business,' Leon cut in grimly. 'What I and my shareholders are interested in is the reintroduction of Francine's most famous scent and the addition of an equally successful new creation! Using modern production methods—'

'I will never create a perfume made in such a way!' Sadie told him passionately. 'To me, synthetic scents are an abhorrence. They are a mockery of everything a true scent should be. A great fragrance can only be made from natural ingredients. It does not just reflect its origins, it also reflects and highlights the…certain essential properties of its wearer…'

'Certain properties?' The dark eyebrows rose mockingly. 'You mean it reflects and highlights a woman's sensuality?'

To her disgust, Sadie realised that she was actually blushing!

'Sadie, you are totally out of step with what's happening today in the perfume business,' Raoul objected angrily.

'No, Raoul,' Sadie argued back, glad to have an excuse to turn away from Leon and focus on her cousin instead. 'You are the one who is out of step. The mass perfume market may still be governed by chemically produced products, but at the top end of the market there is an increasing demand for traditionally produced perfumes. If either of you two had done your homework you would both know this,' Sadie told them fiercely. 'And the fact that you do not know it, the fact that you have not done your homework, makes me have very serious doubts about the ultimate success of any new product you might launch.'

Whilst Raoul was beginning to bluster an angry protest, it was Leon's reaction that interested her more, Sadie acknowledged. His mouth had tightened into a hard line and he was frowning at her.

'Mass-market perfume is big business,' he told her harshly. 'The production of a perfume which can only be afforded by a few élite buyers does not interest me.'

'Well, it should,' Sadie countered. 'Because it is the scent worn by the élite buyers that the mass-market buyers most want to wear themselves. And why shouldn't they aspire to do so? Why should they be fobbed off with a synthetic substitute that is never going to come anywhere near equating to the real thing?'

'Perhaps because the synthetic substitute is affordable and the real thing is not,' Leon told her pungently.

'You say that, but it could be!' Sadie claimed immediately. 'It is perfectly feasible for high-quality natural perfumes to be made at a reasonable cost. But of course the profit margin on them would be much smaller, and that is the real reason why big business like you refuse to produce them. Because profit is all that matters to you. You and men like you are as…as soulless as…as…synthetic perfume!' Sadie told him passionately.

'Is that a fact?'

The silky tone of Leon's voice made Sadie quiver inwardly with wariness, but she refused to heed her body's own protective warning, eyeing Leon defiantly.

'Well, you, of course, would be in a perfect position to judge me, wouldn't you? Having met me how often? Twice?'

'Three times,' Sadie corrected him, and then felt her body burn with self-conscious heat as he looked thoughtfully at her.

'Three times?'

'How many times I've seen you is an irrelevance.' Sadie overrode him.

'The world's opinion of the status of the corporation you run and its aims and beliefs are written about publicly and frequently in the financial press, and—'

'The financial press?' Leon stopped her. 'They report company and corporation policy. They do not make it,' he told her acidly.

'I don't care what you say,' Sadie protested emotionally. 'Raoul already knows my views on his plans to sell Francine to you—against my wishes. In fact I came here hoping that I might be able to dissuade him, but I can see that there is no hope of that! I cannot stop him from selling to you, since he is the majority shareholder, but there is no way that I would ever—ever…prostitute my…my gift of a good "nose" for perfume by selling that to you!'

Abruptly Sadie realised how silent both men had become. Raoul was looking angry and embarrassed, whilst Leon…

The chill was back in his green eyes, but strangely now there was a glow beneath it, a glitter like the beginning of the Northern lights on ice, all white fire shimmer and danger, a warning of a strength and a power that secretly she already felt vulnerably in awe of.

Which was all the more reason why she should not give in to him, Sadie told herself militantly.

'Stirring words. Pity they don't seem to have been matched by your actions!'

Leon's cool words were every bit as chillingly dangerous as the look he had given her. Outraged, Sadie turned to look to Raoul for support, but her cousin was out of earshot on the other side of the room, searching through some papers on his desk.

Leaning closer to her, Leon continued with steely venom, 'When I saw you at the trade fair it was quite obvious that you were—'

'That was Raoul's idea,' Sadie protested defensively.

'Raoul's idea, Francine's perfume—and your body. As a matter of interest, what kind of response, other than the obvious, did that cheap sideshow you were putting on generate? I am, of course, asking about the amount of sales it generated, and not the number of offers you received for your body!'

Sadie glared at him.

'How dare you say that? I had no idea that men would assume I was also available.' Her mouth compressed with anger whilst her face burned hotly with sharply remembered shame.

'No idea?' The contempt in his eyes left her sensitivities burned raw. 'Oh, come on. You can't expect me to believe that! You paraded yourself openly and deliberately, wearing—'

Sadie had had enough.

'I was perfectly respectably dressed, and if I'd had any idea that what I had assumed to be a collection of professional businessmen would behave like...like a pack of...of...animals, I would never, ever have allowed Raoul to persuade me into helping him.'

How could her cousin even think of selling Francine to this man? To this...this monster?

With a change of tack so swift and unexpected that it caught her totally off guard, Leon demanded, 'That scent you're wearing today—what is it?'

Immediately Sadie tilted her chin and eyed him defiantly.

'It's a perfume of my own.'

'I like it,' Leon told her crisply. 'Indeed, I should have thought that it would be a highly marketable addition to the Francine name. In fact, I am surprised that you are not already marketing it!'

Anger flashed in Sadie's eyes, turning them as brilliant a gold as the sun streaming in through the dusty windows.

'This scent was created by me for my own personal use.'

'It's an original formula of your own devising?'

Sadie frowned. Why was he asking her so many questions? He was beginning to seriously annoy her!

'Not exactly,' she admitted haughtily. 'It's actually based on a one-time famous Francine perfume called Myrrh.'

Sadie stopped speaking as the dark eyebrows snapped together and she was treated to a frowning look.

'Myrrh...I see!'

In the warning-packed silence that followed Sadie could feel her nerve-ends tightening.

'Aren't I right in thinking that that was Francine's most exclusive and successful scent?' Leon asked smoothly.

Now it was Sadie's turn to frown.

'Yes, it was,' she acknowledged. 'You have done your research well,' she admitted, unable to resist adding a little acidly, 'Or rather someone has.'

No doubt a man like him paid other people to provide him with whatever information he needed! He could certainly afford to do so, after all!

'You say that the scent you are wearing is based on Francine's Myrrh? I am surprised that you allowed Sadie to tamper with something so valuable and irreplaceable, Raoul,' he announced to Raoul, looking over Sadie's head towards her cousin.

Infuriated as much by his manner as his words, it gave Sadie a great deal of satisfaction to tell him coldly, 'Actually, Raoul has no power to "allow" anyone to do a thing with the original Myrrh formula, since her father left it to my grandmother and she left it to me! A fact which I'm sure Raoul intended to share with you in the near future.'

Sadie saw immediately that Leon had not been told that she owned the Myrrh formula. He looked at her, his mouth thinning, before turning and demanding, 'So you own one-third of Francine and the Myrrh formula?'

'Yes,' Sadie confirmed emphatically, with a great deal of satisfaction.

'This is a matter I shall need to discuss with my lawyers. The Myrrh name, in my opinion, belongs to Francine, and—'

'And the Myrrh scent belongs to me,' Sadie informed him angrily. 'If you think that you are going to browbeat and bully me with threats of lawyers, then let me tell you that you cannot. I'm going, Raoul,' she told her cousin shortly. 'I've wasted enough time here!'

'Sadie—' Raoul began to protest, but Sadie ignored him, crossing the room and pulling open the heavy door.

Her visit, Sadie acknowledged bitterly as she got back to her car, had been a complete waste—not just of her time, but more importantly of her hope and her desire to some-how persuade Raoul not to sell the business.

She attempted to soothe her spirits and her senses by walking through the old town, along the narrow streets that wound between wonderful old seventeenth- and eighteenth-century buildings, pausing to glance in shop windows before stepping out of the sunlight into the shadows until she had finally made her leisurely way to the principal square at the top of the old town.

The Place aux Aires housed a daily market of fresh flowers and regional foods. However, it was so late in the day that the flowers and food had all been sold by now, and the stallholders were packing up for the day. She decided to find a café in the arcade that lined one long side of the square and drink a cup of coffee whilst she admired the pretty three-tiered fountain which graced the square.

Down below where she had parked she could see the empty shell of one of the town's old distilleries, neglected and unused now, in these modern times—thanks to men like Leon! Before getting into her car something made her stop and look up towards the window to Raoul's of-fice.

Her whole body stiffened as she saw Leon standing there, looking down at her.

Angrily she held his gaze, determined not to be the

first one to look away, her concentration only broken when another driver, anxious for her to vacate her parking spot, beeped his horn to attract her attention.

In the dusty silence of the room the two men looked at one another.

'Look, Leon,' Raoul began breezily, 'I know what you must be thinking, but I promise you that everything will be fine. I'll talk to her. She'll come round. You'll see. Of course it would help if you were a bit more, well…friendly towards her! The woman hasn't been born who doesn't respond to a bit of coaxing and flattery,' Raoul told him.

Silently Leon studied him before saying gently, 'Friendly? Well, I assume that you know your cousin far better than I do, Raoul. Although I wouldn't have thought…'

'Oh, Sadie is okay.' Raoul gave a small shrug. 'Of course, she's had her own way all her life—been spoiled and indulged. Her grandmother saw to that! She married into a wealthy English family.'

He gave another dismissive shrug, neglecting to add that that wealth had been lost long before Sadie's birth!

'There's nothing to worry about, Leon,' Raoul continued confidently. 'Sadie's a bit naïve. She gets all fired up and on her high horse, all moralistic at times, that's all. I put it down to the fact that she was virtually brought up by her grandmother! Sadie's a bit old-fashioned, if you know what I mean, but I can soon talk her round! She's just not had much to do with men, of course— thanks to her grandmother.'

'Oh, yes, that would explain it,' Leon murmured suavely, but Raoul was oblivious to his sarcasm.

'Leave everything to me, Leon!' he continued arrogantly.

Leon frowned. It was becoming increasingly obvious to him that Sadie was in a very vulnerable position where Raoul and the business were concerned. Had she been a member of *his* family... But of course she was not, and there was no way he could afford to let his Greek ancestry urge him into the self-elected role of protective paterfamilias towards her! Indeed, there was no reason why he should concern himself about her in any way—not after the open hostility she had shown him!

His frown deepened. Hostility wasn't something Leon was used to women exhibiting towards him. Quite the opposite. There had never been a woman he had needed to pursue, and he certainly wasn't going to start chasing one who had made it plain that she didn't want him! Of course he wasn't! No, all he felt was pique and chagrin; these were emotions so unimportant that he wasn't even going to bother acknowledging them, never mind responding to them!

What *was* important—almost vital—was securing the acquisition of Francine. Leon had understood from Raoul when they had first discussed the matter that in acquiring Francine he would also be acquiring its existing scent formulae, including that for Myrrh, and the perfume-creating skills of Sadie herself. Now it seemed that Raoul had not been entirely honest with him.

'Everything will be fine, Leon. I promise you,' Raoul repeated insistently. 'All we need to do is convince Sadie that you'll let her use her precious natural ingredients and she'll be eating out of your hand and begging you to let her concoct a new perfume for you.'

'I'm afraid that isn't an option, Raoul. The cost alone of simply acquiring natural raw products would give my board a collective heart attack! It just isn't commercially viable to produce a mass-market scent by traditional methods.'

'Well, maybe not. But you don't have to tell her that, do you?' Raoul challenged him.

'Are you suggesting that I should deliberately lie to her?'

'You want the Myrrh formula and you want her to work for you, don't you?' Raoul asked him shrewdly.

Leon looked away from him briefly before demanding curtly, 'Raoul, why wasn't I informed about your cousin's views—and, more specifically, that she owned the formula for Myrrh?'

Raoul gave a dismissive shrug

'I didn't think it was that important. You only asked me for a list of the perfumes my father had sold off. Anyway, like you, I am sure you could prove that legally the formula really belongs to the business. After all, a man with your resources can afford the very best of lawyers—lawyers who can prove anything. Sadie hasn't the money to take you on in court, but of course it will save you a lot of fuss if she gives in and hands it over to you—and I promise you that if you play it my way she will!'

'You seem remarkably unconcerned about your cousin, if I may say so,' Leon commented dryly.

Carelessly, and without any trace of embarrassment, Raoul told him, 'Certainly I am not as concerned for her as I am for myself. Why should I be? We've only been in contact for the last few months. I need to sell Francine, Leon. If not to you then to someone else. And there is no way I am going to let Sadie or anyone else interfere with that.'

'I think I'd prefer to speak with your cousin myself,'

Leon announced coolly, adding warningly, 'It's true that I want Sadie's expertise, and that I want the Myrrh formula, but there's no way I would agree to her being deceived about my future plans for the business. I'm afraid that in my book honesty can never be sacrificed for expediency!'

Initially, when he had seen Sadie at the trade fair, Leon had assumed that she was made much in the same mould as her cousin. But now he wasn't nearly so sure.

But he could not afford the luxury of sympathy, Leon warned himself, and unless he had misjudged her Sadie would certainly not welcome receiving it from him.

Raoul gave a careless shrug.

'Fine—if that's what you want to do. After all, you're going to be the boss!'

Going to be, but was not as yet, Raoul reminded himself angrily after Leon had gone.

There was no way he was going to allow Sadie to mess up this deal for him, and no way he was going to risk leaving it to Leon to persuade his cousin to change her mind. Not when Raoul knew that he could do so much more easily and quickly.

In the privacy of his elegant hotel suite, Leon completed the telephone conversation he had been having with his chief executive in Sydney and then went to stand in front of the large window that opened out onto his private balcony.

Sadie's ownership of the Myrrh formula was a complication he had not anticipated, as was Sadie herself. But he had no intention of using Raoul's suggested underhand tactics to rectify it! Underhandedness and deceit were weapons of engagement that were never employed in the Stapinopolous business empire—even though once they had been used against it to devastating and almost totally destructive effect.

Leon's expression hardened. Those dark years when his family had almost lost the business were behind them now, but they had left their mark on him. However, right now it wasn't the past he was thinking about so much as...

A little grimly Leon acknowledged that he wasn't sure which had distracted him the most—the tantalising length of Sadie's slim legs encased in the jeans she had been wearing, or the intensity with which her eyes had reflected her every emotion.

She was, he decided grimly, impossibly stubborn, fiercely passionate and hopelessly idealistic. She was a go-it-aloner, a renegade from the conventional business and profit-focused world of modern perfumes. She was, in short, trouble every which way there was. A zealot, a would-be prophet, intent on stirring up all kinds of disorder and destined to cause chaos!

She would make his board of directors shake in their corporate shoes and question his financial judgement for even thinking about wanting to get involved in a business in which she played even the smallest part.

Did she really believe that it was feasible to produce what amounted to a handmade scent in the quantities needed to satisfy a mass-market appetite at an affordable price, using old-fashioned methods and natural raw materials?

He was already facing opposition from some members of his board over his plans to acquire Francine—but it was an opposition he fully intended to quash! An opposition he *had* to quash if he was not to find himself in danger of being voted off his own board!

'Why Francine?' one of his co-directors had demanded

belligerently. 'Hell, Leon, there are dozens of other perfume houses in far better financial condition, with more
assets, and—'

'It is precisely because Francine is Francine that I want
it,' Leon had countered coolly. 'The name has a certain
resonance. An allure. And because of its current run-
down state we can acquire it at a reasonable cost and
build up a completely new profile for it. The new
Francine perfume, when it comes on the market, is going
to be *the* perfume to wear.'

'The new Francine perfume?' one of the others had
questioned. 'Hell, Leon, if there's to be a new perfume
why buy the damned outfit at all? Why not just get some
chemist to come up with a new perfume for us and get
some actress or model to front it for us? That's what
everyone else is doing.'

'Which is exactly why it is not going to be what we
shall do,' Leon had responded briskly.

He was taking a very big gamble. He knew that. For
every classic fragrance there were a hundred perfumes
that had been forgotten, buried in obscurity. Leon wasn't
a fool. He knew that he had his detractors and his ene-
mies in the shark-infested waters of the business world
in which he lived; he knew too that there were also those
who were simply plain jealous of his success. And all of
them, whatever their motivation, would enjoy seeing him
fail and fall.

Launching a new perfume was always a risk, even for
a well-established perfume house with a stable of existing
popular products. All Francine had was a name and a
couple of old-fashioned formulae.

A couple, but not Myrrh, it now seemed.

Broodingly, Leon turned his back on the view. On the
bedside table amongst his personal possessions was a

small framed photograph. Going over to it, he picked it up and studied the delicately pretty feminine features of its subject, a sombre expression darkening his eyes.

The Sadies of this world didn't really know what life was all about. Handed a silver spoon at birth, they could take what they wanted from life as a right.

Was she really oblivious to the fact that only a small handful of women could afford the luxury of the kind of scents she blended? Or did she simply not care?

Well, he cared. He cared one hell of a lot—as she was about to discover!

As she drove past the flower fields belonging to Pierre, Sadie exhaled a deep breath of pleasure and satisfaction. Pleasure because both the sight and the scent of growing flowers always lifted her spirits, and satisfaction because she had the power to prevent the Greek Destroyer from wrecking the precious heritage her grandmother had passed on to her.

Pierre and his brother grew both jasmine and roses. A swift, delicate-fingered person could pick half a kilo of the jasmine blossoms in an hour, and the picked blossoms sold at a hefty price—as Sadie had good cause to know. The delicacy of the jasmine flower meant that it required year-round care by humans rather than machines. And in the rose fields stood the precious, wonderful Rose de Mai, from which the rose absolute which Sadie used in her perfumes was made.

Pierre and his wife Jeannette came hurrying out to the car to welcome Sadie, embracing her affectionately.

'So Francine is to be sold and soon you will be creating a fine new perfume for the new owners? That is excellent news. A talent such as yours should be recognised and allowed to truly shine. I am already looking forward to saying that I know the creator of the next classic scent,' Pierre announced teasingly, once Sadie was seated at the scrubbed kitchen table, drinking the coffee Jeannette had made for her.

Sadie frowned as she listened to him. She had expected Pierre to share her own feelings towards the sale of the business, instead of which he was making it plain that he thought it was an excellent opportunity for her.

'It is true that Leon…he…the would-be owner does wish me to create a new perfume—but, Pierre, he is only interested in mass-market perfumes made out of chemical ingredients,' Sadie objected.

Pierre shrugged. 'He is a businessman, as we all must be these days, and perhaps not totally *au fait* with the complexities of our business. He does not have your knowledge perhaps, *petite*. Therefore it is up to you, in the name and memory of your *grandmère*, to help him,' Pierre pronounced sagely.

'Help him!' Sadie's voice was a squeak of female outrage. 'I would rather—' she began, and then stopped as Pierre overrode her.

'But you must do so,' he said calmly. 'For if people like yourself do not give their knowledge and their expertise to those who are coming new into the business then how are we to go on? This is a wonderful opportunity for you Sadie!' Pierre repeated emphatically.

'It is?' Sadie stared at him whilst Pierre nodded his head in vigorous confirmation.

'Indeed it is, and your grandmother would be the first to say so if she were here. Ah, I can remember hearing her tell her father that she longed for the House of Francine to produce a new perfume—a fragrance which would rival that of the most famous perfumery.'

'You heard her say that?' Sadie swallowed the emotional lump which was suddenly blocking her throat. She had loved her grandmother so much, and she knew how much Francine had meant to her.

'You are indeed fortunate to have been given such an opportunity,' Pierre was telling her.

'I am?' Sadie struggled to marshal all the objections she had had no difficulty in hurling at Leon's head. 'But I prefer to work on a one-to-one basis with my clients,' she managed to point out.

'Pff...' Pierre gave a Gallic thrust of his shoulders. 'Filmstars and the like—they come and go and are as changeable and fickle as a mistral wind! They would quite happily take your perfume and claim it as their own creation if it suited them, and just as easily turn to someone else.'

A little reluctantly Sadie was forced to acknowledge that what he was saying had a grain of truth to it. Right now her own perfumes were very popular, but that could all change overnight. And if it did...

She frowned. What was she trying to tell herself? Surely she wasn't actually going to give in—to sell out—let Leon walk all over her?

But what if Pierre was right? What if she could create a wonderful new perfume—so wonderful and so popular that the whole world would want to wear it?

Sadie began to feel slightly dizzy, almost drugged with her own surging excitement, with the thought of fulfilling her grandmother's unexpectedly revealed dream.

But Sadie was no fool. She knew perfectly well that it was impossible to mass-produce a perfume created only out of natural ingredients, which meant...

'I can't do it, Pierre,' she told him, shaking her head. 'You know how I feel about synthetic scents.'

Pierre nodded. 'Indeed, we all feel the same, but these

are modern times and it is impossible to mass-produce a
scent from natural materials alone. There has to be a
compromise... But think of what a triumph it would be
were you to create one based on a perfect combination
of old and new, natural and synthetic.'

'No one has ever managed to do that,' Sadie objected.

'Until now,' Pierre told her slyly.

Giddily Sadie tried to clear her head.

'Do you really think that I can do it?' she asked Pierre
shakily.

'Of a certainty! If not you, then who else? You have
the history and the knowledge, the experience, the tenderness, the understanding...You have a gift and, like a
truly exceptional perfume, it is only waiting to be released in order to charm everyone who experiences it!'

Sadie stared at him in bemusement. She felt as though
she was riding a rollercoaster of emotions and thoughts.
Could she do it? Could she create a perfume to rival that
of the very greatest of houses?

She could almost see it in her mind's eye. She would
call her perfume Francine.... It would have a similar base
to Myrrh, but be a little lighter, delicate enough to make
everyone who smelled it move closer to its wearer in
order to breathe it again. It would be sensual and yet
joyously teasing, flirtatious but still serious—a woman's
perfume, passionate, charming, enticing... It would be a
scent her grandmother would have been proud for her to
create!

To her surprise, Sadie discovered that she was on her
feet and halfway towards the kitchen door.

'I must go, Pierre,' she told him dizzily.

She would need to make sure that Leon knew she was
not to be messed with, of course. And she'd make it clear
that she must be given carte blanche where the creation

of her scent was concerned. There was no way that Leon was going to overrule her or dictate to her, and she fully intended to make that plain to him. The scent would be her creation and would bear the Francine name. It would, Sadie decided, her heart singing, restore to the house of Francine its old status and glory. It would be her abiding gift of love to her grandmother!

CHAPTER THREE

SADIE picked up the telephone message Raoul had left, asking her to come back to Grasse so that they could talk, as she got into her car.

Still under the heady influence of listening to Pierre, she sent Raoul a text message informing him that she was on her way.

This time Raoul himself opened the door to her, hugging her warmly and apologising to her for their earlier quarrel before she could so much as say a single word.

'You promised me that we would be able to talk about selling the business before we met with Leon,' Sadie reminded him warily.

'I know, I know…' Raoul was all but wringing his hands as he ushered her solicitously into the salon.

It was such a shame that the house was so run-down and neglected, Sadie reflected for the second time that day. It had so much potential, and could in the right hands be turned into the most wonderful family home. Emotionally she looked out into the courtyard, trying to imagine her grandmother playing there as a little girl. But bemusingly, as the sunlight glittered on the droplets of water from the fountain, the child she suddenly visualised toddling across the ancient paved stones was not a miniature version of her grandmother but instead a sturdy, dark-haired green-eyed little boy, who looked shockingly like…

Her whole body heating in the sudden surge of recognition that burned through her, Sadie dragged her trapped gaze away from the courtyard. Why on earth had she imagined Leon's baby boy there? And, even more disturbing, why had she felt that unmistakable sharp maternal tug on her own heartstrings as she did so?

She did not want Leon's child. Why, the very thought was—

'Sadie? Come back! You aren't listening to me.'

There was a note of distinct peevishness in Raoul's voice. Guiltily Sadie turned round to look at him.

'I'm sorry. What were you saying?'

'I was just trying to tell you that after you left I had a long talk with Leon and explained to him that if he was serious about wanting to buy Francine and having you on board as well, then he was going to have to compromise on a few things.'

Sadie blinked as she listened to him.

'You did?' she exclaimed, unable to hide her astonishment. She had been expecting to hear Raoul verbally persuading her, if not actually bullying her into changing her mind.

'I did,' Raoul confirmed. 'I know you and I haven't always seen eye to eye over Francine, Sadie, but I have to say that, listening to you today, I began to realise that you were making some very valid points. And I have said as much to Leon.'

Her cousin's unexpected support was leaving Sadie momentarily lost for words.

'I…see…' she managed to say. 'And how did Leon react to that?'

'Well, at first, of course, he was reluctant to agree with me—and I'll be honest with you, Sadie, it took me a hell of a long time to bring him round to seeing my side of the argument. In the end I had to remind him that unless he wanted to alienate you completely he was just going to have to compromise…'

'I'm sure he loved that,' Sadie could not help murmuring dryly.

'Well, he is a businessman, after all, and he is now prepared to concede that if you agree to the sale, and provided you work for Francine, then he is prepared to allow you to base any new perfume you create on natural products.'

'Base?' Sadie queried cautiously, whilst her heart felt as though it was bouncing around inside her chest in excitement and relief.

Unbelievably, Raoul had taken her side, her part, and had managed to convince Leon that she was right!

'Well, you will have to negotiate with him to see how much of any new perfume can be natural products and how much chemically manufactured. And, of course, he will want access to the Myrrh formula.'

'Access, maybe—but I am not prepared to hand over ownership,' Sadie shot back immediately.

Raoul made no response, his expression suddenly becoming almost theatrically anxious.

'Sadie, I have not wanted to mention this. I do have my pride after all.' He looked away from her and rubbed his hand over his eyes. 'But I'm afraid that I haven't been entirely…honest with you about…about certain things.'

Sadie waited.

'The fact is that…well, I have got myself in a bit of a financial mess. And if I can't sell Francine to Leon then…'

'Then?' Sadie prompted him, dry-mouthed. They might only have met one another relatively recently, but he was still her cousin, Sadie reminded herself loyally. She might not approve of the things he did, or the way he lived his life, but she couldn't help but be emotionally affected by the way he had come to her support against Leon.

'Francine is virtually bankrupt—and so am I. Worse than that, I have commitments....'

'Commitments?' Sadie repeated uneasily.

'All right, if you will have it, debts,' Raoul admitted, flinging out one arm in a gesture of open despair. 'I have debts, Sadie. There! I have been forced to tell you what I had hoped not to have to do. I am in your hands now, Sadie, and if you don't help me by agreeing not just to this sale but to giving your expertise to Francine then I shall be facing financial ruin.'

Somewhere in the back of Sadie's mind a tiny warning bell rang. It was a small, sharp and instinctive feeling that Raoul was not being either totally honest or totally genuine. But loyally she refused to listen to it. Even so, a little hesitantly, she began, 'I...I...' and then stopped.

Raoul swung round and exclaimed joyously, 'You'll do it? Oh, Sadie, thank you. Thank you.' He was holding her in his arms. Hugging her, kissing her on both cheeks and then again as his pleasure and relief overwhelmed him. 'I cannot tell you what this means to me.'

There were actually tears in his eyes, as well as in his voice, Sadie recognised.

'You don't know what a weight off my shoulders it will be to get this contract signed...and to get away from here,' he added, giving the dusty room a dismissive, disparaging look.

'Get away?' Sadie queried.

'Yes. This place is obviously part of the deal, and quite frankly I am relieved that it is. I cannot wait to buy myself a decent modern apartment. But first I have to make a short trip...a family matter...an elderly relative on my mother's side. She lives outside Paris in...in straitened circumstances. She is my godmother, and I want to do a little something to help her. Your agreement to the sale of Francine means that I shall be able to do so!'

He cleared his throat and his voice thickened. 'I shall let Leon know what you have said. I can't tell you how much your agreement means to me, Sadie. With the money I receive from Leon I shall be able to see that Tante Amelie receives the care she needs. It is the least I can do. And you, Sadie—I expect you will be wanting to return to your own home. There will be much for you to do there, I know, before you begin working for Francine and Leon!'

Sadie frowned. She supposed she should not have been surprised to discover that her grandmother's childhood home was to be included in the sale of the business, but she owned that she was surprised by Raoul's revelations about his ailing godmother! And she would have to return to Pembroke, of course. But she had not planned to do so as yet.

'Won't Leon want to…to discuss his plans with me?' she questioned Raoul.

'Yes, indeed, but not right now. I suspect he will want to wait until after the formalities of the contract being signed for that.'

Disconcerted, Sadie digested her disappointment at the thought of not seeing Leon again for some time. She hadn't actually wanted to see him, had she? That wasn't why she was changing her mind, was it? Because…

No, of course it wasn't! How could it be? She barely knew the man!

Guessing from the way he kept looking at his watch that Raoul had other things to do, Sadie took her leave of him.

She might as well see out her stay in France, she decided, as she got into her car. And then if Leon did want to discuss anything with her over the next couple of days she would be on hand.

Her decision was based entirely on common sense, she assured herself as she pulled out into the traffic. Common sense. That was all…nothing else, she assured herself firmly.

Raoul waited until he was sure that Sadie had gone before telephoning Leon, his fingers drumming impatiently on the wall as he waited for Leon to answer his call. When he did, Raoul began immediately.

'I've spoken to Sadie, and it is just as I said it would be, Leon,' Raoul announced boastfully. 'I soon made her see reason. All you need to do now is get the contracts organised. Oh, by the way, speaking of the contracts—I was wondering…is there any way you could let me have an advance on the buyout figure? Only I've got a couple of obligations I'd like to get cleared up.'

Leon frowned as he listened to Raoul. He knew all about Raoul's debts, having had him thoroughly investigated prior to their negotiations. Illogically, he acknowledged that whilst he was relieved to hear that Raoul had managed to talk Sadie round, he also felt surprised, and almost a little bit disappointed that she had given in to her cousin so easily. Somehow he had expected her to put up more of a fight!

Suspiciously, he challenged Raoul.

'You haven't forgotten what I said to you about my not being agreeable to changing my decision on the ingredients of any new scent she creates, have you, Raoul?'

'Of course not,' Raoul responded promptly.

'Did she say why she had changed her mind?' Leon probed.

On the other end of the line Raoul frowned in irritation. Leon was asking for too many questions. Why on earth couldn't he simply accept what he was saying to him?

'She's a woman, Leon,' Raoul told him. 'Who knows why they do the things they do? About that advance... I need to leave Grasse for a few days, and...'

'I shall arrange for five hundred thousand euros to be transferred into your account today, Raoul.'

'Five hundred thousand—that is all?'

He could hear the disappointment in the other man's voice.

'Five hundred thousand,' Leon confirmed grimly. 'Take it or leave it!'

After Raoul had rung off, Leon stared frowningly through the open glass door of his suite. His attention was not focused on the stunning view that lay beyond his private balcony, but instead on something or rather someone that the male core of his memory found even more stunning.

Sadie!

It still surprised him that she had changed her mind and given in, agreeing not just to the sale of Francine to him but also agreed to work for him as well. Somehow it seemed a little out of character. Almost as if she'd submitted to him...

Hastily he dragged his thoughts back from the brink they were careering towards and reminded himself that he had work to do!

Since leaving Grasse earlier he had spent far more time than he wanted to admit thinking about her! And not just because of the problems she was causing him with the takeover. Not just? Be honest, he derided himself Not at all! No, the reason she had gained so much control inside

his head was quite simply because she, or rather his reaction to her, his awareness of her, his desire for her, had
assumed far too much control of his senses!

To put it bluntly, he ached for her in a way that had
not just caught him off guard, but was also actively making him...

Making him what? Making him want to rewind life
right back to that second when he had first seen her in
Cannes, so that he could do what every male instinct his
body was packed with had urged him to do then? Pick
her up in his arms, get her the hell out of there and take
her somewhere where....

It was at times like this that his Greek blood was most
at odds with his Australian upbringing, Leon acknowledged wryly. Right now, hormonally he was quite definitely all Greek male, but cerebrally—thank heaven—a
part of him remained an Aussie businessman! And that
was the part of him he needed most to focus on!

He had certainly enjoyed focusing on Sadie, he mused.
He had never liked over-thin women, and Sadie was just
right—her waist so tiny he could span it with his hands,
her hips sexily curved, her legs long...long enough to
wrap right around him when he...and her breasts. Ah,
her breasts... Just the thought of touching them, holding
them, brushing his lips against their tender quivering
crests and then...

Leon gave a low groan and closed his eyes. Bad mistake, since immediately a vision of Sadie formed behind
his shuttered eyelids. He must be going crazy—either that
or he was well on his way to falling head over heels in
love with her.

In love? In lust, more like! Anyway, falling in love
right now was a complication he definitely did not need

in his life. Unlike Sadie. He needed *her* all right. In his life. In his arms. In his bed…

Raoul had told him that she was going back to England and Leon told himself that he ought to be glad!

His grandmother would certainly have enjoyed seeing him in the state of turmoil he was in right now!

Thinking of his grandmother made Leon frown again. He had been just fourteen when she died. A sensitive age, which was no doubt why—

His mobile phone rang, breaking his train of thought.

Was she doing the right thing? Sadie asked herself soberly as she parked her car in the hotel car park and made her way to her room.

She wished passionately that her grandmother were here for her to talk to. Would she approve of what she was doing? The wave of euphoria which had carried her back to Grasse had receded now, leaving her feeling shaky and insecure. What if she couldn't create a saleable perfume? And, even if she did, what made her think that her scent could succeed where so many others had failed? They lived in a different world now from the one in which the classic scents had been created. Consumers were more demanding, more fickle—but if she could succeed…if she could create a new scent that would take the world by storm and…

She was beginning to feel light-headed with excitement again. What if, between them, she and Leon…?

Between them? She and Leon? A fresh surge of excitement gripped her, but this one had nothing whatsoever to do with the creation of a new scent!

Why didn't she give in and admit it to herself? She had been attracted to Leon the first moment she had seen him.

Attracted to him! To describe her feelings as mere attraction was like trying to compare cologne with full-strength perfume.

Her heart started to thud, her palms suddenly becoming damp. Why was it that the look in one particular man's eyes could make a woman feel so…? Hot-cheeked, Sadie acknowledged that she did not want to explore just what it was that Leon made her feel right now! At least not in public.

'I just hope that I'm doing the right thing.'

Sadie's voice wobbled a little, and she held her mobile just that little bit tighter as she voiced her uncertainty to her friend.

On the other end of the line Mary responded bracingly.

'Well, it certainly sounds to me as though you are. Sometimes you just have to follow your instincts and your heart, Sadie, no matter how risky it might seem.'

Her heart! That organ started to thump erratically at the thought that she had betrayed herself so easily to her friend. How could Mary have guessed from what she had told her about her emergent feelings for Leon? She had barely mentioned him!

'Your kind of work isn't merely a career choice, Sadie, it's a vocation, and when a person has your kind of talent—well, then they need to be able to fulfil the need it gives them and follow the direction of their heart, rather than make cerebral decisions!'

Her work! Mary was talking about her work, not about Leon!

'It is a once in a lifetime opportunity,' Sadie agreed excitedly. 'But—'

'No more buts,' Mary told her firmly. 'You go for it, girl!'

She had spent longer talking to her friend on the telephone than she had realised, Sadie recognised ten minutes after she had ended the call, when the grumbling protest of her stomach made her look at her watch. It was almost eight o'clock and she hadn't eaten since breakfast!

Showering quickly, Sadie redressed in an elegant taupe silk dress she had spotted in an expensive boutique's sale in Paris, slipping her bare feet into a pair of kitten-heeled sandals and gathering up a cream cashmere wrap just in case the evening air proved chilly.

It was only a five-minute walk from the rooms to the main hotel, and as Sadie picked her way along the prettily illuminated path and down the several flights of stone steps she paused to look out across the valley, to where the lights of the town twinkled in the distance.

As she crossed the car park *en route* for the hotel foyer she noticed that it was busy with cars, but thought no more about it, smiling briefly at the receptionist as she made her way across the tiled floor and then walked down the stairs and through the lower level foyer into the cocktail bar.

It had bemused her a little the first time she had walked into this bar, to recognise that it was styled very much in the manner of a gracious English country house—even to the extent of having a log-burning fire—but this hotel was not occupied merely in the summer, she acknowledged, but all the year round by those who wished to use its spa facilities. The cocktail bar was certainly very comfortable and welcoming.

The lower foyer, through which she had just walked, had elegant French windows which opened out onto a large paved patio area where guests could sit at wrought-iron tables and look out across the valley. Tonight the patio was crowded with several large groups of diners,

Sadie noticed as she headed for the entrance to the dining room and the *maître d'*.

'A table for dinner? *Madame*, I am sorry but that is not possible. We are fully booked,' he told her when she asked for a table.

Sadie stared at him.

'But I am a hotel resident,' she protested. Delicious food smells from the meal being served to a table of diners just inside the doorway were informing her just how very hungry she really was. Her stomach was actually growling.

The *maître d'* looked sorrowful and spread his hands.

'I am so sorry, but I think you will have seen in your room that hotel guests are requested to make prior reservations for dinner. We are a Michelin-starred restaurant, and many people drive out from Cannes to eat here.'

Sadie's heart was sinking deeper with every word he said. It was true that there was a notice in her room warning guests about the limited availability of tables for dinner.

'There are several very good restaurants in the old town of Mougins,' the *maître d'* informed her helpfully. 'It is only a short walk from here, and a very pretty place. It gets many tourists.'

Sadie sighed. Whilst she didn't mind eating alone in a hotel restaurant, she was loath to do so further afield. She *had* planned to visit the old town of Mougins, but during the daytime.

Ruefully she acknowledged that she ought to have pre-booked her dinner reservation, and realized that she was now going to have to return to her room and order a meal there, from Room Service. She had just thanked the *maître d'* and was making her way through the now extremely busy bar, when she suddenly saw Leon on the other side of the room.

He was walking towards her and had obviously seen her. Immediately her face lit up, a giddy sensation, a heady mixture of thrilling excitement, shock, and pleasure, flooding her body with breathless delight.

'Leon!' she exclaimed as he came towards her. 'What are you doing here?'

His calm, 'Actually, I'm staying here,' took her thrilled delight down a few notches, and she had to control her expression to stop herself from betraying her disappointment. He had not come looking for her, as she had originally deliriously believed.

'And you?' he queried. 'Are you dining here?'

He looked and sounded so coolly remote that her heart banged uncomfortably against her chest wall whilst she battled against the feeling of disappointment that was filling her.

The reality of him was so different from the fantasies she had been building inside her head all afternoon. He looked so austere, so disapproving and remote, so very much the man she remembered from their first encounter—right down to the immaculate shirt and suit.

The happiness and expectation that had fuelled her day was leaking out of her, and she was miserably conscious of the way in which Leon was looking over her shoulder and beyond her, as though in search of someone! Another woman perhaps? Did he have a dinner date?

Lifting her chin she told him bravely, 'Actually, no, I'm not dining here this evening, Coincidentally, I am also staying here.' There was no way she wanted him thinking she had booked in because she knew he was staying at this hotel. After all, she hadn't realized that he was. 'But unfortunately—obviously unlike you—I ne-

glected to make a reservation for dinner. The *maître d'*
has suggested that I walk into the old town and—'

'What? On your own? You are doing no such thing.'
Leon stopped her authoritatively 'I'm surprised that he
suggested such a thing to a woman on her own. You *are*
on your own, I take it?'

He wasn't looking over her shoulder any more. In fact
he was looking right at her, and his eyes, like his voice,
had warmed—as though…as though…

'Yes. Yes, I am…' Sadie agreed weakly. 'I… Whoops.'
She gave a small gasp as a new crowd of people pressed
into the confined space of the bar, one of whom inadvertently bumping into her and causing her to stagger slightly.

Immediately Leon reached out for her, drawing her
towards him. So close to him, in fact, that all it would
have taken for their bodies to actually touch would be
for her to take one good deep breath. And, even though
she was in no real danger of being pushed or crushed by
the crowd, his arm was still curled protectively around
her.

'Look, it's getting like a beer garden in here,' he told
her. 'Since I've got a table booked, why don't you join
me?'

'Oh, no!' Sadie protested immediately. 'I didn't tell
you because—'

'I did!' Leon told her softly.

The cold ice she had previously seen in his eyes had
melted and turned into… Dizzily, she acknowledged that
she could not find the right words to describe the incredible heat and sensuality that was burning in the green
gaze he'd turned on her. All she could think of was what
it was doing to her…

'Do you think that's a good idea?' Sadie couldn't help protesting.

'Why shouldn't it be?' Leon retaliated.

Sadie could think of a hundred reasons, all of which had to do with the fact that she was already dangerously aware of him and potentially responsive to him, without doing something that was bound to encourage her vulnerable emotions to start rioting totally out of control!

'Well, in view of the professional situation between us…' she began a little lamely, not wanting to admit to him the real reason why she felt that having dinner with him might not be a good idea.

But Leon wouldn't allow her to continue, saying immediately, 'Why don't we draw a line under all of that and start again? Call a truce? I've spoken to Raoul…'

Even though she knew she was being idiotic, Sadie couldn't quite suppress her small spurt of disappointment when she realised that Leon was talking to her as a business colleague, not as a woman he wanted to get to know personally.

'Oh, have you?' she answered him.

'I have,' he confirmed, 'and I can't tell you how pleased I am to hear about your decision, Sadie.'

'It seemed the best thing to do.' Sadie paused, wanting to tell him how pleased she was that he had backed down over the use of natural raw materials. But before she could continue Leon shook his head.

'Part of the truce is no business talk tonight.'

'You never said that before.'

'Didn't I?' The corners of his eyes crinkled with amusement. He really was heart-stoppingly sexy, Sadie acknowledged giddily. 'Ah, well, I'm saying it now!'

'But if we don't talk about business, then what—?'

Sadie stopped and blushed as she saw the way he was looking at her.

'Oh, I think we'll find that we have plenty of things to say to one another,' Leon told her softly.

Sadie didn't make any reply. She was far too conscious of the fact that she was dangerously close to wanting much more from him than a simple business relationship!

He was looking away from her and in the direction of the *maître d'* who was hurrying over. Turning towards him, Leon said something quietly and the other man ushered them both to Leon's table.

Sadie could see the subtle feminine interested looks Leon was attracting from the women diners at the other tables as they were led to their own. Predictably, he had been given a table in a prime position, and as the waiter pulled out a chair for her Sadie couldn't help feeling glad that she had chosen to wear her silk dress. It might not be as dramatic as some of the outfits several of the other women were wearing, but thanks to her grandmother she knew how to choose clothes that suited her.

Sadie had barely opened her menu when another waiter arrived, carrying a bottle of champagne and two glasses.

Wide-eyed, she looked at Leon.

'I hope you don't mind,' he told her softly. 'Only it seemed appropriate. To celebrate.'

Sadie couldn't drag her gaze away from his. Why on earth had she ever thought his eyes cold? They were anything but. And as for his smile... A funny aching sensation had begun to spread from the direction of her heart all the way down through her body right into her toes, making her curl them protectively inside her sandals!

'Well, yes...' she agreed, trying to sound nonchalant and sophisticated. 'Only Raoul did say it could be a few days before the contracts were ready for us all to sign, and since he isn't here...'

The smile curling Leon's mouth deepened and his eyes started to crinkle at the corners.

'It wasn't the prospect of us signing the contracts I wanted to celebrate,' he told her in a voice that sounded like dark melting chocolate.

'It...it wasn't...?' Agitatedly, Sadie picked up her glass of champagne.

'No, it wasn't,' Leon agreed, watching her with a gaze so sensual and exciting that Sadie just knew her whole body was about to start quivering with delight in response to it.

'Aren't you going to ask me what I *am* celebrating?' he prompted huskily.

'I...er...' Sadie took a deep gulp of her champagne and then gasped as the bubbles hit the back of her throat and exploded. She coughed and put her glass down.

'I'm sorry,' she apologised, her face burning at her own lack of sophistication.

'What's wrong? Don't you like champagne?' Leon teased her.

'Well, I do,' Sadie told him. 'Only I'm not much of a drinker, really. I suppose it comes of having been brought up by my grandmother... She was a bit old-fashioned about such things by modern standards.'

'Why did your grandmother bring you up?'

He was frowning now, but not in a disapproving or condemnatory way, Sadie noticed. No, he was looking at her as though he was genuinely interested in discovering more about her! A sweetly sharp thrill of excitement spun through her.

'My mother died shortly after I was born, and Dad— well, he had to work. So Grandmère brought me up, and then Dad remarried.' She paused awkwardly, not wanting him to think she was trying to make him feel sympathetic towards her. 'Well, Melanie—my stepmother—she was younger than Dad, and I don't think she was too keen on the idea of taking on a soon-to-be teenage stepdaughter. Anyway, I was happy to stay with Grandmère.'

'I see...'

He was looking at her in the most direct and yet somehow very tender way, Sadie recognised. A way that made her feel as though she could almost tell him just how hurt she had felt, knowing that her stepmother didn't want her and that her father did not love her enough to insist that she was allowed to be a part of their lives.

'I too had a very close relationship with my grandmother,' Leon told her quietly.

For a moment they looked at one another in silence. They were, Sadie recognised, two people suddenly discovering that they had more in common than they had realised.

'Your grandmother was Greek, wasn't she?' Sadie asked hesitantly, not wanting to pry and yet suddenly desperate to learn as much about him as she could, for him to be the one to tell her!

'Yes. Like you, with your grandmother, I was very close to her. My parents both worked in the business my father was building, and my grandmother lived with us and looked after me. She died when I was fourteen.' His frown deepened. 'It was a very bad time for the family.'

'You still miss her?' Sadie guessed.

'Yes,' he agreed gruffly. 'She didn't have the easiest of lives—' His mouth twisted a little bitterly. 'And that is an understatement. She had an extremely hard life. Her parents emigrated to Australia to escape from poverty at home. Her mother died before they reached Sydney and her father was so grief stricken that he began to drink. My grandmother brought up her brothers and sisters virtually single-handed, and looked after her father as well, when she was little more than a child herself! She was just twelve when they arrived in Australia, and twenty-four when she married my grandfather. She was working as a ladies' maid when he met her, and in those days anyone in service was not allowed to get married. She wouldn't leave her job because she still had her father to support.'

'She must have been a wonderful person,' Sadie told him softly.

'She was,' he agreed.

There was a look in his eyes she couldn't analyse, Sadie acknowledged. A look which held bitterness and anger. A look which for some reason right now he seemed to be directing right at her!

'You're wearing your perfume,' he said abruptly changing the subject

Sadie nodded her head, trying not to betray the fact she was pleased he had noticed.

'Is it very different from the original Myrrh?'

'A little,' she told him, the realisation that his interest had been of a business rather than a personal nature turning her pleasure to disappointment. Rather briskly, she added, 'The original perfume, like most perfumes of its time, was much stronger than women want to wear today—and, of course, very expensive.'

'Expensive and exclusive,' Leon agreed curtly. 'In fact, a luxury that most ordinary women could never hope to enjoy!'

To Sadie's bewilderment his expression as well as his voice once again suddenly changed, becoming closed and forbidding.

'Have you decided want you want to eat yet?' he asked grimly.

Sadie looked at him, tempted to ask what it was she had said that had caused him to withdraw so sharply from her, but instead she simply told him very coolly and distantly that, yes, she was ready to order.

'How old were you when you first knew that you had a "nose"?'

Their first course had just arrived, and Sadie looked across at Leon a little warily. But whatever it was that had caused that momentary harsh bleakness to harden his expression had gone, and he was once more smiling warmly at her.

'I don't know,' she admitted. 'I just sort of grew up knowing that I wanted to create perfume. My grandmother encouraged me, of course. She was born at the wrong time, I think, looking back now. She would have loved to have taken over the business, but as a girl with a brother that was just not an option.'

'I have gathered that there was some discord between them,' Leon acknowledged, and he looked encouragingly at her, obviously wanting to learn more.

'My great-uncle was a gambler, and he ran down the business to finance his gambling habit. My grandmother hated what he did, and I think she ended up hating him too,' Sadie admitted. 'A rift developed between them which was exacerbated by the fact that my grandmother had married an Englishman and lived so far away from him. Still, she felt so passionately about the business…'

'A passion which she obviously passed on to you,' Leon interrupted her.

Sadie smiled.

'My grandmother was a very passionate person.'

'And so, I imagine, are you. Very passionate!'

Across the table their glances met and locked. Sadie discovered she was only able to breathe shallowly, her heart bouncing frantically around her chest, making her feel as though she wanted to press her hands to her body to keep it still.

The silence between them, the intimacy of their locked gazes, was the most exciting sensation she had ever experienced, she acknowledged dizzily. Her food was completely forgotten—Leon was her food, her need, her every sustenance both physical and emotional. If he were to reach out now, take hold of her hand and lead her from the table, she knew beyond any doubt that she would go with him.

'You can't possibly know that. I…' Her voice was a papery dry whisper, a muted husk of sound, her eyes huge, her pupils dilated.

'I do know it.' Leon stopped her. His own voice was tense, low and raw with an open hunger that made Sadie shudder violently.

'I know exactly how you will feel in my arms, Sadie, how you will taste, how passionately you will respond to me in my bed.'

What the hell was he doing? Leon wondered savagely as he heard what he was saying almost as though he was standing outside himself and listening. From the moment he had taken over the family business on his twenty-first birthday, Leon had dedicated himself totally to its success. Nothing and no one had ever threatened to come between him and that dedication—until now!

For the first time in his life Leon could feel himself being pulled in different directions emotionally. Had he gone completely mad? Totally lost the plot? Okay, so

Sadie was one delectably desirable woman. But that didn't mean...

The way she was looking at him made his body clench, and a surge of desire as fierce as the kick of a mule powered through his belly.

This wasn't something he had written down in his mental checklist of life goals. Not now and quite definitely not ever with *this* particular woman!

So why wasn't he doing something about it? Why wasn't he getting a grip and forcing his unwanted desire for her to shrivel into nothing? Because he didn't want to or because he couldn't do so? Because he was already in way way over his head and not even thinking about trying to save himself?

A small shudder ripped through Sadie, openly visible to him, and his own body reacted. Responded! Hell, but no woman had affected him like this in public since he had left his teenage days behind him. It was a damn good job that the table covered the visible evidence of his arousal.

He moved a little uncomfortably in his seat, cursing softly to himself.

Sadie held her breath as she saw the way Leon's eyes burned with sexual awareness as he monitored her reaction.

She could hardly breathe normally, never mind think of eating! Frantically she tried to come up with something banal to say, to extinguish the almost palpable aura of sexual heat surrounding them. But her brain was simply refusing to co-operate. If she didn't manage to break the sensual intensity of the gaze they were sharing Sadie didn't know what might happen! Or, rather, she knew perfectly well what her body was hoping would happen!

And that knowledge was making her feel both more excited than she had ever felt in her whole life and more
apprehensive as well!

Someone at a nearby table pushed back their chair, and
the scraping noise caused Leon to look in that direction.
Dizzily Sadie dragged great gulps of air into her lungs
and picked up her fork.

CHAPTER FOUR

SINCE Leon had already determined to put things between them back on a sensible, businesslike footing at the very first chance he got, why, when Sadie had taken the opportunity to do exactly that, was he reacting as though she was somehow challenging him? And why was he actively looking for ways to break through the social barriers she had thrown up and return things to a much more personal level? Leon asked himself derisively.

He had never thought of himself as the kind of man so needy, and lacking in self-esteem as to have to verbally force a woman to be aware of him sexually, but right now...

He looked at Sadie's mouth. It was soft and full, and if she was wearing any lipstick it was so natural as to be virtually indiscernible. He hated kissing women who caked their mouths in red grease! Kissing Sadie's mouth, in fact kissing any bit of Sadie, would be a pleasure he would give his eye teeth for right now!

Desperate to bring her rioting emotions and desires under control, Sadie waited until their main course had been served before clearing her throat and asking politely, 'What made you decide to buy Francine?'

For a moment she thought that he wasn't going to reply, but then he looked at her and her heart did a foolish somersault.

'It just seemed a natural progression. We are a luxury goods group, after all.' Right now he didn't want to discuss his business affairs with Sadie. In fact he didn't really want to talk about anything with her at all. At the moment the kind of communication he wanted to share with Sadie involved using their lips for something much more intimate than phrasing words!

Although Leon had spoken naturally enough in answer to her question, Sadie had felt as though he was measuring his words, as if somehow he was having to guard what he said, she reflected. But she was guiltily aware that, although she had been listening to his words, a wickedly wanton streak in herself she had not realised she possessed had been focusing on Leon's mouth in an altogether far too intimate way!

'We made a deal that we weren't going to talk about business,' Leon reminded her.

Sadie's heart banged so loudly against her ribs that she was too worried that he might have heard it to think about anything else.

'This steak is the best I've tasted in a long time,' Leon told Sadie enthusiastically.

He had been caught slightly on the hop by Sadie's unexpected question about his reasons for acquiring Francine. Wanting her was one thing. Discussing his grandmother with her was another! He knew that it was his own pride that made him feel so immediately protective of his grandmother, so unwilling to discuss the real reason why he so much wanted to acquire Francine and Myrrh.

The truth was that he had never forgotten how he had felt as a youngster, when his grandmother had told him the story of how when she had been a ladies' maid she had yearned to be able to wear the exotic and expensive perfume worn by her mistress.

'It was called Myrrh,' his grandmother had told him with a sigh, 'and it was the most beautiful perfume ever.'

'Couldn't you have bought some?' his younger self had asked her naïvely.

She had smiled sadly and shaken her head, ruffling his hair with a hand gnarled and deformed by years of hard domestic work.

'Leon, just one small bottle would have cost more than I would have earned in five years,' she had told him. 'Perfume like that wasn't created for women like me!'

As he had seen the look in her eyes Leon had sworn there and then that one day his grandmother would own a bottle of the best and the most expensive perfume in the world, and that he would buy it for her. Only she had died before he had been able to make good that promise. But he had never forgotten that he had made it, and never ceased regretting that he hadn't been able to keep it. And he had certainly never forgotten *why* he had made it, which was why he'd felt so antagonistic towards Sadie's original refusal to create a new perfume that would be inexpensive enough for every woman to wear and enjoy.

But fortunately Sadie had seen sense, and at last the Myrrh scent was going to belong to him! It was too late for his grandmother to enjoy, but at least he would have the satisfaction of knowing that the grandson of the woman who hadn't been able to afford to buy the smallest bottle of the scent now owned the whole company! And if it was the last thing he did he intended to make sure that every woman who wanted to would be able to afford to wear a Francine perfume!

And so he had deliberately not told his board the reasons for his determination to acquire Francine. There was no way he was going to make himself vulnerable to anyone by admitting that he had been motivated to buy Francine out of sentiment. He would never hand out that kind of information and give others the opportunity to crucify him! As they undoubtedly would. The business world he operated in traded in financial gains, not emotional ones. And it only respected the men who made those financial gains.

Leon had grown up in a tough world, watching his parents struggling to establish the business—and then, just when the business had been on the verge of becoming very profitable, he'd seen them very nearly lose it. The shock and stress of that event had undermined his father's health and left him permanently weakened physically. Witnessing such traumatic events had given Leon a fierce, youthful resolve to do all he could to protect his family, to make the business so financially stable and secure that he would never again have to see his father's face grey with defeat and despair, or his mother's eyes shining with frightened tears.

He might have taken his parents' business and built it into the successful and profitable empire it was today, he might be a billionaire whose wealth could open any door for him, but deep down inside there was a part of him that still felt the anguish and the anger he had experienced as a fourteen-year-old, witnessing his parents' fear, just as he still remembered listening to his grandmother describe how her poverty had sometimes humiliated her.

His children would be told all about their great-grandmother, and they would be brought up to respect and revere her memory, to understand that money could not buy spirit or character or love. If Sadie objected to that then she was not the woman he believed her to be...

Leon put down his cutlery with a clatter that made Sadie stare at him in confusion and wonder just what had caused that look of arrested shock she could see in his eyes. But before she could question him, however, he had distracted her by asking if she had as yet tried any of the hotel's spa facilities.

'No I haven't,' she admitted. 'Have you?'

'No,' Leon acknowledged. 'There hasn't really been time.'

Sadie gave a small but very luxurious sigh. It was over an hour since they had finished their meal and come into the bar, where Leon had escorted her over to one of the seductively comfortable squashy sofas before going to order their drinks.

They were the only people left there, apart from the bar staff, and the logs on the fire had burned down to glowing ashes. She couldn't say just what she and Leon had talked about—the time had flown by on wings of exultation and delight. It was almost as though Leon could actually sense what she was thinking—so much so that every time she had been tempted to forget their pact and talk to him about her excited plans for the future, and the new perfume she hoped to create, he'd somehow stopped her, sidelining their conversation into another direction. And all the time…all the time…every minute, every second, he had been looking at her in such a way that…

'It looks like we've outstayed our welcome,' Leon told her now, with an amused look at the barman, very purposefully cleaning up. 'I'll walk you back to your room,' he added as Sadie stood up.

Outside it was cool enough for her to be glad she had brought her wrap—and she was even more pleased when without a word Leon took it from her and draped it gently over her shoulders. Was it her imagination or did his fingers really stroke slowly against her bare skin before he stepped back from her?

The path which wound up along the hillside and through the gardens was well illuminated by the strategically placed lighting. The sky was a blue-black dome of velvet, sprinkled with diamond-bright stars, with the thin sliver of a crescent moon.

The path curved and slipped between a small stand of trees into a hidden grove of scented darkness, which took Sadie by surprise, causing her to half stumble on an unseen step.

Immediately Leon reached out to steady her.

'Thanks.' Although the ground was in darkness there was enough light from the moon for her to see his features. The intensity of his gaze her made her heart thump frantically. 'I didn't realise there was a step there.' It was disconcerting to know how at odds with the way she was feeling the bland mundanity of her words was.

'No. I'm surprised the hotel management hasn't had this area better lit. Surprised, but extremely pleased,' Leon told her rawly.

'Pleased?' Was he actually saying what she thought he was saying? Sadie's heart was doing more than merely thumping now; it was practically turning excited cartwheels! Instinctively she looked up at Leon, and the hungry look in his eyes caused the whole world to spin dizzily round her. She stood very still.

Slowly Leon lowered his head, his mouth seeking her own. Silently she waited, hardly daring to breathe in case she broke the spell that was binding them together in the magical and intimate darkness.

His lips touched hers, firm, warm, sure and knowledgeable, making her feel...

Making her feel like a woman, Sadie acknowledged giddily. Like a very desirable woman.

Strong male hands drew her closer, one resting in the

small of her back, the other lifting to her neck, sliding beneath her hair, supporting her head as the pressure of his kiss tipped it backwards.

Sadie exhaled a disbelieving shaky whisper of breath before eagerly parting her lips to the probing thrust of Leon's tongue. She could feel the solid trunk of a tree behind her shoulders, and yet had no memory of having stepped backwards. Leon's hand had left the small of her back and travelled to the rounded curve of her bottom, urging her into his own body.

With a fierce thrill of delight she recognised his arousal, her body reacting to it with a sensual abandon that had her pushing her hips against him, revelling in the immediate and passionate response of his hands and his mouth as he gripped her harder and thrust his tongue deeper into the eager softness of her mouth.

Her own arms were wrapped tightly around him now, her breasts sensitised by the movement of her body against his. In her mind she could already picture his hands covering their nakedness, feel the fierce tug of his mouth against her nipples.

She shuddered violently at her own thoughts. A sharp spike of shock pierced through her, only to be overwhelmed by a fresh wave of aching longing as Leon pressed her even more closely to his body.

He felt excitingly hard and... Instinctively Sadie's mind shied away from what she was thinking, imagining...

She wasn't in the habit of assessing a man's virility in terms of shape and size, and she most certainly wasn't in the habit of getting excited about them—or him!

What had happened to her normal reserve? Not to mention the moral objections...the sheer common sense she should be heeding?

Leon's mouth was moving along her jaw and towards her ear, leaving a trail of delicate kisses that filled her with stunning delight. Dizzily Sadie acknowledged that just the whisper of his breath...his lips against her skin...was sending her crazy. Not that he was exactly immune to the reaction he was arousing in her, judging by the way he was gripping her hips and pulling her tightly against his body, Sadie realised with a fierce thrill of female pleasure.

'The way you're making me feel I could take you here and now, do you know that?' Leon groaned against her ear, confirming her thoughts and sending her pulse rocketing out of control whilst the images inside her head became even more explicit and steamy.

Again she wondered—where was her normal, sane and sensible self that should have been objecting sharply and immediately to what he was saying? Why was she moving her body even closer to his instead of pulling herself away?

Sadie didn't know, and what was more she didn't care. In fact, if Leon chose to put his threat into action, she didn't think she would be able to object. Object...? She was aching so badly for him that...

Now it was her turn to moan out loud with delight as his hand moved up her body and cupped her breast. Just the feel of his thumb-tip rubbing sensuously across her tight, aching nipple made her bite on her bottom lip to stop herself from begging him to take off her top and expose her breast to his gaze, his touch and the hot, hard caress of his mouth.

Frantically she tensed her muscles, squeezing her thighs together as she felt the surge of longing rocket through her.

As though he guessed what was happening to her,

Leon cupped her hip, his fingers kneading her rhythmically.

She was leaning fully against the tree now, letting it take the weight of her body whilst Leon's hands sensitively explored every inch of her, making her quiver from head to foot in open longing.

When his hand stroked gently between her legs she groaned huskily and shuddered.

'Sadie…' As Leon took her hand and placed it against his own body she almost sobbed with pleasure. Her hands were long and slender, but the hard swollen length of him extended beyond her outstretched fingertips. Sadie closed her eyes, pleasure a dark velvet blanket of sensuality behind her eyelids. She ached as though she had a fever for the feel of him inside her. She'd had no idea there could be desire like this—instant, immediate, hot and hungry, a need that burned everything else into oblivion and drove a person relentlessly until it was sated.

No doubt in Leon's eyes, she decided helplessly, she was totally unworldly and naïve not to have experienced something like this before. Unlike him!

How many times…how many women…? That thought burned through her in a hot agony of molten jealousy that stiffened her whole body.

'Sadie?'

Suddenly they both heard voices somewhere lower down the path. Immediately Leon released her and bent to pick up the shawl which had fallen from her shoulders.

Tucking her hand through his arm, he guided her back to the path. She was shaking so much she suspected she would have stumbled if he hadn't been holding on to her.

Unable to keep her feelings to herself, she burst out emotionally, 'I don't believe this is happening.'

'You don't believe or you don't want to believe it?'
Leon challenged her.

Tiny tremors of reaction were still seizing her body,
and Sadie knew that Leon must be aware of them. What
an idiot he must think her, to get in such a state over a
mere kiss. Only for her it hadn't been just a kiss, had it?
For her...

'It's all right, Sadie,' she heard him telling her gently,
when she was unable to answer his question. 'Will it help
if I admit that I've been caught as much off guard by
what happened back there as you? I can't pretend that I
haven't spent all evening imagining what it would be like
to take you to bed, but...'

'I...I don't do things like this,' Sadie told him stiffly,
suddenly feeling exposed and vulnerable. 'I don't make
a habit of...of this sort of thing. You might...'

'I might what?' he asked, disconcerting her when he
guessed accurately. 'Were you thinking that I might go
to bed with a different woman every night of the week?
Is that what you're trying to say?'

Embarrassed, Sadie shook her head.

'I don't have any right to...to pry into your private
life,' she told him awkwardly. 'It's just that I don't want
you to think that I...'

'I haven't been to bed with a woman in over five
years,' Leon told her curtly. 'I don't happen to approve
of anyone sleeping around just for the hell of it. It's cheap
and it's a health hazard. What happened tonight was—'

'You don't have to explain. I understand!' Sadie
rushed in quickly. He was going to tell her that it had
been a mistake, that things had got out of hand.

'You do? I wish to hell that I could say that,' Leon
came back at her with harsh grimness. 'Right now—' he
stopped and shook his head whilst Sadie held her breath,

aching to have him complete what he had been going to say, and at the same time a little fearful in case he did!

They had almost reached the door to her room.

'Do you have any plans for tomorrow?' Leon asked her abruptly as he stood in front of her.

They were almost as close as they had been earlier, when he had kissed her. If she were to just shift her weight from one foot to the other she would be even closer!

Sadie looked at him. Her body was already overruling the cautious anxieties of her heart and the stern warnings of her head, telling her very forcibly that the only plans it wanted to have, included Leon and preferably complete privacy!

'Well, no...not really.' As her heart jumped and thumped around her ribcage, with an adrenalin-fuelled cocktail of complex emotions, Sadie berated herself inwardly. Why on earth hadn't she told him she was already busy, as she would normally have done? What was happening to her? Never in her life had she chosen danger over safety. It just wasn't her style!

Maybe it hadn't been, a little voice inside her head mocked her, but that had been before she'd met Leon!

'I'm driving out to see a *mas* I'm renting for the summer tomorrow. Why don't you come with me?'

'You're spending the whole summer here?' Sadie commented, unable to conceal her envy at the thought of being able to spend weeks on end enjoying the sunshine in a *mas*, as Provençal farmhouses were called.

Yes...I have a variety of business interests on the continent, and the farmhouse I am planning to rent would make an excellent base for me to work from.'

They were outside her door now, and the light on the

wall illuminated Sadie's expression as she looked up at him.

'A farmhouse?' she questioned, a little uncertainly.

'You don't sound very enthusiastic,' Leon commented wryly. 'What's wrong? Don't you like the countryside?' he asked her.

Immediately Sadie shook her head.

'No, I love it,' she told him vehemently.

'So?' The querying rise of Leon's eyebrows warned her that he intended to get an answer.

'Well, it's just that… Well, I just didn't think that you would be a country person. One always assumes, somehow, that a businessman will be city-based.' Sadie began, and then stopped, biting her lip.

But to her relief Leon didn't take offence at her comment, simply shrugging his shoulders and telling her easily, 'I do have an apartment in Sydney, it's true. It's convenient for business, but given the choice I'd much rather spend my time at the winery my parents own, way out in the country. They're retired now, or supposed to be, but Dad's already talking about putting new vines in and upgrading their wine, despite the fact that he's got a bad heart and ought to be taking things easy!' He stopped and apologised. 'Sorry, you don't want to hear about my family.'

Sadie flicked her tongue-tip over her lips, aching to admit that there was nothing she wanted to learn about more—unless it was every tiny detail about Leon himself. What made him laugh, what kind of food he liked, which side of the bed he liked to sleep on…where he most liked to be touched and kissed…where…

'Well?' she heard him demanding softly.

Her face flared hot pink as for an instant she thought he had somehow read her mind, but then she realised he was waiting for her to respond to his invitation. She ought to turn it down, her own sense of self-preservation told her that, but instead of doing so she heard herself saying huskily, 'Thank you, yes. I…I'd love to join you.' To join him. To join *with* him…to…!

'Good!'

The look he gave her sent a thrill of dangerous pleasure zinging right through her. Helplessly she clenched her muscles against it, against the betraying sexual shudder she could feel gripping her.

Leon was smiling at her, his mouth curling up at the corners in the way that made her long to throw her arms around him and kiss every delicious centimetre of those tempting warm male lips. Especially where they curled so fascinatingly into the smile that made her heart somersault and sent a dizzying rush of pleasure showering through her.

Hastily Sadie averted her gaze from his mouth and tried instead to focus on a point somewhere beyond his left shoulder. But she was still excruciatingly conscious of him, and of her own longing for him. Where had it come from, this savage, clawing, aching, longing that had hit her out of nowhere, left her drugged, doped, dependent on the proximity of him?

When she had contemplated the prospect of falling in love in the past her mental meanderings had never come anywhere near encompassing anything like this! And they had certainly never allowed her to imagine anyone like Leon!

'Hell, Sadie, will you please stop looking at me like that?' Leon demanded savagely. 'Because if you don't I'm going to have to kiss you, and I warn you that if I do I'm not going to want to stop at just kissing you…' he continued fiercely.

Her face bright red, Sadie asked him quickly, 'I…what time shall I meet you in the morning?' She held her breath, not sure if she wanted Leon to stop speaking so erotically to her or not.

'Well, from my point of view it will probably facilitate matters if we have breakfast together,' Leon began.

'Together?' Sadie could hear the squeak of panic in her voice.

'I meant in the dining room, of course,' Leon assured her blandly. 'Unless…'

'Oh, the dining room. Yes, of course. Yes…er…what time? I…'

Listening to herself gabbling, Sadie wondered if Leon knew just how much she was longing to have the courage to simply reach out and wrap her arms around him, to stand on tiptoe and press her body the entire length of his whilst she kissed him in a way that would leave him in no doubt whatsoever about where she most wanted to have breakfast with him tomorrow morning!

Before he could guess what she was thinking she opened her handbag and searched for her key.

Ten minutes later, safely inside her room on her own, with the door locked, she told herself that it was relief she was feeling that Leon hadn't pushed or pressed to be allowed to come in with her—and not disappointment.

Still, she would be seeing him in the morning. Blissfully she hugged that thought to her, lost in a dreamy fantasy of sensual blue skies and an even more sensual man.

CHAPTER FIVE

'THAT'S what I like to see—a woman who enjoys her food.'

Sadie's toes curled into her shoes as Leon's warmly approving gaze embraced her.

He had telephoned her at seven o'clock, the ringing bringing her out of the shower, to ask her if she was awake and suggest that they meet up in the restaurant at eight.

'Awake—of course I'm awake,' she had responded indignantly, adding without thinking, 'I was actually in the shower.'

There was a small silence, and then Leon's voice, like warm honey melting down the telephone line, as he'd said thickly, 'I wish you hadn't told me that, Sadie!'

He hadn't said anything else, but Sadie had known immediately that he was picturing her naked—and what was more she had been doing some pretty sensual visualisation of the two of them together herself!

Just the thought of Leon naked in the shower with her was enough to make her skin prickle in sensual hunger.

She had dressed at top speed, donning a clean white tee shirt and a pair of beige linen cut-offs, and some white and beige trainers for comfort. A beige raffia bag embroidered with white daisies and her sunglasses had completed her preparations.

Leon had been waiting for her in the foyer of the hotel. Like her, he was casually dressed, his tee shirt revealing warmly tanned and strongly muscled arms.

'Good.' He smiled approvingly at her. 'I'm glad you've dressed casually. The *mas* is in a fairly remote place, and although it has its own swimming pool, and overlooks the sea itself, I've picked it because of its country location.'

Now, as she finished her fruit and reached for the delicious croissant she had selected from the lavish buffet table, Sadie turned to Leon and mentioned hesitantly, 'Raoul told me that your company will be acquiring the house in Grasse as well as the business attached to it.'

She couldn't help thinking how much this would have upset her grandmother. She had often told Sadie whilst she was growing up how much she missed her childhood home. Sadie had been too young then to suggest that her grandmother lower her pride and make contact with her brother, with a view to visiting Grasse and the house.

'You should see it, Sadie,' she had told her vehemently. 'It is as much a part of your heritage as your "nose".' When your grandfather saved me from the Germans and brought me to England I had no idea that I would never return to Grasse. My father would have been so angry and hurt if he had known what my brother did.'

Sadie had tried to find words to comfort her, but she had seen how much her grandmother had missed her home.

'Yes, that is part of the deal,' Leon agreed, picking up the coffee pot and refilling her empty cup for her.

'What will you do with it? Will you keep it or sell it?' Sadie asked him, wondering what it was about seeing such a strong sexy man performing this small domestic chore that made her insides melt.

'I don't know yet, and anyway the decision won't be

entirely mine to make. Why?' Leon questioned, giving her a keen look.

'No reason,' Sadie answered him hesitantly. Despite the physical intimacy they had shared she didn't feel mentally close enough to him to talk more about her grandmother.

Her reticence owed more to her own loyalty to her grandmother than a reluctance to confide in Leon. She was well aware that an outsider who had not known her grandmother might question her stubbornness in refusing to have anything to do with her estranged brother. And, for reasons she was not prepared to delve deeply into, it was becoming increasingly important to Sadie that Leon felt warmly and sympathetically towards the grandmother she had loved so much. After all, how could she give her love completely to a man who did not understand and accept Grandmère's little foibles?

Leon was still looking at her, with one dark eyebrow raised and an expression in his eyes that told her he knew she was being evasive.

Ruefully, she gave a small shrug.

'It's just that—well, there is so much family history attached to the house. I just think it would be very sad if it were to be sold off, or converted into offices or apartments like so many of the older buildings have been. If you were going to…to dispose of it…'

'You'd want first chance to buy it?' Leon guessed, wondering why, if she did want the property, she had not asked for it to be included in the package he was having put together for her in part exchange for the very generous lump sum she would be receiving for her share of the business.

Immediately Sadie shook her head.

'I'd love to,' she admitted, wrinkling her nose a little

as she added, 'But there's no way I could afford it. Even in its run-down state it would still be expensive, and I just don't have that kind of money. Not even if I sold my home in England.'

Leon frowned as he listened to her. Raoul had implied to him that Sadie came from a wealthy background—'pampered and spoiled' had been just two of the words he had used to describe her. Even if Raoul had been lying, the sum he had agreed to pay him for the business and the property was, in his opinion, on the dangerous side of generous—and he knew that his board would agree with him.

Sadie would by virtue of her one-third holding in Francine receive one-third of that money. When he included in that sum the extra amount he had now offered, via Raoul, to pay in respect of Sadie giving up her own business to join the company, he was looking at a very large amount indeed—and Sadie's share was well in excess of what he knew to be the value of the Grasse property.

It was on the tip of his tongue to challenge her statement, and a small frown wrinkled his forehead as he contemplated what might lie behind Sadie's seemingly artless comment.

Could she actually be angling for him to offer to hand over the Grasse property to her? Somehow he hadn't thought of her as a person who was either manipulative or grasping—unlike her cousin. But he was enough of a businessman to respect the fact that she was in a position where, if she chose to do so, she could set an extremely high value on her expertise.

Unusually for Raoul, he had been unexpectedly and unhelpfully vague about what he thought Sadie's financial requirements might be for joining Francine, and so

Leon had sought the advice of a local firm of head-hunters, asking them what the going rate for a person of Sadie's skills would be. Once they had told him he had decided that in view of the fact she was giving up her stance on natural raw materials, and agreeing to create a new perfume, he had added a large extra amount onto the sum he had informed his legal team he would be paying her as a salary.

If she was after the Grasse house as an additional 'sweetener', though, she was going to be disappointed!

Aware of his unexpected and certainly unwanted withdrawal from her, but totally unaware of what Leon was thinking, Sadie questioned lightly, 'Is something wrong?'

'No, nothing at all,' Leon assured her smoothly. 'If you're ready, we ought to make a start. The *mas* is a good three hours' drive away.'

Relieved to see the sombre look replaced by a much warmer one, Sadie nodded her head.

The tables on the open air terrace of the restaurant where they had eaten their breakfast were filling up with other guests now, and Sadie was glad that they'd eaten early enough to have virtually had the place to themselves.

This hotel would make a wonderful venue for honeymoons, she acknowledged as she stood up and Leon came to pull her chair back for her. What with its spa facilities and suites with their own private hot tubs. If she and Leon were sharing such a suite...

As he saw her eyes darken and her face flush, Leon wondered what it was that had brought that soft look to Sadie's eyes and caused her sudden intake of breath.

Standing close to her now, breathing in the warm scent of her, he wondered if he was being entirely wise in choosing to spend a whole day with her—especially after last night! And it wasn't the fiercely passionate kiss they had exchanged before going their separate ways he was thinking about, but the hours afterwards, when he had lain awake in bed, aching for her so much that he'd had to grit his teeth against the sheer intensity of it, and will the hard, angry throb of his erection to subside.

When Leon picked up the keys for the hire car he had ordered from the foyer, the receptionist announced, 'The hire car firm has asked me to apologise to you because unfortunately they have not been able to supply you with the car you requested. They have instead delivered a smaller one. Apparently there was a mix-up at the main office, and with Cannes being so busy with a big trade fair...'

Sadie could see that Leon was frowning a little, and so she offered calmingly, 'As there are only the two of us the size of the car doesn't really matter, does it?'

Leon took the keys from the receptionist and turned to smile warmly at her.

'Does having such a good nature come naturally to you, or do you have to work at it?' he teased her gently as he took her arm and guided her out into the warm morning sunshine.

Sadie cast him a wry look.

'You didn't give me the impression that you thought I had a good nature when we first met,' she reminded him dryly.

'Ah.' Leon gave her a droll look. 'But that was before.'

'Before what?' Sadie couldn't resist asking as he led her towards the small compact hire car parked just outside the main entrance.

Bending his head towards her, Leon replied wickedly, 'Before I kissed you.' He was playing with fire and he knew it, but suddenly he felt happier than he had felt in a long long time.

Speechlessly Sadie got into the passenger seat. Leon was quite definitely flirting with her, and somehow she didn't think that he was the type of man to flirt with every woman he met. No, when Leon flirted, it was because…

Because what? Because he wanted to idle away a few spare days enjoying a brief sexual liaison? Sadie shivered, as though the words 'brief' and 'liaison' were lumps of ice someone had dropped down her back.

It really was a compact car, she acknowledged ruefully a few minutes later, as she saw the way that Leon was practically folded over the steering wheel.

'In Australia we wouldn't give something of this size to our kids in case we were convicted of child abuse,' he told her in disgust as he inserted the key into the ignition.

Sadie laughed.

'I thought it was only Texas where everything was bigger than anywhere else,' she teased him, but her laughter turned into a small anxious frown as the car refused to start.

Cursing beneath his breath, Leon tried again—and this time, to Sadie's relief, the engine fired.

The farmhouse Leon was planning to rent for the summer was in the Massif de l'Estérel region of Provence, a beautiful mountainous area made up of the volcanic rock porphyry. The sides of the mountains were cloaked in forests of pine and cork oaks. Sadie felt a thrill of excitement at the thought of visiting such a beautiful area, and an even sharper one at the thought of visiting it with Leon.

However, because of some roadworks in the centre of Mougins they had to take a circuitous route in order to get to the road that would take them up into the region.

As they drove through the countryside surrounding Mougins Sadie couldn't resist pointing out to Leon the fields full of flowers grown for the perfume industry.

'How can anything made in a laboratory come anywhere near rivalling the scent of these?' she asked him passionately, gesturing towards fields of roses and jasmine.

'No, it doesn't,' Leon agreed with a glinting look towards her. 'For one thing with a chemically based scent there's no risk of the final product differing from batch to batch because the sun shone for three days less one year! And that means that when a woman buys a chemically created perfume she can be sure she is getting exactly the same scent that was in her previous bottle—and at an affordable price!'

Sadie's forehead puckered into a frown. From listening to Leon it would be easy to imagine that he had not changed his stance at all on the creation of the new perfume. Or was he simply trying to bait her?

She opened her mouth to vigorously defend her own stance, but Leon shook his head and gave her a meaningful look.

'Remember our pact?' he warned her.

Sadie laughed, but inwardly she couldn't help wishing that she could talk with him about her excitement and enthusiasm for her work on creating their new perfume. *Their* new perfume... She was also aching to get to work on the old-fashioned men's cologne produced by Francine, to update it, to make out of it a scent that was intensely male...a fragrance that would for ever and always be for her the mark of the man she was so passionately drawn to. Leon's scent...

Dreamily she let her imagination go to work! She would name it Leon—in her own secret thoughts if not in public—and it would be topaz-dark in hue, leonine, discreet, sensual, strong, earthy and rich, yet with a touch of coolness and hauteur, a fragrant suggestion of the pale green ice that was Leon's eyes! Leon…Leon… The bottle would be tall and round, wide enough for a man's hand to grip comfortably and feel at ease with…

Guiltily Sadie snatched her recklessly wayward thoughts back to reality.

Leon was an excellent driver in whose care she felt extremely safe, and she was pleased when he praised her map-reading skills and thanked her for finding them a shorter route to the motorway.

'I dare say this wretched slug of a car will mean that it will take us longer to get there than I had expected,' Leon warned her once they reached the right road. 'And heaven alone knows how it will cope with climbing the mountains.'

Sadie gave him a rueful look. Although he was complaining, he was not doing so in a bad-tempered manner, rather a wryly resigned one. It increased her growing respect for him to see that he could control his reaction to difficult situations.

In fact, as she was quickly discovering, time spent in Leon's company was such a blissful experience that merely sitting beside him inside a car made her feel happier than she suspected, as a sane modern woman, she had any right to be feeling.

As Leon had predicted, the small car laboured wretchedly up the steep mountain roads, but Sadie was too entranced by their surroundings and her companion to care. She had read in the guide book provided with the car that the porphyry rock that formed the mountains held colours which ranged from the deepest red in Cap Roux through to blue in Agay, where the Romans had made the column shafts for their monuments in Provence, to green, yellow, purple and grey. But to actually glimpse these rich colours through the deep green screen of the forest made her catch her breath in awe, unable to resist drawing Leon's attention to what she had seen.

'They are awesome,' he agreed, his expression deliberately teasing as he added, 'That is unless you have seen Ayers Rock!'

'Oh, you.' Sadie pulled a face at him and then stopped, her eyes misting a little with emotion as she realised how easy and natural she felt with him—just as though she had known him for years...

From somewhere deep inside her the words 'soul mates' rose up and would not be denied. Soul mate. Wasn't that truly what every single human being longed for? To meet their own one and only soul mate? To be with their special-once-in-a-lifetime person who was their fate and their destiny?

A tiny little shiver quivered through her.

'Cold?' Leon asked, frowning and reaching out to the air-conditioning control.

Sadie shook her head, but a small perverse part of her was pleased when he turned his head to give her a searching look, and then, and only then, seemed prepared to accept her statement. Ridiculously, she knew—given her age and the fact that she had looked after herself for so long—it gave her a tiny thrill of pleasure to know that he was so concerned for her comfort. Perhaps another woman might have accused him of being stereotypically male but Sadie admitted she was actually enjoying the sensation of being cared for.

'Does it look from the map as though it's much further?' Leon asked with a small frown as the car crawled up yet another steep hill.

Obligingly, Sadie checked the map. Ironically, it gave her as much pleasure to be treated as an equal partner in their shared venture as it had done only seconds ago to feel he regarded her as someone in need of his care and protection.

'Well, it's going on for twenty miles to the village you mentioned,' she told him.

'In that case we'd better stop for some lunch. Is there anywhere before then?' Leon asked.

'We should be coming up to a place called the Auberge des Adrets soon,' Sadie informed him, looking at the guidebook again. 'It was once supposed to be the favourite haunt of some highwayman named Gaspard de Besse. But there's a small town a little bit further on,' she added. 'Why don't we stop there and buy some food? Then we can eat when we get to the *mas*.'

When Leon shot her a surprised look Sadie back-pedalled a little, telling him, 'You said that it was un-occupied, so I thought in view of the time it's taking us to get there... But if you would rather eat at a restau-rant...'

'No...buying our own stuff is fine by me. In fact I think it's a great idea,' Leon assured her immediately.

'Well, we should be reaching the town soon,' Sadie assured him.

Watching her as she concentrated on the guidebook, diligently checking that they were travelling in the right direction, Leon admitted that he could not think of a time when he had last enjoyed himself so much—couldn't re-member a time when he had enjoyed a woman's com-pany so much. Back home, the women he occasionally dated would have thrown a fit had he suggested taking them anywhere other than the most expensive and fashionable places to eat. And when he did, eating was the last thing they actually did.

They tended to parade up and down in their designer clothes, apply lipstick to their already vermilioned mouths whilst checking out the other occupants of the tables in their compact mirrors. They'd wave to their friends with long polished nails, whilst pouting complaints to him that they couldn't possibly drink anything other than the most expensive champagne. Oh, yes they did all that! But eat? Never!

Oh, they would certainly order the most expensive dishes on the menu, all right, but then refuse to eat them, protesting about calories and fat content. If there was one thing Leon hated it was seeing good food wasted—a hang-up from his upbringing, no doubt, when his grandmother had often regaled him with stories of how poor she and his grandfather had been, and how one joint of meat had been made to last a whole week.

Sadie wasn't like the spoiled society women he had previously dated, though. Last night and this morning she had eaten her food with every evidence of enjoyment. And somehow he found just watching her doing that far more sexually stirring than watching a stick-thin model-type toying irritably with a piece of designer greenery.

And surely a woman with a healthy appetite for food would have an equally healthy appetite for life's other sensual pleasures?

Leon recognised that his thoughts were about to surge dangerously out of control.

'I think the town is coming up now,' Sadie warned him

As he nodded his head in acknowledgement, Leon reflected ruefully that the town wasn't on its own!

* * *

'You've bought enough food to feed at least a dozen people.' Sadie laughed, shaking her head in mock disapproval as she and Leon headed back to the car. Both of them were carrying the purchases Leon had insisted on making.

He'd excitedly bought long sticks of French bread, freshly baked that morning, some local cheese and fruit, some olives, and some cold meats from the local *charcuterie*, some delicious delicacies from the patisserie, and even a bottle of red wine, as well as some water. It was a feast fit for any king

But Leon wasn't a king, he was a billionaire, Sadie reminded herself as they reached the car. No wonder he had looked at her in such surprise when she had suggested they buy food and virtually picnic at the *mas*.

'What's wrong?' Leon demanded, making her jump as she realised that he was watching her.

The genuine concern in his voice and the perceptiveness of the look he was giving her brought Sadie to a standstill in the middle of the empty street.

'Sadie?'

The intensity with which Leon spoke her name as he raised one hand to her face, gently tucking an errant strand of hair behind her ear, caused Sadie to tremble from head to foot, the paper bag she was clutching in her arms shaking with her.

Very gently Leon's hand stroked down the side of her head, before resting on her neck, his thumb massaging the delicate flesh just behind her ear in a way, to judge from the concerned look in his eyes, Sadie suspected he had intended to be comforting and reassuring, but in fact was anything but. Her whole body leapt into shocking, aroused life immediately, her tremors increasing.

What on earth must Leon think of her? He must be used to sophisticated, experienced woman who did not react like inexperienced and over-excited teenagers the moment he touched them. Inexperienced...

Sadie pulled her mind back from the word like a mother protectively pulling a child's fingers back from an open flame.

Leon's hand was still cupping the side of her head, and somehow Sadie managed to make herself look directly into his eyes.

The look in their deep, deep depths was making her feel dizzy, holding her in thrall.

'Have I told you, yet, Sadie, just what a very exceptional person I think you are?'

Exceptional? Her? Sadie tried to remind herself of who he was and why she was with him, but the slow, gentle movement of his hand against her scalp was overheating her thoughts as well as her body. Beneath her clothes she could feel it reacting to him, her breasts filling with liquid aching need, her nipples tightening, flaunting their desire as they pushed hungrily against the fine silk of her bra. Low down in her stomach her muscles tightened, whilst the female core of her swelled and moistened.

Tiny beads of perspiration dampened her hairline and upper lip—and they were not caused by the heat of the sun, Sadie noted ruefully as she made a valiant attempt to behave as though she was perfectly accustomed to such a situation.

Leon looked closely at her as the soft, incredibly long dark lashes concealed Sadie's eyes from him. He could feel the tiny convulsive tremors of her body. They ran through his fingertips and up his arm, and from there right the whole way through him, to every last inch and single cell of him. He had never ever met a woman who made him feel like this, who aroused in him such a complex tangle of emotions and desires.

Within the space of a single heartbeat she could send him from the most intense physical need he could ever remember feeling to the most protective and tender realisation of just how vulnerable she was. In one breath she could make him want to be both poacher and gamekeeper. Right now, here in this hot little street, he could quite easily lean her against the nearest wall and take her in the most primitive, hungry male way there was—yes, and make her ache with the need he felt for every single heartbeat. But at the same time he also wanted to wrap a cloak of protection around her that would prevent any male eyes from ever looking lustfully on her, any male desire from ever hurting her.

Including his own?

Leon had never met a woman who made him feel that so much in life that was simple and easily affordable was somehow also invaluably pleasurable. Apart, perhaps, from his grandmother, She had also relished the simple and inexpensive things in life.

Suddenly Sadie pulled away from him.

Looking down at her, Leon growled. 'Do you have any idea how very, very tempted I am to kiss you?'

Sadie granted herself ten wonderful seconds in which to absorb the blissful delight that hearing these words gave her, and then another ten just because it felt so good. Then, in case she dangerously gave away how shamelessly she wanted him to kiss her, she turned away from him and started to hurry to where they had parked the car.

Leon watched her. He could still feel the warmth of her neat, delicately shaped head on his palm, the softness of her hair and her skin. As she walked away from him he watched the awesome femaleness in the movement of her body with male appreciation—and a very physical male response—only just managing to suppress a small growl of possessiveness as he contemplated the effect of her neatly rounded derrière on other vulnerable members of his sex who were witnessing it as she walked past them.

It was his duty, surely, to protect them from such vulnerability—and the temptation which accompanied it! For the sake of his own sex, Sadie needed a man in her life and a ring on her finger! A ring? His ring?

Now, where the hell had that thought come from?

They had to call at the local garage before leaving the town, to put more petrol in the car, and Leon frowned as he saw the way the driver of a car on the other side of the pumps paused to give Sadie a lingeringly appreciative second look before getting back into his vehicle.

'Seems like you've made a conquest,' he commented dryly to Sadie as he put the key in the ignition.

'It's probably my hair,' she answered matter-of-factly. She had already noticed how often local men looked at her blonde locks.

'Yeah, and the rest,' she thought she heard Leon mutter beneath his breath. But as she turned to look at him she realised that the car was as it had been this morning, when Leon had first attempted to start it—refusing to start!

Sadie held her breath as he tried again, and then again, To her relief, on the fourth attempt the engine fired.

CHAPTER SIX

HALF an hour later Sadie looked out of the passenger window and caught her first glimpse of the sea, way, way down below them—foam-capped, blue-green, dipping to denser all-blue where it met the horizon.

Automatically she gave a small exclamation of pleasure.

'Want a closer look?' Leon offered, moving to pull over to the side of the road, where there was a convenient parking space.

Sadie was tempted, but she knew that it was taking them much longer to reach the *mas* than Leon had expected. If they were to stop she knew she would also be tempted to look for a path down the steep cliff, so that she could sink her toes into the untouched golden sand of the small, perfect half-moon-shaped beach which was just visible below them. And of course once on that beach she would definitely need to at least dip her feet into the sea itself!

The thought of the two of them sharing the privacy of that small beach, even perhaps picnicking there, with the food they had bought, made her long to accept Leon's suggestion. Sternly she reminded herself of the reason they were here, and the fact that that she was an adult and not a child.

Leon was still waiting for her to reply. Regretfully, she shook her head.

Recognising the wistfulness in her expression, Leon twitched his mouth in amusement. But, like her, he was conscious of how long the journey was taking them. At this rate they would no sooner have reached the *mas* than it would be time to turn back! Nevertheless... The thought of being alone with Sadie on that small deserted beach was a very tempting one. A very, very tempting one indeed!

Deliberately suppressing it, he put his foot down a little harder on the accelerator. The small car struggled to respond, chugging valiantly up the steep incline.

'Not much further now,' Leon assured Sadie as they turned off the coast road and onto a narrower road which would take them to the *mas*.

About ten minutes after leaving that road, and driving down a private lane, they found it. A small cosy spread of red-roofed, warmth-washed buildings, perched half-way up the hillside and facing out to sea.

Leon brought the car to a halt outside it, and neither of them spoke as they both gazed at the *mas*.

Without a word Leon pressed the automatic buttons and opened their car windows—as though he had guessed what she was thinking, Sadie reflected as she breathed in the wonderfully pure air. Even up here, at this height, she would have sworn she could smell and taste the sea.

Lavender shrubs scented the air with their flowers, and the silvery-grey trunk of a wisteria leaned heavily against the golden walls of the *mas*, its branches covered in soft feathery leaves. A scattering of obviously self-seeded semi-wild flowers threw up their heads in warm bursts of colour that broke up the green of the grass, and beyond the *mas* Sadie could see a small olive grove. But what really caught her eye was the low wall, bordered with an informal hedge of orange trees, beyond which she could see the enticing sparkle of water. The *mas* had a swimming pool! And not just any swimming pool, but one of the stunning modern infinity pools that had recently become so fashionable. From where she was looking, it really did seem as though the water in the pool actually merged with the sea, so that the sparkling blue water seemed to stretch into infinity.

The whole place combined a perfect blend of traditional and modern design, Sadie recognised. If this place was hers she knew there was no way she could ever bear to let it to anyone else.

'Oh, how beautiful!' Her soft, delighted words broke the silence and had Leon turning his head to look at her.

'This is the first time I've actually seen it.' His voice sounded gruff and slightly hoarse, as though he was as affected by the wild, private beauty of the *mas* as she was herself, but trying in a manlike way to hide it. 'In the flesh, I mean,' he amended. 'The agent sent me photographs and a video. I told him I wanted somewhere private, and this place is certainly that.'

'It's heavenly,' Sadie told him, so caught up in the spell of the place that she had opened the car door and stepped out without even realising she had done so.

A soft breeze stroked over her skin and instinctively she held her face up to the sun, closing her eyes as she basked in its warmth.

Turning to Leon, and gesturing widely with her arms to encompass the *mas*, the land and the sea and sky beyond it, she told him huskily, 'This is what perfume is all about—flowers, earth, air, sea, capturing the scents of nature. No laboratory-produced chemical can ever reproduce this!' she finished passionately.

Sombrely Leon watched her. The breeze was moulding her clothes to her body, highlighting its curves. He was tempted to challenge her statement, to remind her that she herself had now agreed to work with man-made scents, but he was reluctant to introduce a note of conflict into their day. In her eyes he could see how intensely she felt, and irrevocably he knew that he wanted to share that passion and, dangerously, he wanted *her*.

'Let's take a look inside.'

The harshness of Leon's voice made Sadie frown. Had he thought her foolish and over-emotional to feel the way she did about their surroundings? He was waiting for her, and so silently she fell into step beside him.

Inside, the *mas* was every bit as perfect as it was outside—at least in Sadie's opinion. The large country-style kitchen opened out onto a shady secluded patio, complete with a family-sized table and chairs, the patio itself ornamented with tubs of geraniums and an old-fashioned water pump.

The long, sprawling building also housed a cosy TV room, as well as a formal dining room and a wonderfully large and elegant sitting room, which ran the full width of the house and had windows on either side.

Upstairs there were five good-sized bedroom, each with its own bathroom. Every room was furnished simply but with style. With each step she took Sadie found herself envying whoever it was who owned it—especially when Leon told her that the land attached to the *mas* extended right down to the sea and included its own private beach.

'It's absolutely wonderful,' she told him.

'You like it?'

'How could anyone not?' Sadie responded ruefully. 'If it was mine, I don't think I could bear to let it out to someone else.'

As soon as she had finished speaking Leon found that he was actually making mental plans to get in touch with the letting agent and find out if the owners would be prepared to sell! After all, it would make sense for him to have a permanent base in Europe—especially now that they were taking over Francine.

Come off it, he derided himself. That isn't why you want it, and you damn well know it. No. It wasn't himself, dressed in a business suit and working alone on his laptop, he was envisaging. It was he and Sadie, and what they were doing had nothing whatsoever to do with work or laptops!

'Well, I don't know about you, but I am ready for that food we bought,' Leon told Sadie, hastily banishing his wayward thoughts. He looked at his watch and added ruefully, 'Do you realise that it's already half past three?'

Sadie hadn't realised, as she had been far too entranced by the house to think about the time.

'Where would you like to eat? Inside or out?' Leon asked her.

'Oh, outside—if that's okay with you?' Sadie responded immediately.

'By the pool?' Leon guessed.

Sadie gave him an eloquent look of confirmation, her eyes shining with pleasure. Watching her, Leon didn't know how the hell he was managing to stop himself from taking hold of her and kissing her until that look of shining pleasure became one of liquid desire.

'It's a pity we didn't bring our swimming things,' Sadie regretted innocently, as she looked longingly at the pool.

'Who says we need them?' Leon teased her softly, laughing outright as he saw her expression.

'What? Don't tell me you've never been skinny-dipping?' He grinned in disbelief. 'You live by the sea, don't you?'

Sadie shook her head vehemently.

'I certainly have not,' she told him firmly, but the expression in her eyes was a little wistful.

The mere thought of swimming naked with Leon in the soft warm water of the pool was sending her imagination into definitely x-rated regions, and making her pulse bounce excitement though her body. Protectively, she hid her reaction from Leon. Her grandmother had been of a generation that believed that it was a man's role to pursue a woman, most definitely not the woman's to pursue him. And although Sadie knew such teachings were outmoded now, a little bit of her still clung to them. Perhaps it was as a consequence of that that her own sexual experience was rather limited—or at least she suspected that in Leon's eyes it would be.

'I was brought up by my grandmother, remember,' she defended, when she saw his expression. 'And besides,' she added dryly, 'the water off the coast of Pembroke is extremely cold.'

Ten minutes later, as they unpacked the food which Leon had brought from the kitchen where they had stored it, Sadie realised just how hungry she was.

'No, thanks,' she refused, shaking her head and covering the wine glass Leon had found as he reached for the wine he had bought.

He raised his eyebrows and teased her. 'Why not? Are you afraid that it might weaken your grandmother-induced resolve enough for you to want to try skinny-dipping after all?'

He was just teasing her. Sadie knew that. After all, he couldn't know how much she wanted him…

Refusing to rise to his bait, she firmly dismissed the tormenting erotic images from her mind and told him calmly, 'You can't have any wine because you're driving, and I don't want to drink any without you. It doesn't seem fair.'

The look she could see in his eyes as he replaced the bottle and reached for one of water instead confused her.

As he poured them both a glass of water, Leon noted that Sadie was constantly surprising and challenging not only his original assessment of her, but also his understanding of women in general. In refusing to drink any wine because he could not share in the pleasure she had shown a genuine kindness of nature which he admitted was seriously denting the barriers he had felt he needed to put up against her. Denting it? Get real, he advised himself derisively. She had damn near demolished it wholesale!

'Mmm...those olives look good,' Leon commented hungrily as he watched Sadie opening the small carton containing them.

'Want one?' she responded immediately, picking one up without thinking about the sensual intimacy of her action as she offered to feed it to him.

The look he gave her made her suddenly conscious of the heat prickling on her back, and even more aware of the heat trickling through her body. She hadn't meant to be provocative, but right now the way he was looking at her made her feel as though she were Eve, offering Adam that apple!

However, before she could retract either her words or the olive, Leon's hand snaked out and his fingers curled softly around her wrist, making her heart bounce around inside her chest as though it were on a piece of elastic. How could such a small gesture, such a simple touch, have such a powerful and erotic effect upon her? She might not be sexually experienced, but she wasn't totally naïve! Somewhere at the back of her mind the knowledge surfaced that a part of her had known from the minute she had set eyes on him that Leon was going to affect her like this.

Dizzily she noted how cool Leon's hold was, and how potentially strong. Her wrist felt so fragile in his grip. She could feel his thumb pressing against her pulse-point and her heart gave a violently convulsive jerk.

Without her even wanting it, never mind being able to do a thing to stop him, Leon had lifted her hand to his mouth. Her eyes rounded, their colour darkening as her gaze followed his every movement. Helplessly, she watched as his lips parted, encompassing not just the juicy pitted black olive but her fingertips as well.

Her own lips parted involuntarily, her mouth going dry as a fierce ache burst into life inside her.

The sensation of Leon's tongue curling over her fingers and then thrusting between to remove the olive made her go light-headed with desire. Her heart was pumping as ferociously as though she had just run up a steep moun-tainside. Shockingly explicit images were forming inside her head, and waves of liquid desire were shafting through her body like bolts of lightning. The thumb pressed so close to her pulse must surely be registering its erratic beat.

The olive had gone from her fingers, but Leon's tongue had not! It was lapping slowly and surely, with deliberate sensuality, at her flesh, removing the satin covering of olive oil.

'Mmm,' she heard Leon whisper throatily, glancing up into her eyes as he did so and giving her a wicked look. 'Very more-ish!'

Sadie's eyes opened wide and her face turned a vivid

shade of pink. He wasn't, she suspected, referring to the olive!

His tongue laved her fingers one more time with lingering thoroughness, and then he lifted his head to look at her, whilst his hand slid down over her wrist to cover hers, folding her fingers into her palm and slowly stroking her small fist as he asked her softly, 'Are you sure you don't want a glass of wine?'

Emphatically Sadie shook her head and tried to repossess her hand. She was intoxicated enough as it was, without drinking wine! The sensuality of what he had done had sent her blood into a cloud of fizzy bubbles as it raced round her veins.

Watching her, Leon was instinctively and sharply aware of her sexual naïveté, and that knowledge sent a huge reactionary surge of corresponding male arousal thundering through him.

He had never been promiscuous, but naturally as a young man he had gone through the normal stages of sexual experimentation and exploration. Since hitting his late twenties, though, he had given up on sexual exploration as a means of expressing himself as a man. However, the majority of women he met were very open about the fact that they were extremely sexually experienced. They seemed to think that he would enjoy the results of that experience. Perhaps like Sadie he had been imbued with a lot of his own grandmother's moral beliefs.

There was also, Leon acknowledged, enough Greek heritage in him to make him find such women more of a turn-off than a turn-on. His realisation that Sadie was clearly quite inexperienced was producing within him the same effect as applying a lighted match to dry tinder—very dry tinder, he recognised grimly.

Whether it was unacceptable in today's modern climate or not, there was something within him, something
in his blood, that found the knowledge that there would
be much he would have the pleasure of showing her extremely attractive! Extremely attractive and insistently
arousing, as his body was making very, very plain!

He was delighted that potentially they had the summer
ahead of them to get to know one another. He would
make it his business to be sure he spent as much time in
France as he could, and he would see to it that Sadie also
needed to be there, for constant 'consultations' regarding
the new perfume she would be creating for them.

Still watching her, he discovered that he was toying
with ways and means of re-vamping the Grasse house
and outbuildings, and insisting that it was essential that
Sadie worked from there on the perfume.

That way their relationship could grow easily and naturally, and when they came to make a full commitment
to one another it would be—

A full commitment?

Leon underwent a moment of wry introspection and
self-searching. He was Greek enough to feel very
strongly that he only wanted to make a full commitment
to one woman and for that partnership to be for ever.
And he was modern-minded enough to know that that
kind of commitment couldn't be based solely on sexual
and emotional desire, but had to be based on mutual trust,
honesty and respect as well.

He had met too many women who were ready to say
anything to get what they wanted. No way could he ever
give his love and his life to a woman like that!

As he looked at Sadie he was uncomfortably aware
that whilst his thoughts might be logical and under control, his feelings and his body were no such thing. The

way he was feeling right now meant that the sooner they left the *mas* the better! The combination of Sadie, solitude and his own sexual longing for her right now were putting his self-control under far too much strain!

With that in mind, he stood up, frowning.

What was Leon thinking? Sadie wondered, watching him uncertainly. Two minutes ago he had been behaving towards her in a way that had quite definitely been very sexual. Now he was looking at her with a sternness that seemed to suggest she had done something wrong!

Perhaps he thought she had been deliberately provocative?

She quickly got to her feet herself, her pleasure in the day flattened by Leon's expression.

'I think it's time we made a move,' Leon announced grimly, adding under his breath so that Sadie couldn't hear him, 'Before it's too late!'

'You want us to leave now?' Sadie couldn't stop herself from questioning in disbelief. And then, when Leon made no response, she protested crossly, 'It might have escaped your notice, but I haven't had anything to eat yet.'

'You can eat in the car,' Leon told her unequivocally, bending down to pick up the bottle of wine as he did so.

The sky above them was still cloudlessly blue, the sea in the distance a deeper but just as storm-free hue. The lightest of breezes stirred the flowers, and the only sound on the clear air was the lazy hum of bees. So why did Sadie suddenly feel as though a very dangerous and threatening storm was imminent? she wondered miserably. Why did she feel as though the sky had turned dark and the coldest of icy winds was piercing her heart? Why?

Did she really need to ask herself that? she questioned

herself derisively whilst she stared at Leon's departing back as he walked towards the car. If ever a man's back was indicative of tightly reined in anger and cold savagery, then that back was Leon's!

Why on earth hadn't she had the sense to think first, before stupidly, idiotically, senselessly offering him that olive? Her face burned a self-contemptuous red. Of course he was bound to have thought she was coming on to him! But if he had thought that then why hadn't he simply rejected her immediately? Why on earth had he deliberately emphasised the sensuality of the moment in the way that he had? Had it been her own lack of experience that had put him off? Sadie wasn't entirely unfamiliar with the type of man who valued a woman purely on her sexual experience and availability, but naïvely she had believed that Leon was far above that kind of thing!

After a brief visit to the bathroom, to prepare herself for the journey and to reinforce to herself all the reasons why she should cease to feel anything whatsoever for Leon, she was ready to join him in the car.

Pulling on her seat beat, she remained resolutely silent as Leon moved to start the car—and continued to be so during the five unsuccessful attempts that followed the first.

However, when Leon finally unlocked the bonnet and got out, lifting it up to peer into the innards of the vehicle, Sadie felt anxious enough to ask, 'What is it? What's wrong?'

'God knows,' came back Leon's terse response. 'I'm no mechanic, but I suspect it's the battery. I'm going to have to ring the car hire people and get them to sort something out for us.'

Leon snapped the bonnet closed and came back to the car to get his mobile phone.

Five minutes later Sadie held her breath as she heard Leon demand ominously into his mobile, 'What do you mean, you can't supply me with a substitute?'

There was a brief pause before he cut in acidly, 'Look, I don't give a damn how busy you are, or how impossible it is for you to get a car out here to me until tomorrow. I would have thought any organisation that considered itself as anything approaching professional would have had the common sense to make sure it had enough vehicles to cover this extra busy period. Hell!' he swore bitterly as he held the instrument away from his ear. 'The line's breaking up,' he told Sadie grimly.

They tried to contact the hire firm on three successive occasions, both with Leon's mobile and Sadie's, and eventually managed to get through. But once again the hire car firm insisted that they were not able to provide Leon with a substitute vehicle until the following morning.

'Well, at least we've got the *mas* to stay in,' Sadie pointed out.

Leon was staring grimly out to sea.

'Yeah, great,' he agreed nastily

The toxicity of his silence was burning Sadie's sensitive nerve-endings.

'Look, I can see that you don't want to be here with me—' she began.

'For heaven's sake, Sadie.' Leon stopped her savagely. 'Don't you understand? It isn't what I *don't* want that's bothering me. It's what I *do* want.'

Sadie's forehead crinkled with her lack of understanding.

'I can see that you want to get back,' she began warily, 'but I don't—'

Leon groaned.

'No, Sadie!' he interrupted bluntly. 'What I want isn't to get back—although hell knows it damn well ought to be. What I want is you!'

His angry words seemed to hang in the enclosed space of the car, reverberating in her ears.

Her? He wanted her?

Sadie tried to say something, but her throat was too dry and the words stuck there. She swallowed and managed to squeak, 'You want me? But—'

'Yes. I want you!' Leon confirmed thickly. 'Every damned intoxicating, aggravating, delicious, sensual inch of you,' he ground out in fierce despair.

Head spinning, Sadie wondered at the strength of the feeling gripping her. What would Leon say if she told him that she fully reciprocated? What would he do?

'Have you any idea just what kind of hell it's going to be for me, having to spend the night here with you— alone. Just the two of us!' Leon emphasised tightly. 'Just the two of us!'

When she didn't say anything, he demanded harshly, 'Didn't last night tell you anything? Show you? Warn you. I could hardly keep my hands off you then!'

Sadie had had enough.

'Would it be such a terrible thing if you didn't?' she asked him bravely.

Leon stared at her, expression on his face hardening his eyes glittering green fire.

'I'm going to pretend I didn't hear that,' he told her grittily.

Sadie wasn't going to give in—no way, not now!

'Why?' she challenged him softly

'Why?'

She could hear raw anger in his voice, threaded with disbelief.

'I can't believe you're asking me that,' he told her flatly. 'I mean, you do know what I'm talking about, don't you? I'm a man, Sadie, and to put it in its bluntest terms, if I come anywhere near you feeling like I do right now... Wanting you like I do right now... Hell, Sadie, all it would take would be just for me to smell the scent of you, never mind touch you! And if I did touch you—'

The look of male hunger he was giving her made Sadie quiver from head to foot!

Grimly he continued, 'Well, let's just say I can't pretend that I am going to be able to stop at a few kisses this time.'

Sadie took a deep breath. Life was offering her an opportunity, and she realised she wanted to seize it with both hands. Right now she couldn't think of anything she wanted more than to make love with Leon. To touch him! Breathe him! Know him in every way that there was! What she was thinking...feeling...wanting...shocked her— but it excited her as well, she admitted.

Leon didn't look excited, though; far from it! The green glacier look was back in his eyes, sending her heart to a thudding drumbeat of a standstill.

How could he speak to her in the way he just had? How could he say the things he just had? How could he make her feel the way he just had and then look at her with that cold iciness in his eyes?

'Look, let's not mince matters,' Leon told her harshly. 'I don't go in for immediate sexual gratification, or casual sex, and before you try to tell me anything different I'm damn sure you don't either!'

Casual sex! Sadie could feel the raw acid taste of her

own shocked pain. It swamped her in a savage wave that tensed her whole body and washed the colour from her face.

Instinctively she wanted to hide what she was feeling from Leon, but somehow she just couldn't find the strength to turn away from him. She could feel her skin prickling with awareness as he looked at her.

When Leon saw Sadie's revealing expression he cursed under his breath and pushed his hand through his hair.

'We've both got one hell of a lot going on in our lives right now,' he told her brusquely. 'I want you, Sadie. Make no mistake about that. But, hell, Sadie,' he swore, when she continued to look at him with an open expression of anguished pain in her eyes, 'can't you see that I'm trying my hardest to protect you? Can't you see that I'm struggling to do the decent thing? Feeling the way I do right now...wanting you the way I do right now...' He groaned. 'Having to spend the night alone here with you is the last thing I need.'

Sadie told herself that she wouldn't have been a woman if she hadn't felt a very satisfying spurt of sensual pleasure at Leon's admission. Far more dangerous, though, was the even stronger surge of excitement that speared through her, and the knowledge that, high-minded though Leon's intentions were, an unexpectedly wicked part of her was strongly tempted to put them to the test. In the hope that they failed!

Hastily she looked away from him, in case that all-seeing gaze of his might somehow guess what she was thinking. Thoroughly bemused by what she was feeling, Sadie shrugged her shoulders and told Leon huskily, 'Well, no matter what either of us feels about it, we don't have any alternative. We are going to have to spend the night here!'

There—that should hopefully convince him that she wasn't secretly pleased that they were going to be here together alone...

'Sadie, I give you my word that you'll be perfectly safe,' Leon told her rawly.

As she turned away from him and started to walk back towards the *mas*, Sadie admitted to herself that she wasn't at all sure that 'safe' was what she wanted to be. In fact she knew that it wasn't! Not when the alternative was a blissful night spent in Leon's arms, enjoying and exploring Leon's body, having him explore hers...all of hers, with his hands and his mouth and...

Guiltily Sadie quickened her step as her whole body melted on a wave of unstoppable longing. Leon would be a wonderful lover. Somehow she already knew that. And her body wanted him to be its lover—*wanted* him to be! She had to stand still as her body reacted to her thoughts with a shocking surge of need.

Watching her, Leon discovered to his chagrin that he was actually grinding his teeth in frustration as a surge of hot male hunger gripped him. Fiercely he tried to resist the impulse to remember how she had felt in his arms last night when he had kissed her. He had given Sadie his word that he wouldn't touch her, and he fully intended to keep it!

Briefly he looked away from her, battling against himself when he discovered that his body was telling him very determinedly and openly just how much it opposed what he had decided.

Already it was tormenting him with dangerous thoughts and even more dangerous images of what it would feel like to share the pleasure of love with Sadie, of what it would be like to share the heat of desire with her, and the intimacy of knowing one another's bodies!

God, but he wanted her, Leon realised savagely—which was exactly why he would have given anything, paid anything, not to have to spend the night here at the *mas* with her.

He was a man of honour, and seducing her...

Seducing her. Leon leaned against the car and gave in to the fierce tide of heat that ripped through him.

He would undress her slowly, uncovering her inch by inch, touching her, stroking her, reassuring her as he kissed the soft sweetness of her skin, her throat, and that delicate delicious spot just behind her ear, her jaw, her eyelids and then her mouth.

Leon closed his eyes and tried to fight the surge of arousal engulfing him. But it was impossible. He could feel the immediate stiffening of his body and cursed himself beneath his breath, relieved that Sadie was too far away from him to be aware of his reaction.

But even knowing what his thoughts were doing wasn't enough to stop them. Not now...

He would kiss Sadie slowly and chastely, waiting until she was ready for the intimate exploration of his tongue. Somehow he would find a way to control his need to thrust it hotly into the sweetness of her mouth. And then, once she had accepted him there, he would start to explore her body, the delicate curve of her arm just above her elbow, the inside of her wrist, the soft slope of her neck where it met her shoulder. And her breasts...

Leon felt the fierce thrusting reaction of his own body, saw when he looked down where his erection strained against the cloth of his jeans. Inside them he was hard and aching, so tumescent that it hurt.

Sadie had already reached the *mas*. He knew he ought

to follow her, but his need for her was devouring him—
and if he did...if he even got within breathing distance
of her right now, never mind close enough to touch her,
Leon knew that he wouldn't be able to trust himself to
keep the promise he had made to her.

Just the thought of cupping the soft weight of her
breasts in his hands, of exploring them, running his fingertip around that place where the creamy paleness gave
way to the deeper pinkness of her aureole before rising
up to the nipple itself, was sending him crazy with longing.

His erection throbbed and pulsed. Inside his head, his
hand was already travelling down her body, stroking her
thighs, easing them apart, exploring the soft warmth of
the full swollen lips protecting her sex with gentle reassurance before sliding between them to probe the moist
excitement of her, and then...

Leon groaned out aloud and sliced a mental guillotine
down across his thoughts. If he continued like this he
wouldn't be able to walk as far as the house, never mind
do anything else, he told himself grittily.

He didn't just want Sadie, he admitted angrily. He
damn well loved her as well!

And loving her meant that he wanted to protect her.
Not just from any other man who might dare to take
advantage of her, but from himself!

He was in this so deep he might as well give up right
now, Leon admitted. But he couldn't afford to. Not until
he had got the takeover sorted.

He was glad that Sadie had seen sense with regard to
his plans for Francine. His board would not have been
too pleased, to say the least, had he had to institute potentially expensive and—even worse—long drawn-out legal proceedings against Sadie to prove that the Myrrh

perfume formula belonged legally to Francine. He needed that formula, Leon admitted, and he needed it badly—because he wanted to make good the vow he had made in his grandmother's name and memory: that women the world over would be able to enjoy and afford the perfume she had so longed for as a young woman.

When that had been done he could give himself time to court Sadie, and to love her. Not until then. And right now he had the night to get through!

At least they weren't going to starve whilst they waited for their replacement vehicle. Thanks to Sadie. Leon closed his eyes, reliving that moment when she had handed him the olive. An innocent Eve, indeed!

His erection stiffened and once again he muttered an imprecation under his breath. He was thirty-four years old, for heaven's sake, and well past the age when he ought to be getting a hard-on just thinking about sex.

But he wasn't just thinking about sex. He was thinking about Sadie! And he was thinking about love! Thinking about it. Aching for it—and for Sadie!

CHAPTER SEVEN

IT WAS gone eleven o'clock. In the kitchen of the *mas*, Sadie suppressed a small yawn and cast a wary look at Leon.

They had eaten a meal together earlier in the evening, and Leon had once again refused any of the wine—although why he should have done so Sadie had no idea, since he was not going to be driving after all.

She had had some, though! To give her the resilience to get through the evening? To help her to block out the savage and aching longing driving through her, urging her to take the kind of provocative sexual action she would normally not just have totally deplored but refused to even consider? Her? Seduce Leon? Her brain said no way, but her emotions and her body ached. If only...

Luckily, all the beds in the *mas* possessed bedclothes, and Leon had managed to turn on the hot water, so at least she would be able to have a shower before she went to bed.

A shelf of books in the TV room should have provided her with some means of passing the time and removing herself from Leon's presence, but stubbornly, and with alcohol-underpinned courage, she had refused to do so, remaining instead in the kitchen even though it was now over two hours since they had finished eating.

'You're tired,' Leon announced in a clipped voice. 'Why don't you go to bed?'

Why didn't she remove her unwanted company from his presence was more like it, Sadie reflected bitterly, but she kept her thoughts to herself as she smothered another yawn. She *was* tired, she admitted, but strangely she was reluctant to leave the kitchen.

Strangely? Since when had it been remotely strange for a woman in love to want to leave the company of the man she loved? Sadie derided herself mentally.

A woman in love? She was in love with Leon? Well, wasn't she? *Wasn't* she?

All right, she admitted angrily. All right! But that didn't mean…

That didn't mean what? she questioned herself mercilessly. That didn't mean that right now she just ached to leave her chair and go over to him and wrap her arms around him? To kiss her way all along his jaw and tease her fingers through his hair? She wanted to taste the texture of his skin and explore the deliciously tempting outline of his mouth, whilst her free hand tugged his tee shirt out of his jeans and slid beneath it to feel the male strength of his chest, and then—

Frantically Sadie fought to reign in her rioting thoughts! Her face was burning, she knew, and no wonder. Perhaps it might be wiser if she *did* go to bed!

'You're right,' she told Leon huskily. 'I am tired. I will go to bed.'

Yes, she needed to get away from him before her body went totally out of control with longing and she ended up making a grab for him and putting her wanton thoughts into action!

Defiantly, she poured herself another glass of wine and picked it up. She had lied about being tired. She was far too wound up emotionally for sleep, but perhaps the wine would help her to do so.

Leon exhaled his pent-up breath in a savage sigh as he watched Sadie walk away from him. Morning couldn't come fast enough for him. How the hell was he supposed to do anything so mundane as sleep when he knew that Sadie was lying there in the next room?

No way was he tired yet. He decided he would walk round the gardens of the *mas* and try and get his feelings under control.

Gathering up the underwear she had rinsed out, Sadie padded naked from the bathroom to the bedroom. The *mas* was certainly well equipped, and she was enjoying the luxury it provided. She envied Leon his stay here.

She found she couldn't get Leon out of her head as she restlessly prowled around the bedroom, the glass of wine forgotten. And besides, a mere glass of wine wasn't capable of subduing her longing…her love…

Leon stared back towards the *mas*. Sadie would be in bed by now. The savagery of the need that gripped him tensed his jaw. He could see the swimming pool, the water shimmering in the moonlight. His body needed cooling down and his thoughts needed exorcising!

He reached the side of the pool in a few strides, stripping off his clothes by the edge, and launching himself into a neat dive that sliced the water almost silently.

A fierce front crawl took him the length of the pool and back.

Still wide awake, Sadie went to her bedroom window. It looked out onto the pool area of the garden, and her whole body stiffened as she saw Leon in the water.

She watched him for several seconds before going into her bathroom and pulling on the bathrobe she had found there.

Like a sleepwalker she opened her bedroom door and made her way quietly and purposefully through the *mas*.

When she reached the pool, Leon was swimming towards the opposite side. Calmly she took off the robe and left it beside the pool. Unlike Leon, she did not dive into the pool, preferring instead to slide her body into its deliciously warm water.

She was a good swimmer. Her stroke was perhaps not as powerful as Leon's, but still very accomplished and sleek, and it carried her speedily through the water to where Leon was just executing his turn.

She could see the look in his eyes as she reached him and put her feet down on the tiled floor of the pool. Here at the shallow end the water was just lapping the lower curves of her breasts, nudging erotically at her nipples before retreating to expose them fully, its touch a sensually warm caress that heightened her already aroused senses.

'Sadie—'

She could hear the harsh warning in his voice but she ignored it. Up above them the sky was a midnight-blue cover sprinkled with brilliant white diamond stars. Sea and pool merged into a shimmering infinity, reflecting the brilliance of the moon. Nightscape lighting had turned the gardens of the *mas* into a place of mystery and fantasy.

The only sound to disturb the warm silence were the lap of the water and their own breathing. Leon's was measured, but harsh, as though he was fighting to control it, and her own was so rapid with excitement that it was making her feel almost faint. Leon was standing up in the water, with his back against the tiles, and Sadie could see his expression quite clearly. He looked, she thought giddily, like some Greek god come to life, with his dark hair and strong chiselled features. And his body… Her heart did a dangerous slalom from what felt like a great height, and then skidded to a thudding halt against her ribs.

Leon's body, she admitted, gulping in air, was just the most sexy male body she had ever seen in her life! She had thought that bodies like Leon's only came courtesy of a Michaelangelo or a Leonardo. His torso was a perfect V shape, his shoulders impressively broad, his chest solid but not overly muscled, tapering into his waist. She itched to spread her fingers across his chest and to savour the silky warmth of the soft darkness of his body hair. Her heated gaze dropped helplessly to where the narrow line of hair disappeared beneath the water. Like her, he was naked…

Sadie could feel her breasts swelling and her nipples tightening. Her body quivered, agitating the water around her. Unable to stop herself, she moved closer to Leon and silently raised one trembling hand to his body.

'Sadie.' Leon's low-voiced growl warned her of her danger, but she refused to stop. The pleasure of touching him was going to her head like champagne.

She took another step closer and then pressed both her hands flat against his chest. Lifting her head, she touched her tongue-tip to the hollow at the base of his throat, savouring the hot, salt male taste of him.

Lost in what she was doing, she didn't see the storm signals or smell the dangerous scent of brimstone in the air. One minute she was standing in front of Leon, shivering with the knowledge that all that was keeping them apart was the soft surge of the water whilst her lips closed on the fierce pulse in his throat, and the next she was literally being imprisoned by Leon's arms as they wrapped themselves punishingly around her and his curses rang savagely in her ears.

'Are you crazy?' she heard him demanding furiously. 'Do you know what you're doing? Do you think I'm made of stone?'

Stone... No, of course not. Leon was all wonderful gorgeous, sexy, woman-arousing, hunky maleness, all hard muscles and solid flesh, excitingly scored with that enticing line of hair that her fingers just ached to explore, Sadie decided feverishly.

She wasn't even aware that she had spoken her thoughts out loud until she felt Leon's teeth nip sharply at her ear and heard him tell her rawly, 'That's it. You've just sent my self-control into lunar orbit. Hell, Sadie!'

His hands gripped her, his fingers biting into the soft flesh of her buttocks as he dragged her through the water and into his own body.

The feel of him against her skin to skin turned her belly soft with hot desire. Impetuously she moved her hips against him, reaching up to wrap her arms around his neck and pull his mouth down towards her own.

She knew that she ought to be shocked by the brazenness of her own behaviour, but instead something inside her was urging her on,

Leon's mouth was on hers and no way was the kiss he was giving her reinforcing the verbal protests and denials he had given earlier.

He was kissing her with a hot passion that more than matched her own, his hands rhythmically kneading her buttocks as he did so.

She could feel him against her, excitingly hard, as his erection rubbed stiffly against her belly. Even the movement of the water seemed to echo the rhythmic thrusts of their bodies as her hips responded to the pressure of his hands, pulling them together.

The reflection of the stars and moon danced on the rocking water. Helplessly Sadie closed her eyes to its mesmerising glitter, only to be subjected to the even more mesmeric effect of Leon's kiss.

She could feel her whole body responding to its passionate demand as she arched up on her toes and pressed herself into him. Her bare breasts were rubbing against his chest, her nipples so aroused by their contact with his body that fierce spirals of sensation coiled from them to flicker like lightning through her.

Their bodies were slickly wet from the pool water, but the heat inside her was generating another kind of wetness within the swelling lips that protected her sex. And not just a wetness, but an ache. Such an ache that she found herself wrapping her arms even more tightly around Leon's neck as she ground her hips into him in open female demand. Her body ached—hurt even—with her need for him.

'You want me here...now?' she could hear Leon demanding thickly as he wrenched his mouth from hers.

Deprived of contact with his mouth, Sadie began to kiss and lick her way along his throat, savouring every taste of him. When she reached his jaw she ran her fingertips experimentally over the shaved line of his beard, exhilarated by the sensually rough feel of him.

His sex, when she touched it, would feel just the opposite—smooth and sleek, the skin tight where it strained over his erection.

Her whole body began to burn and shake, and she made a small, very female growl low in her throat as she nipped urgently at Leon's ear.

Did he really need to hear her say the words? Couldn't he see? Couldn't he feel what was happening to her?

She slid her hands into his hair and tugged it until he once more bent his head towards her.

Against his lips she told him fiercely, 'Yes. I want you. Yes, here—and yes, now!'

She punctuated each word with a kiss, gasping as Leon cut off her breath with her last word, taking her mouth with a savage primitive hunger that sent her blood roaring through her veins and made her weak with reciprocal longing.

His hands were touching her everywhere. Stroking her shoulders, her arms, cupping her breasts and then kneading them with loving attention until she was shuddering pre-orgasmically with hot rivulets of pleasure.

The feel of the pads of his thumbs against her nipples made her cry out—a low, guttural sound that had his hands slipping down, one to grasp the side of her waist, the other stroking over her stomach and then lower, parting the swollen lips of her sex and stroking against her wet eagerness.

At no time in her life had there ever been anything like this! There never had been and never would be again, Sadie acknowledged dizzily as her body responded to Leon's sensual stroking touch with violent, almost climactic little shudders of pleasure.

Instinctively she reached for him, clasping him in her hand, her eyes widening in shock as she realised that she could not fully encompass him.

He felt hot and hard, his sex swollen. Shockingly, she had a sudden savage, surging ache of need to have the feel of him against her lips, to caress and explore him, slowly and thoroughly, but she knew her own body wasn't going to wait for much longer.

As though she had verbalised her urgency and need to him, Leon suddenly grasped her by the waist and lifted her against him.

Eagerly Sadie opened her legs and wrapped them around him, gasping with pleasure as she felt the first thrust of him within her, urging him to move faster and deeper as she clung to him, offering the full pleasure of her body.

The water around them was pounding against the side of the pool in increasingly fast waves, but Sadie wasn't aware of the movement of the water, only the rhythm of their bodies as they rocked together in frantic, desperate need. She could feel the tight circling of her orgasm beginning, her stomach and her thighs tensing as she reached for it, crying out her pleas and praise to Leon.

She could see the rictus mask of his face above her as he drove harder and deeper into her eager flesh. Voluptuously it tightened around him, increasing the intensity of their pleasure.

'Yes...*Yes!*' she moaned. 'Yes. Just like that, Leon... just like that... Mmm...yes. Just—'

The broken sob of her voice was suspended as her whole body tensed and then exploded in a fierce succession of rhythmic contractions.

She could feel the hot surge of Leon's own release pulsing into the warm darkness of her body.

Release, bliss...peace...

She could feel how much she was shaking as she clung to Leon, knowing she was not actually capable of standing on her own two feet.

She felt his lips brush against the dampness of her face.

'Tears?' he whispered. 'I hope they are tears of pleasure?'

'Do you need to ask?' Sadie challenged huskily.

He lifted her out of the water and put her on the side of the pool. Still trembling in the aftermath of her orgasm, she watched as he hauled himself out.

'Stay there,' he ordered her gently.

Dreamily she watched as he went and picked up her discarded robe, returning with it and wrapping her in it.

'Time for bed,' he told her softly, and then he swung her up into his arms and carried her inside.

CHAPTER EIGHT

'BUT this is your bedroom,' Sadie whispered, after he had pushed open the door and carried her over to the bed.

'So it is!' Leon agreed softly. 'Where else did you think you were going to spend the night? Unless, of course, you'd prefer to sleep alone?'

Bravely Sadie met the look he was giving her head-on. No way was she going to pretend that what had just happened between them meant nothing to her, had simply been a mere sexual indulgence.

'I want to sleep with you,' she told him huskily.

'And I certainly want to sleep with you,' Leon told her back, only just managing to restrain himself from adding *for the rest of my life*.

He hadn't been able to believe what was happening when she had come to him in the pool. Just thinking about it now made his body start to harden again.

'I need a shower,' Sadie whispered. 'The pool water...'

'I need one too,' Leon replied, giving her a smokily sensual look as he leaned down towards her and grasped her hand, pulling her gently to her feet and informing her, 'The bathroom's this way, and the shower is plenty big enough for two.'

Sadie knew that he had felt the small quiver of excitement that ran through her body because he turned to look at her, his gaze fastening on her mouth and then dropping very deliberately to her breasts, where her nipples were flaunting their arousal.

He was right about the shower, she noted as she

stepped into the bathroom. The owners of the *mas* had obviously spared no expense in equipping this room. It was larger than her own, with a separate wet area which housed a purpose-built shower.

The water in the pool had left her skin feeling slightly tight and dry, and it was bliss to step into the shower and feel the body-height jets pumping warm, clean water against her skin.

'Want me to do your back for you?'

There was a look in Leon's eyes that made her whole body tingle with excitement. The shower was designed so that it was perfectly possible to wash one's own back, but Sadie had no intention of pointing this fact out to Leon...

She nodded her head and turned her back to him.

The silky-soft feel of the expensive body mousse Leon was massaging into her skin made her sigh in appreciative pleasure. The resultant foam slipped down her legs and floated on the tiles. His hands were moving lower now...beyond her waist. Sadie held her breath and closed her eyes. Her whole body was quivering with expectation and longing. Now that it knew the pleasure Leon would give it, it wanted him all the more.

His fingertips brushed the front of her thigh, and the soft quiver became an involuntary and uncontrollable convulsive shudder. She could feel Leon's lips nuzzling the back of her neck, just below her ear. His hands moved with aching slowness up over the front of her body towards her breasts.

With a small moan Sadie pressed back against him.

'What is it?' he murmured against the ear. 'Do you want me to stop?'

His hands were doing incredible things to her breasts, making her ache for the feel of his mouth against her tight, eager nipples. But Leon did not seem to share her own surging urgency. Instead he continued to stroke and caress her, nibbling little kisses against her neck, sliding his hands over her soap-slicked body. His touch was arousing her to such a frantic pitch that she moaned sharply in frustration and opened her legs, mentally begging him to touch her intimately.

'What is it?' he asked again softly, when her ecstatic writhings wouldn't be stilled. 'What do you want?'

'You know,' Sadie moaned, desperate to grab hold of his hand and place it against her body, but unable to do so because of the way he was still stroking her.

'Tell me,' Leon urged huskily. 'Tell me what you want me to do, Sadie. Show me how you want me to touch you…how you want me to love you… Is it this you want?' he asked warmly as his hand caressed the curve of her hip and slid down over her belly before cupping her sex.

Sadie gasped as she felt the impatient swell of her body, too wrought up to be able to tell Leon what was happening to her. But somehow he knew, she realised, because he turned her round and stared down into her wild open eyes as his fingers answered the urgent need of her body and the fierce, tight explosion of her orgasm brought her into trembling release.

Sadie was awake, but she did not want to open her eyes just in case it had all been only a dream and Leon wasn't actually in bed beside her after all. She knew it must be morning, even with her eyes closed. Somehow she could feel the brightness of the day through her eyelids. If Leon wasn't there…

Cautiously she moved her body, still heavy and soft with satisfaction and love.

Love! Her heart turned over inside her chest. She loved
Leon so much... Just the thought of him was enough
to—

She stiffened abruptly as the restless movements of her
body brought her into contact with warm male flesh. It
had happened! She hadn't just imagined it! Leon was
here!

Bubbles of joy and excitement fizzed through her
blood. With her eyes still closed Sadie nestled closer to
him, fitting her body into the curve of his. She could
smell the warm, musky scent of him—and it was more
aphrodisiacal than any man-made perfume. The soft hair
on his chest was tickling her nose. Tenderly she rubbed
her lips against his skin, delighting in the secret stolen
pleasure of being able to do so whilst he was still asleep.
Smiling to herself, she stroked her fingertip lazily along
his arm, so different from her own, all powerful muscles
and sinews.

Against her body she could feel his stirring. A female
shiver of pleasure slowly caressed her own body.

Snuggling further down his body, she teased her
tongue-tip around his navel, her hand reaching out to
touch and then hold him. It was an extraordinarily sensual
and tender thing to feel him growing within her hold, at
once both vulnerable and powerful.

Experimentally she started to caress him, enjoying his
body's response to her and rewarding it with a soft kiss.

This was an intimacy she hadn't imagined she would
ever want to experience, but suddenly she knew just how
much she did. The brief touch of her lips became a more
intimate and sensual exploration.

'Enjoying yourself?'

The low, groaned words shocked through her. Lifting
her head, she turned to look up at Leon. She had been

so lost in the enjoyment of what she was doing that she hadn't even realised he was awake.

'I…'

'I certainly was,' he told her thickly, his voice soft with pleasure, 'so don't let me stop you…'

'What time will they be bringing the replacement hire car?' Sadie asked Leon drowsily as she responded to the slow drift of his hands on her body.

They had made love, and then slept, and now Leon was caressing her again.

'Soon,' he told her wryly, removing his hand with obvious reluctance. 'I suppose we'd better make a move.'

There was a note in his voice that made Sadie look enquiringly at him.

'I swore that there was no way I was going to let this happen,' he told her ruefully.

'But you wanted it to?' Sadie questioned him.

'Do you really need to ask?' Leon responded, his voice wry with self-mockery.

Leon's mobile rang as he walked into his hotel room several hours later. He'd just left Sadie at her own room.

'Brad.' He smiled as he recognised the voice of his godfather, the company's and his own solicitor. 'I was going to ring you later, to give you an update on what's happening with the Francine acquisition. Yes, I know things are taking longer than we originally expected,' Leon agreed, still smiling. 'There's been a bit of a complication with the junior shareholder, made more difficult by the fact that she almost backed out of the deal.'

Briefly Leon explained to his godfather exactly what had happened. His smile turned to a frown as he heard Brad asking worriedly, 'What do you mean? We aren't talking about the woman we saw at the trade fair, are we, Leon? Because she looked to me...' He took a pause, and then went on even more worriedly, 'Your father almost lost the business and the shirt off his back, thanks to a conniving, lying woman, Leon, and by the sounds of it you're in danger of having the same thing happen to you!'

'Brad, Sadie isn't like that,' Leon stopped him curtly.

'How can you know that, Leon? You've already said that she's causing problems.'

'Brad, Sadie is not another Miranda.'

'You can't be sure of that, Leon. You're carrying a mighty heavy responsibility on your shoulders—we both know that! Hell, you're a man, Leon, and only human. I understand that. But if you're wrong, you don't need me to tell you how much damage that could do to the business.'

'You worry too much, Brad,' Leon told his godfather affectionately before ending the call, but his frown deepened as he walked over to the window. No matter what his personal feelings for Sadie were, he could not afford to do anything that might put the business at risk.

Sadie was not another Miranda Stanton. He was sure of it. But what if he was wrong? Whatever risks he was prepared to take with his own emotions, he was not prepared to take any with the financial security of the business.

Miranda Stanton!

He had been fourteen, and still mourning his grandmother, when to everyone's shock his father's business partner had died of a heart attack.

Andy and his father had been at school together, and even though the business had originally been Leon's father's idea, he had generously offered Andy a share in it.

They had started out with nothing, but by the time Leon was thirteen the business was beginning to do very well.

And then Andy had got married—to a much younger woman—who none of them had liked.

'If a woman has gold-digger written all over her then that woman is Miranda!' Leon could remember his mother sighing.

Leon could also remember his father coming home one night and telling his mother that he had to go and see the bank. Andy was in a bit of a financial mess, due to Miranda's insistence on an expensive lifestyle, and had asked Leon's father to buy him out of their business.

Generously, because of Andy's desperation, Leon's father had given him the money before the legal documents confirming the buy-out had been signed. A week later, whilst on holiday with Miranda, Andy had had a heart attack and died. And a week after that Miranda had informed Leon's father that she wanted and intended to have the full cash value of Andy's half-share in the business.

It had been useless for Leon's father to protest that Andy had already had the money, and she had known about it. She had pointed out that Leon's father had no legal documentation to prove it.

Leon's father had not given up easily. The matter had even gone to court. But of course legally there had been no proof.

In order to buy her out and meet his legal costs Leon's father had had to mortgage the business up to the hilt, and sell the family home. The family had gone from living in comfort to living from hand to mouth. His parents' smiling faces had become pinched and strained.

Leon had hated Miranda for what she had done to his family. He had vowed then and there that what had happened to his father would never happen to him! And now here was Brad, suggesting that Sadie was potentially another Miranda!

It wasn't true, of course, Leon assured himself. That stubbornness she displayed was defensive rather than manipulative. But a cautionary inner voice reminded him sharply that she had hinted to him about wanting the Grasse property. And there had been all that fuss she had made, both about the Myrrh formula and the creation of a new scent. He had believed her motives to be genuine, if somewhat idealistic and simplistic, but if he was wrong…

It was hardly unknown for an acquisitive woman to use sex to get what she wanted.

Sadie wasn't like that, though!

His intimacy with her was interfering with his analytical abilities as well as potentially threatening to screw up the deal and his life, Leon admitted grimly.

'Face it,' he told himself brutally. 'You've got yourself in way too deep.'

Way, way too deep, he realised.

The best thing he could do right now, he conceded reluctantly, in fact the only thing he could do right now, was to back off and put some space between himself and Sadie.

When the deal had gone through tomorrow, once he had Francine and the Myrrh formula and had fulfilled his duty to the business, then things would be different.

On their way back from the *mas*, he and Sadie had talked briefly about the takeover.

'The legal side of things is pretty well sorted out,' Leon had explained. 'You, Raoul and I sign the papers tomorrow, but first I've told my people to organise an immediate press conference to announce the takeover. It will put an end to all the speculation and gossip that's been going on. I want you to be there, of course, as you're a big part of what will be happening. I'll be making an announcement to the effect that you're going to be working on a new scent under the Francine name, and that we are going to reintroduce a modern version of Mrryh. Unfortunately, virtually as soon as that the press conference is over, I'm going to have to fly back to Australia, via Italy. I've got to see the new designer we're taking on to head the fashion division.'

Leon had felt the beginnings of a sharp ache at the thought of leaving her, but now, he told himself, he was relieved.

Back in her hotel room, Sadie waited, hoping that Leon would ring. He had told her on the way back that he had business matters to attend to, and she understood that, of course, but surely in view of the intimacy they had shared he would also want to be with her as much as possible, before they had to go their separate ways?

Impulsively Sadie went to her door and opened it.

Leon frowned as he opened his door to Sadie's knock.

Smiling tenderly at him, Sadie told him, 'I know you said you had business to attend to, but I thought I could at least be with you—and then, perhaps…'

Her voice trailed away as she saw the way Leon was frowning.

'Leon?' she began uncertainly.

What had happened to the passionate, sensual man she had known so intimately at the *mas*? She could not see anything of him here, in the grim rejection of Leon's reaction to her now.

Anxious and bewildered, Sadie struggled to understand what was happening.

'If it's a bad time…'

Helplessly she looked at him, unable to hide what she was feeling.

As he saw the look in Sadie's eyes Leon's first instinct was to go to her and take her in his arms, but somehow he managed to suppress it. Brad's warning had resurrected some very painful memories. Sadie might not be Miranda, but there were some very complicated issues between them, and there was no way he could allow his own emotions to rule his head now.

'I've got a lot of work to catch up on, Sadie,' he informed her curtly, turning his back on her as he spoke so that he couldn't look into her eyes and be tempted beyond his own self-control.

Reminding himself of his responsibilities to the business, he took a deep breath.

'What happened between us at the *mas*…' he began.

Sadie could not let him go on. Ice-cold anguish and pain were seeping agonisingly through her whole body, filling her with a mixture of anger and disbelief. Only the knowledge that if she remained in Leon's room she would be brutally humiliated made her stop him with a cold stare.

'You don't need to say any more, Leon. I understand perfectly what you mean.'

Not trusting herself to say any more, she whirled round and left.

She felt hot, cold and sick with the pain of being rejected. Burning with anger, she felt torn between two totally conflicting sets of emotions—hating Leon and yet at the same time fully aware of just how much she actually loved him.

Grimly, Leon stared at the empty space where Sadie had been standing. He told himself that he was glad she had left. If she hadn't... Helplessly he moved towards where she had been standing, treacherously allowing himself to breathe in the air still scented by her presence.

She was a passionately and infuriatingly stubborn woman who had the potential to make his life one hell of a lot more complicated than he wanted it to be! And also a lot more pleasurable. It would certainly be more filled with love, with all the things he had denied himself during the years he had focused on building up the business and securing what had been so nearly lost to his family.

Leon's expression became even more grim. He just did not have time for this now. He had to secure Francine— if he didn't, his board would have his guts for breakfast. If he gave in and allowed his feelings for Sadie to take him over and rule his life, how the hell was he going to be able to concentrate wholly on the business? And if he didn't...

Somewhere deep inside him a small, unfamiliar voice asked if he really wanted to devote the rest of his life to the conglomerate...if he wouldn't really rather build a loving relationship than a fat balance sheet. But Leon refused to listen to it.

Sadie stared unseeingly around her room. Leon had rejected her! Her face burned fiercely at the recollection of just how determined and obvious that rejection had been! He had used her and then dropped her, she stormed in furious inward anger, but somehow a part of her recognised that that did not ring true. If Leon had simply wanted a brief sexual fling he could have found someone much more up for that sort of thing than her.

So why had he cast her aside, then, if it wasn't because of that? she demanded of herself, lashing her anger with the whip of her own self-contempt and misery. Why was she trying to find excuses for him? He couldn't have made it plainer that he didn't want her. Sadie felt even more humiliated as she relived his reaction to her uninvited arrival at his room.

Painful as the experiment had been, she discovered that a treacherous part of her had recorded every minute detail about him with a lover's intensity—even small things, like the movement of his hands as he had backed away from her. Were those really the same hands that had drawn her so close, held her so tenderly and touched her so intimately? The harshness of his voice—the same voice which had whispered smokily to her of desire and longing, the same voice which had rung out into the night at the height of passion…. Sadie shivered as she remembered the way his gaze had hardened over her, that same gaze which so very recently had melted and then burned with heat and longing…

What had happened? Why had he changed so abruptly? Instinctively Sadie knew that there was no point in her trying to ask him. His body language had told her exactly how he wanted things to be between them—with as much distance as possible!

Her own pride flared into bitter life. Very well! If that was what he wanted, then that was what he was going to get.

Her emotions were in total confusion, Sadie recognised achingly. She had believed they were falling in love with one another, but now Leon was telling her that he just didn't want to know, that he had changed his mind and that he did not want to build a relationship with her after all.

And, what was more, in telling her that he had also implied that he still expected them to share a business relationship!

One part of her—the part of her which had given him her love and her trust and had had that love rejected—was demanding that she protect herself by having nothing more to do with Leon—ever! But Sadie prided herself on her professionalism, and in her opinion it would just not be morally acceptable for her to back out of the contract negotiations now, just because Leon had rejected her emotionally.

She was in between the proverbial rock and hard place, and her poor heart was being badly hurt by them both!

Perhaps once the contracts had been signed and she became involved in her new role she would be too busy to worry about Leon. Too involved in the excitement of what she was doing to have any time to spare to think about him and how much he had hurt her. In fact, there was no 'perhaps' about it, Sadie decided firmly. That was the way things were going to be! There was no way was she going to languish around nursing a broken heart!

CHAPTER NINE

SHE was, Sadie knew, a little bit late and an awful lot on edge for this morning's press conference—and both her lateness and her edginess were down to one person and one alone. Leon himself!

She was late because if it hadn't been for the fact that she had to be here nothing would have dragged her anywhere she might have to see him. It had taken a hard-fought internal battle to enable herself to put her personal feelings to one side. And, having done so, she was on edge—just in case when she did see him the love she knew full well she still felt for him overwhelmed her and led her into subjecting herself to even more humiliation.

One of the small army of PR people Leon had obviously hired spotted her and bustled purposefully towards her.

'Yes, I'm Sadie,' she admitted, on being questioned. 'Is my cousin Raoul here yet?'

'Yes, I believe he is. If you will come with me, please?'

The press conference that Leon's publicity people had organised was turning out to be a far larger affair than Sadie had expected, and was being held at the house in Grasse—which would still go into Leon's possession with the signing of legal documents later on in the day.

Now, as she looked round the main salon of the house and out into the courtyard, Sadie could only be unwillingly impressed by the transformation Leon's people had managed to achieve in such a short space of time.

Granted, the massed displays of freshly cut flowers helped to draw the eye away from the house's shabbiness, but it had been a master stroke to have some of the old advertisements for Francine perfumes framed and hung on the walls.

Still following the PR girl, Sadie froze suddenly as she looked towards the small stage that had been erected at one end of the room and saw Leon.

The first thing she had done after Leon's rejection of her had been to book herself into a different hotel. She'd chosen a small *pension* in Grasse itself, so that she would not have to run the risk of coming into contact with him. However, she was now discovering that the sight of him after several hours of not seeing him was having much the same effect as the sight of water was likely to have on a man lost in the desert!

He was standing with his back to her, and despite the anger she could still feel burning inside her, her gaze homed in on him like a missile, greedily gathering up every bit of information it could to stockpile inside her heart for the Leon-empty days that lay ahead!

She, who had always always been able to see another person's point of view, was so angry and hurt that she could not extend that generosity to Leon. She felt as though she hated him, but she knew that she loved him! And because of that she pitied herself.

From his position on the small stage—a position he assured himself he had not chosen simply because it gave him an uninterrupted view of anyone entering the room— Leon had witnessed Sadie's arrival, and the manner in which she was so obviously ignoring him. His mouth compressed. He had virtually lost a full nights' sleep— and not because his second in command on the board had telephoned to warn him that another board member, who had been the most keenly opposed to the acquisition of Francine had been demanding to know what was causing the delay, and prophesying that Leon had made a dangerous error in judgement.

No, it wasn't Kevin Linton's fierce antagonism or questioning of his business acumen and judgement that had kept Leon awake last night. Sadie was solely responsible for that! And right now he was sorely tempted to go over to her and remind her in whatever way it took—and so far as he was concerned the more physically intimate the better—of just why she should not ignore him! He ached so badly for her that right now...

Leon's jaw tightened even further. Up until now nothing, no one had had the power to come between him and his dedication to the business. And for it to be Sadie, a woman his solicitor had already cautioned him against...

But Brad didn't know Sadie as he knew her, and Leon swore he never would! No other man ever would, if Leon had his way. No other man would be allowed to so much as look at her, never mind—

Abruptly Leon recognised that he was out of control, that his emotions were careering wildly down a one-way street and that if he didn't get a hold of them...

Out of the corner of his eye he saw a man approaching Sadie, smiling at her, reaching out his hand to touch her... A red mist exploded inside Leon's head. His heart was thumping, adrenalin flooding his body. He wanted—

At Leon's side, the head of the PR company interrupted his dangerous flow of thoughts.

'I think everyone is here. We should begin the conference, I think. The press are beginning to grow impatient...'

At the same moment, this mystery man was raising

Sadie's hand to his lips. The PR executive frowned in confusion as she heard Leon give a low, muted growl of male anger.

'Merci, Monsieur Fontaine,' Sadie said politely, thanking the man who had been praising the scent she was wearing. Still smiling, she firmly extracted her hand from his grasp.

'Come on, Sadie. Leon wants us both up on the stage,' Raoul announced, suddenly appearing at her side and taking hold of her arm.

Sadie could feel the PR executive and Leon looking at them as she and Raoul approached the stage. Immediately she averted her face, looking very deliberately past Leon, her chin lifting with haughty female pride.

Out of the corner of her eye she caught a glimpse of the icy, brief look Leon gave her. From out of nowhere, Sadie jealously wondered, would the elegant Frenchwoman at his side be the one to share his bed tonight?

The pain that tore at her almost made her cry out loud!

Unable to stop herself, she watched as Leon strode to the front of the stage and picked up the microphone.

'I hope this is going to be quick,' Raoul muttered at her side. 'The sooner Leon's cheque is in my pocket the happier I shall be! I must say you don't look very happy for someone who's about to pocket a couple of million euros!'

'Francine means far more to me than money, Raoul,' Sadie reminded her cousin in a determined whisper. 'You know that. If it wasn't—'

A fierce 'shush' from one of the hovering PR personnel made Sadie go red and stop speaking, to concentrate instead on what Leon was saying to the assembled press.

Determinedly Sadie tried not to be aware of him, not to think about him, not to remember. But as fierce as her anger was, her love was even fiercer, and helplessly she turned her head to look longingly towards him, taking advantage of his audience's concentration on what he was saying to gaze hungrily at his dark-suited back view.

Just watching him made her whole body quiver with aching need.

Leon had reached the end of his short speech confirming the takeover.

Someone from the floor called up.

'Are you intending to keep the Francine name?'

'Of course,' Leon responded immediately.

'And the Francine perfumes?' someone else challenged him, 'What about them?

'So far as I am concerned there is only one Francine perfume,' Leon responded coolly, 'and that is Myrrh. I am delighted to be able to tell you that the great-great-great-granddaughter of the founder of the house is going to be working for us—not only on adapting the Myrrh formula to suit modern-day tastes, but also on creating a new perfume under the Francine name. As you will all know, Sadie Roberts is already well regarded in the business as a gifted creator of exclusive scents, and I am delighted to be able to introduce her to you as Francine's new creative director.'

As Leon turned to look at her, Sadie stood up on cue and walked towards him, knowing that he intended to introduce her to the audience.

He had extended his hand towards her in what appeared to be a gesture of warmth and appreciation, but Sadie deliberately stopped just short of it—and him—and for her pains received a look from him that threatened to collapse her fragile pride into dust.

Turning his head so that no one else could hear him, he said softly, 'This is a business arena we are in today, Sadie, not a personal one.'

Equally softly, Sadie hissed back, 'There is no personal arena for us any more, Leon.'

Whilst their gazes were still locked in silent combat, one of the reporters in the audience called, 'As you say, we know of Mademoiselle Sadie, but surely it is true that she only creates perfumes made from natural sources? Are we to understand that from now on Francine perfumes are to be created in the same way?'

Sadie took a deep breath, wholly professional now as she waited confidently for her moment to make public the compromise she and Leon had reached—publicly for Francine, but privately in her heart for her grandmother. But before she could say anything Leon had reached for the microphone.

'No, the new Francine perfumes will be scents that will be affordable for every woman who wishes to wear them, and for that reason they will—in common with most modern perfume houses—be created without the need for expensive and sometimes unreliable raw materials.'

Rigid with disbelief, Sadie drew in her breath, the audience momentarily forgotten as she turned to Leon and burst out, white-faced with fury, 'How can you say that? You know I would *never* agree to work wholly with synthetics!'

The press conference was over, the eagerly curious audience having been hurriedly despatched by the PR company, and Sadie and Leon were confronting one another across the upstairs room of the house where they had first officially met.

'How could you do that?' Sadie demanded bitterly,

swinging round from where she had been looking out of the window to face Leon. 'How could you lie like that?'

'Lie?' Leon stopped her, his voice ominously quiet. 'I haven't lied, Sadie. You assured Raoul that you were in agreement with my plans. You accepted both that the Myrrh perfume rightly belongs to Francine and that you were willing to work on revamping its formula and creating a new perfume using man-made materials.'

Sadie had never looked more beautiful or more desirable to him than she did right now, Leon acknowledged, and he felt the stomach-clenching kick of his own fierce need thrust through his body.

'I assured Raoul of no such thing!' Sadie insisted. She felt almost incandescent with shock and rage, barely able to speak for the ferocity of her fury. She knew she'd been lied to and deceived—and not just by her cousin!

'You must have known that I would never, ever give such an agreement,' she threw at Leon passionately. 'I can't believe you can possibly have thought that I would ever agree to work exclusively with synthetics when you know how important it is to me...'

Leon couldn't believe what he was hearing. This was his worst nightmare scenario come to life! There he was, facing a stubborn, emotional woman who threatened the security of his business.

Just wait until Kevin Linton got to hear about this! He had been opposed to the Francine acquisition right from the start, stating that it simply did not have legs, and now, Leon realised bitterly, his adversary might be right.

'You tricked me,' she told him fiercely.

'I tricked you!' Leon snapped, adding, 'It seems to me that it's very convenient for you that Raoul is nowhere to be found!'

'Convenient for *me*?' Sadie felt as though she might

explode with the ferocity of her rage and sense of ill-usage. 'Raoul assured me that you were willing to compromise, to allow me to create a perfume that was a blend of both naturals and synthetics—a perfume that—'

'What? You expected me to let you create a perfume for selfish women with too much money who don't give a damn about anyone other than themselves? No way. Not now. Not ever!' Leon told her, shaking his head to emphasise his feelings. 'I thought I'd already made it plain to you, Sadie, that I want a perfume that all women can enjoy.'

'All women?' Sadie's lip curled in furious contempt. 'You don't give a damn about my sex, Leon. All you care about is making money—well rest assured you aren't going to make any from me, or from the Myrrh formula!'

Leon had had enough! Before he could stop himself he was reaching for Sadie and wrapping his arms around her, smothering her angry, heated words with the equally heated pressure of his mouth.

For one single heartbeat Sadie tried to resist him, but it was impossible. A hot tide of longing was already surging through her, obliterating her defences as it did so. Helplessly she clung to him, returning his kiss with equal intensity. Their mouths meshed, their bodies defying the pressure of their mutual anger.

'Sadie, you've got to see reason,' Leon growled against her mouth.

'*I've* got to see reason?' Immediately Sadie pulled back from him, her breasts rising and falling with the rapidity of her aroused breathing.

'You verbally agreed to sign our contract, and morally—'

'Morally, nothing,' Sadie declared, incensed, still try-ing to come down from the emotional impact of his kiss.

Leon froze. Suddenly he was fourteen again, witness-ing the argument between his father and Miranda. 'Mor-ally?' She had laughed mockingly. 'Legally, you have nothing! Now legally *he* had nothing. There was no wit-ness to her verbal agreement, no contract, no Myrrh and no Sadie.

Anger, despair and the sharpest pain he had ever known roiled inside him.

'My God, Brad was right to warn me. You are another Miranda Stanton,' he burst out, white-faced.

His words barely registered in Sadie's consciousness. Suddenly she was sick to her stomach as a horrible thought hit her. Had Leon taken her to bed in a cold-blooded attempt to soften her up? Had he ultimately in-tended to persuade her to create a wholly synthetic per-fume?

Torn apart by her pain, she told him emptily, 'I will never, ever create a synthetic perfume, Leon. Never!'

Without waiting for his reply she turned and walked unsteadily out of the room.

Leon stared after Sadie's departing back and tried to fight down his own emotions. Suddenly he had the most intense longing to go after her and stop her—tell her... Tell her what? That he was afraid he might love her? Tell her about Miranda Stanton and that he dreaded that she might be just like her? That he was afraid she might somehow tempt him into putting his love for her before his responsibility towards the business? That he was ter-rified that if he touched her now he would tell her she could create her damned perfume out of the stars in the sky and he would drag them down out of it for her if only she would tell him she loved him back?

Oh, Kevin would love that!

He needed a straitjacket!

He needed...

Leon gave a groan as his memory provided him with a very detailed and illuminating image of just exactly what he *did* need. That was Sadie, soft, warm, naked, willing and loving in his arms—whispering to him, kissing him, holding him, telling him things that would send him plain crazy and then putting those words into actions, sweet, hot, sexy promises of intimate pleasure that...

Leon ground his teeth in savage frustration. Without Sadie and the Myrrh formula Francine was doomed to failure. And if it failed it would cost his group of companies millions of pounds and a public loss of face from which there could be no recovery.

His own position and his own fortune were unassailable, but Leon was all too aware of the vulnerability of those who had invested in his companies and in him. He had a moral obligation to his shareholders that he had to put ahead of his own feelings.

CHAPTER TEN

GRIMLY Leon put down his mobile. He had been trying to get in touch with Raoul for the last four days—ever since he had returned to Sydney, in fact—but there was just no answer either to his calls or his e-mails.

From the modern offices of Stapinopolous Inc. Leon could look down onto the harbour, but the fabulous view before him could not hold his attention today.

'Could I have a word, Leon?'

Blanking his thoughts, Leon shot Kevin Linton an assessing look.

'Not if you want to regurgitate everything we've already discussed, Kev,' he answered calmly.

'Hell, Leon. You're talking to me as though we're on opposite sides of the fence! No one has the interest of this corporation at heart more than me; you know that!'

'I also know, Kev, that so far you've tried to block just about every expansion programme we've adopted, and—'

'Leon, we're an Aussie business and, yeah, I think we should stay that way. All this tomfoolery about buying into stuff in Europe. I just don't get it.'

'We live in a shrinking world, Kev. From a TV programme beamed out across it, viewers can see and want a thousand products—that's a fact I don't need to prove. We're already well-established in the market, but if we are to expand...'

'Leon, I know what you're saying—but to buy a rundown perfume business...' Kevin shook his head. 'It seems to me that you've made a real error or judgement—especially when we take into account the fact that the deal hasn't gone through yet, and all on account of this woman!'

'The deal will go through,' Leon told him tersely. 'And "this woman" as you call her is—' Leon stopped, his heart doing a slow, painful somersault. This woman was *his* woman. And she had got so far inside his head and his heart that he could barely function without her.

'Well, it's your reputation that's lying on the line, Leon, not mine. But I have to tell you there's no way I will agree to being held to ransom and having to pay out good money for something we could damn well hire a chemist to make for us for peanuts.'

Somehow Leon managed to hold on to his temper. He had made it perfectly clear to Kevin why they were buying Francine and right now he was in no mood for Kevin's favourite kind of power-game-playing.

'And this woman—the one who's causing us all this trouble. Honestly, Leon, she sounds like a real bitch from hell.'

'Sadie is no such thing!'

Leon had spoken before he could stop himself, leaping immediately and instinctively to Sadie's defence in a way that shocked him just as much as it had obviously surprised his co-director.

Why was he so bent on defending a woman who had caused him so much trouble? Because he was a fool, that was why! Or because deep down inside himself he knew—just knew—that Sadie was not another Miranda? Not matter how much the facts might suggest that she was.

After Kevin had gone Leon wondered broodingly what he was doing, spending so much time thinking about

Sadie over there in Europe, when there was so much that was surely more important that needed his attention right here in Sydney.

The truth was, though, that he just could not get her out of his head. Instead of thinking about his upcoming meeting with Mario Testare, the designer he had head-hunted to take charge of the ageing fashion house he had taken over five years ago, and the meeting he had planned with CEO of the luxury leather goods arm of the business, all he could think about was Sadie, he acknowledged angrily.

There hadn't been a single second in his life when Leon had envisaged himself in this kind of situation. Marriage, children—yes, he wanted both—one day. He was part Greek, after all. But falling in love, and the intensity of emotion Sadie aroused in him—these were just not part of his game plan at all.

Sadie! Hell, he was thinking about her again! Only because of his concern over the problems she had caused by refusing to sign the contract, Leon assured himself firmly.

But it wasn't just her signature on that contract he needed. What he also needed was her mouth on his, her body in his arms, her soft, sexy voice whispering those things in his ear that made him just ache to—

Stop that, he warned himself sternly. What he absolutely *had* to have was her agreement to creating a new perfume. A saleable, affordable perfume. And that perfume had to be made from synthetics. Didn't it? Though in the heat of their argument Sadie had implied that she was prepared to compromise, and to work on creating a blended scent.

Yes, and it would be a blended scent with so many

expensive ingredients that it would be far too expensive for any mass market, Leon told himself firmly.

But what if there were some way such a perfume could be created at an affordable cost? What if he could find a way to prove that to himself and to his board? Maybe then…

Why was he was wasting time he didn't have allowing his thoughts to dwell on the most aggravating and impossible woman God had ever created?

He picked up his mobile. He suspected that Raoul was not taking his calls because he was afraid Leon would call in the advance he had given him against the acquisition. Leon knew that he had to take on Francine now, thanks to Kevin, or face the possibility of a vote of no confidence from his own board. And to that end he needed to speak with Raoul. And with Sadie!

Frowning, he put down his mobile. If Raoul would not answer his calls then there was only one thing he could do!

Striding across his office, he sat down and buzzed for his secretary.

'Book me a flight to Nice, will you, please?'

'And a hotel?' his secretary asked. 'Do you want to stay in Mougins again, or…?'

Leon hesitated. Mougins. That was where he and Sadie…

Sadie stared in disbelief at the e-mail she had just received. It was a request—no, not a request but a demand, and a very tersely worded one at that—from Leon, insisting that she present herself in Grasse 'in order that a discussion can take place to resolve current difficulties.'

Just knowing that Leon had sent the e-mail was causing her heart to thud and her whole body to react. If a

mere e-mail from him could fill her with such a savage
mixture of longing pain and anger then what was the
reality of him likely to do?

Cravenly, she was tempted to simply ignore the message. But logically she knew that she couldn't.

Whilst she was still staring at the screen her telephone
rang.

As she picked up the receiver she heard Raoul's voice
exclaiming urgently, 'Sadie! I need to talk to you!'

'I've got Leon's e-mail, Raoul, and if you're phoning
to try and persuade me to talk with him—' Sadie began.

But Raoul cut across her, announcing grimly, 'Sadie,
you've got to help me. If you don't Leon could take me
to court and claim back the money he's advanced me
against the acquisition of Francine—and if he does that
I'm in real trouble.'

So, Raoul had lied to her and about her, Sadie told
herself. But he was still her cousin, and oddly it was
easier to forgive him than it was for her to forgive Leon.
Because Leon had hurt her so much more? Or because
she loved Leon so much more?

Just don't go there, she advised herself.

'Raoul, nothing's changed,' she warned her cousin. 'I
will not allow Leon to have the Myrrh formula, and neither will I create a synthetic perfume for him.'

'Sadie, all he wants to discuss is the acquisition of
Francine,' Raoul reassured her. 'Nothing more than that.
And if you don't agree to sell to him, Sadie, I'm going
to be in one hell of a mess.'

'If you're lying to me again, Raoul—' Sadie began,
but she knew that she was weakening and she suspected
that Raoul knew it too.

By the time she had replaced the receiver she had
agreed to go back to France.

*   *   *

'What's wrong?' Mary asked Sadie sympathetically, whilst her teenage niece Caroline, who was visiting her, gleefully explored Sadie's workroom. 'Still brooding about Leon? You haven't been able to put what happened with him behind you, have you? Despite what you said to me!'

Sadie had, of course, told Mary everything that had happened in France with Leon. Well, almost everything! She had been so upset on her return to Pembroke that she had not been able to stop herself from pouring her heart out to her. Then, she had claimed that she was going to make herself believe that she hadn't even met Leon, never mind fallen so deeply in love with him! But, as Mary had just pointed out, forgetting Leon had proved to be impossible!

'It doesn't matter how I feel, Mary. I told you what he said to me, how all he wants is for me to create a synthetic scent for him. I shall never do that! Never!' she announced doggedly.

'I've agreed to go to France to see him, but that's for Raoul's sake. If Leon thinks he can make me change my mind...'

Mary gave her a shrewd look.

'Please don't take this the wrong way, Sadie. You're my friend, and the last thing I want to do is to hurt or offend you, but it seems to me from all that you have said about Leon that the two of you are perfectly matched and both as stubborn as one another!' she said gently.

Whilst Sadie glowered, unwilling to accept her friend's assessment, Mary went on ruefully. 'Love on its own isn't enough, you know.' She insisted semi-severely. 'There has to be a willingness to understand and accept one's other half's point of view. Haven't either of you heard of the word ''compromise''?'

Before Sadie could answer, Caroline came out of the workroom to join them.

'Sadie, that perfume you're wearing is delicious,' she began longingly. 'Isn't there any way you could create something similar but not quite as expensive?' she asked plaintively. 'Something that a poor student like me could afford?'

After Mary and Caroline had gone Sadie went into her workroom. Caroline's comments about her perfume had struck home and made her feel a little bit guilty. Of course it was only natural that any woman would want to be able to wear a 'good' scent, but Caroline's innocent question had forced Sadie to reassess her own stance and ask herself if there really was a way man-made scents could be blended to create a good perfume that would be within the means of all women.

It wasn't because she wanted to give in to Leon that she was thinking like this, trying to find a way to make an expensive traditional perfume more financially accessible, Sadie assured herself. It was just that the look of longing in Caroline's eyes had made her see things differently. It would certainly be a challenge for her!

But nowhere near as much of a challenge as winning Leon's love!

Angry with herself, Sadie paced her workroom floor. What kind of woman was she to want to win the love of a man who had so humiliatingly rejected her?

She tried to make herself focus on her work, but all she could think of was Leon and that final destructive scene between them.

Had he any idea just how much he had shocked and hurt her? Accusing her of...

Sadie frowned, suddenly remembering just what he had said to her. *'You are another Miranda Stanton.'*

Who was Miranda Stanton? And what did she have to do with Leon's rejection of her?

Sadie stared at her computer and then quickly began to type, her fingers trembling slightly.

By the time Sadie had finished re-reading the information her computer search had brought up for the third time she was having to swallow hard to suppress her tears of compassion.

The story of what had happened had been laid bare for her through newspaper archive accounts, but reading it had not shocked her as much as the one photograph she had seen of a fourteen-year-old Leon, so tall that he had been almost shoulder to shoulder with his father, his gaze fixed on his father's face.

What a dreadful time that must have been for the whole family; what a dreadful thing Miranda Stanton had done. And what an appalling insult Leon had hurled at her when he had drawn a parallel between this woman and herself! Torn between exasperation, anger and aching love, Sadie didn't know whether to run towards her upcoming meeting in France with Leon, or to run from it!

CHAPTER ELEVEN

THE sun might be shining down warmly, but its heat wasn't enough to melt the ice-cold despair and pain lodged in her heart, Sadie realised sadly as she stepped out of her taxi and looked up at the front of the Mougins hotel, which was where Leon had elected to hold their meeting.

Sadie wished he had chosen anywhere but here—the place where she had begun to love him and where she had believed he had begun to love her in return.

She was early for her meeting with Leon and Raoul, and she was tired—she hadn't been sleeping properly at home, and last night, after her arrival at the small hotel in Cannes where she was staying, every time she had managed to fall asleep she had ended up dreaming about Leon! And what dreams they had been! Her face grew hot at the memory of them. But nowhere near as hot as her body had been last night!

She had nearly half an hour to waste before her meeting, so Sadie thought she might as well wander through the hotel's gardens. But she would not follow the path where Leon had kissed her for the first time!

On the balcony of his suite Leon tensed as he looked out of the window and saw Sadie slowly walking through the garden. He tried to close his mind and his heart to the effect the sight of her was having on him, but it was impossible! His body had already made its feelings perfectly clear.

161

As he watched he saw Sadie turn and start in the opposite direction.

Unable to stop himself, he left his balcony, taking the flight of stone steps that led directly into the gardens two at a time, and calling out her name as he followed her down the path.

The moment she heard Leon calling her name Sadie froze. Somehow she made herself turn round and confront him.

He looked grimly forbidding, and for a moment her own resolve faltered. This was a business meeting—nothing more, she reminded herself. If she had hopes and dreams that were not going to be fulfilled, then she had only herself to blame.

Silently she fell into step beside him, careful to keep a clear distance between their bodies and he escorted her back towards his suite.

'Is Raoul here?' she asked, and then frowned as her mobile rang.

Excusing herself, she fished it out of her bag, her frown deepening when she realised that the caller was Raoul himself.

'Sadie—I just thought I'd let you know that I have decided it's best if you and Leon sort out your differences alone. Leon knows that I am not the one holding up completion of the acquisition. And you know how very important it is to me that this deal goes through. As your cousin, I beg you to remember this and to—'

'Raoul, I am with Leon now,' Sadie interrupted him sharply. 'Where are you? Why aren't you—?'

She gave a small hiss of exasperation as Raoul immediately ended the call.

'That was Raoul,' she told Leon. 'He—'

'I gathered what he said,' Leon informed her curtly.

They had reached the stone staircase now, and Leon stood to one side to allow Sadie to precede him. Warily, she did so.

'Raoul wants me to agree to sell my share of the business to you,' she told Leon. 'I understand that you have advanced certain monies to him and that legally you are entitled to demand their repayment in full.'

'And so, to protect Raoul from such a fate, you are willing to—?'

'I am willing to sell my share of Francine to you, Leon. That is all I offer. Nothing else.'

She had just started to mount the steps but stopped, turning to look at him. He was still a couple of stairs lower, and Sadie suddenly became aware that they were on the same eye level.

Disconcertingly, she realised that Leon's gaze had dropped to her mouth. And that her mouth had suddenly become soft and eager with the memory of his kisses. Sadie could swear she felt her lips warming and parting, almost pouting as they gloried in Leon's visual attention.

And what was sauce for the goose…

Whilst Leon's attention was so engaged there was nothing to stop her from looking at him…at his face, his skin, his own mouth.

She was losing it, and in a big, big way, Sadie recognised helplessly when she heard herself give a small betraying moan as she leaned hungrily towards him.

'Sadie!'

Was that a warning to stay away from him, or a warning that he could not…?

'Sadie?'

'Leon…' Sadie was shocked to discover herself murmuring his name against his jaw, and to note that she was wrapped wonderfully and blissfully tightly in his arms.

She was perfectly sure that if she turned her head, like this...

A shock of savagely hot pleasure burned through her as she returned the fierce passion of Leon's kiss, somehow managing to wriggle her arms free so that she could fling them around him to hold him as tightly as he was holding her.

The unashamed hardness of his arousal against her body reminded her vividly of last night's dreams. But this wasn't a dream. This was wonderfully, gorgeously real!

Behind her closed eyelids, Sadie could see a bed, a large, wonderful bed, in a shadowy private room. And on those bed she could see Leon naked, aroused, reaching for her...

Leon, who had rejected her, who had compared her to a woman he hated...a woman who—

'No!'

Fiercely, Sadie pushed Leon away.

'This isn't why I'm here, Leon,' she told him firmly, quickly turning her head so that he wouldn't have the opportunity to look into her eyes and see just how very vulnerable to him she actually was. After all, she had her pride, didn't she? She wasn't going to give him the opportunity to reject her a second time, was she?

'As I've already said, for Raoul's sake I am prepared to sell my share of Francine to you. So, now you've got what you want, if you don't mind I—'

'Got what I want? And if I haven't got everything I want?' Leon asked softly.

Sadie could feel her heart hammering against her ribcage This wasn't a verbal prelude to a declaration of love or a plea for understanding and forgiveness, she told herself quickly. So there was no point in her stupid heart hoping that it was. Leon just wasn't that kind of man. Leon didn't want her. He wanted...

'I haven't changed my mind about the Myrrh formula, Leon—that formula was entrusted to me by my grand-mother. Its history meant a great deal to her. If I were to sell it or change it in any way—' Her mouth twisted with bitter sadness. 'But of course I can hardly expect you to understand how I feel, can I? After all, in your eyes I'm another Miranda Stanton. I knew from your tone of voice that you were insulting me, Leon, but I didn't realise just how much until I read up on just what she had done! I can understand how frightened and vulnerable you must have felt when she—'

'I felt no such thing!'

The harshness in his voice made Sadie turn her head to look at him. It was obvious that she had found a chink in his emotional armour, but that knowledge made her feel more sad than triumphant.

'Have you any idea how I felt, knowing you had com-pared me to her Leon? A woman so morally deficient, a woman who delighted in hurting others, in cheating them for her own selfish ends?'

Every word Sadie said was making Leon feel increas-ingly uncomfortable and angry. He had spent the whole of the previous two days talking with one of the French perfume industry's foremost chemists, trying to find out if there was a way that he and Sadie could reach a com-promise over the creation of a new scent, so that he could tell her... But clearly all she wanted to do was touch an old but still raw wound he had no wish to have prodded and probed.

'Sadie, I know you're no Miranda. I...' He pushed his hand into his hair and gave a small exasperated shrug.

'Oh, you say that now, Leon, when you want me to

agree to sell my share in Francine,' Sadie told him coldly. 'But there really isn't any need for you to lie to me. I've already told you I—'

'Lie to you! What the hell—! My God, Sadie I'm doing my damnedest to build bridges here, but as fast as I try you go pulling them down.'

'I've had enough of this,' Sadie told him. 'I'm not a complete fool, Leon—no matter what you might think. I can do simple maths and add up two and two, you know. You think that every woman you come across in business is potentially another Miranda, and I can understand why you're afraid of history repeating itself, but—'

'Hell and damn it, Sadie, I am not afraid of anything or anyone,' Leon growled savagely. 'And right now you are seriously off topic.'

'Yes, you are, Leon,' Sadie countered simply. 'You're afraid now and you will continue to be afraid all your life—unless you learn to let go of the past and—'

Sadie gave a small gasp of shock as suddenly she was in Leon's arms and the words she had been about to speak were smothered by the hot pressure of his mouth grinding down fiercely on hers.

She ought to stop him. She knew that. Or at least her head knew it. Her body might know it, but if it did it certainly didn't seem to care, because it was reacting to him with love-crazed enthusiasm: her lips softening and parting, her tongue stroking hungrily against his, her arms lifting to hold him equally as tightly as he was holding her. Her body was pressing itself into him, her hips grinding achingly against the hard thrust of his erection.

The sound of their breathing, the soft little sighs and moans of pleasure Sadie was giving and the thick, raw muffled responses from Leon filled the air around them.

Dizzily Sadie acknowledged that if this was war no way was she going to sue for peace!

When Leon's hand cupped her breast she moaned an appreciative response. When she tugged his shirt free of his jeans and allowed her hands the pleasure of caressing his warm bare skin he returned the compliment by sliding his hand beneath her tee shirt with gratifying impatience and eagerness.

Her nipple pushed eagerly against the thin fabric of her bra, seeking the skin to skin touch of his hand just as eagerly as his erection was demanding hers.

Between hungrily passionate kisses their clothes were quickly and mutually discarded. The desk was behind them and Sadie murmured in approval as Leon made good use of it, by lifting her onto it.

The warm sunlight through the window dusted gold over Leon's warmly tanned skin, finding in the dark shadowing of hair glints of tawny warmth. Sadie clung to him as he reached for her, wrapping herself tightly around him, welcoming each hungry thrust of his body within her own, encouraging his deeper and deeper penetration of her as her need for him rocketed out of control.

They came together quickly and ferociously, the explosion of pleasure inside her leaving Sadie's body trembling.

As the heat left her body and the red burst of need clouding her brain lifted, she wondered bleakly what on earth she had done. But as she made to pull away from Leon he pulled her closer, cradling her against his body.

'No. I want you here with me, Sadie. In my arms. Heaven knows I've dreamed about holding you in them damn near every night since we've been apart.'

Silently Sadie looked at him. Her heart had begun to jump giddily around inside her ribcage, and she wanted to tell it to stop, to realise as she did that Leon was afraid of the commitment it ached for them to share.

'And in my bed!' Leon was continuing, his voice growing thicker with every word. 'Not just now, tonight, but every night, Sadie. You were right when you accused me of being afraid,' he told her abruptly. 'But what I'm most afraid of right now is loving you, Sadie. I want you in my life full-time, with all that entails. You could never be another Miranda. I knew that all along. But to have you back out of the deal I'd spent so much time putting together, knowing how my board were likely to react when some of them had been against the whole thing from the start…'

'What happened to your father must have been hard for you,' Sadie said quietly.

She could see from the look in Leon's eyes that a part of him wanted to back off from this kind of discussion, but to Sadie it was important that they talked about it. '*Very* hard for you,' she added with soft encouragement, waiting, wanting him to open up to her and allow her into his pain.

The look on his face said that she had gone too far, trespassed too far, but Sadie wasn't about to back off!

They had shared one very important kind of intimacy, the kind of intimacy where she had opened herself to him as a woman, and now it was time for him to open himself to her as a man!

'Hard?' His mouth twisted bitterly. 'I was fourteen and my father was my hero. He had worked damn near a ten-hour day seven days a week to get the business off the ground. You should have seen the pride in his face the day he took my mother and me to see the house he had bought for us. That meant so much to him. That he was able to provide for us, to give my mother all the things she'd had to do without whilst he was getting the business up and running. He told me that one day I would take over from him...but not until I'd been to college and seen a bit of the world. He wanted me to have the opportunities he hadn't been able to have himself! And then Andy died, and Miranda...' Leon paused. 'That was hard, seeing my father going virtually overnight from a man of pride and self-respect to someone...'

Unable to stop herself, Sadie reached out and covered Leon's hand with her own in a gesture of womanly comfort and understanding.

'You must have felt very angry, and very afraid.' she said gently. When he looked at her she added, 'You were only a boy, Leon. Fourteen...'

'Fourteen is only four years off manhood,' Leon told her curtly. 'What happened then made me the man I am today, Sadie. A man who always puts the security of the business ahead of everything else in my life.'

He paused to look at her before adding gruffly, 'And then you came along, and suddenly...What was happening between us wasn't in my game plan—and you were a woman I was involved with on a business footing. When I was with you, you blew my ability to rationalise clean out of the water. All I wanted...all I needed was you. Don't you see?' he growled. 'What was happening between us pushed me off base and made me feel...'

'Vulnerable?' she suggested softly.

For a moment she thought he wasn't going to reply.

This man, *her* man, she acknowledged with a tiny shiver of fierce pleasure, was quite definitely one tough alpha male.

'If you want to put it that way,' he agreed, almost grudgingly.

'And that was why you rejected me?'

Sadie didn't wait for his reply; she could see it in his eyes. The best way to teach someone was by example, she reminded herself. And, that being the case, if she wanted Leon to talk to her about his feelings perhaps she would talk about her own first!

Taking a deep breath, she asked him slowly, 'Have you any idea what rejection does to a woman, or at least to this woman, when she's given herself in love to the man she thinks shares her feelings? When she's already planning their future together, even imagining having his babies? Only to be told that she's got it wrong, that he doesn't want her; that he doesn't share her feelings?'

'You were doing that? Imagining having my babies?' His voice was thick with awe, raw with emotion. 'You were imagining…?'

As he took her in his arms, Leon whispered against her mouth, 'We've got to find a way to make this work, Sadie. We will find a way!'

Pushing him away, Sadie warned him, 'I won't change my mind about the Myrrh formula, Leon. Nor about working with synthetics.'

Leon brushed his thumb against Sadie's lips.

'No words now, Sadie. Not when there is so much I want to communicate to you in so many other ways— with my hands, with my mouth, with my body!' he added sensuously as he felt her lips open to caress the hard pad of his thumb.

Tomorrow he would tell her about his meeting with the chemist, and that he planned to put to his board the proposal that they invest in creating a scent which would combine the best of both natural ingredients and synthetic that could be afforded by women all over the world. But right now he had far, far more important things on his mind than mere business!

As her tongue probed the ridges of flesh on Leon's thumb, Sadie opened her arms to him, moaning with pleasure as he bent his head to her breast and started to feather delirium-inducing caresses against its taut peak.

CHAPTER TWELVE

'YES, Raoul. I've told Leon that I'm prepared to sell him my share of Francine,' Sadie confirmed patiently into her mobile.

She was still in Leon's suite at the hotel, having spent the entire night with him, and her body throbbed blissfully with that very special physical ache that comes with sexual fulfilment.

Leon had left half an hour earlier, telling her that he had a meeting to go to but insisting that she was to stay until he returned.

'We have a great deal to talk about,' he had whispered as he kissed her. 'And I do not mean the Francine contract!'

Sadie's mouth curled into a happy smile now as she spoke to her cousin.

'I've also told Leon that I haven't changed my mind about either the Myrrh formula or creating a new synthetic scent for him,' she warned Raoul.

'Well, he won't be bothered about that,' Raoul interrupted her carelessly. 'I've heard that he's already in negotiation with Arnaud Lebrun, and he's supposed to be the best chemist in the whole of the perfume industry. If you want my opinion, you've been a fool to turn down the kind of opportunity Leon would have given you and your career, but it was your choice! Lebrun will give Leon what he wants! But at least you've had the sense to agree to sell your share of Francine to Leon,' Raul continued, oblivious to the deathblow he had dealt her.

Numbly, Sadie ended the call. Logically there was no valid reason why she should feel the way she was right now! Leon had every right to hire someone else to do what she had refused to do. But last night he had told her that they would find a way to work things out, and she had believed that he'd meant he was prepared to compromise, just as she was herself.

But she could not have been more wrong.

Once again pain, anger, desolation and a feeling of betrayal filled her. These were now familiar, destructive and unwanted feelings for Sadie. Feelings she had told herself—and believed—in Leon's arms last night that she would never experience again.

And what made it all so much worse was that Leon hadn't even warned her what he was planning to do. In bed last night he had as good as told her he loved her. But how could he when…?

She was on the point of leaving when Leon walked into the suite.

When she made no move to go to him, and then stepped back out of arm's reach when he came to her, he stood still and frowned.

'What is it? What's wrong?' He asked immediately.

'Was your appointment today with Arnaud Lebrun?' she challenged him.

'Yes, it was. But—'

Sadie felt sick with shock and pain.

'Leon, this just isn't going to work between us!' she told him fiercely.

'Last night I thought that perhaps… That given what I believed we felt for one another we might be able to reach a compromise with regard to Francine's new scent. But though I know that logically I have no right to feel this way because you have approached Lebrun to create

a new perfume for you. I just wish you had told me—
that's all. I had hoped that you were prepared to meet me
halfway. I just wish that you cared enough—not just
about me, but about my professional opinion, my work
ethic—to want to find that compromise, just as I want to
find it with you! But now…'

'Sadie—'

'No. It's no good. Being involved sexually with you
is just not enough for me. And I don't even think that
being involved with you emotionally is either. I'm a modern woman, Leon. I want to play a full role in my partner's life. I want my own career too.'

'Sadie, I went to see Lebrun to ask his advice about
the feasibility of creating a new scent that was a combination of natural materials and synthetics, that was all!
He's the best in the business and I wanted to see not only
if he thought if it could be done but also if it *was* done
if it could be done within a budget that would make it
affordable to every woman who wanted to wear it. I'd
already decided that I was going to strong-arm my board,
even put money in myself, if that was what it took to get
the thing off the ground. And do you know why I was
doing all that, Sadie? Do you know why I've been pacing
my bedroom floor at night and staring out of my damn
office window instead of concentrating on my business?
Do you even care why? Or are you so damned intent on
being right that you just can't see beyond that? I did it
for you…for my love for you and our future together. It
was for *you*, Sadie!'

As she stared at him in silence Sadie felt sure she could
hear the tiny sound of something precious breaking.

'You should have trusted me,' Leon told her angrily,
confirming her thoughts. 'But, no…'

Battling against her tears, Sadie gazed at him.

'Yes, you're right—I should,' she agreed quietly. 'But that goes both ways, Leon. We're two people who feel very strongly about certain things inside ourselves. I love you, and—'

'And I damn well love *you*,' Leon growled, giving her a look that made her ache to run into his arms and demand to be told that nothing else mattered other than that love.

But even love could not shut out reality and the world for ever. Buried problems had a way of growing and erupting, and if she and Leon could not reach a compromise…if they could not trust one another now, when their love was new…

'I asked Lebrun for his opinion because I wanted to come to you and tell you that I had changed my mind. I wanted to give you that change of mind as a gift of my love, Sadie.'

'I would rather you had given me your trust and treated me as an equal, not as a child to be given "gifts",' Sadie told him huskily.

But somehow she had moved, and so had he, and they were once more in each other's arms. From there it was just a few short, passionate moves to the bed, their discarded clothing littering the floor as they took refuge in the thing that bound them most securely together both physically and emotionally.

Through the blur of her tears Sadie saw the scratches she had left on Leon's back, scarlet weals of passion, inflicted in an agony of ecstasy he had induced and shared.

'We can't go on like this,' she whispered in despair. 'How can we be like this with one another when we don't trust each other? What's happening to us now is killing me, Leon, and I'm afraid that it will kill our love as well.'

'I know what you're saying,' Leon agreed. 'We need to start afresh, Sadie. Without any hidden agenda between us. I want you to create a new scent for Francine, but you will have to create it within a certain budget. You need time to think about whether or not you want to do that. And you need time to learn to trust me as well. What do you say to us having three months apart? I know how I feel about you, but you have to trust me, Sadie, and right now I don't believe that you do.'

'Three months apart sounds a good idea to me,' Sadie told him hollowly.

She was lying! Oh, how she was lying! The very thought of spending three *hours* apart from Leon right now was almost more than she could bear, but her pride would not allow her to say so. Why hadn't he just talked to her, instead of consulting Lebrun? Didn't *he* trust *her*?

Listening to Sadie agree to his plan, Leon clenched his jaw. How could he be such a fool? Right now what he longed to do more than anything else was pick Sadie up and carry her off somewhere he could have her all to himself—and for ever!

CHAPTER THIRTEEN

SADIE'S hand trembled as she stoppered the small precious bottle and wrapped it carefully in bubble wrap.

Her ticket was booked and there was no way she was going to give in to the nervousness and self-doubt that were making her hands tremble so much.

But what if, when she got to France, Leon reminded her that it was only three weeks since they had last been together and refused to see her? What if he insisted that they stick to their agreement not to see one another for three months? Or what if he had changed his mind altogether and simply no longer wanted her? What if…?

Sadie impatiently dismissed her wayward thoughts. Her flight was booked and her bag packed. Now all she needed to do was to place this precious phial of hope and love and compromise in her bag.

She was waiting in the departure lounge when her mobile rang. Answering it, she way surprised to hear Mary's voice.

'Sadie, where are you?' Mary demanded.

'At the airport,' Sadie replied. 'My flight has just been called, Mary.' She stood up to go and join the queue lining up for boarding.

'Stop right where you are,' she heard Mary urging. 'And if you aren't sitting down then I think you ought to be!' she added dramatically, pausing theatrically before continuing, 'You've got a visitor, Sadie.'

'A visitor?'

Sadie felt her hand start to tremble and then her whole

body as the small burst of aching disbelief inside her flowered warmly into hope.

Her mouth dry, she begged. 'Is it…is it Leon, Mary?'

It couldn't be, of course, and she was every kind of fool for even thinking that it might be, but…

'You'd just better come home,' Mary answered her obliquely. 'And you'd better get back here fast, because if you don't I might just be tempted to make off with him myself.'

It was the longest drive of Sadie's life! Mary hadn't said specifically that it was Leon who was her visitor, but Sadie hoped and prayed with every mile passing that it was. And that he would wait. And that he would listen. And that he would still want her. And… Her heart jerked, the uneven beat sending her pulse-rate scattering live bolts of nervous excitement through her body.

Please let it be Leon.

It was dark when she finally arrived home, and at first Sadie didn't see the dusty black Mercedes pulled to one side of her drive.

She was still focusing on it when the door of the house opened and Leon came walking out. How had he got in? Sadie momentarily wondered. Mary, of course! She had a spare key!

'Le—'

She didn't even get as far as finishing saying his name before she was dragged into his arms and kissed until she could hardly breathe.

'It *is* you. You *are* here!' she whispered shakily She was too thrilled to bother to hide her joy. 'Mary wouldn't say, but I hoped, and… Leon. Mmm…' She protested as he started to kiss her again, until somehow she discovered that they were both inside her house and the door was closed firmly behind them, shutting out the outside world.

'Let me look at you,' Leon demanded rawly, cupping her face and studying her features. 'You've lost weight,' he accused her gruffly.

'A little,' Sadie admitted, still breathless from his kisses. Inside her body the ache of longing which had begun pulsing there long before she had even got as far as the airport, never mind learned that Leon was here in her home, had become a demanding urge of embarrassing intensity. To try to ease it she shifted her weight from one foot to the other, and then gasped as she inadvertently bumped into him.

The feel of him against her sent the pulsing ache into hungry overdrive. Helplessly her hand went to his chest, then his waist before moving lower, unable to wait for the feel of the erection she could already see pushing against his jeans.

'Sadie,' she heard him growl protestingly, but she was beyond listening—had been beyond anything but satisfying her need for him from the moment she had seen him walking towards her.

She felt him tense and then shudder as she touched him, his reaction making her bolder—bold enough, in fact, to hold his gaze with her own as he groaned and covered her hand with his.

Now it was his gaze that was imprisoning her, just as it was her turn to shudder in mute response to the need they were both feeling.

'What you're doing right now, Sadie, is just about enough to push me over the edge,' Leon warned her huskily, bending his head to brush her lips with his own as he added, 'So if that isn't what you want…'

Purposefully he lifted his hand from hers, and just as

purposefully Sadie left hers where it was, covering the bulge under his jeans.

He had stopped kissing her and was simply looking at her with those dizzying green eyes. She started to tremble, and then flicked her tongue-tip nervously against her lips. As she did so for some reason her gaze dropped to Leon's crotch.

A raw sound like a cross between a roar and a groan warned her that she had tripped the danger switch, but before she could do anything Leon had grabbed hold of her, picking her up and swinging her into his arms.

'Which way is the bedroom?' he demanded thickly. 'And you'd better tell me damned quick, Sadie, otherwise it's going to have to be that kitchen table I can see right through there.'

As Sadie nodded numbly in the direction of the hallway leading to the stairs Leon acknowledged that he no longer gave a single damn about Francine or even Myrrh, and that right now the only thing…the only person that mattered to him was the woman he was holding in his arms. And he fully intended telling her so. There weren't going to be any more misunderstandings, no more misinformation! From now on he was planning to tell her every day of their lives how much he loved her.

How could he ever have risked losing her?

'You can't carry me all the way upstairs, Leon!' Sadie protested, but she still clung to him, revelling in the close contact she was enjoying.

'You just watch me!' he told her. 'On second thoughts, the kitchen table it is. There isn't any way I'm about to let you go! Not now, Sadie, and not ever.'

When he laid her down on her long pine table Sadie managed to find the conscience to remind him, 'About Francine, Leon…'

'Francine, nothing,' Leon growled. 'Right now the only perfume that's on my mind, Sadie, is yours!' he emphasised in a muffled voice, and he buried his face against her throat and started to kiss his way along it, unfastening the buttons on her shirt as he did so.

When she felt him slip his hand inside it and peel back the fabric of her bra to reveal the hard point of her nipple Sadie shuddered in wanton delight.

'You like this?' Leon demanded, watching her reaction as he rubbed his thumb against the aching crest of flesh. 'Like it?'

Sadie wondered hazily if Leon could translate the whimpered sound of pleasure she made, but patently he could, because he made a deep satisfied response in his own throat and then bent his lips to her breast, urging her thickly, 'And this? Do you like this too, Sadie?'

As Sadie's body arched, she frantically pulled open Leon's shirt. Her hands clung to his shoulders, her nails digging helplessly into his flesh, and Sadie could only give an incoherent moan. But Leon didn't need to hear any words. The way she was responding to him told him everything he needed to know.

The instant Leon's free hand stroked between her legs Sadie parted them. Inside her head she was already anticipating what was to come, her mind full of remembered images of intense sensuality.

Leon was tugging her jeans free of her legs, kneeling up on the table, his torso exposed where his shirt had been ripped open, Sadie recognised, her eyes widening as she stared at the torn fabric. Had she done that? And those scratches she could just see on his shoulder…had she inflicted those?

Leon had finished removing her jeans. He bent to remove her thin lace low-rise briefs.

Sadie closed her eyes in wanton pleasure as she felt the heat of his breath against her skin. Leon was sliding his hands beneath the lace. Her breath caught in her throat on a sob of pleasure.

'What is it, Sadie?' Leon was demanding huskily.

She could feel the heat of his breath on the soft triangle of curls beneath the lace. And then she could feel the light brush of his lips, teasing her, tantalising her with their promise of what she was already aching for...

'You want this?' he whispered, as his hands tugged away the lace and she was free to spread her legs in a wide vee of liquid female longing, inviting him to part the swollen lips of her sex and taste the sweet juice of her love.

The touch of Leon's tongue against the eager ridge of flesh that was her sensual centre sent Sadie wild. The firm lap of his tongue was taking her to heaven—beyond heaven, she acknowledged, as her body twisted and convulsed and the pleasure built up inside her to the point where she knew she was not going to be able to control it.

Leon's tongue lapped and stroked until Sadie could bear no more. Her whole body clenched, the muscles in her thighs tightening against Leon's hands as he held her.

As the first spasm of her orgasm began Leon raised his head and looked at her, watching her pleasure, making her focus wide-eyed on his gaze as it held her and demanded that she expose herself to him totally and completely.

As the quivers finally eased out of her body Sadie remembered there was something she had to tell him. Something important. Looking at him, she whispered with love-drugged urgency, 'Leon, the Myrrh formula—'

'Not now.' He stopped her, shaking his head and lowering his body to rest alongside her own. Tenderly he cupped her chin and started to kiss her, little gentle kisses that melted her insides.

'There's something I want to tell you first. I love you, and I need you, and if it means giving up the whole damn conglomerate to have you in my life then that is what I intend to do!'

'Oh, Leon!' Sadie protested mistily.

The look in his eyes as he bent over her and kissed her made her own prick with tears.

Slowly he released her mouth, his attention distracted by the sudden tightening of the nipple closest to him. Leon rewarded its demand with the lazy brush of his lips and the not so lazy lap of his tongue.

Immediately Sadie curled her toes, a small gasp of shocked pleasure parting her lips. Surely not again? Not so…so…immediately and intensely?

She made another small sound and reached for Leon.

The feel of him inside her filled her with a pleasure which went way beyond anything physical. Just holding him there was surely the most intense emotional experience she had ever had, Sadie acknowledged.

'More, Leon,' she demanded with female hunger. 'More…yes…just like that. Just like that…' she moaned as she urged him deeper and deeper within her, wrapping him tightly with the wet warmth of her flesh.

'Sadie!' Leon warned her, but her body was already eager for his climax, matching it and capturing him as he pulsed thickly inside her.

She was almost asleep when Leon pulled her up and they made their way up to bed. He tucked her into his side and pulled the bedclothes over them. But even in her sleep Sadie was not prepared to let him go.

Curled into his body, she rested one of her hand on

him. Not that she needed to hold him. Before he had fallen asleep Leon had thrown a possessive male leg over Sadie's body, imprisoning her where he intended to keep her. At his side. For ever.

When Sadie woke up she was on her own, the side of the bed next to her empty and cold—but nowhere near as cold as her heart.

Frantically she threw back the bedclothes and rushed to the window. The Mercedes was still outside!

Then she heard a sound from downstairs. Quickly she looked for something to put on. The first thing that caught her eye was Leon's discarded shirt. Pulling it on, she paused to breathe in the smell of him.

As she tried to fasten it up she realised that one of the buttons was missing and that one of the buttonholes was torn. Guiltily she remembered how that had happened! She had done it last night, in her eagerness to get to Leon's body!

Padding downstairs, she went into the kitchen, where she could smell coffee brewing. But Leon wasn't there. And then she saw him across the hallway in her sitting room. Holding her grandmother's photograph.

Even though she could have sworn she had not made a sound, he turned and looked at her.

'Your grandmother?' he asked.

Silently Sadie nodded her head.

Putting the photograph back, Leon came towards her.

'Where were you going yesterday?' he asked.

Sadie looked at him

'To find you,' she admitted. And, turning away from him, she went to where she had left her bag the previous evening. Opening it, she removed the bubble-wrapped packet. 'And to give you this,' she added, handing the package to him.

'What is it?' Frowning, Leon unwrapped it and stared at the small glass phial in his hand.

'I...' Sadie took a deep breath. 'You weren't the only one looking for...for a compromise. It's a new Myrrh perfume,' she told him huskily. 'I...I made it here in my workshop. It's a...' She stopped and discovered that her whole body was shaking. Lifting her head, she looked at him. 'It's a blend of raw material and...and synthetics.' She bit her lip.

For a long time she thought he simply wasn't going to speak. His whole attention was concentrated on the small bottle he was holding. But then suddenly he raised his head, and in the green eyes and on the black lashes Sadie could see quite openly the glitter of strong male tears.

'You did this for me?' Leon demanded.

'For us,' Sadie corrected him, her own gaze blurring.

'Oh, Sadie.' Leon groaned, kissing her softly and then saying against her lips, 'Sadie, I love you. Will you marry me? You'd better,' he advised when she looked at him.

'For one thing I just couldn't bear it if you don't, and for another...' He bent his head and whispered in her ear, 'After last night, I feel in nine months' time there could be a very good reason why you and I should be man and wife!'

'A baby?' Sadie blinked away her tears.

'Mmm...we could try for twins if you like,' Leon teased her.

It took several seconds for his meaning to sink through Sadie's euphoric happiness. When it did she gave him an old-fashioned look.

'Certainly not,' she told him primly. 'Well, at least not until I've had a cup of coffee…'

'You can have a cup of coffee…when I've had you…' Leon promised sexily.

EPILOGUE

'AND so what have you called the new baby?' the excited reporter asked Sadie eagerly.

Bright-eyed, she looked at Leon, who was standing by her side.

'Well, I think we've decided on Petit Bébé.' Sadie answered her, straight-faced.

She and Leon had worked hard to come up with an original name for the range of baby products they were launching under the Francine name. The range had gone into production just about the same time as Sadie herself, and the results of both efforts were on display in the Grasse house now. The Petit Bébé range of babycare products in their attractive modern packaging, and the equally modern and attractively packaged identical twin daughters Sadie had given birth to six weeks before.

'See, I told you it could be twins,' Leon had murmured when Sadie had gone for the scan which had revealed the fact that she was carrying two babies.

And despite the fact that she was a recently married woman and a mother-to-be Sadie had blushed deeply at the look in his eyes, remembering just how and where those babies had been conceived.

'I wonder which of them is the kitchen table baby,' Leon whispered teasingly to her when the press conference was over.

'Neither or both,' Sadie responded firmly. 'After all, they are identical twins.'

Still smiling at her, Leon bent his head to kiss her.

The Demetrios Virgin

PENNY JORDAN

CHAPTER ONE

'FOUR forty-five.' Saskia grimaced as she hurried across the foyer of the office block where she worked, heading for the exit. She was already running late and didn't have time to pause when the receptionist called out. 'Sneaking off early... Lucky you!'

Andreas frowned as he heard the receptionist's comment. He was standing waiting for the executive lift and the woman who was leaving hadn't seen him, but he had seen her: a stunningly leggy brunette with just that gleam of red-gold in her dark locks that hinted at fieriness. He immediately checked the direction of his thoughts. The complication of a man to woman entanglement was the last thing he needed right now, and besides...

His frown deepened. Since he had managed to persuade his grandfather to semi-retire from the hotel chain which Andreas now ran, the older man had begun a relentless campaign to persuade and even coerce Andreas into marrying a second cousin. Such a marriage, in his grandfather's eyes, would unite not just the two branches of the family but the wealth of the family shipping line—inherited by his cousin—with that of the hotel chain.

Fortunately Andreas knew that at heart his grandfather was far more swayed by emotion than he liked

5

to admit. After all, he had allowed his daughter, Andreas's mother, to marry an Englishman.

The somewhat clumsy attempts to promote a match between Andreas and his cousin Athena would merely afford Andreas some moments of wry amusement if it were not for one all-important fact—which was that Athena herself was even keener on the match than his grandfather. She had made her intentions, her *desires*, quite plain. Athena was a widow seven years his senior, with two children from her first marriage to another wealthy Greek, and Andreas suspected that it might have been Athena herself who had put the ridiculous idea of a marriage between them in his grandfather's head in the first place.

The lift had reached the penthouse floor and Andreas got out. This wasn't the time for him to be thinking about his personal affairs. *They* could wait. He was due to fly out to the Aegean island his grandfather owned, and where the family holidayed together, in less than a fortnight's time, but first his grandfather wanted a detailed report from him on his proposals to turn the flagging British hotel chain they had recently bought into as successful an enterprise as the rest of the hotels they owned.

Even though Andreas had become the company's chief executive, his grandfather still felt the need to challenge his business decisions. Still, the acquisition would ultimately be a good one—the chain-owned hotels were very run down and old fashioned, but had excellent locations.

Although officially he was not due to arrive at the chain's head office until tomorrow, Andreas had opted to do so this afternoon instead, and it looked as though he had just discovered one way at least in which profitability could be improved, he decided grimly, if all the staff were in the habit of 'sneaking off early', like the young woman he had just seen...

Sneaking off early! Saskia grimaced as she managed to hail a cruising taxi. If only! She had been at her desk for seven-thirty this morning, as she had been every morning for the last month, and neither had she had a lunch hour, but they had all been warned that Demetrios Hotels, who had taken over their own small chain, were relentless when it came to pruning costs. Tomorrow morning they were all due to meet their new boss for the first time, and Saskia wasn't exactly looking forward to the occasion. There had been a lot of talk about cutbacks and there had also been grapevine rumours about how very formidable Andreas Latimer was.

'The old man, his grandfather, had a reputation for running a tight ship, and if anything the grandson is even worse.'

'They both favour a "the guest is always right even when wrong" policy, and woe betide any employee who forgets it. Which is, of course, why their hotels are so popular...and so profitable,'

That had been the general gist of the gossip Saskia had heard.

Her taxi was drawing up outside the restaurant she had asked to be taken to. Hastily she delved into her handbag for her purse, paying the driver and then hurrying quickly inside.

'Oh, Saskia—*there* you are. We thought you weren't going to make it.'

'I'm sorry,' Saskia apologised to her best friend as she slipped into the spare seat at the table for three in the Italian restaurant where they had arranged to meet.

'There's been a panic on at work,' she explained. 'The new boss arrives tomorrow.' She pulled a face, wrinkling the elegant length of her dainty nose and screwing up her thick-lashed aquamarine eyes. She paused as she saw that her friend wasn't really listening, and that her normally happy, gentle face looked strained and unhappy.

'What's wrong?' she asked immediately.

'I was just telling Lorraine how upset I am,' Megan answered, indicating the third member of their trio, Megan's cousin Lorraine, an older woman with a brisk, businesslike expression and a slightly jaded air.

'Upset?' Saskia queried, a small frown marring the elegant oval of her face as she pushed her long hair back and reached hungrily for a bread roll. She was starving!

'It's Mark,' Megan said, her voice shaking a little and her brown eyes full of quiet despair.

'Mark?' Saskia repeated, putting down her roll so that she could concentrate on her friend. 'But I thought the two of you were about to announce your engagement.'

'Yes, we were…we are… At least, Mark wants to…' Megan began, and then stopped when Lorraine took over.

'Megan thinks he's involved with someone else…' she told Saskia grimly. 'Two-timing her.'

Older than Megan and Saskia by almost a decade,

and with a broken marriage behind her, Lorraine was inclined to be angrily contemptuous of the male sex.

'Oh, surely not, Megan,' Saskia protested. 'You told me yourself how much Mark loves you.'

'Well, yes, that's what I thought,' Megan agreed, 'Especially when he said that he wanted us to become engaged. But...he keeps getting these phone calls. And if I answer the phone whoever's ringing just hangs up. There've been three this week and when I ask him who it is he says it's just a wrong number.'

'Well, perhaps it is,' Saskia tried to reassure her, but Megan shook her head.

'No, it isn't. Mark keeps on hanging around by the phone, and last night he was talking on his mobile when I walked in and the moment he saw me he ended the call.'

'Have you *asked* him what's going on?' Saskia questioned her in concern.

'Yes. He says I'm just imagining it,' Megan told her unhappily.

'A classic male ploy,' Lorraine announced vigorously with grim satisfaction. 'My ex did everything to convince me that I was becoming paranoid and then what does he do? He moves in with his secretary, if you please!'

'I just wish that Mark would be honest with me,' Megan told Saskia, her eyes starting to fill with tears. 'If there *is* someone else...I... I just can't believe he's doing this... I thought he loved me...'

'I'm sure he does,' Saskia tried to comfort her. She had not as yet met her friend's new partner, but from what Megan had told her about him Saskia felt he sounded perfect for her.

'Well, there's one sure way to find out,' Lorraine announced. 'I read an article about it. There's this agency, and if you've got suspicions about your partner's fidelity you go to them and they send a girl to try to seduce him. That's what you should do,' she told Megan crisply.

'Oh, no, I couldn't,' Megan protested.

'You must,' Lorraine insisted forcefully. 'It's the only way you'll ever know whether or not you can trust him. I wish I'd been able to do something like that before I got married. You *must* do it,' she repeated. 'It's the only way you'll ever be sure. Mark is struggling to make ends meet since he started up his own business, Megan, and you've got that money you inherited from your great-aunt.'

Saskia's heart sank a little as she listened. Much as she loved her friend, she knew that Megan was inclined to allow herself to be dominated by her older and more worldly cousin. Saskia had nothing against Lorraine, indeed she liked her, but she knew from past experience that once Lorraine got the bit between her teeth there was no stopping her. She was fiercely determined to do things her own way, which Saskia suspected was at least part of the reason for the breakdown of her marriage. But right now, sympathetic though Saskia was to Megan's unhappiness, she was hungry…very hungry… She eyed the menu longingly.

'Well, it does *sound* a sensible idea,' Megan was agreeing. 'But I doubt there's an agency like that in Hilford.'

'Who needs an agency?' Lorraine responded. 'What *you* need is a stunningly gorgeous friend who Mark hasn't met and who can attempt to seduce him. If he responds…'

'A stunningly gorgeous friend?' Megan was musing. 'You mean like Saskia?'

Two pairs of female eyes studied Saskia whilst she gave in to her hunger and bit into her roll.

'Exactly,' Lorraine breathed fervently. 'Saskia would be perfect.'

'What?' Saskia almost choked on her bread. 'You *can't* be serious,' she protested. 'Oh, no, no way…' She objected when she saw the determination in Lorraine's eyes and the pleading in Megan's. 'No way at all.'

'Meg, this is crazy, you must see that,' she coaxed, trying to appeal to her friend's common sense and her conscience as she added winningly, 'How *could* you do something like that to Mark? You love him.'

'How can she risk committing herself to him unless she knows she can trust him?' Lorraine interjected sharply, adding emphatically, 'Good, that's settled. What we need to do now is to decide just where Saskia can accidentally run into Mark and put our plan into action.'

'Well, tonight is his boys' night out,' Megan ventured. 'And last night he said that they were planning to go to that new wine bar that's just opened. A friend of his knows the owner.'

'I can't do it,' Saskia protested. 'It…it's…it's immoral,' she added. She looked apologetically at Megan as she shook her head and told her, 'Meg, I'm sorry, but…'

'I should have thought you would *want* to help Megan, Saskia, to protect her happiness. Especially after all *she's* done for *you*...' Lorraine pointed out sharply.

Saskia worried guiltily at her bottom lip with her pretty white teeth. Lorraine was right. She *did* owe Megan a massive favour.

Six months ago, when they had been trying to fight off the Demetrios takeover bid, she had been working late every evening and at weekends as well. Her grandmother, who had brought her up following the breakdown of her young parents' marriage, had become seriously ill with a viral infection and Megan, who was a nurse, had given up her spare time and some of her holiday entitlement to care for the old lady.

Saskia shuddered to think even now of the potentially dangerous outcome of her grandmother's illness if Megan hadn't been there to nurse her. It had been on Saskia's conscience ever since that she owed her friend a debt she could never repay. Saskia adored her grandmother, who had provided her with a loving and stable home background when she had needed it the most. Her mother, who had given birth to Saskia at seventeen was a distant figure in her life, and her father, her grandmother's son, had become a remote stranger to both of them, living as he now did in China, with his second wife and young family.

'I know you don't approve, Saskia,' Megan was saying quietly to her, 'but I *have* to know that I can trust Mark.' Her soft eyes filled with tears. 'He means *so* much to me. He's everything I've *ever* wanted in a man. But...he dated so many girls before he met me, before he moved here, when he lived in London.' She paused. 'He swears that none of them ever meant anything serious to him and that he loves me.'

Privately Saskia wasn't sure that she could even begin to think about committing herself to a relationship with a man without being able to trust him—and trust him to such an extent that there would be no need for her to use any underhand methods to test his fidelity. But then she acknowledged that she was perhaps a trifle more wary of love than her friend. After all, her parents had believed themselves to be in love when they had run away to get married and conceived her, but within two years of doing so they had parted, leaving her grandmother with the responsibility of bringing her up.

Her grandmother! Now, as she looked at Meg's tearstained face, she knew she had no option but to go along with Lorraine's scheme.

'All right,' she agreed fatalistically. 'I'll do it.'

After Megan had finished thanking her she told her wryly, 'You'll have to describe your Mark to me, Megan, otherwise I shan't be able to recognise him.'

'Oh, yes, you will,' Megan said fervently with a small ecstatic sigh. 'He'll be the best-looking man there. He's gorgeous, Saskia…fantastically good-looking, with thick dark hair and the most sexy mouth you've ever seen. Oh, and he'll be wearing a blue shirt—to match his eyes. He always does. I bought them for him.'

'What time is he likely to get there?' Saskia asked Megan practically, instead of voicing her feelings.

'My car's in the garage at the moment, and since Gran's house is quite a way out of town…'

'Don't worry about that. I'll drive you there,' Lorraine volunteered, much to Saskia's surprise. Lorraine wasn't known to be over-generous—with anything!

'Yes, and Lorraine will pick you up later and take you home. Won't you, Lorraine?' Megan insisted with unexpected firmness. 'There's no taxi rank close to the wine bar and you don't want to be waiting for a mini-cab.'

A waiter was hovering, waiting to take their order, but bossily Lorraine shook her head, telling Megan and Saskia firmly, 'There won't be time for us to eat now. Saskia will have to get home and get ready. What time *is* Mark likely to go to the wine bar Megan?' she asked her cousin.

'About eight-thirty, I should think,' Megan answered.

'Right, then you need to get there for nine, Saskia,' Lorraine informed her, 'So I'll pick you up at half-eight.'

Two hours later Saskia was just coming downstairs when she heard the front doorbell. Her grandmother was away, spending several weeks with her sister in Bath. A little nervously Saskia smoothed down the skirt of her black suit and went to open the door.

Only Lorraine was standing outside. They had agreed that it would be silly to take the risk of Megan being seen and recognised. Now, as Lorraine studied her, Saskia could see the older woman beginning to frown.

'You'll have to wear something else,' she told Saskia sharply. 'You look far too businesslike and unapproachable in that suit. Mark's got to think you're approachable—remember. And I really think you ought to wear a different lipstick…red, perhaps, and more eye make-up. Look, if you don't believe me then read this.' Lorraine thrust an open magazine beneath Saskia's nose.

Reluctantly Saskia skimmed through the article, a small frown pleating her forehead as she read of the lengths the agency was prepared to have its girls go to in order to test the faithfulness of its clients' men.

'I can't do any of this,' she told Lorraine firmly. 'And as for my suit…'

Stepping into the hall and closing the front door behind her, Lorraine stood squarely in front of Saskia and told her vehemently, 'You have to—for Megan's sake. Can't you see what's happening to her, the danger she's in? She's totally besotted with this man; she's barely known him four months and already she's talking about handing over the whole of her inheritance to him…marrying him…having children with him. Do you know how much her great-aunt left her?' she added grimly.

Silently Saskia shook her head. She knew how surprised and shocked Megan had been when she had learned that she was the sole beneficiary under her great-aunt's will, but tactfully she had not asked her friend just how much money was involved.

Lorraine, it seemed, had not had similar qualms.

'Megan inherited nearly three million pounds,' she told Saskia, nodding her head in grim pleasure as she saw Saskia's expression.

'*Now* do you see how important it is that we do everything we can to protect her? I've tried to warn her umpteen times that her precious Mark might not be all he tries to make out he is, but she just won't listen. Now, thank goodness, she's caught him out and he's showing his true colours. For her sake, Saskia, you just do everything you can to prove how unworthy he is. Just imagine what it would do to her if he not only broke her heart but stole all her money as well. She'd be left with nothing.'

Saskia could imagine it all too well. Her grandmother had only a small pension to live on and Saskia, mindful of the sacrifices her grandmother had made when she was growing up, to make sure she did not go without the treats enjoyed by her peers, contributed as much as she could financially to their small household.

The thought of losing her financial independence and the sense of security that earning money of her own gave her was one that was both abhorrent and frightening to her, and Lorraine's revelations suddenly gave her not just the impetus but a real desire to do everything she could to protect her friend.

Megan, dear sweet trusting Megan, who still worked as a nurse despite her inheritance, deserved to find a man, a partner, who was truly worthy of her. And if this Mark wasn't... Well, perhaps then it would be for the best if her friend found out sooner rather than later.

'Perhaps if you took off the jacket of your suit,' Lorraine was saying now. 'You must have some kind of sexy summer top you could wear...or even just...'

She stopped as she saw Saskia's expression.

'Summer top, yes,' Saskia agreed. 'Sexy...no!'

As she saw the look on Lorraine's face Saskia suppressed a small sigh. It was pointless trying to explain to a woman like Lorraine that when nature had given one the kind of assets it had given Saskia, one learned very young that they could be something of a double-edged sword. To put it more bluntly, men—in Saskia's experience—did not need the double overload of seeing her body clad in 'sexy' clothes to encourage them to look twice at her. And in most cases to want to do much more than merely look!

'You must have *something*,' Lorraine urged, refusing to be defeated. 'A cardigan. You must have a cardigan—you could wear it sort of unbuttoned...'

'A cardigan? Yes, I have a cardigan,' Saskia agreed. She had bought it halfway through their cold spring when they had been on an economy drive at work and the heating had been turned off. But as for wearing it unbuttoned...!

'And red lipstick,' Lorraine was insisting, 'and more eye make-up. You'll have to let him know that you find him attractive...' She paused as Saskia lifted her eyebrows. 'It's for Megan's sake.'

In the end it was almost nine o'clock before they left the house, due to Lorraine's insistence that Saskia had to reapply her make-up with a far heavier hand than she would normally have used.

Uncomfortably Saskia refused to look at her reflection in the hall mirror. All that lipstick! It felt sticky, gooey, and as Lorraine drove her towards Hilford she had to force herself to resist the temptation to wipe it off. As for the unbuttoned cardigan she was wearing beneath her suit jacket—well, the moment she was inside the wine bar and out of Lorraine's sight she was going to refasten every single one of the top three buttons Lorraine had demanded that she left undone. True, they did nothing more than merely hint at a cleavage, but even that was far more of a provocation than Saskia would normally have allowed.

'We're here,' Lorraine announced as she pulled up outside the wine bar. 'I'll pick you up at eleven— that should give you plenty of time. Remember,' Lorraine hissed determinedly as Saskia got out of the car, 'We're doing this for Megan.'

We? But before Saskia could say anything Lorraine was driving off.

A man walking in the opposite direction paused on the pavement to give her an admiring glance. Automatically Saskia distanced herself from him and turned away, mentally squaring her shoulders as she headed for the entrance to the wine bar.

Lorraine had given her a long list of instructions, most of which had made Saskia cringe inwardly, and already her courage was beginning to desert her. There was no way she could go in there and pout and flirt in the enticing way that Lorraine had informed her she had to do. But if she didn't poor Megan could end up having her heart broken and her inheritance cheated away from her.

Taking a deep breath, Saskia pulled open the wine bar door.

CHAPTER TWO

ANDREAS saw Saskia the moment she walked in. He was seated at the bar, which was now being besieged by a crowd of young men who had come in just ahead of her. He could have stayed in and eaten in the office block's penthouse apartment—or even driven to the closest of their new acquisitions—but he had already endured two lengthy phone calls he would rather not have had this evening: one from his grandfather and another from Athena. So he had decided to go somewhere where neither of them could get in touch with him, having deliberately 'forgotten' to bring his mobile with him.

He hadn't been in a particularly good mood when he had arrived at the wine bar. Such places were not to his taste.

He liked good food served in comfortable sur-roundings where one could talk and think with ease, and there was also enough Greek in him for him to prefer somewhere more family centred and less of an obvious trawling ground for members of the opposite sex.

Thinking of the opposite sex made his mouth harden. Athena was becoming more and more brazen in her attempts to convince him that they should be together. He had been fifteen the first time he had been exposed to Athena's sexual aggression, and she had been twenty-two and about to be married.

He frowned as he watched Saskia. She was standing just inside the doorway, studying the room as
though she was looking for someone. She turned her
head and the light fell on her smoothly glossed lips.

Andreas sucked in his breath as he fought to control his unwanted reaction to her. What the hell was
he doing? She was so damned obvious with that almost but not quite scarlet lipstick that he ought to be
laughing, not… Not what? he asked himself causti-
cally. Not wanting…lusting…

A strong surge of self-disgust lashed him. He had
recognised her, of course. It was the girl from this
afternoon, the one the receptionist had congratulated
on her early departure from work. Then she had been
wearing a minimum of make-up. Now… He eyed her
lipsticked mouth and kohl-enhanced eyes grimly. She
was wearing a suit with a short skirt…a very short
skirt, he observed as she moved and he caught sight
of the length of her sheer black tights-clad legs. A
very, very short skirt!

As the turned-over waistband of her once respectably knee-length skirt made its presence felt, Saskia
grimaced. Once she had found Mark she fully intended to make her way to the cloakroom and return
her skirt to its normal length. It had been Lorraine,
of course, who had insisted on shortening it.

'I can't go out like *that*,' Saskia had yelped.

'Don't be ridiculous,' Lorraine had derided her.
'That's nothing. Haven't you seen pictures from the
sixties?'

'That was then,' Saskia had informed her firmly
without letting her finish, but Lorraine had refused
to give in and in the end Saskia had shrugged her

shoulders and comforted herself with the knowledge that once Lorraine was out of sight she could do what she liked with her skirt. The cardigan too was making her feel uncomfortable, and unwittingly she started to toy with the first of its unfastened buttons.

As he watched her Andreas's eyes narrowed. God, but she was obvious, drawing attention to her breasts like that... And what breasts! Andreas discovered that he was starting to grind his teeth and, more importantly, that he was totally unable to take his eyes off Saskia...

Sensing that she was being watched, Saskia turned round and then froze as her searching gaze clashed head-on with Andreas's hard-eyed stare.

For a breath of time Saskia was totally dazed, such was the effect of Andreas's raw masculinity on her. Her heart was pounding, her mouth dry, her body... Helplessly transfixed, she fought desperately against what she was feeling—against what she was not allowed to feel. For this was Megan's Mark—it had to be. She could not really be experiencing what her emotions were telling her she was experiencing, she denied in panic. Not a woman like her, and not for this man, Megan's man!

No other man in the place came anywhere near matching the description Megan had given her as closely as this one did. Mentally she ticked off Megan's euphoric description of him—one Saskia had previously put down to the near ravings of a woman besottedly in love. Gorgeous, fantastically good-looking, sexy... Oh, and he would be wearing a blue shirt, Megan had told her, to match his eyes. Well, Saskia couldn't make out the colour of his eyes across the dimly lit distance that separated them, but she could certainly see that Megan had been right on every other count and her heart sank. So this was Megan's Mark. No wonder she was worrying so anxiously that he might be being unfaithful to her... A man who looked like this one did would have women pursuing him in droves.

Funny, but Megan hadn't mentioned the most important thing of all about him, which wasn't just that he was so spectacularly and sexually male but that he emanated a profound and intense air of authority that bordered almost on arrogance; it had struck Saskia the moment she had looked at him. That and the look of discreet male inspection quickly followed by a reactive resultant look of contemptuous disapproval.

That look... How *dare* he look at her like that? Suddenly all the doubts she had been harbouring about what she had agreed to do were vanquished.

Lorraine was right to be suspicious of such a man's motives, especially where a naïve, gentle, unworldly girl like Megan was concerned. Saskia didn't trust him one little bit. Megan needed a man who would appreciate her gentleness and treat her correspondingly. This man was powerful, daunting, awesome—and looking at him was, as Saskia was beginning to discover, something of a physical compulsion. She couldn't take her eyes off him. But that was just because she disliked him so much, she assured herself quickly, because she was so intensely aware of how very right Lorraine had been to want to test his loyalty to Megan.

Determinedly quelling the butterflies fluttering in

her stomach, Saskia took a deep breath, mentally reminding herself of what she had read in the article Lorraine had thrust under her nose. Then she had been horrified, repulsed by the lengths the girls hired by the agency were prepared to go to in order to entice and entrap their quarry into self-betrayal. It had even crossed her mind that no mere man could possibly find the strength to resist the kind of deliberate temptation those girls offered—everything from the most intense type of verbal flattery right up to outright offers of sex itself, although thankfully offers had been all they were.

A man like this one, though, must be used to women—attractive women—throwing themselves at him. 'He dated so many girls before he met me,' Megan had said innocently.

Saskia would just bet that he had. Megan was a honey, and Saskia loved her with a fierce loyalty, but even she had to admit that her friend did not possess the kind of glamorous instant eye appeal she suspected a man like this one would look for. But perhaps that was what he loved about her—the fact that she was so shy and homely. If he loved her... Well, that was up to Saskia to prove...or disprove...wasn't it?

With the light of battle shining in her eyes, Saskia made her way towards him.

Andreas watched her progress with a mixture of curiosity and disappointment. She was heading for him. He knew that, but the cool hauteur with which she not only ignored the interested looks she was collecting from other men as she did so but almost seemed not to notice them, was every bit as contrived as the unfastened buttons of the top she was wearing. It had to be! Andreas knew the type. He should do. After all, Athena...

'Oh, I'm sorry,' Saskia apologised as she reached Andreas's side and 'accidentally' stumbled against him. Straightening up, she stood next to him at the bar, giving him a winsomely apologetic smile as she moved so close to him that he could smell her scent... Not her perfume, which was light and floral, unexpectedly, but her *scent*, ...the soft, honey-sweet headily sensual and erotic scent that was her. And like a fool he was actually breathing it in, getting almost drunk on it...letting his senses react to it...to her...

Lorraine had coached her on her best approach and Saskia had memorised it, grimacing with loathing and distaste as she did so.

Andreas forced himself to step back from her and put some distance between them, but the bar was crowded and it was impossible for him to move away altogether, so instead he asked her coldly, 'I'm sorry...do I know you?'

His voice and demeanour were, he knew, cutting enough to make it plain that he knew what she was up to. Although why on earth a woman who looked like this one needed to trawl bars looking for men to pick up he had no idea. Or rather he did, but he preferred not to examine it too closely. There were women, as he already knew to his cost, who would do anything for money...anything...with anyone...

But Saskia was facing him now, her lipstick-glossed mouth parting in a smile he could see was forced as she purred, 'Er, no, actually, you don't…but I'm hoping that soon you will.'

Saskia was relieved that the bar was so dimly lit. She could feel the heat of her burning face. She had *never* in her most private thoughts even contemplated coming on to a man like this, never mind envisaged that she might actually do so. Quickly she hurried on to the next part of her prepared speech, parting her lips in what she hoped was a temptingly provocative smile whilst carefully running her tongue-tip over them.

Yuck! But all that lipstick felt repulsive.

'Aren't you going to ask me if I'd like a drink?' she invited coyly, batting her eyelashes in what she hoped was an appropriately enticing manner. 'I love the colour of your shirt,' she added huskily as she leaned closer. 'It matches your eyes…'

'If you think that you must be colour blind; my eyes are grey,' Andreas told her tersely. She was beginning to make him feel very angry. Her obviousness was nothing short of contemptible. But nothing like as contemptible as his own ridiculous reaction to her. What was he? A boy of eighteen? He was supposed to be a man…a mature, sophisticated, experienced, worldly man of thirty-odd—and yet here he was, reacting, *responding*, to the pathetically tired and jaded sexual tricks she was playing on him as eagerly as though… As though what? As though there was nothing he wanted to do right now more than take her to bed, to feel the hot urgency of her body beneath his, to hear her cry out his name through lips swollen with the mutual passion of their shared kisses whilst he…

'Look,' he told her sharply, cutting off the supply of lifeblood to his unwanted fantasies by the simple act of refusing to allow himself to think about them, 'you're making a big mistake.'

'Oh, no,' Saskia protested anxiously as he started to turn away from her. By rights she should simply accept what he was saying and go back to Megan and tell her that her beloved Mark was everything he was supposed to be. But an instinct she couldn't analyse was telling her that despite all the evidence to the contrary he was tempted. *Any* man could be tempted, she tried to tell herself fairly, but something inside her refused to allow her to listen.

'*You* could never be a mistake,' she purred suggestively. 'To any woman...'

Fatuously Andreas wondered if he had gone completely mad. To even think of desiring a woman who was openly propositioning him was anathema to everything he believed in. How could he possibly be even remotely attracted to her? He wasn't, of course. It was impossible. And as for that sudden inexplicable urge he had had to take her home with him, where she would be safe from the kind of attention her make-up and behaviour were bound to attract. Well, now he knew he *must* be seriously losing it.

If there was one thing he despised it was women like this one. Not that he preferred them to be demure or virginal. No. What he found most attractive was a woman who was proud to be herself and who expected his sex to respect her right to be what she was. The kind of woman who would automatically eschew any act that involved her presenting herself as some kind of sexual plaything and who would just as determinedly turn her back on any man who wanted her to behave that way. This woman...

'I'm sorry,' he told her, making it verbally plain that he was no such thing by the cold tone of his voice, 'but you're wasting your time. And time, as I can see,' he continued in a deceptively gentle voice, 'has to be money for a woman like you. So why don't you go away and find someone else who will be... er...more receptive to what you've got on offer than I am?'

White-faced, Saskia watched as he turned away from her and thrust his way towards the door. He had rejected her...refused her. He had... He had... Painfully she swallowed. He had proved that he was faithful to Megan and he had... He had looked at her as though...as though... Like a little girl, Saskia wiped the back of her hand across her lipsticked mouth, grimacing as she saw the stain the high-coloured gloss had left there.

'Hi there, gorgeous. Can I buy you a drink?'

Numbly she shook her head, ignoring the sour look the man who had approached was giving her as she stared at the door. There was no sign of Megan's man. He had gone—and she was glad. Of course she was. How could she not be? And she would be delighted to be able to report to Megan and Lorraine that Mark had not succumbed to her.

She glanced at her watch, her heart sinking. She still had over an hour to go before she met Lorraine. There was no way she could stay here in the bar on her own, attracting attention. Quickly she headed for the ladies. There was something she had to do.

In the cloakroom she fastened her cardigan and

wiped her face clean of the last of the red lipstick
and the kohl eye-liner, replacing them both with her
normal choice of make-up—a discreet application of
taupe eye-shadow and a soft berry-coloured lipstick—and coiling up her long hair into a neat chi-
gnon. Then she waited in the ladies' room until an
inspection of her watch told her she could finally
leave.

This time as she made her way through the
crowded bar it was a very different type of look that
Saskia collected from the men who watched her ad-
miringly.

To her relief Lorraine was parked outside, waiting
for her.

'Well?' she demanded eagerly as Saskia opened
the car door and got in.

'Nothing,' Saskia told her, shaking her head. 'He
turned me down flat.'

'What?'

'Lorraine, careful…' Saskia cried out warningly as
the other woman almost backed into the car behind
her in shock.

'You mustn't have tried hard enough,' Lorraine
told her bossily.

'I can assure you that I tried as hard as anyone
could,' Saskia corrected her wryly.

'Did he *mention* Megan…tell you that he was spoken for?' Lorraine questioned her.

'No!' Saskia shook her head. 'But I promise you
he made it plain that he wasn't interested. He looked
at me…' She stopped and swallowed, unwilling to
think about, never mind tell anyone else, just how
Megan's beloved had looked at her. For some odd

reason she refused to define just to remember the icy
contempt she had seen in his eyes made her tremble
between anger and pain.

'Where *is* Megan?' she asked Lorraine.

'She was called in unexpectedly to work an extra
shift. She rang to let me know and I said we'd drive
straight over to her place and meet up with her there.'

Saskia smiled wanly. By rights she knew she
ought to be feeling far happier than she actually was.
Though out of the three of them she suspected that
Megan would be the only one who would actually
be pleased to learn that her Mark had determinedly
refused to be tempted.

Her Mark. *Megan's* Mark. There was a bitter taste
in Saskia's mouth and her heart felt like a heavy
lump of lead inside her chest.

What on earth was the matter with her? She
couldn't possibly be jealous of Megan, could she?
No! She couldn't be…she *must* not be!

'Are you sure you tried hard enough?' Lorraine
was asking her sternly.

'I said everything you told me to say,' Saskia told
her truthfully.

'And he didn't make any kind of response?'

Saskia could tell that Lorraine didn't believe her.

'Oh, he made a response,' she admitted grimly. 'It
just wasn't the kind…' She stopped and then told her
flatly, 'He wasn't interested, Lorraine. He must really
love Megan.'

'Yes, if he prefers her to you he must,' Lorraine
agreed bluntly. 'She's a dear, and I love her, but
there's no way… You don't think he could have

guessed what you were doing do you? No way he could have known…?'

'No, I don't,' Saskia denied. She was beginning to feel tired, almost aching with a sharp, painful need to be on her own. The last thing she wanted right now was to deal with someone like Lorraine, but she owed it to Megan to reassure her that she could trust Mark.

As they pulled up outside Megan's house Saskia saw that her car was parked outside. Her stomach muscles started to clench as she got out of Lorraine's car and walked up the garden path. Megan and Mark. Even their names sounded cosy together, redolent of domesticity…of marital comfort. And yet…if ever she'd met a man who was neither domesticated nor cosy it had been Megan's Mark. There had been an air of primitive raw maleness about him, an aura of power and sexuality, a sense that in his arms a woman could…*would*…touch such sensual heights of delight and pleasure that she would never be quite the same person again.

Saskia tensed. What on earth was she thinking? Mark belonged to Megan—her best friend, the friend to whom she owed her grandmother's life and good health.

Megan had obviously seen them arrive and was opening the door before they reached it, her face wreathed in smiles.

'It's all right,' Saskia told her hollowly. 'Mark didn't…'

'I know…I know…' Megan beamed as she ushered them inside. 'He came to see me at work and explained everything. Oh, I've been such an idiot…

Why on earth I didn't guess what he was planning I just don't know. We leave next week. He'd even told them at work what he was planning…that was the reason for all those calls. Plus the girl at the travel agency kept phoning. Oh, Saskia, I can't believe it. I've always longed to go to the Caribbean, and for Mark to have booked us such a wonderful holiday… The place we're going to specialises in holidays for couples. I'm so sorry you had a wasted evening. I tried to ring you but you'd already left. I thought you might have got here sooner. After all, once you'd realised that Mark wasn't at the wine bar…' She stopped as she saw the look on both her cousin's and Saskia's faces.

'What is it?' she asked them uncertainly.

'*You* said that you'd spoken to Mark,' Lorraine was saying tersely to Saskia.

'I did…' Saskia insisted. 'He was just as you described him to us, Megan…'

She stopped as Megan shook her head firmly.

'Mark wasn't there, Sas,' she repeated. 'He was with me at work. He arrived at half past eight and Sister gave me some time off so that we could talk. He'd guessed how upset I was and he'd decided that he would have to tell me what he was planning. He said he knew he couldn't have kept the secret for very much longer anyway,' she added fondly.

'And before you say a word,' she said firmly to her cousin, 'Mark is paying for everything himself.'

Saskia leaned weakly against the wall. If the man she had come on to hadn't been Megan's Mark, then just who on earth had he been? Her face became even paler. She had come on to a man she didn't know…a total and complete stranger…a man who… She swallowed nauseously, remembering the way she had looked, the way she had behaved…the things she had said. Thank God he was a stranger. Thank God she would never have to see him again.

'Sas, you don't look well,' she could hear Megan saying solicitously. 'What is it?'

'Nothing,' she fibbed, but Lorraine had already guessed what she was thinking.

'Well, if the man in the wine bar wasn't Mark then who on earth was he?' She demanded sharply.

'Who indeed?' Saskia echoed hollowly.

CHAPTER THREE

To SASKIA's dismay she heard the town hall clock striking eight a.m. as she hurried to work. She had intended to be in extra early this morning but unfortunately she had overslept—a direct result of the previous evening's events and the fact that initially she had been mentally agonising so much over what she had done that she had been unable to get to sleep.

Officially she might not be due to be at her desk until nine a.m., but in this modern age that was not the way things worked, especially when one's hold on one's job was already dangerously precarious.

'There are bound to be cutbacks…redundancies,' the head of Saskia's department had warned them all, and Saskia, as she'd listened to him, had been sharply conscious that as the newest member of the team she was the one whose job was most in line to be cut back. It would be virtually impossible for her to get another job with the same kind of prospects in Hilford, and if she moved away to London that would mean her grandmother would be left on her own. At sixty-five her grandmother was not precisely old—far from it—and she had a large circle of friends, but the illness had left Saskia feeling afraid for her. Saskia felt she owed her such a huge debt, not only for bringing her up but for giving her so much love.

As she hurried into the foyer she asked Emma, the receptionist, anxiously, 'Has he arrived yet?'

There was no need to qualify who she meant by 'he', and Emma gave her a slightly superior smile as she replied, 'Actually he arrived yesterday. He's upstairs now,' she added smugly, 'interviewing everyone.' Her smugness and superiority gave way to a smile of pure feminine appreciation as she sighed. 'Just wait until you see him. He's gorgeous…with a great big capital G.'

She rolled her eyes expressively whilst Saskia gave her a wan smile.

She now had her own special and private—very private—blueprint of what a gorgeous man looked like, and she doubted that their new Greek boss came anywhere near to matching it.

'Typically, though, mind you,' the receptionist continued, oblivious to Saskia's desire to hurry to her office, 'he's already spoken for. Or at least he soon will be. I was talking to the receptionist at their group's head office and she told me that his grandfather wants him to marry his cousin. She's mega-wealthy and—'

'I'm sorry, Emma, but I must go,' Saskia interrupted her firmly. Office gossip, like office politics, was something Saskia had no wish to involve herself in, and besides… If their new boss was already interviewing people she didn't want to earn herself any black marks by not being at her desk when he sent for her.

Her office was on the third floor, an open plan space where she worked with five other people. Their boss had his own glass-walled section, but right now both it and the general office itself were empty.

Just as she was wondering what to do the outer door swung open and her boss, followed by the rest of her colleagues, came into the room.

'Ah, Saskia, there you are,' her boss greeted her.

'Yes. I had intended to be here earlier...' Saskia began, but Gordon Jarman was shaking his head.

'Don't explain now,' he told her sharply. 'You'd better get upstairs to the executive suite. Mr Latimer's secretary will be expecting you. Apparently he wants to interview everyone, both individually and with their co-department members, and he wasn't too pleased that you weren't here...'

Without allowing Saskia to say anything, Gordon turned on his heel and went into his office, leaving her with no option but to head for the lift. It was unlike Gordon to be so sharp. He was normally a very laid back sort of person. Saskia could feel the nervous feeling in her tummy increasing as she contemplated the kind of attitude Andreas Latimer must have adopted towards his new employees to cause such a reaction in her normally unflappable boss.

The executive suite was unfamiliar territory to Saskia. The only previous occasions on which she had entered it had been when she had gone for her initial interview and then, more recently, when the whole staff had been informed of the success of the Demetrios takeover bid.

A little uncertainly she got out of the lift and walked towards the door marked 'Personal Assistant to the Chief Executive'.

Madge Fielding, the previous owner's secretary,

had retired when the takeover bid's success had been announced, and when Saskia saw the elegantly groomed dark-haired woman seated behind Madge's desk she assumed that the new owner must have brought his PA with him from Demetrios head office.

Nervously Saskia gave her name, and started to explain that she worked for Gordon Jarman, but the PA waved her explanation aside, consulting a list in front of her instead and then saying coldly, without lifting her head from it, 'Saskia? Yes. You're late. Mr Latimer does not like... In fact I'm not sure...' She stopped and eyed Saskia with a disapproving frown. 'He may not have time to interview you now,' she warned, before picking up the phone and announcing in a very different tone of voice from the one she had used to address Saskia, 'Ms. Rodgers is here now, Andreas. Do you still want to see her?

'You *can* go in,' she informed Saskia. 'It's the door over there...'

Feeling like a naughty child, Saskia forced herself not to react, heading instead for the door the PA had indicated and knocking briefly on it before turning the handle and walking in.

As she stepped into the office the bright sunlight streaming in through the large windows momentarily dazzled her. All she could make out was the hazy outline of a man standing in front of the glass with his back to her, the brilliance of the sunlight making it impossible for her to see any more.

But Andreas could see Saskia. It hadn't surprised him that she should choose to arrive at work later than her colleagues; after all, he knew how she spent her evenings. What had surprised him had been the genuinely high esteem in which he had discovered she was held both by her immediate boss and her co-workers. It seemed that when it came to giving that extra metre, going that extra distance, Saskia was always the first to do so and the first to do whatever she could to help out her colleagues.

'Yes, it is perhaps unusual in a young graduate,' her boss had agreed when Andreas had questioned his praise of Saskia. 'But then she has been brought up by her grandmother and perhaps because of that her values and sense of obligation towards others are those of an older generation. As you can see from my report on her, her work is excellent and so are her qualifications.'

And she's a stunningly attractive young woman who seems to know how to use her undeniable 'assets' to her own advantage, Andreas had reflected inwardly, but Gordon Jarman had continued to enthuse about Saskia's dedication to her work, her kindness to her fellow employees, her ability to integrate herself into a team and work diligently at whatever task she was given, and her popularity with other members of the workforce.

After studying the progress reports her team leader and Gordon himself had made on her, and the photograph in her file, Andreas had been forced to concede that if he hadn't seen for himself last night the way Saskia could look and behave he would probably have accepted Gordon's glowing report at face value.

She was quite plainly a woman who knew how to handle his sex, even if with him she had made an error of judgement.

This morning, for instance, she had completely metamorphosed back into the dedicated young woman forging a career for herself—neatly suited, her hair elegantly sleeked back, her face free of all but the lightest touch of make-up. Andreas started to frown as his body suddenly and very urgently and unwontedly reminded him of the female allure of the body that was today concealed discreetly beneath a prim navy business suit.

Didn't he already have enough problems to contend with? Last night after returning from the wine bar he had received a telephone call from his mother, anxiously warning him that his grandfather was on the warpath.

'He had dinner with some of his old cronies last night and apparently they were all boasting about the deals they had recently pulled off. You know what they're like.' She had sighed. 'And your grandfather was told by one of them that he had high hopes of his son winning Athena's hand…'

'Good luck to him,' Andreas had told his mother uncompromisingly. 'I hope he does. That at least will get her and Grandfather off my back.'

'Well, yes,' his mother had agreed doubtfully. 'But at the moment it seems to have made him even more determined to promote a marriage between the two of you. And, of course, now that he's half retired he's got more time on his hands to plan and fret… It's such a pity that there isn't already someone in your life.' She had sighed again, adding with a chuckle, 'I honestly believe that the hope of a great-grandchild would thrill him so much that he'd quickly forget he'd ever wanted you to marry Athena!'

Someone else in his life? Had it really been exasperation and the headache he knew lay ahead of him with their new acquisition that had prompted him into making the rashest statement of his life in telling his mother, 'What makes you think there *isn't* someone?'

There had been a startled pause, just long enough for him to curse himself mentally but not for him to recall his impetuous words, before his mother had demanded in excitement, 'You mean there *is*? Oh, Andreas! Who? *When* are we going to meet her? Who is she? How did you…? Oh, darling, how wonderful. Your grandfather *will* be thrilled. Olympia, guess what…'

He had then heard her telling his sister.

He had tried to put a brake on their excitement, to warn them that he was only talking in 'ifs' and 'buts', but neither of them had been prepared to listen. Neither had his grandfather this morning, when he had rung at the ungodly hour of five o'clock to demand to know when he was to meet his grandson's fiancée.

Fiancée… How the hell his mother and sister had managed to translate an off the cuff remark made in irritation into a real live fiancée Andreas had no idea, but he did know that unless he produced this mythical creature he was going to be in very big trouble.

'You'll be bringing her to the island with you, of course,' his grandfather had announced, and his words had been a command and not a question.

What the hell was he going to do? He had eight

days in which to find a prospective fiancée and make it clear to her that their 'engagement' was nothing more than a convenient fiction. Eight days and she would have to be a good enough actress to fool not just his grandfather but his mother and sisters as well.

Irritably he moved out of the sunlight's direct beam, turning round so that Saskia saw him properly for the first time.

There was no opportunity for her to conceal her shock, or the soft winded gasp of dismay that escaped her discreetly glossed lips as her face paled and then flooded with burning hot colour.

'You!' she choked as she backed instinctively towards the door, her memories of the previous night flooding her brain and with them the sure knowledge that she was about to lose her job.

She certainly was an excellent actress, Andreas acknowledged as he observed her reaction—and in more ways than one. Her demeanour this morning was totally different from the way she had presented herself last night. But then no doubt she *was* horrified to discover that he was the man she had so blatantly propositioned. Even so, that look of sick dismay darkening her eyes and the way her soft bottom lip was trembling despite her attempts to stop it... Oh, yes, she was a first-rate actress—*a first-rate actress*!

Suddenly Andreas could see a welcome gleam of light at the end of the dark tunnel of his current problem. Oh, yes, indeed, a very definite beam of light.

'So Ms Rodgers.' Andreas began flaying into Saskia's already shredded self-confidence with all the delicacy of a surgeon expertly slicing through layer after layer of skin, muscle and bone. 'I have read the report Gordon Jarman has written on you and I must congratulate you. It seems that you've persuaded him to think very highly of you. That's quite an accomplishment for an employee so new and young. Especially one who adopts such an unconventional and, shall we say, elastic attitude towards time-keeping...leaving earlier than her colleagues in the evening and arriving later than them in the morning.'

'Leaving *early*?' Saskia stared at him, fighting to recover her composure. How had he known about *that*?

As though he had read her mind, he told her softly, 'I was in the foyer when you left...quite some time before your official finishing time.'

'But that was...' Saskia began indignantly.

However, Andreas did not allow her to finish, shaking his head and telling her coolly, 'No excuses, please. They might work on Gordon Jarman, but unfortunately for you they will not work with me. After all, I have seen how you comport yourself when you are not at work. Unless...' He frowned, his mouth hardening as he studied her with icy derision. 'Unless, of course, *that* is the reason he has given you such an unusually excellent report...'

'No!' Saskia denied straight away. 'No! I don't... Last night was a mistake,' she protested. 'I...'

'Yes, I'm afraid it was,' Andreas agreed, adding smoothly, 'For you at least. I appreciate that the salary you are paid is relatively small, but my grandfather would be extremely unhappy to learn that a member of our staff is having to boost her income in a way that can only reflect extremely badly on our company.' Giving her a thin smile he went on with deceptive amiability, 'How very fortunate for you that it wasn't in one of *our* hotels that you were…er… plying your trade and—'

'How dare you?' Saskia interrupted him furiously, her cheeks bright scarlet and her mouth a mutinous soft bow. Pride burned rebelliously in her eyes.

'How dare I? Rather I should say to you, how dare *you*,' Andreas contradicted her sharply, his earlier air of pleasantness instantly replaced by a hard look of contemptuous anger as he told her grimly, 'Apart from the unedifying moral implications of what you were doing, or rather attempting to do, has it ever occurred to you to consider the physical danger you could be putting yourself in? Women like you…'

He paused and changed tack, catching her off guard as he went on in a much gentler tone, 'I understand from your boss that you are very anxious to maintain your employment with us.'

'Yes. Yes, I am,' Saskia admitted huskily. There was no use denying what he was saying. She had already discussed her feelings and fears about the prospect of being made redundant with Gordon Jarman, and he had obviously recorded them and passed them on to Andreas. To deny them now would only convince him she was a liar—as well as everything else!

'Look… Please, I can explain about last night,' she told him desperately, pride giving way to panic. 'I know how it must have looked, but it wasn't… I didn't…' She stopped as she saw from his expression that he wasn't prepared even to listen to her, never mind believe her.

A part of her was forced to acknowledge that she

could hardly blame him…nor convince him either, unless she dragged Lorraine and Megan into his office to support her and she had far too much pride to do that. Besides, Megan wasn't capable of thinking of anything or anyone right now other than Mark and her upcoming Caribbean holiday, and as for Lorraine… Well, Saskia could guess how the older woman would revel in the situation Saskia now found herself in.

'A wise decision,' Andreas told her gently when she stopped speaking. 'You see, I despise a liar even more than I do a woman who…' Now it was his turn to stop, but Saskia knew what he was thinking.

Her face burned even more hotly, which made it disconcerting for her when he suddenly said abruptly, 'I've got a proposition I want to put to you.'

As she made a strangled sound of shock in her throat he steepled his fingers together and looked at her over them, like a sleek, well-fed predator watching a small piece of prey it was enjoying tormenting.

'What kind of proposition?' she asked him warily, but the heavy sledgehammer strokes of her heart against her ribs warned her that she probably already knew the answer—just as she knew why she was filled with such a shocking mixture of excitement and revulsion.

'Oh, not the kind you are probably most familiar with,' Andreas was telling her softly. 'I've read that some professional young women get a kick out of acting the part of harlots…'

'I was doing no such thing,' Saskia began heatedly, but he stopped her.

'I was there—remember?' he said sharply. 'If my

grandfather knew how you had behaved he would demand your instant dismissal.' His grandfather might have ceded most of the control of the business to Andreas, but Andreas could see from Saskia's expression that she still believed him.

'You don't *have* to tell him.' He could see the effort it cost her to swallow her pride and add a reluctant tremulous, 'Please...'

'I don't *have* to,' he agreed 'But whether or not I do depends on your response to my proposition.'

'That's blackmail,' Saskia protested.

'Almost as old a profession as the one you were engaging in last night,' Andreas agreed silkily.

Saskia began to panic. Against all the odds there was only one thing he could possibly want from her, unlikely though that was. After all, last night she had given him every reason to assume...to believe... But that had been when she had thought he was Mark, and if he would just allow her to explain...

Fear kicked through her, fuelling a panic that rushed her headlong into telling him aggressively, 'I'm surprised that a man like you needs to blackmail a woman into having sex with him. And there's no way that I...'

'Sex?' he questioned, completely astounding her by throwing back his head and laughing out loud. When he had stopped, he repeated, 'Sex?' adding disparagingly, 'With you? No way! It isn't *sex* I want from you,' he told her coolly.

'Not sex? Then...then what is it?' Saskia demanded shakily.

'What I want from you,' Andreas informed her

calmly, 'is your time and your agreement to pose as my fiancée.'

'What?' Saskia stared at him. 'You're mad,' she told him in disbelief.

'No, not mad,' Andreas corrected her sternly. 'But I am very determined not to be coerced into the marriage my grandfather wants to arrange for me. And, as my dear mother has so rightly reminded me, the best way to do that is to convince him that I am in love with someone else. That is the only way I can stop this ridiculous campaign of his.'

'You want *me*…to pose…as *your*…fiancée?' Saskia spaced the words out carefully, as though she wasn't sure she had heard them correctly, and then, when she saw the confirmation in his face, she denied fiercely, 'No. No way. No way at all!'

'No?' Andreas questioned with remarkable amiability. 'Then I'm afraid you leave me with no alternative but to inform you that there is a strong—a very strong possibility that we shall have to let you go as part of our regrettable but necessary cutbacks. I hope I make myself clear.'

'No! You can't do that…' Saskia began, and then stopped as she saw the cynical way he was looking at her.

She was wasting her time. There was no way he was even going to listen to her, never mind believe her. He didn't *want* to believe her. It didn't suit his plans to believe her…she could see that. And if she refused to accede to his commands then she knew that he was fully capable of carrying out his threat against her. Saskia swallowed. She was well and truly trapped, with no way whatsoever of escaping.

'Well?' Andreas mocked her. 'You still haven't given me your reply. Do you agree to my proposition, or…?'

Saskia swallowed the bitter taste of bile and defeat lodged in her throat. Her voice sounded raw, rasping…it hurt her to speak but she tried to hold up her head as she told him miserably, 'I agree.'

'Excellent. For form's sake I suggest that we invent a previously secret accidental meeting between us—perhaps when I visited Hilford prior to our takeover. Because of the negotiations for the takeover we have kept our relationship…our love for one another…a secret. But now…now there is no need for secrecy any more, and to prove it, and to celebrate our freedom today I shall take you out for lunch.'

He frowned and paused. 'We shall be flying out to the Aegean at the end of next week and there are things we shall be expected to know about one another's background!'

'Flying out to *where*?' Saskia gasped. 'No, I can't. My grandmother…'

Andreas had heard from Gordon Jarman that she lived with her grandmother, and now one eyebrow rose as he questioned silkily, 'You are engaged to me now, my beloved, surely *I* am of more importance than your grandmother? She will, I know, be surprised about our relationship, but I am sure she will appreciate just why we had to keep our love for one another to ourselves. If you wish I am perfectly prepared to come with you when you explain…everything to her…'

'No!' Saskia denied in panic. 'There's no need anyway. She's in Bath at the moment, staying with her sister. She's going to be there for the next few weeks. You can't do this,' she told him in agitation. 'Your grandfather is bound to guess that we're not...that we don't... And...'

'But he must *not* be *allowed* to guess any such thing,' Andreas told her gently. 'You are an excellent actress, as I have already seen for myself, and I'm sure you will be able to find a way of convincing him that we *are* and we *do*, and should you feel that you do need some assistance to that end...' His eyes darkened and Saskia immediately took a step backwards, her face flaming with embarrassed colour as she saw the way he was looking at her.

'Very nice,' he told her softly, 'But perhaps it might not be wise to overdo the shy, virginal bit. My grandfather is no fool. I doubt that he will expect a man of my age to have fallen passionately in love with a woman who is not equally sexually aware. I am, after all, half-Greek, and passion is very much a factor of the male Greek personality and psyche.'

Saskia wanted to turn and run away. The situation was becoming worse by the minute. What, she wondered fatalistically, would Andreas do if he ever learned that she was not 'sexually aware', as he had termed it, and that in fact her only experience of sex and passion was limited to a few chaste kisses and fumbled embraces? She had her parents to thank for her caution as a teenager where sexual experimentation had been concerned, of course. Their rash behaviour had led to her dreading that she might repeat their foolishness. But there was, of course, no way that Andreas could ever know that!

'It's now almost ten,' Andreas informed her

briskly, looking at his watch. 'I suggest you go back to your office and at one p.m. I'll come down for you and take you out to lunch. The sooner we make our relationship public now, the better.'

As he spoke he was moving towards her. Immediately Saskia started to panic, gasping out loud in shock as the door opened to admit his PA in the same heartbeat as Andreas reached out and manacled Saskia's fragile wrist-bone in the firm grip of his fingers and thumb.

His skin was dark, tanned, but not so much so that one would automatically guess at his Greek blood, Saskia recognised. His eyes *were* grey, she now saw, and not blue as she had so blush-makingly suggested last night, and they added to the confusion as to what nationality he might be, whilst his hair, though very, very dark, was thick and straight. There was, though, some whisper of his ancient lineage in his high cheekbones, classically sculptured jaw and aquiline nose. They definitely belonged to some arrogant, aristocratic ancient Greek nobleman, and he would, she suspected, be very much inclined to dominate those around him, to stamp his authority on everything he did—and everyone he met.

'Oh, Andreas,' the PA was exclaiming, looking in flustered disbelief at the way her boss was drawing Saskia closer to him, 'I'm sorry to interrupt you but your grandfather has been on—twice!'

'I shall ring my grandfather back shortly,' Andreas responded smoothly, adding equally smoothly, 'Oh, and I don't want any appointments or any interruptions from one to two-thirty today. I shall be taking my fiancée to lunch.'

As he spoke he turned to Saskia and gave her such a look of melting tender sensuality, so completely redolent of an impatient lover barely able to control his desire for her, that for a breath of time she was almost taken in herself. She could only stare back at him as though she had been hypnotised. If he had given her a look like that last night... Stop it, she warned herself immediately, shaken by the unexpected thought.

But if his behaviour was shocking her it was shocking his PA even more, she recognised as the other woman gave a small choked gurgle and then shook her head when Andreas asked her urbanely if anything was wrong.

'No. I was just... That is... No...not at all...'

'Good. Oh, and one more thing. I want you to book an extra seat on my flight to Athens next week. Next to mine...for Saskia...' Turning away from his PA he told Saskia huskily, 'I can't wait to introduce you to my family, especially my grandfather. But first...'

Before Saskia could guess what he intended to do he lifted her hand to his mouth, palm facing upwards. As she felt the warmth of his breath skimming her skin Saskia started to tremble, her breath coming in quick, short bursts. She felt dizzy, breathless, filled with a mixture of elation, excitement and shock, a sense of somehow having stepped outside herself and become another person, entered another life—a life that was far more exciting than her own, a life that could lead to the kind of dangerous, magical, awe-inspiring experiences that she had previously thought could never be hers.

Giddily she could hear Andreas telling her huskily, 'First, my darling, we must find something pretty to adorn this bare finger of yours. My grandfather would not approve if I took you home without a ring that states very clearly my intentions.'

Saskia could hear quite plainly the PA's sudden shocked indrawn breath, but once again the other woman could not be any more shocked than she was herself. Andreas had claimed that she was a good actress, but he was no slouch in that department himself. The look that he was giving her right now alone, never mind the things he had said...

After his PA had scuttled out of his office, closing the door behind her, she told him shakily, 'You do realise, don't you, that by lunchtime it will be all over the office?'

'All over the office?' he repeated, giving her a desirous look. 'My dear, I shall be very surprised and even more disappointed if our news has not travelled a good deal further than that.'

When she gave him an uncomprehending look he explained briefly, 'By lunchtime I fully expect it to have travelled at least as far as Athens...'

'To your grandfather,' Saskia guessed.

'Amongst others,' Andreas agreed coolly, without enlightening her as to who such 'others' might be.

Unexpectedly there were suddenly dozens of questions she wanted to ask him: about his family, as well as his grandfather, and the island he intended to take her to, and about the woman his grandfather wanted him to marry. She had a vague idea that Greeks were very interested in protecting family interests and according to Emma his cousin was 'mega wealthy', as was Andreas himself.

Somehow, without knowing quite how it had happened, she discovered that Andreas had released her hand and that she was walking through the door he had opened for her.

'Ready, Saskia?'

Saskia felt the embarrassed colour start to seep up under her skin as Andreas approached her desk. Her colleagues were studiously avoiding looking openly at them but Saskia knew perfectly well that they were the cynosure of their attention. How could they not be?

'Gordon, I'm afraid that Saskia is going to be late back from lunch,' Andreas was announcing to her bemused boss as he came out from his office.

'Have you told him our news yet, darling,' Andreas asked her lovingly.

'Er...no...' Saskia couldn't bring herself to look directly at him.

'Saskia,' she could hear her boss saying weakly as he looked on disbelievingly, 'I don't understand...'

He would understand even less if she tried to explain to him what was *really* happening, Saskia acknowledged bleakly. It seemed to her that it was a very unfair thing to do to deceive the man who had been so kind to her but what alternative did she really have.

'You mustn't blame Saskia,' Andreas was saying protectively. 'I'm afraid I'm the one who's at fault. I insisted that our relationship should be kept a secret until the outcome of our takeover bid became public.

I didn't want Saskia to be accused of having conflicting loyalties—and I must tell you, Gordon, that she insisted that any kind of discussion about the takeover was off-limits between us... Mind you, talking about work was not exactly *my* number one priority when we were together,' Andreas admitted, with a sensual look at Saskia that made her face burn even more hotly and caused more than one audible and envious gasp from her female co-workers.

'Why did you have to do *that*?' Saskia demanded fretfully the moment they were alone and out of earshot.

'Do what?' Andreas responded unhelpfully.

'You know perfectly well what I mean,' Saskia protested. 'Why couldn't we just have met somewhere?'

'In secret?' He looked more bored now than amorous, his eyebrows drawing together as he frowned impatiently down at her. He was a good deal taller than her, well over six foot, and it hurt her neck a little, craning to look up at him. She wished he wouldn't walk so close to her; it made her feel uncomfortable and on edge and somehow aware of herself as a woman in a way that wasn't familiar to her.

'Haven't I already made it plain to you that the whole object of this exercise is to bring our relationship into the public domain? Which is why—' He smiled grimly at Saskia as he broke off from what he was saying to tell her silkily, 'I've booked a table at the wine bar for lunch. I ate there last night and I have to say that the food was excellent—even if what happened later was less...palatable...'

Suddenly Saskia had had enough.

'Look, I keep trying to tell you, last night was a mistake. I...'

'I completely agree with you,' Andreas assured her. 'It *was* a mistake...*your* mistake...and whilst we're on the subject, let me warn you, Saskia, if you *ever* manifest anything similar whilst you are engaged to *me*, if you ever even *look* at another man...' He stopped as he saw the shock widening her eyes.

'I'm half-Greek, my dear,' he reminded her softly. 'And when it comes to *my* woman, I'm more Greek than I am British...very much more...'

'I'm *not* your woman,' was the only response Saskia found she could make.

'No,' he agreed cynically. 'You belong to any man who can afford you, don't you, in reality? But...' He stopped again as he heard the sharp sound of protest she made, her face white and then red as her emotions overwhelmed her self-control.

'You have no right to speak to me like that,' Saskia told him thickly.

'No right? But surely as your fiancée I have *every* right,' Andreas taunted her, and then, before she could stop him, he reached out and ran one long finger beneath her lower eyelashes, collecting on it the angry humiliated tears that had just fallen. 'Tears?' he mocked her. 'My dear, you are an even better actress then I thought.'

They had reached the wine bar and Saskia was forced to struggle to control her emotions as he opened the door and drew her inside.

'I don't want anything to eat. I'm not hungry,' she told him flatly once they had been shown to their table.

'Sulking?' he asked her succinctly. 'I can't force you to eat, but I certainly don't intend to deny *myself* the pleasure of enjoying a good meal.'

'There are things we have to discuss,' he added in a cool, businesslike voice as he picked up the menu she had ignored and read it. 'I know most of your personal details from your file, but if we are to convince my family and especially my grandfather that we are lovers, then there are other things I shall need to know...and things you will need to know about me.'

Lovers... Saskia just managed to stop herself from shuddering openly. If she had to accede to his blackmail then she was going to have to learn to play the game by his rules or risk being totally destroyed by him.

'Lovers.' She gave him a bleak smile. 'I thought Greek families didn't approve of sex before marriage.'

'Not for their *own* daughters,' he agreed blandly. 'But since you are *not* Greek, and since *I* am half-British I am sure that my grandfather will be more...tolerant...'

'But he wouldn't be tolerant if you were engaged to your cousin?' Saskia pressed, not sure why she was doing so and even less sure just why the thought of his cousin should arouse such a sensation of pain and hostility within her.

'Athena, my cousin, is a *widow*, a previously married woman, and naturally my grandfather...' He paused and then told her dryly, 'Besides, Athena herself would never accept my grandfather's interference in any aspect of her life. She is a very formidable woman.'

'She's a *widow*?' For some reason Saskia had assumed that this cousin was a young girl. It had never occurred to her that she might already have been married.

'A widow,' Andreas confirmed. 'With two teenage children.'

'Teenage!'

'She married at twenty-two,' Andreas told her with a shrug. 'That was almost twenty years ago.'

Saskia's eyes widened as she did her sums. Athena was obviously older than Andreas. A lonely and no doubt vulnerable woman who was being pressurised into a second marriage she perhaps did not want, Saskia decided sympathetically.

'However, you need not concern yourself too much with Athena, since it is doubtful that you will meet her. She lives a very peripatetic existence. She has homes in Athens, New York and Paris and spends much of her time travelling between them, as well as running the shipping line she inherited.'

A shipping line and a hotel chain. No wonder Andreas's grandfather was so anxious for them to marry. It amazed Saskia that Andreas was not equally keen on the match, especially knowing the hard bargain he had driven over the takeover.

As though he had guessed what she was thinking, he leaned towards her and told her grittily, 'Unlike you, *I* am not prepared to sell myself.'

'I was *not* selling myself,' Saskia denied hotly, and then frowned as the waiter approached their table carrying two plates of delicious-looking food.

'I didn't order a meal,' she began as he set one of them down in front of her and the other in front of Andreas.

'No. I ordered it for you,' Andreas told her. 'I don't like to see my women looking like skinny semi-starved rabbits. A Greek man may be permitted to beat his wife, but he would never stoop to starving her.'

'Beat…' Saskia began rising to the bait and then stopped as she saw the glint in his eyes and realised that he was teasing her.

'I suspect you are the kind of woman, Saskia, who would drive a saint, never mind a mere mortal man, to be driven to subdue you, to master you and then to wish that he had had the strength to master himself instead.'

Saskia shivered as the raw sensuality of what he was saying hit her like a jolt of powerful electricity. What was it about him that made her so acutely aware of him, so nervously on edge?

More to distract herself than anything else she started to eat, unaware of the ruefully amused look Andreas gave her as she did so. If he didn't know better he would have said that she was as inexperienced as a virgin. The merest allusion to anything sexual was enough to have her trembling with reaction, unable to meet his gaze. It was just as well that he knew it was all an act, otherwise… Otherwise what? Otherwise he might be savagely tempted to put his words into actions, to see if she trembled as deliciously when he touched her as she did when he spoke to her.

To counter what he was feeling he began to speak to her in a crisp, businesslike voice.

'There are certain things you will need to know about my family background if you are going to convince my grandfather that we are in love.'

He proceeded to give her a breakdown of his immediate family, adding a few cautionary comments about his grandfather's health.

'Which does not mean that he is not one hundred and fifty per cent on the ball. If anything, the fact that he is now prevented from working so much means that he is even more ferociously determined to interfere in my life than he was before. He tells my mother that he is afraid he will die before I give him any great-grandchildren. If that is not blackmail I don't know what is,' Andreas growled.

'It's obviously a family vice,' Saskia told him mock sweetly, earning herself a look that she refused to allow to make her quake in her shoes.

'Ultimately, of course, our engagement will have to be broken,' Andreas told her unnecessarily. 'No doubt our sojourn on the island will reveal certain aspects of our characters that we shall find mutually unappealing, and on our return to England we shall bring our engagement to an end. But at least I shall have bought myself some time…and hopefully Athena will have decided to accept one of the many suitors my grandfather says are only too willing to become her second husband.'

'And if she doesn't?' Saskia felt impelled to ask.

'*If* she doesn't, we shall just have to delay ending our engagement until either she does or I find an alternative way of convincing my grandfather that one of my sisters can provide him with his great-grandchildren.'

'You don't *ever* want to marry?' Saskia was startled into asking.

'Well, let's just say that since I have reached the age of thirty-five without meeting a woman who has made me feel my life is unliveable without her by my side, I somehow doubt that I am likely to do so now. Falling in love is a young man's extravagance. In a man past thirty it is more of a vain folly.'

'My father fell in love with my mother when he was seventeen,' Saskia couldn't stop herself from telling him. 'They ran away together…' Her eyes clouded. 'It was a mistake. They fell out of love with one another before I was born. An older man would at least have had some sense of responsibility towards the life he had helped to create. My father was still a child himself.'

'He abandoned you?' Andreas asked her, frowning.

'They both did,' Saskia told him tersely. 'If it hadn't been for my grandmother I would have ended up in a children's home.'

Soberly Andreas watched her. Was *that* why she went trawling bars for men? Was she searching for the male love she felt she had been denied by her father? His desire to exonerate her from her behaviour irritated him. *Why* was he trying to make excuses for her? Surely he hadn't actually been taken in by those tears earlier.

'It's time for us to leave,' he told her brusquely.

CHAPTER FOUR

IF SOMEONE had told her two weeks ago that she would be leaving behind her everything that was familiar to fly to an unknown Greek island in the company of an equally unknown man to whom she was supposed to be engaged Saskia would have shaken her head in denial and amusement—which just went to show!

Which just went to show what a combination of male arrogance, self-belief and determination could do, especially when it was allied to the kind of control that one particular male had over her, Saskia fretted darkly.

In less than fifteen minutes' time Andreas would be picking her up in his Mercedes for the first leg of their journey to Aphrodite, the island Andreas's grandfather had bought for his wife and named after the goddess of love.

'Theirs was a love match but one that had the approval of both families,' Andreas had told Saskia when he had been briefing her about his background.

A love match...unlike *their* bogus engagement. Just being a party to that kind of deceit, even though it was against her will, made Saskia feel uncomfortable, but nowhere near as uncomfortable as she had felt when she had had to telephone her grandmother and lie to her, saying that she was going away on business.

Andreas had tried to insist that she inform her grandmother of their engagement, but Saskia had refused.

'*You* may be happy to lie to your family about our supposed ''relationship'',' she had told him with a look of smoky-eyed despair. 'But I *can't* lie to my grandmother about something so…' She hadn't been able to go on, unwilling to betray herself by admitting to Andreas that her grandmother would never believe that Saskia had committed herself and her future to a man without loving him.

Once the fall-out from the news of her 'engagement' had subsided at work, her colleagues had treated her with both wary caution and distance. She was now the boss's fiancée and as such no longer really 'one of them'.

All in all Saskia had spent the week feeling increasingly isolated and frightened, but she was too proud to say anything to anyone—a hang-up, she suspected, from the days of her childhood, when the fact that her parents' story was so widely known, coupled with the way she had been dumped on her grandmother, had made her feel different, distanced from her schoolmates, who had all seemed to have proper mummies and daddies.

Not that anyone could have loved her more than her grandmother had done, as Saskia was the first to acknowledge now. Her home background had in reality been just as loving and stable, if not more so, than that of the majority of her peers.

She gave a small surreptitious look at her watch. Less than five minutes to go. Her heart thumped heavily. Her packed suitcase was ready and waiting in the hall. She had agonised over what she ought to take and in the end had compromised with a mixture of the summer holiday clothes she had bought three years previously, when she and Megan had gone to Portugal together, plus some of her lightweight office outfits.

She hadn't seen Andreas since he had taken her out for lunch—not that she had minded *that*! No indeed! He had been attending a gruelling schedule of business meetings—dealing, if the trickles of gossip that had filtered through the grapevine were anything to go by, heroically with the problems posed by the challenging situation the hotels had fallen into prior to the takeover.

'He's visited every single one of our hotels,' Saskia had heard from one admiring source. 'And he's been through every single aspect of the way they're being run—and guess what?'

Saskia, who had been on the edge of the group who'd been listening eagerly to this story, had swallowed uncomfortably, expecting to hear that Andreas had instituted a programme of mass sackings in order to halt the flood of unprofitable expenses, but to her astonishment instead she had heard, 'He's told everyone that their job is safe, provided they can meet the targets he's going to be setting. Everywhere he's been he's given the staff a pep talk, told them how much he values the acquisition his group has made and how he personally is going to be held responsible by the board of directors if he can't turn it into a profit-making asset.'

The gossip was that Andreas had a way with him that had his new employees not only swearing allegiance but apparently praising him to the skies as well.

Well, they obviously hadn't witnessed the side to his character she had done, was all that Saskia had been able to think as she listened a little bitterly to everyone's almost euphoric praise of him.

It was ten-thirty now, and he wasn't... Saskia tensed as she suddenly saw the large Mercedes pulling up outside her grandmother's house. Right on time! But of course Andreas would not waste a precious second of his time unless he had to, especially not on her!

By the time he had reached the front door she had opened it and was standing waiting for him, her suitcase in one hand and her door key in the other.

'What's that?'

She could see the way he was frowning as he looked down at her inexpensive case and immediately pride flared through her sharpening her own voice as she answered him with a curt, 'My suitcase.'

'Give it to me,' he instructed her briefly.

'I can carry it myself,' Saskia informed him grittily.

'I'm sure you can,' Andreas agreed, equally grimly. 'But...'

'But what?' Saskia challenged him angrily. 'But Greek men do not allow women to carry their own luggage nor to be independent from them in any way?'

Saskia could see from the way Andreas's mouth tightened that he did not like what she had said. For some perverse reason she felt driven to challenge him, even though a part of her shrank from the storm signals she could see flashing in his eyes.

'I'm afraid in this instance you should perhaps blame my English father rather than my Greek mother,' he told her icily. 'The English public school he insisted I was sent to believed in what is now considered to be an outdated code of good manners for its pupils.' He gave her a thin, unfriendly look. 'One word of warning to you. My grandfather is inclined to be old-fashioned about such things. He will not understand your modern insistence on politically correct behaviour, and whilst you are on the island…'

'I have to do as *you* tell me,' Saskia finished bitterly for him.

If this was a taste of what the next few weeks were going to be like she didn't know how she was going to survive them. Still, at least there would be one benefit of their obvious hostility to one another. No one who would be observing them together would be surprised when they decided to end their 'engagement'.

'Our flight leaves Heathrow at nine tomorrow morning, so we will need to leave the apartment early,' Andreas informed Saskia once they were in the car.

'The *apartment*?' Saskia questioned him warily immediately.

'Yes,' Andreas confirmed. 'I have an apartment in London. We shall be staying there tonight. This afternoon we shall spend shopping.'

'Shopping…?' Saskia began to interrupt, but Andreas overruled her.

'Yes, shopping,' he told her cautiously. 'You will need an engagement ring, and...' He paused and gave her a brief skimming look of assessment and dismissal that made her itch to demand that he stop the car immediately. Oh, how she would love to be able to tell him that she had changed her mind...that there was no way she was going to give in to his blackmail. But she knew there was no way she could.

'You will need more suitable clothes.'

'If you mean holiday clothes,' Saskia began, 'they are in my case, and...'

'No, I do not mean "holiday" clothes.' Andreas stopped her grimly. 'I am an independently wealthy man, Saskia; you don't need me to tell you that. Your department's investigations prior to our takeover must have informed you to the nearest hundred thousand pounds what my asset value is. My grandfather is a millionaire many times over, and my mother and my sisters are used to buying their clothes from the world's top designers, even though none of them are what could be considered to be fashion victims or shopaholics. Naturally, as my fiancée...'

Without allowing him to finish Saskia took a deep, angry breath and told him dangerously, 'If you think that I am going to let *you* buy my clothes...'

With only the briefest of pauses Andreas took control of the situation from her by asking smoothly, 'Why not? After all, you were prepared to let me buy your *body*. Me or indeed any other man who was prepared to pay for it.'

'No! That's not true,' Saskia denied with a shocked gasp.

'Very good,' Andreas mocked her. 'But you can

save the special effects for my family. I know *exactly* what you are—remember. Think of these clothes as a perk of your job.' He gave her a thin, unkind smile. 'However, having said that, I have to add that I shall want to vet whatever you wish to purchase. The image I want you to convey to my family as my fiancée is one of elegance and good taste.'

'What are you trying to suggest?' Saskia hissed furiously at him. 'That left to my own devices I might choose something more suited to a…?' She stopped, unable to bring herself to voice the words burning a painful brand in her thoughts.

To her bemusement, instead of saying them for her Andreas said coolly, 'You are obviously not used to buying expensive clothes and there is no way I want you indulging in some kind of idiotic unnecessary economy which would negate the whole purpose of the exercise. I don't want you buying clothes more suitable for a young woman on a modest salary than the fiancée of an extremely wealthy man,' he informed her bluntly, in case she had not understood him the first time.

For once Saskia could think of nothing to say, but inside she was a bundle of fury and shame. There was no way she could stop Andreas from carrying out his plans, she knew that, but she fully intended to keep a mental record of everything he spent so that ultimately she could repay him, even if doing so totally depleted the small nest egg she had been carefully saving.

'No more objections?' Andreas enquired smoothly. 'Good, because I promise you, Saskia, I mean to have my way—even if that entails dressing you and undressing you myself to get it. Make no mistake, when we arrive on Aphrodite you will be arriving as my fiancée.'

As he drove down the slipway onto the motorway and the powerful car picked up speed Saskia decided diplomatically that quarrelling with him whilst he was driving at such a speed would be very foolish indeed. It was over half an hour later before she recognised that, in her anxiety to reject Andreas's claimed right to decide what she should wear, she had neglected to deal with the more important issue of her discomfort at the idea of spending the night with him.

But what did she really have to fear? Certainly not any sexual advances from Andreas. He had, after all, made it shamingly plain what he thought of her sexual morals.

She had far too much pride to admit to him that she felt daunted and apprehensive at the thought of sharing the intimacy of an apartment with him. On the island it would be different. There they would be with his family and the staff who ran the large villa complex he said his grandfather had had built on it.

No, she would be wise to grit her teeth and say nothing rather than risk exposing herself to his disbelief and mocking contempt by expressing her anxieties.

As she waited for the chauffeur to load her luggage into the boot of her hired limousine Athena tapped one slender expensively shod foot impatiently.

The moment she had heard the news that Andreas was engaged and about to bring his fiancée to

Aphrodite on an official visit to meet his family she had sprung into action. Fortunately an engagement was not a marriage, and she certainly intended to make sure that *this* engagement never made it as far as a wedding.

She knew why Andreas had done it, of course. He was, after all, Greek to the very marrow of his bones—even if he chose to insist on everyone acknowledging his British blood—and like any Greek man, indeed any *man* he had an inborn need to be the one in control.

His claim to be in love with this other woman was simply his way of showing that control, rejecting the marriage to her which was so very dear to his grandfather's heart and to her own.

As the limousine sped away from the kerb she leaned forward and gave the driver the address of a prestigious apartment block overlooking the river. She herself did not maintain a home in London; she preferred New York's social life and the Paris shops.

Andreas might think he had outmanoeuvred her by announcing his engagement to this undoubtedly cold and sexless English fiancée. Well, she would soon bring an end to that, and make sure that he knew where his real interests lay. After all, how could he possibly resist *her*? She had everything he could want, and he certainly had everything *she* wanted.

It was a pity he had managed to prevent her from outbidding him for this latest acquisition. Ownership of the hotels themselves meant nothing to her *per se*, but it would have been an excellent bait to dangle in front of him since he obviously set a great deal of store by them. Why, she could not understand. But then in many ways there were a considerable number of things about Andreas that she did not understand. It was one of the things that made him so desirable to her. Athena had always coveted that which seemed to be out of reach.

The first time she had realised she wanted Andreas he had been fifteen and she had been on the verge of marrying her husband. She smiled wantonly to herself, licking her lips. At fifteen Andreas, although a boy, had been as tall as a man and as broad, with a superbly fit young body, and so indescribably good-looking that the sight of him had made her melt with lust.

She had done her best to seduce him but he had managed to resist her and then, within a month of deciding that she wanted him, she had been married.

At twenty-two she had not been a young bride by Greek standards, and she had been carefully stalking her husband-to-be for some time. Older than her by a decade, and immensely wealthy, he had played a cat and mouse game with her for well over a year before he had finally capitulated. There had certainly been no way she was going to give up the marriage she had worked so hard for for the passion she felt for Andreas, a mere boy.

But then fate had stepped in. Her husband had died unexpectedly and she had been left a widow. A very rich widow...a very rich and sexually hungry widow. And Andreas was now a man—and what a man!

The only thing that was keeping them apart was Andreas's pride. It had to be. What other reason could he possibly have for resisting her advances?

As the limousine pulled up at the address she had

given the driver Athena examined her reflection in the neat mirrors fitted into the Rolls's interior. That discreet nip and tuck she had had last year had been well worth the prince's ransom she had paid the American plastic surgeon. She could quite easily pass for a woman in her early thirties now.

Her jet-black hair had been cut and styled by one of the world's top hairdressers, her skin glowed from the expensive creams lavished on it, her make-up was immaculate and emphasised the slanting dark-ness of her eyes, her toe and fingernails gleamed richly with dark red polish.

A smile of satisfaction curved her mouth. No, there was no way Andreas's dreary little fiancée—an office girl, someone he had supposedly fallen in love with during the negotiations to buy out the hotel chain—could compete with her. Athena's eyes hard-ened. This girl, whoever she was, would soon learn what a mistake she had made in trying to lay claim on the man *Athena* wanted. What a very, very big mistake!

As she left the limousine the perfume she had es-pecially blended for her in Paris moved with her, a heavy, musky cloud of sexuality.

Her teenage daughters loathed it, and were con-stantly begging her to change it, but she had no in-tention of doing so. It was her signature, the essence of herself as a woman. Andreas's English fiancée no doubt wore something dull and insipid such as lavender water!

'I'll leave the car here,' Andreas told Saskia as he swung the Mercedes into a multi-storey car park right in the centre of the city. Saskia's eyes widened as she saw the tariff pinned up by the barrier. She would never have dreamed of paying so much to park a car, but the rich, as they said, were different.

Just how different she came to realise during the course of the afternoon, as Andreas guided her into a series of shops the like of which Saskia had never imagined existed. And in each one the very aura of his presence seemed to draw from the sales assistants the kind of reverential reaction that made Saskia tighten her lips. She could see the female admiration and speculation in their eyes as a series of outfits was produced for his inspection. For *his* inspection— not *hers*, Saskia recognised and her sense of helpless frustration and resentment grew with each shop they visited.

'I'm not a doll or a child,' she exploded outside one of them, when she had flatly refused to even try on the cream trouser suit the salesgirl had gushingly declared would be perfect for her.

'No? Well, you're certainly giving a wonderful imitation of behaving like one,' Andreas responded grimly. 'That suit was—'

'That suit was over one thousand pounds,' Saskia interrupted him grittily. 'There's no *way* I would ever pay that kind of money for an outfit… not even my wedding dress!'

When Andreas started to laugh she glared furiously at him, demanding, 'What's so funny?'

'You are,' he told her uncompromisingly. 'My dear Saskia, have you really any idea of the kind of wedding dress you would get for under a thousand pounds?'

'No, I haven't,' Saskia admitted. 'But I do know that I'd never feel comfortable wearing clothes the cost of which would feed a small country, and neither is an expensive wedding dress any guarantee of a good marriage.'

'Oh, spare me the right-on lectures,' Andreas broke in in exasperation. 'Have you ever thought of how many people would be without jobs if everyone went around wearing sackcloth and ashes, as you obviously would have them do?'

'That's not fair,' Saskia defended herself. She was, after all, feminine enough to like good clothes and to want to look her best, and in that trouser suit she *would* undeniably have looked good, she admitted inwardly. But she was acutely conscious of the fact that every penny Andreas spent on her she would have to repay.

'I don't know why you're insisting on doing this,' she told Andreas rebelliously. 'I don't *need* any clothes; I've already told you that. And there's certainly no need for you to throw your money around to impress me.'

'You or anyone else,' Andreas cut in sharply, dark bands of colour burning across his cheekbones in a visual warning to her that she had angered him.

'I am a businessman, Saskia. Throwing money around for *any* reason is not something I do, least of all in an attempt to impress a woman who could easily be bought for less than half the price of that trouser suit. Oh, no, you don't,' he cautioned her softly, reaching out to catch hold of the hand she had automatically lifted.

He was holding her wrist in such a tight grip that

Saskia could actually see her fingers going white, but her pride wouldn't allow her to tell him that he was hurting her. It also wouldn't allow her to acknowledge that she had momentarily let her feelings get out of control, and it was only when she suddenly started to sway, white-faced with pain and shock, that Andreas realised what was happening. He released her wrist with a muffled curse and then start to chafe life back into her hand.

'Why didn't you *tell* me I was hurting you so much?' he grated. 'You have bones as fragile as a bird's.'

Even now, with his dark head bent over her tingling hand whilst he massaged it expertly to bring the blood stinging back into her veins, Saskia couldn't allow herself to weaken and claim his compassion.

'I didn't want to spoil your fun,' she told him sharply. 'You were obviously *enjoying* hurting me.'

She tensed when she heard the oath he gave as he released her completely, and tensed again at the sternness in his voice, one look of grim determination in his eyes as he said, 'This has gone far enough. You are behaving like a child. First a harlot and now a child. There is only *one* role I want to see you play from now on, Saskia, and that is the one we have already agreed upon. I'll warn you now. If you do or say *anything* to make my family suspect that ours is not a true love match I shall make you very sorry for it. Do you understand me?'

'Yes, I understand you,' Saskia agreed woodenly.

'I mean what I say,' Andreas warned her. 'And it won't just be the Demetrios chain you won't be able to work for. If you flout me, Saskia, I'll see to it that you will never be able to work *anywhere* again. An accountant who can't be trusted and who has been dismissed on suspicion of stealing is not one that anyone will want to employ.'

'You can't do that,' Saskia whispered, white-faced, but she knew all too well that he could.

She hated him now…really hated him, and when in the next shop he marched her into she saw the salesgirl's eyes widening in breathless sexual interest, she reflected mentally that the other girl was welcome to him…more than welcome!

It was late in the afternoon before Andreas finally decided that Saskia had a wardrobe suitable for his fiancée.

At their last port of call he had called upon the services of the store's personal shopper who, with relentless efficiency, had provided Saskia with the kind of clothes that she had previously only ever seen in glossy magazines.

She had tried to reject everything the shopper had produced, but on each occasion apart from one Andreas had overruled her. The only time they had been in accord had been when the shopper had brought out a bikini which she had announced was perfect for Saskia's colouring and destination. The minuteness of the triangles which were supposed to cover her modesty had made Saskia's eyes widen in disbelief—and they had widened even more when she had discreetly managed to study the price tag.

'I couldn't possibly swim in that,' she had blurted out.

'*Swim* in it?' The other woman had looked stunned. 'Good heavens, no, of course not. This isn't for *swimming* in. And, look, this is the wrap that goes with it. Isn't it divine?' she had purred, producing a length of silky fragile fabric embellished with sequins.

As she'd seen the four-figure price on the wrap Saskia had thought she might actually faint with disbelief, but to her relief and surprise Andreas had also shaken his head.

'That is *not* the kind of outfit I would wish my fiancée to wear,' he had told the shopper bluntly, adding, just in case she had not fully understood him, 'Saskia's body is eye-catching enough without her needing to embellish it with an outfit more suitable for a call girl.'

The shopper diplomatically had not pressed the issue, but instead had gone away, returning with several swimsuits.

Saskia had picked the cheapest of them, unwillingly allowing Andreas to add a matching wrap.

Whilst he'd been settling the bill and making arrangements for everything to be delivered to his riverside apartment Saskia had drunk the coffee the personal shopper had organised for her.

Perhaps it was because she hadn't really eaten anything all day that she was feeling so lightheaded and anxious, she decided. It couldn't surely be because she and Andreas were now going to go to his apartment, where they would be alone—could it?

'There's an excellent restaurant close to the apartment block,' Andreas informed Saskia, once they were in the car and he was driving her towards the dockland area where his apartment was situated. 'I'll arrange to have a meal sent in and...'

'No,' Saskia protested immediately. 'I'd rather eat out.'

She could see that Andreas was frowning.

'I don't think that's a good idea,' he told her flatly. 'A woman on her own, especially a woman like you, is bound to attract attention, and besides, you look tired. I have to go out, and I have no idea what time I will be back.'

Andreas was going out. Saskia could feel her anxiety easing. Her feet ached from the unaccustomed pavement-pounding and her brain was exhausted with the effort of keeping a running tab on just how much money Andreas, and therefore she, had spent.

Far more than she had wanted to spend. So much that just thinking about it was making her feel distinctly ill. Wretchedly she acknowledged that there would be precious little left of her hard-earned little nest egg once she had repaid Andreas what he had spent.

Tiredly Saskia followed Andreas through the underground car park and into the foyer of the apartment block. A special key was needed to use the lift, which glided upwards so smoothly that Saskia's eyes rounded in shock when it came to a standstill. She had not even realised that they were moving.

'It's this way,' Andreas told her, touching her arm and guiding her towards one of the four doorways opening off the entrance lobby. He was carrying her case, which he put down as he unlocked the door, motioning to Saskia to precede him into the elegant space beyond it.

CHAPTER FIVE

THE first thing that struck Saskia about Andreas's apartment was not the very expensive modern art hanging on the hallway's walls but its smell—a musky, throat-closing, shockingly overpowering scent which stung her nostrils and made her tense.

That Andreas was equally aware of it she was in no doubt. Saskia could see him pause and lift his head, like a hunting panther sniffing the air.

'Hell... Hell and damnation,' she heard him mutter ferociously beneath his breath, and then, to her shock, he thrust open the door into the huge-windowed living space that lay beyond the lobby and took hold of her. His fingers bit into the soft flesh of her arms, his breath a warning whisper against her lips as his eyes blazed down into the unguarded shocked softness of hers, dark as obsidian, hard as flint, commanding...warning...

'Alone at last. How you have enjoyed teasing me today, my loved one, but now I have you to myself and I can exact what punishment on you I wish...'

The soft crooning tone of his voice as much as his words scattered what was left of her senses, leaving Saskia clinging weakly to him as the shock ripped through her in a floodtide. Then his mouth was covering hers, silencing the protest she was trying to make, his lips moulding, shaping, coaxing, *seducing* hers with an expertise that flattened her defences as effectively as an atom bomb.

Incoherently Saskia whispered his name, trying to insist on a cessation of what he was doing and an explanation for it. But her lips, her mouth, her senses, unused to so much sensual stimulation, were defying reason and caution and everything else that Saskia's bemused brain was trying to tell them. Her frozen shock melted beneath the heat of the pleasure Andreas's hungry passionate expertise was showing her, and her lips softened and trembled into an unguarded, uninhibited response.

Without being aware of what she was doing Saskia strained to get closer to Andreas, standing on tiptoe so that she could cling ardently to the delicious pleasure of his kiss. Her hands on his arms registered the sheer size and inflexibility of the muscles beneath them whilst her heart pounded in awed inexperienced shock at the intensity of what she was feeling.

Even more than she could smell that musky, overpowering female perfume, she could smell Andreas himself. His heat…his passion…his maleness… And shockingly something in her, something she hadn't known existed, was responding to it just as her lips were responding to him…just as *she* was responding to him, swaying into his arms compliantly, her body urging him to draw her close, to let her feel the rest of his male strength.

Dizzily Saskia opened the eyes she had closed at the first touch of his mouth on hers, shivering as she saw the sparks of raw sensuality darting like lightning from his eyes as he stared down at her. It was like hanging way above the earth in a dizzying, death-defying place where she could feel her danger and yet at the same time know somehow she would be safe.

'You love like an innocent…a virgin…' Andreas was telling her huskily, and as he did so the sparks glittering in his eyes intensified, as though he found something very satisfying about such a notion.

Helplessly Saskia stared back at him. Her heart was thudding frantically fast and her body was filled with an unfamiliar shocking ache that was a physical need to have him touch her, to have his hand run slowly over her skin and reach right through it to that place where her unfamiliar ache began, so that he could surround and soothe it. Somehow just thinking about him doing such a thing *increased* the ache to a pounding throb, a wild, primitive beat that made her moan and sway even closer to him.

'You like that… You want me…'

As he spoke to her she could hear and feel the urgency in his voice, could feel his arousal. Eagerly she pressed closer to him, only to freeze as she suddenly heard a woman's voice demanding sharply, 'Andreas? Aren't you going to introduce me?'

Immediately she realised what she was doing and shame flooded through her, but as she tried to pull away, desperate to conceal her confusion, Andreas held on to her, forcing her to stay where she was, forcing her even more closely into his body so that somehow she was leaning against him, as though…as though…

She trembled as she felt the powerful thrust of his leg between her own, her face burning hotly with embarrassed colour as she realised the sexual connotation that their pose suggested. But it seemed that the woman who was watching them was not similarly self-conscious.

Saskia caught her breath as Andreas allowed her to turn her head and look at the woman.

She was tall and dark-haired, everything about her immaculately groomed, but despite the warmth of her olive skin and the ripe richness of her painted mouth and nails Saskia shivered as she sensed her innate coldness.

'Athena,' Andreas was demanding shortly, 'how did *you* get in here?'

'I have a key. Have you forgotten?' the other woman purred.

The sloe-eyed look she gave Andreas and the way she was managing to totally exclude Saskia both from their conversation and from her line of vision left Saskia ruefully reflecting on her earlier mental picture of a devastated widow being too grief-stricken at the loss of her husband to prevent herself from being bullied into a second marriage.

No one would ever bully *this* woman into any-thing...and as for her being grief-stricken—there was only one emotion Saskia could see in those dark eyes and it had nothing to do with grief.

She forced down the sudden surge of nausea that burned in her throat as she witnessed the look of pure condensed lust that Athena was giving Andreas. Saskia had never imagined, never mind seen, a woman looking at a man in such a powerfully and openly predatory sexual way.

Now she could understand why Andreas had felt in need of a mock fiancée to protect himself, but

what she could not understand was how on earth
Andreas could resist the other woman's desire for
him.

She was blindingly sensually attractive, and obviously wanted Andreas. And surely that was what
all men fantasised about—a woman whose sexual appetite for them could never be satiated.

Naively Saskia assumed that only her own sex
would be put off by Athena's intrinsic coldness and
by the lack of any real loving emotion in her make-
up.

Andreas had obviously kissed Saskia because he
had guessed that Athena was in the apartment, and
now that the other woman was standing so close to
them both Saskia knew how he had known. That
perfume of hers was as unmistakable as it was unappealing.

'Aren't you going to say how pleased you are to
see me?' Athena was pouting as she moved closer to
Andreas. 'Your grandfather is very upset about your
engagement. You know what he was hoping for,' she
added meaningfully, before turning to Saskia and
saying dismissively, 'Oh, I'm sorry. I didn't mean to
hurt your feelings, but I'm sure Andreas must have
warned you how difficult it is going to be for all his
family, especially for his grandfather, to accept
you…'

'Athena,' Andreas was saying warningly, and
Saskia could well imagine how she *would* have felt
to be confronted by such a statement, if she and
Andreas were genuinely engaged.

'But it's the truth,' Athena was continuing unre-
pentantly, and she shrugged her shoulders, the move-

ment drawing attention to the fullness of her breasts. Breasts which Saskia could quite easily see were naked and unfettered beneath the fine cotton shirt she was wearing.

Quickly she averted her gaze from the sight of Athena's flauntingly erect nipples, not daring to allow herself to look at Andreas. Surely no man could resist the demand that those nipples were making on his attention...his concentration...his admiration for their perfection and sexuality. Her own breasts were well shaped and firm, but her nipples did not have that flamboyant fullness that the other woman's possessed and, even if they had, Saskia knew that she would have felt embarrassed about making such a public display of them.

But then perhaps Athena's display was meant *only* for Andreas...perhaps it was meant to be a reminder to him of intimacies they might already have shared. She did, after all, have the key to his apartment, and she certainly seemed to want to make it plain to Saskia that there was a very special intimacy between the two of them.

As though in confirmation of Saskia's thoughts, Athena suddenly leaned forward, putting one manicured hand against Andreas's face and effectively coming between them. With a sultry suggestiveness she said softly, 'Aren't you going to kiss me? You normally do, and I'm sure your fiancée understands that in Greece family relationships...family *loyalties* are very, very important.'

'What Saskia understands is that I love her and I want her to be my wife,' Andreas informed Athena curtly, stepping back from her and taking Saskia with him. As he held her in front of him and closed his arms around her, tucking her head against his shoulder, Saskia reminded herself just *why* he was doing so and just what her role was supposed to be.

'How sweet!' Athena pronounced, giving Saskia an icy look before turning back to Andreas and telling him insincerely, 'I hate to cast a shadow on your happiness, Andreas, but your grandfather really isn't very pleased with you at all at the moment. He was telling me how concerned he is about the way you're handling this recent takeover. Of course *I* understand how important it must be to you to establish your own mark on the business, to prove yourself, so to speak, but the acquisition of this hotel chain really was quite foolhardy, as is this decision of yours to keep on all the existing staff.

'You'll never make a profit doing that,' she scolded him mock sweetly. 'I must say, though, having had the opportunity to look a little deeper into the finances of the chain, I'm glad I pulled out of putting in my own bid. Although of course I *can* afford to lose the odd million or so. What a pity it is, Andreas, that you didn't accept my offer to run the shipping line for me. That would have given you much more scope than working as your grandfather's errand boy.'

Saskia felt herself tensing as she absorbed the insult Athena had just delivered, but to her astonishment Andreas seemed completely unmoved by it. Yet *she* only had to make the merest observation and he fired up at her with so much anger.

'As you already well know, Athena,' he responded, almost good-humouredly, 'It was my *grandfather's* decision to buy the British hotel chain and it was one I endorsed. As for its future profitability... My research confirms that there is an excellent market for a chain of luxurious hotels in Britain, especially when it can boast first-class leisure facilities and a top-notch chef—which is what I am going to ensure that our chain has.

'And as for the financial implications of keeping on the existing staff—Saskia is an accountant, and I'm sure she'll be able to tell you—as you should know yourself, being a businesswoman—that in the long run it would cost more in redundancy payments to get rid of the staff than it will cost to continue employing them. Natural wastage and pending retirement will reduce their number quite dramatically over the next few years, and, where appropriate, those who wish to stay on will be given the opportunity to relocate and retrain. The leisure clubs we intend to open in each hotel alone will take up virtually all of the slack in our staffing levels.

'However, Saskia and I are leaving for Athens tomorrow. We've had a busy day today and, if you'll excuse us, tonight is going to be a very special night for us.'

As Saskia tensed Andreas tightened his hold on her warningly as he repeated, 'A *very* special night. Which reminds me...'

Still holding onto Saskia with one hand, he reached inside his jacket pocket with the other to remove a small jeweller's box.

'I collected this. It should be small enough for you now.'

Before Saskia could say anything he was slipping

the box back into his jacket, telling her softly, 'We'll find out later...'

In the living area beyond the lobby a telephone had started to ring. Releasing her, Andreas went to answer it, leaving Saskia on her own with Athena.

'It won't last,' Athena told her venomously as she walked past Saskia towards the door. 'He won't marry you. He and I were destined to be together. He *knows* that. It's just his pride that makes him fight his destiny. You might as well give him up now, because I promise you *I* shall never do so.'

She meant it, Saskia could see that, and for the first time she actually felt a small shaft of sympathy for Andreas. Sympathy for a man who was treating her the way Andreas was? For a man who had misjudged her the way he had? She must be crazy, Saskia derided herself grimly.

Apprehensively Saskia watched as the new suitcases, which were now carefully packed with her new clothes, were loaded onto the conveyor belt. The airline representative was checking their passports.

On her finger the ring Andreas had given her the previous evening glittered brilliantly.

'It's amazing how good fake diamonds can look these days, isn't it?' she had chattered nervously when Andreas had taken it from its box. She'd tried to disguise from him how edgy and unhappy she felt about wearing a ring on the finger that she had imagined would only ever bear a ring given to her by the man she loved, a ring she would wear forever.

'Is it?' Andreas had responded almost contemptuously. 'I wouldn't know.'

His comment had set all her inner alarm bells ringing and she had demanded anxiously, 'This... It isn't real, is it?'

His expression had given her her answer.

'It *is*!' She had swallowed, unable to drag her gaze away from the fiery sparkle of the magnificent solitaire.

'Athena would have spotted a fake diamond immediately,' Andreas had told her dismissively when she'd tried to protest that she didn't want the responsibility of wearing something of such obvious value.

'If she can spot a fake *diamond* so easily,' she had felt driven to ask him warily, 'then surely she will be able to spot a fake fiancée.'

'Athena deals in hard facts, not emotions,' had been Andreas's answer.

Hard facts, Saskia reflected now, remembering that brief conversation. Like the kiss Andreas had given her last night, knowing Athena would witness it. Andreas himself had made no mention of what he had done, but Saskia had known that her guess as to why he had done it was correct when, immediately after he had ended his telephone call, he had switched on the apartment's air conditioning with the grim comment, 'We need some fresh air in here.'

Later, Andreas had gone out, as promised, and, after picking at the meal he had ordered her, Saskia had gone to bed—alone.

'How long will it take us to reach Aphrodite?' Saskia asked Andreas as they boarded their flight.

'On this occasion it will take longer than normal,'

Andreas answered as the stewardess showed them to their seats—first-class seats, Saskia noted with a small frisson of nervous awe. She had never flown first class before, never really done anything that might have equipped her to feel at home in the rarefied stratosphere of the mega-wealthy that Andreas and his family obviously inhabited.

'Once we arrive in Athens I'm afraid I shall have to leave you to occupy yourself for a few hours before we continue with our journey. That was my grandfather who rang last night. He wants to see me.'

'He won't be at the island?' Saskia asked.

'Not immediately. His heart condition means that he has to undergo regular check-ups—a precautionary measure only, thank goodness—and they will keep him in Athens for the next day or so.'

'Athena told me she doesn't believe that our relationship will last. She believes that the two of you are destined to be together,' Saskia said.

'She's trying to intimidate you,' Andreas responded, the smile he had given the attentive stewardess replaced by a harsh frown.

Impulsively Saskia allowed the sympathy she had unexpectedly felt for him the previous evening to take precedence over her own feelings. Turning towards him, she said softly, 'But surely if you explained to your grandfather how you feel he would understand and accept that you can't be expected to marry a woman you don't…you don't want to marry…'

'My grandfather is as stubborn as a mule. He's also one hell of a lot more vulnerable than he thinks…than any of us want him to think. His heart condition...' He gave a small sigh. 'At the moment it's stable, but it is important that he—and we—keep his stress levels down. If I told him that I didn't want to marry Athena without producing you as a substitute he would immediately become very stressed indeed. It isn't just that by marrying Athena as he wishes I would attach her fortune and assets to our own, my grandfather is also a man to whom male descendants are of paramount importance.

'My elder sister already has two daughters, and Athena also has two. My grandfather is desperate for me, as his direct male descendent, to produce the next male generation...a great-grandson.'

'But even if you did marry Athena there would be no guarantee that you would even have children, never mind sons,' Saskia protested.

'Why are you laughing at me?' she demanded in chagrin as she saw the mirth crinkling Andreas's eyes and a gust of warmly amused male laughter filled the small space between them.

'Saskia, for a woman of your experience you can be very, very naïve. You should *never* suggest to any man, and most *especially* not a Greek one, that he may not be able to father a son!'

As the plane suddenly started to lift into the sky Saskia automatically clutched at her arm-rests, and then tensed in shock as she felt the hard male warmth of Andreas's hand wrapping around her own.

'Scared of flying?' he asked her in amusement. 'You shouldn't be. It's the safest form of transport there is.'

'I know that,' Saskia responded waspishly. 'It's

just…well, it's just that flying seems so…so unnatural, and if…'

'If God had intended man to fly he'd have given him wings,' Andreas offered her wryly. 'Well, Icarus tried that option.'

'I always think that's such a sad story.' Saskia shivered, her eyes shadowing. 'Especially for his poor father.'

'Mmm…' Andreas agreed, before asking her, 'Am I to take it from that comment that you're a student of Greek mythology?'

'Well, not precisely a student,' Saskia admitted, 'but my grandmother used to read me stories from a book on Greek mythology when I was little and I always found the stories fascinating…even though they nearly always made me cry.'

Abruptly she stopped speaking as she realised two things. The first was that they were now completely airborne, and the second was…her own bemused awareness of how good it felt actually to have Andreas's large hand clasping her own. It was enough to make her face sting with self-conscious colour and she hastily wriggled her hand free, just as the stewardess came up to offer them a glass of champagne.

'Champagne!' Saskia's eyes widened as she took a sip from the glass Andreas was holding out to her and she gasped as the delicious bubbles exploded against her taste buds.

It had to be the champagne that was making her feel so relaxed and so…so…laid-back, Saskia decided hazily a little later, and when the captain announced that they were coming in to land she was

surprised to realise how quickly the time had flown—
and how much she had enjoyed the conversation she
and Andreas had shared. She was even more surprised to discover how easy it was to slip her hand
into the reassuring hold of Andreas's as the plane's
wheels hit the tarmac and the pilot applied reverse
thrust to slow them down.

'I can either have our driver take you to the family
apartment in Athens, where you can rest whilst I see
my grandfather, or, if you prefer, I can arrange for
him to drive you on a sightseeing tour,' Andreas offered, casually lifting their cases off the luggage car-
ousel.

He was wearing a pair of plain light-coloured trousers and a cool, very fine white cotton short-sleeved
shirt, and for some indefinable reason it did odd
things to Saskia's normally very sensible female
senses to witness the way the muscles hardened in
his arms as he swung their cases on to the ground.
Very odd things, she acknowledged giddily as the
discreet smile of flirtatious invitation she intercepted
from a solitary woman traveller caused her instinctively to move possessively closer to him.

What on earth was happening to her? It *must* be
the champagne...or the heat...or perhaps both! Yes,
that was it, she decided feverishly, grateful to have
found a sensible explanation for her unfamiliar behaviour. After all, there was no reason why she
should feel possessive about Andreas. Yesterday
morning she had hated him...loathed him... In fact
she had been dreading her enforced time as his 'fiancée'—and she still was, of course. Of course! It
was just that...

Well, having met Athena it was only natural that she should feel *some* sympathy for him. And she had been fascinated by the stories he had told her during the flight—stories which had been told to him by older members of his Greek family and which were a wonderful mix of myth and folklore. And it was a very pleasant experience not to have to struggle with heavy luggage. Normally when she went away she was either with a group of friends or with her grandmother, and...

'Saskia...?'

Guiltily Saskia realised that Andreas was still waiting for an answer to his question.

'Oh, I'd much prefer to see something of the city,' she answered.

'Well, you won't have a lot of time,' Andreas warned her. 'Our pilot will already have filed his flight plan.'

Saskia already knew that they would be flying out to the island in a small plane privately owned by Andreas's grandfather, and what had impressed her far more than Andreas's casual reference to the plane had been his mention of the fact that he himself was qualified to fly.

'Unfortunately I had to give it up. I can't spare the amount of hours now that I believe are needed to keep myself up to speed and in practice, and besides, my insurance company were extremely wary about insuring me,' he'd added ruefully.

'It's this way,' he told her now, placing his hand on her shoulder as he turned her in the right direction.

Out of the corner of her eye Saskia caught a

glimpse of their reflections in a mirrored column and immediately tensed. What was she *doing* leaning against Andreas like that? As though...as though she *liked* being there...as though she was enjoying playing the helpless fragile female to his strong muscular male.

Immediately she pulled away from him and squared her shoulders.

'Athena would have loved to have seen you do that,' he told her sharply, the disapproval clear in his voice.

'We're supposed to be in love, Saskia...remember?'

'Athena isn't here,' she responded quickly.

'No, thank God,' he agreed. 'But we don't know who might accidentally observe us. We're a *couple*— very much in love—newly engaged...and you're about to fly to my home to meet my family. Don't you think it's natural that—?'

'That I should feel nervous and intimidated...worried about whether or not they'll think I'm good enough for you.' Saskia interrupted him angrily, her pride stung by what he was suggesting. 'And what am I supposed to do? Cling desperately and despairingly to you...afraid of their rejection...afraid of *losing* you...just because—'

She stopped as she saw the blank impatient look Andreas was giving her.

'What I was about to say,' he told her grimly, 'was don't you think it's only natural that I should want to hold you close to me and equally that *you* should want that same intimacy? That as lovers we *should* want always to be physically in touch with one another?' He paused. 'And as for what you have just said, I'm a man of thirty-five, long past the age of needing *anyone's* approval of what I do or who I love.'

'But you don't...' Saskia began, and then stopped as she realised what she had been about to say. Andreas hardly needed *her* to tell him that he didn't love her.

'I don't what?' he prompted her, but she shook her head, refusing to answer him.

'So you want to see the Acropolis first?' Andreas checked with Saskia before getting out of the limousine, having first given the driver some instructions in Greek.

'Yes,' Saskia confirmed.

'I have told Spiros to make sure you are at the airport in time for our flight. He will take care of you. I am sorry to have to leave you to your own devices,' Andreas apologised formally, suddenly making Saskia sharply aware of his mixed cultural heritage.

She recognised how at home he looked here, and yet, at the same time, how much he stood out from the other men she could see. He was taller, for one thing, and his skin, whilst tanned, was not as dark, and of course his eyes would always give away his Northern European blood.

Saskia gave a small emotional sigh as she finally turned her back on the Acropolis and started to walk away. She had managed to persuade the driver that she would be perfectly safe on her own, but only after a good deal of insistence, and she had enjoyed her solitude as she had absorbed the aura of the ancient building in awed appreciation.

Now, though, it was time for her to go. She could see the limousine waiting where she had expected, but to her consternation there was no sign of its driver.

There *was* a man standing close to the vehicle, though, white-haired and elderly. Saskia frowned as she recognised that he seemed to be in some distress, one hand pressed against his side as though he was in pain. A brief examination of the street confirmed that it was empty, apart from the old man and herself. Saskia automatically hurried towards him, anxious for his well-being.

'Are you all right?' she asked in concern as she reached him. 'You don't look well.'

To her relief he answered her in English, assuring her, 'It is nothing...the heat—a small pain. I have perhaps walked further than I should...'

Saskia was still anxious. It *was* hot. He did not look well, and there was certainly no way she could possibly leave him on his own, but there was still no sign of her driver or anyone else who might be able to help, and she had no idea how long it would take them to get to the airport.

'It's *very* hot,' she told the old man gently, not wanting to hurt his pride, 'and it can be very tiring to walk in such heat. I have a car...and...and a driver... Perhaps we could give you a lift?' As she spoke she was searching the street anxiously. Where *was* her driver? Andreas would be furious with her if she was late for their flight, but there was no way she could leave without first ensuring that the old man was alright.

'You have a car? This car?' he guessed, gesturing towards the parked limousine.

'Well, it isn't *mine*,' Saskia found herself feeling obliged to tell him. 'It belongs to...to someone I know. Do you live very far away?'

He had stopped holding his side now and she could see that his colour looked healthier and that his breathing was easier.

'You are very kind,' he told her with a smile, 'But I too have a car...and a driver...' His smile broadened and for some reason Saskia felt almost as though he was laughing a little at her.

'You are a very kind girl to worry yourself so much on behalf of an old man.'

There *was* a car parked further down the street, Saskia realised, but it was some distance away.

'Is *that* your car?' she asked him. 'Shall I get the driver?'

'No,' he denied immediately. 'I can walk.'

Without giving him any opportunity to refuse, Saskia went to his side and said gently, 'Perhaps you will allow me to walk with you to it...' Levelly she met and held the look he was giving her.

'Perhaps I should,' he capitulated.

It took longer to reach the car than Saskia had expected, mainly because the old man was plainly in more distress than he wanted to admit. As they reached the car Saskia was relieved to see the driver's door open and the driver get out, immediately hurrying towards them and addressing some words to her companion in fast Greek. The old man was now starting to look very much better, holding himself upright and speaking sternly to the driver.

'He fusses like an old woman,' he complained testily in English to Saskia, adding warmly, 'Thank you, my dear, I am *very* pleased to have met you. But you should not be walking the streets of Athens on your own,' he told her sternly. 'And I shall—' Abruptly he stopped and said something in Greek to his driver, who started to frown and look anxiously up and down the street.

'Yannis will walk back with you to *your* car and wait there with you until your driver returns.'

'Really, there's no need for that,' Saskia protested, but her new-found friend was determinedly insistent.

'There really is no need for you to come with me,' she told the driver once they were out of earshot of the older man. 'I would much rather you stayed with your employer. He looked quite poorly when I saw him in the street.'

To her relief, as she finished speaking she saw that her own driver was getting out of Andreas's car.

'See, there is no need to come any further,' she smiled in relief, and then frowned a little before saying anxiously to him, 'Your employer... It is none of my business I know...but perhaps a visit to a doctor...' She paused uncertainly.

'It is already taken care of,' the driver assured her. 'But he... What do you say? He does not always take anyone's advice...'

His calmness helped to soothe Saskia's concern and ease her conscience about leaving the older man. He was plainly in good hands now, and her own driver was waiting for her.

CHAPTER SIX

SASKIA darted a brief look at Andreas, catching back her gasp of pleasure as she stared out of their plane and down at the blue-green of the Aegean Sea beneath them.

He had been frowning and preoccupied when they had met up at the airport, not even asking her if she had enjoyed her sightseeing trip, and now with every mile that took them closer to his home and family Saskia could feel her tension increasing. It seemed ironic, when she reflected on how she had dreamed of one day spending a holiday in this part of the world, that now that she was actually here she was far too on edge to truly appreciate it.

The starkness of Andreas's expression forced her to ask, more out of politeness than any real concern, she was quick to assure herself, 'Is something wrong? You don't look very happy.'

Immediately Andreas's frown deepened, his gaze sweeping her sharply as he turned to look at her.

'Getting in some practice at playing the devoted fiancée?' he asked her cynically. 'If you're looking for a bonus payment, don't bother.'

Saskia felt a resurgence of her initial hostility towards him.

'Unlike you, I do not evaluate everything I do by how I can best benefit from it,' Saskia shot back furiously. 'I was simply concerned that your meeting hadn't gone very well.'

'*You?* Concerned for *me*? There's only one reason you're here with me, Saskia, and we both know that isn't it.'

What did he expect? Saskia fumed, forcing herself to bite back the angry retort she wanted to make. He had, after all, blackmailed her into being here with him. He was using her for his own ends. He had formed the lowest kind of opinion of her, judged her without allowing her the chance to defend herself or to explain her behaviour, and yet after all that he still seemed to think he could occupy the higher moral ground. Why on earth had she ever felt any sympathy for him? He and Athena deserved one another.

But even as she formed the stubborn angry thought Saskia knew that it wasn't true. She had sensed a deep coldness in Athena, a total lack of regard for any kind of emotion. Andreas might have done and said many things she objected to, but there was a warmly passionate side to him...a *very* passionate side, she acknowledged, trembling a little as she unwillingly remembered the kiss he had given her... Even though it had merely been an act, staged for Athena's benefit he had still made her feel—*connected* at a very deep and personal level. So much so, in fact, that even now, if she were to close her eyes and remember, she could almost feel the hard male pressure of his mouth against her own.

'As a matter of fact my meeting did *not* go well.'

Saskia's eyes opened in surprise as she heard Andreas's abrupt and unexpected admission.

'For a start my grandfather was not there. There

was something else he had to do that was more important, apparently. But unfortunately he did not bother to explain this to me, or to send a message informing me of it until I'd been waiting for him for over half an hour. However, he *had* left instructions that I was to be informed in no uncertain terms that he is not best pleased with me at the moment.'

'Because of me...us?' Saskia hazarded.

'My grandfather knows there is no way I would or could marry a woman I do not love—his own marriage was a love match, as was my parents', even if my mother did have to virtually threaten to elope before she got his approval. When my father died my grandfather admitted how much he admired him. He was a surveyor, and he retained his independence from my grandfather.'

'You must miss him,' Saskia said softly.

'I was fifteen when he died; that was a long time ago. And, unlike you, at least I had the comfort of knowing how much he loved me.'

At first Saskia thought he was being deliberately unkind to her, and instinctively she stiffened in self-defence, but when unexpectedly he covered her folded hands with one of his own she knew that she had misinterpreted his remark.

'The love my grandmother has given me has more than made up for the love I didn't get from my parents,' she told him firmly—and meant it.

His hand was still covering hers...both of hers...and that funny, trembly sensation she had felt inside earlier returned as she looked down at it. Long-fingered, tanned, with well-groomed but not manicured nails, it was very much a man's hand:

large enough to cover both of hers, large enough, too, to hold her securely to him without any visible effort. It was the kind of hand that gave a woman the confidence to know that this man could take care of her and their children. Just as he was the kind of man who would always ensure that his woman and his child were safe and secure.

What on earth was she thinking? Agitatedly Saskia wriggled in her seat, snatching her hands from beneath Andreas's.

'Are you sure this is a good idea?' she asked him slightly breathlessly as she tried to concentrate on the reality of why she was sitting here next to him. 'I mean, if your grandfather already doesn't approve of our engagement...'

It was so long before he replied that Saskia began to think that her question had annoyed him but when he did answer her she recognised that the anger she could see darkening his eyes wasn't directed at her but at Athena.

'Unfortunately Athena claims a blood closeness to my grandfather which he finds flattering. His elder brother, Athena's grandfather, died some years ago and whilst there is no way at all that Athena would allow anyone, least of all my grandfather, to interfere in the way she runs her own financial empire, she flatters and encourages him to the point where his judgement is sometimes not all that it should be. My mother claims that the truth will out, so to speak, and that ultimately my grandfather will see through Athena's machinations.'

'But surely she must realise that you don't want to marry her,' Saskia suggested a little bit uncomfortably. It was so foreign to her own way of behaving to even consider trying to force anyone into a relationship with her that it was hard for her to understand why Athena should be driven to do so.

'Oh, she realises it all right,' Andreas agreed grimly. 'But Athena has never been denied anything she wants, and right now...'

'She wants you,' Saskia concluded for him.

'Yes,' Andreas agreed heavily. 'And, much as I would like to tell her that her desires are not reciprocated, I have to think of my grandfather.'

He stopped speaking as their plane started to lose height, a small smile curling his mouth as he saw Saskia's expression when she looked out of the window down at their destination.

'He can't possibly be intending to put this plane down on that tiny piece of land,' she gasped in disbelief.

'Oh, yes, he can, It's much safer than it looks,' Andreas said reassuringly. 'Look,' he added, directing her attention away from the landing strip and to the breathtaking sprawl of his family villa and the grounds enclosing it.

'Everything is so green,' Saskia told him in bemusement, her eyes widening over the almost perfect oval shape of the small island, the rich green of its gardens and foliage perfectly shown off by the whiteness of its sandy beaches and the wonderful turquoise of the Aegean Sea that lapped them.

'That's because the island has its own plentiful supply of water,' Andreas told her. 'It's far too small to be able to sustain either crops or livestock, which is why it was uninhabited—as you can see it is quite some distance from any of the other islands, the furthest out into the Aegean.'

'It looks perfect,' Saskia breathed. 'Like a pearl drop.'

Andreas laughed, but there was an emotion in his eyes that made Saskia's cheeks flush a little as he told her quietly, 'That was how my grandmother used to describe it.'

Saskia gave a small gasp as the plane suddenly bumped down onto the runway, belatedly realising that Andreas had deliberately distracted her attention away from their imminent landing. He could be so entertaining when he wanted to be, so charming and so easy to be with. A little wistfully she wondered how much difference it would have made to his opinion of her had they met under different circumstances. Then she very firmly pulled her thoughts into order, warning herself that her situation was untenable enough already without making it worse by indulging in ridiculous fantasies and daydreams.

There was a bleak look in Andreas's eyes as he guided Saskia towards the aircraft's exit. There was such a vast contradiction in the way he was perceiving Saskia now and the way he had perceived her the first time he had seen her. For his own emotional peace of mind and security he found himself wishing that she had remained true to his first impression of her. That vulnerability she fought so determinedly and with such pride to conceal touched him in all the ways that a woman of Athena's coldness could never possibly do. Saskia possessed a warmth, a humanity, a womanliness, that his maleness reacted and responded to in the most potentially dangerous way.

Grimly Andreas tried not to allow himself to think about how he had felt when he had kissed her. Initially he had done so purely as an instinctive response to his awareness that Athena was in his apartment—that appalling overpowering scent of hers was instantly recognisable. Quite how she had got hold of a key he had no idea, but he suspected she must have somehow cajoled it from his grandfather. But the kiss he had given Saskia as a means of reinforcing his unavailability to Athena had unexpectedly and unwontedly shown him—*forced* him to acknowledge—something he was still fighting hard to deny.

He didn't *want* to want Saskia. He didn't want it at all, and he certainly didn't want to feel his current desire to protect and reassure her.

Athens had been hot, almost stiflingly so, but here on the island the air had a silky balminess to it that was totally blissful, Saskia decided, shading her eyes from the brilliance of the sun as she reached the ground and looked a little uncertainly at the trio of people waiting to greet them.

Andreas's husky, 'Here you are, darling, you forgot these,' as he handed her a pair of sunglasses threw her into even more confusion, but nowhere near as much as the warm weight of his arm around her as he drew her closer to him and whispered quite audibly, 'Our harsh sunlight is far too strong for those beautiful Celtic eyes of yours.'

Saskia felt her fingers start to tremble as she took the sunglasses from him. They carried a designer logo, she noticed, and were certainly far more expensive than any pair of sunglasses she had ever owned. When Andreas took them back and gently slipped them on for her she discovered that they fitted her perfectly.

'I remembered that we didn't get any in London and I knew you'd need a pair,' he told her quietly, leaning forward to murmur the words into her ear, one arm still around her body and his free hand holding her shoulder as though he would draw her even closer.

To their onlookers they must look very intimate, Saskia recognised, which was no doubt why Andreas had chosen to give them to her in such a manner.

Well, two could play at that game. Without stopping to think about the implications of what she was doing, or to question why she was doing so, Saskia slid her own arm around *his* neck, turning her face up to his as she murmured back, 'Thank you, darling. You really are so thoughtful.'

She had, she recognised on a small spurt of defiant pleasure, surprised him. She could see it in his eyes—and she could see something else as well, something very male and dangerous which made her disengage herself from him hastily and step back. Not that he allowed her to go very far. Somehow he was holding her hand and refusing to let go of it, drawing her towards the small waiting group.

'Mama. This is Saskia...' he announced, introducing Saskia first to the older of the two women.

Warily Saskia studied her, knowing that if she and Andreas were really in love and engaged her heart would be in her mouth as she waited to see whether or not she and Andreas's mother could build a true bond. Physically she looked very much like Athena, although, of course, older. But the similarity ended once Saskia looked into her eyes and saw the warmth there that had been so markedly lacking from Athena's.

There was also a gentleness and sweetness about Andreas's mother, a timidity almost, and intuitively Saskia sensed that she was a woman who, having loved only one man, would never totally cease mourning his loss.

'It's a pleasure to meet you, Mrs Latimer,' Saskia began, but immediately Andreas's mother shook her head chidingly.

'You are going to be my daughter-in-law, Saskia, you must call me something less formal. Helena is my name, or if you wish you may call me Mama, as 'Reas and my daughters do.' As she spoke she leaned forward and placed her hands gently on Saskia's upper arms.

'She is lovely, 'Reas,' she told her son warmly.

'I certainly think so, Mama,' Andreas agreed with a smile.

'I meant inside as well as out,' his mother told him softly.

'And so did I,' Andreas agreed, equally emotionally.

Heavens, but he was a wonderful actor, Saskia acknowledged shakily. If she hadn't known how he really felt about her that look of tender adoration he had given her just now would have…could have… A man like him should know better than to give a vulnerable woman a look like that, she decided indignantly, forgetting for the moment that so far as Andreas was concerned she was anything *but* vulnerable.

'And this is Olympia, my sister,' Andreas continued, turning Saskia towards the younger of the two women. Although she was as darkly Greek as her mother, she too had light coloured eyes and a merry open smile that made Saskia warm instantly to her.

'Heavens, but it's hot down here. Poor Saskia must be melting,' Olympia sympathised.

'You could have waited for us at the villa,' Andreas told her. 'It would have been enough just to have sent a driver with the Land Rover.'

'No, it wouldn't,' Olympia told him starkly, shrugging her shoulders as her mother made a faint sound of protest. She looked anxiously at her, saying, 'Well, he has to know…'

'I have to know what?' Andreas began to frown.

'Athena is here,' his mother told him unhappily. 'She arrived earlier and she…'

'She what?'

'She said that your grandfather had invited her,' his mother continued.

'You know what that means, don't you Andreas?' Olympia interrupted angrily. 'It means that she's bullied Grandfather into saying she could stay. And that's not all…'

'Pia…' her mother began unhappily, but Olympia refused to be silenced.

'She's brought that revolting creep Aristotle with her. She claims that she is right in the middle of an important business deal and that she needs him with her because he's her accountant. If it's so important, how come she had time to be here?' Olympia demanded. 'Oh, but I hate her so. This morning she went on and on about how concerned Grandfather is about the business and how he's been asking her advice because he's worried that you...'

'Pia!' her mother protested again, and this time Andreas's sister did fall silent, but only for a few seconds.

'What I can't understand is why Gramps is so taken in by her,' she burst out, as though unable to contain herself. 'It's obvious what she's doing. She's just trying to get at you, Andreas, because you won't marry her.'

'I'm sorry about this,' Helena Latimer was apologising gently to Saskia. 'It can't be pleasant for you. You haven't met Athena yet, I know—'

'Yes, she has,' Andreas interrupted his mother, explaining when both she and Pia looked at him questioningly, 'Somehow or other she managed to get a key for the London apartment.'

'She's the worst, isn't she?' Pia told Saskia. 'The black widow spider I call her.'

'Pia!' Andreas chided her sharply.

'Mama hasn't told you everything yet,' Pia countered, looking protectively at her mother before continuing, 'Athena has insisted on having the room that Mama had arranged to be prepared for Saskia. It's the one next to your suite—.'

'I tried to stop her, Andreas,' Helena interrupted her daughter unhappily. 'But you know what she's like.'

'She said that Saskia could have the room right down at the end of the corridor. You know, the one we only use as an overspill when absolutely everyone is here. It hasn't even got a proper bed.'

'You'll have to say something to Athena, Andreas.

Make her understand that she can't…that she can't
have that room because Saskia will be using it.'

'No, she won't,' Andreas contradicted his mother
flatly, sliding his arm very firmly around Saskia, im-
prisoningly almost, drawing her right into his body
so that her face was concealed from view as he told
his mother and sister, 'Saskia will be sharing *my*
room…and *my* bed…'

Saskia could sense their shock, even though she
could not see their faces. *Now* she knew why he was
holding her so tightly, preventing anyone else from
seeing her expression or hearing the panicky denial
she was trying to make but which was muffled
against the fine cotton of his shirt.

There was just no way that she was prepared for
anything like this. No way that she could ever be
prepared for it. But her attempts to tell Andreas were
bringing her into even more intimate contact with
him as she tried to look up into his face.

His response to her efforts to attract his attention
made the situation even worse, because when he bent
his head, as though anxious to listen to what she was
saying, her lips inadvertently brushed against his jaw.

It must be a combination of heat and shock that
was sending that melting liquid sensation of weakness swooshing through her, Saskia decided dizzily.
It certainly couldn't be the feel of Andreas's skin
against her lips, nor the dangerous gleam she could
see in his narrowed eyes as they glittered down into
hers. The arm he had around her moved fractionally,
so that the hand that had been resting on her waist
was now somehow just beneath the curve of her

breast, his fingertips splaying against its soft curve and making her...making her...

'Saskia will be sharing your room!' Pia was breathing, verbalising the shock that Saskia herself felt and that she suspected his mother was too embarrassed to voice.

'We *are* engaged...and soon to be married...' Andreas told his sister smoothly, adding in a much rougher, rawer, spine-tinglingly possessive voice, 'Saskia is mine and I intend to make sure that everyone knows it.'

'Especially Aristotle,' Pia guessed. 'I don't know how Athena can endure him,' she continued shuddering. 'He's like a snake, Saskia. All cold and slimy, with horrid little eyes and clammy hands...'

'Athena endures him because of his skill at "creative" accounting,' Andreas informed his sister dryly.

'You mean he's dishonest,' Pia translated pithily.

'You didn't hear that from me,' Andreas warned her as he started to shepherd all three of them towards the waiting Land Rover.

Whilst they had been talking the driver had loaded their luggage, and as he held the door open for his mother, sister and Saskia to get in Saskia heard Andreas asking him about his family, listening interestedly whilst the driver told him with pride about his son who was at university.

'Grandfather was not very pleased at all when Andreas said that he wanted to use the money our father had left him to help pay for the education of our personal household staff,' Pia told Saskia.

'Pia, you aren't being very fair to your grandfather,' her mother objected.

Andreas had done that? Stubbornly Saskia refused to acknowledge that she was impressed by his philanthropy.

Had he really meant what he had said about them sharing a room? He couldn't have done—could he? Personally she didn't care *where* she slept, even if it was a normally unused bedless room, just so long as she occupied it on her own.

'We have both had a long day and I imagine that Saskia is going to want to have a rest before dinner,' Andreas was saying as the Land Rover pulled up in a cool paved courtyard with a central fountain that sent a musical plume of water up into the air to shower back to earth in millions of tiny teardrops.

'I'll make sure everyone knows that you aren't to be disturbed,' his mother responded. 'But perhaps Saskia would like something light to eat and drink…'

Before Saskia could say anything Andreas was answering for her, telling his mother, 'I'll see to that,' before placing his hand beneath Saskia's elbow and telling her in a soft voice in which she suspected only she could hear the underlying threat, 'This way, Saskia…'

CHAPTER SEVEN

'I CAN'T sleep in this room with you!'

Saskia had been able to feel herself trembling as Andreas had whisked her down a confusing maze of corridors. She had known that he must be able to feel her nervousness as well, but somehow she had managed to keep her feelings under control until they were both inside the huge elegant bedroom with the door firmly shut behind them.

Right now, though, she was in no mood to appreciate the cool elegance of her surroundings. Whirling round, she confronted Andreas determinedly. 'No way was *that* part of the deal.'

'The "deal" was that you would act as my fiancée, and that includes doing whatever has to be done to ensure that the act is believable,' he told her angrily.

'I won't sleep here with you,' Saskia protested wildly. 'I don't... I haven't...' She could hardly bear to look at the large king-sized bed as panic filled her, flooding out rationality. She had gone through so much, and now she was hot and tired and very, very afraid. Her emotions threatened to overwhelm her.

Quickly she turned away as she heard Andreas saying, almost mundanely, 'I'm going to have a shower, and if you'll take my advice you'll do the same. Then, when we're both feeling cooler and calmer, we can discuss this whole situation less emotively.'

A shower! With Andreas! Saskia stared at him in mute shocked disbelief. Did he really think that she would…that she could…?

'You can use the bathroom first,' he told her.

First! So he hadn't meant… Relief sagged through her, quickly followed by a furious burst of toxic anger.

'I don't want to use the bathroom at all,' she burst out. 'What I *want* is to be at home. My *own* home, with my own bathroom and my own bedroom. What I want is to be free of this stupid…stupid charade… What I *want*…' She had to stop as her feelings threatened to overwhelm her, but they refused to be contained, spilling out in a furious fierce torrent of angry words. 'How could you let your mother and sister think that you…that we…?' She shook her head, unable to put into words what she wanted to say.

Andreas had no such qualms.

'That we are lovers?' he supplied dramatically for her. 'What else should they think? I'm a man, Saskia, and you and I are supposed to be engaged. And if in reality we were, do you think for one minute that I wouldn't—'

'Want to test the goods before you bought them?' Saskia threw wildly at him. 'Oh, of course, a man like you would be bound to want to do that…to make sure…'

She tensed as she saw the way he was looking at her and the bitter anger in his eyes.

'That kind of comment is typical of a woman like

you,' he ground out. 'Reducing everything to terms of money. Well, let me tell you—'

But Saskia wouldn't let him finish, defending herself sharply instead as she insisted, '*You* were the one who said…'

But Andreas immediately checked her.

'What I said, or rather what I was *trying* to say before you interrupted me,' he told her grittily, 'was that if I genuinely loved you there would be no way I would be able to deny myself—or you—the pleasure of showing that love in the most intimate physical way there is. There would be no way that I could bear to let you out of my sight or my arms, certainly not for the length of a whole night.'

Saskia discovered that she had started to tremble almost violently as his words struck sharply sensitive chords deep within her body that she had not even known existed. Chords that activated a deep core of feminine longing, that brought her dangerously close to the edge of tears she had no idea why she wanted to cry. Panic raced through her veins, flooding out common sense. She could feel her heart thumping frantically with anxiety.

She opened her mouth to tell Andreas that she had changed her mind, that she wanted to go home, that she was not prepared to stay a minute longer, no matter how much he tried to blackmail her into doing so. But her panic didn't stem from any fear of him. No. It was herself she feared now, and the way she was beginning to feel, the thoughts she was beginning to have. She *couldn't* allow herself to feel that way about him. She *couldn't* be attracted to him. He wasn't her type of man at all. She abhorred the way he had treated her, the way he had misjudged her. But the shocking shaft of self-awareness, of longing she had felt as he'd described his desire for the woman he would love wasn't going to be dismissed.

'I can't...' she began, stopping as Andreas held up his hand warningly, silencing her as someone knocked on the door.

Dry-mouthed, Saskia waited whilst he went to open it, watching as their cases were brought in— not by the driver of the Land Rover but by another smaller, older man to whom Andreas was talking in Greek, smiling warmly at him as he did so, and then laughing good-humouredly as the older man looked past him at Saskia herself, before clapping him on the shoulders with a wide, beaming smile.

'What was that all about?' Saskia demanded curiously once he had gone and they were on their own again.

'Stavros was saying that it is high time I had a wife...and that I must lose no time in getting myself a fine boy child,' he added mercilessly.

Saskia could feel herself colouring to the roots of her hair as she looked everywhere but at the king-sized bed in the centre of the room.

Despite the room's air conditioning she felt stifled, unable to breathe...hunted and desperate to escape.

'I'm going to have that shower,' Andreas told her, mundanely breaking into her thoughts, turning away from her as he did so and heading for one of the three doors that opened off the bedroom.

Once he had disappeared Saskia looked at the door to the corridor, longing to have the courage to walk through it and demand that she be flown back immediately to Athens. But if she did she would lose her job—Andreas would make sure of that!

Fiercely Saskia tried to concentrate on something else, *anything* else but the appalling situation she was in. She hated what Andreas was doing to her...what he was making her do. And she hated Andreas himself too...didn't she?

Unable to answer her own question honestly, Saskia studied the view beyond the large patio doors that opened out onto an enclosed courtyard, which itself surrounded a tantalisingly tempting swimming pool complete with its own bubbling spa pool.

Small oases of green plants broke up the paving and the brilliant harshness of the sunlight. Comfortable-looking sun loungers complete with umbrellas offered a lazy way to enjoy the sunshine. The whole scene looked like something out of an exclusive holiday brochure, the kind Saskia had only been able to glance at enviously, knowing such a holiday was way beyond her means. But right now the only place she wanted to be was safe in her own home.

Andreas couldn't really expect her to share a room—never mind a bed—with him. She couldn't do it. She wouldn't...she was so...

'The bathroom's free...'

Saskia froze. She had been so engrossed in her thoughts she hadn't realised that Andreas was in the bedroom with her...standing right behind her, she recognised as she picked up the clean, warm scent of his newly showered body.

'I'll go and sort out something light for you to eat. Dinner won't be for a few hours yet, and if you'll take my advice you'll try to rest for a while. Greeks eat late and go to bed even later.'

'But I thought that we'd be having separate rooms,' Saskia burst out, unable to control her panic any longer. 'I would never have agreed to come here if I'd thought that I'd— No! Don't you dare touch me,' she protested as she felt him moving closer to her, reaching out to her. She wouldn't be able to bear it if he touched her, if he...

Frantically she turned and ran towards the door, but somehow Andreas managed to get there before her, blocking her access to it, taking hold of her, his fingers biting into the soft flesh of her arms.

'What the hell do you think you're doing?' he ground out savagely. 'What exactly is it you're pretending to be so afraid of? This? A woman like you!'

Saskia gasped and shook from head to foot as his arms closed imprisioningly around her and his mouth came down on hers. He was wearing a robe, but as she struggled to break free it was his bare skin she could feel beneath her flaying hands. Warm, damp...hard, his chest roughened by dark hairs. Her hands skittered wildly over his torso, shocked by the intimate unexpected contact with his bare skin, seeking some kind of purchase to thrust him away and finding none.

He was kissing her with an angry passion that made her feel weak, the blood roaring in her head as her brain recognised her inability to deal with the searing experience of so much furiously male arrogant sensuality.

'Stop acting like a novice, an innocent,' Saskia heard him demanding against her mouth. His tongue forced her lips to part for its entry and the hand that was imprisoning her urged her even deeper into the sensual heat of his parted thighs as he leaned back against the door, taking her with him. His free hand was on her body, arrogantly stroking its way up past her waist to the curve of her breast.

Saskia tensed in shock as it cupped her breast, his thumb-pad circling her nipple and somehow enticing it to peak into a shocking bud of delicious wanton pleasure.

She could feel the aroused heat of him like a brand, and beneath her anger she felt a sharp, spiralling stab of female curiosity and excitement...a dangerous surge to conspire with him, to allow her traitorous body to experience even more of the intimacy of their embrace.

Without knowing she had done so she opened her mouth, hesitantly allowing him access to its sweetness, shyly starting to return his kiss and even more shyly allowing her tongue to mesh seductively with his.

'Andreas? Are you in there? It's me, Athena...I need to talk to you.'

Saskia froze as she heard Athena's voice from the other side of the door, but Andreas showed no sign whatsoever of any confusion or embarrassment. Still holding Saskia against him in a grip she could not break, he opened the door and told Athena flatly, 'Not now, Athena. As you can see, Saskia and I are busy.'

'She is with *you*,' Athena snapped angrily, darting Saskia a look of icy venom. 'Why isn't she in her own room?'

'She is,' Andreas returned coolly. 'My room is Saskia's room. My bed...her bed. My body...her...'

'Your grandfather will never allow you to marry her,' Athena breathed, but Andreas was already closing the door, ignoring her insistence that he listen to her.

'Andreas, let me go,' Saskia demanded. She couldn't bear to look at him. Couldn't bear to do anything, least of all think about the way she had responded to him...the way she had encouraged him...

Derisively Andreas watched her.

'Okay, Saskia, that's enough,' he told her. 'I know I told you I wanted you to act like a faithful fiancée, but that does not mean you have to pretend to be an innocent virgin who has never—' Abruptly he stopped, frowning as he mulled over the unwanted suspicions that were striking him as he looked at Saskia's pale face and hunted eyes.

Even though he had let her go she was still shaking, trembling from head to foot, and he could have sworn just now, when he had held her in his arms and kissed her...touched her, that he was the first man to make her feel so...

For a moment he examined what he was thinking, and feeling, and then firmly dismissed his suspicions. There was no way she could be so inexperienced, no way at all. There was enough Greek in him for him to consider that the gift of her virginity, her purity, was one of the greatest gifts a woman could give to the man she loved, but his cultural heritage from his British father and schooling mocked and even deplored such archaic feelings.

Would a woman expect a man to keep himself pure until he met her? No. So why should it be any different for a woman? As a mature man he accepted and respected a woman's right to choose how she dealt with her own sexuality. But he knew too that as a lover, a husband, there would be a deeply, darkly passionate and possessive part of him that yearned to be his beloved's only partner, an ache within him to teach her, show her the delights of sensual love. And right now something about Saskia's reaction to him was sparking off a reaction he was having to fight to control, a response that was pure primitive Greek male. A need!

'I'm not sleeping in this room with you,' Saskia reiterated numbly. 'I'm...'

If she *was* acting then she deserved an Oscar, Andreas decided grimly. But a fiancée who looked terrified at the very thought of being with him was the last thing he needed. He had to calm her down, to calm them both down.

'Come with me,' he commanded, taking hold of her hand and drawing her towards one of the doors that opened off the bedroom.

When he opened it Saskia could see that the room that lay beyond it was furnished as an office, with all the latest technological equipment.

'Will it make you feel any better if I tell you that I intend to sleep in there?' Andreas demanded.

'In there? But it's an office. There's no bed,' Saskia whispered shakily.

'I can bring in one of the sun loungers and sleep on that,' Andreas told her impatiently.

'You mean it...' Saskia was wary, reluctant to trust or believe him.

Andreas nodded his head grimly, wondering why on earth he was allowing his overactive conscience to force him into such a ridiculous situation. He knew there was no way she could possibly be the naïve, frightened innocent she was behaving as though she was.

'But surely someone would notice if you removed a sun bed?' she was asking him uncertainly.

'Only my room opens out onto this pool area. It's my private territory. The main pool which everyone else uses is round the other side of the villa.'

His own private pool. Saskia fought not to be impressed, but obviously she had not fought hard enough, she recognised ruefully as Andreas gave her an impatient look.

'I'm not trying to make a point, Saskia, one-upmanship of that boastful sort is anathema to me. My grandfather may be a millionaire but I most certainly am not.'

It wasn't entirely true, but something about the look in Saskia's eyes made him want to refute any mental criticism she might have that he was some kind of idle playboy, lounging by a swimming pool all day.

'It's just that I happen to like an early-morning swim when I'm here at the villa; my sisters used to claim that I woke them up so I had this pool installed for my own use. Swimming laps helps me to clear my thoughts as well as allowing me to exercise.'

Saskia knew what he was saying, she felt the same about walking. Whenever she was worried about something, or had a problem to mull over, she walked.

As he watched her Andreas asked himself grimly why he was going to so much trouble to calm and reassure her. That frightened heartbeat he had felt thudding so anxiously against his own body just had to have been faked. There was no way it could not have been. Just like that huge-eyed watchfulness.

Saskia bit her lip as she looked away from him. It was obvious that Andreas meant what he said about sleeping in his office, but right now it wasn't their sleeping arrangements that were to the forefront of her mind so much as what was happening during their waking hours—and what she herself had just experienced when he kissed her.

She couldn't have secretly wanted him to kiss her. Surely it was impossible that that could happen without her being consciously aware of it. But what other explanation could there be for the way she had responded to him? her conscience demanded grittily.

'Right,' she could hear Andreas saying dryly, 'now that we've got *that* sorted out I've got some work to do, so why don't you have something to eat and then have a rest?'

'I need to unpack,' Saskia began to protest, but Andreas shook his head.

'One of the maids will do that for you whilst you're resting.'

When he saw her expression he told her softly, 'They work for us, Saskia. They are servants and they work to earn their living just as you and I work to earn ours.'

*   *   *

'Oh, I'm sorry, I didn't wake you, did I?' Pia said *sotto voce*. 'But it will be dinner time soon and I thought you might appreciate some extra time to get ready.'

As Saskia came fully awake and struggled to sit up in the bed she recognised that her unexpected visitor was Andreas's sister Olympia.

The arcane grin that crossed Pia's face as she added, 'We normally dress down here, not up, but Athena is bound to want to make an impact,' made Saskia warm to her friendliness.

'Where's...?' she began anxiously, but didn't get any further than the first word of her enquiry.

'Where's Andreas?' Pia supplied for her, 'Grandfather telephoned to speak to our mother and then he wanted to have a word with Andreas.' She gave a small shrug. 'He's probably still on the phone, and I have to warn you he isn't in a very good mood.' As she saw the way Saskia's eyes became watchful she hastened to assure her. 'Oh, it isn't you. It's Athena. She's brought her accountant with her and Andreas is furious. He can't stand him. None of us can, but Athena insisted that Grandfather invited Aristotle personally.'

As Pia darted about the room, switching on lamps to illuminate the darkness of the Greek evening, Saskia swung her feet to the floor. She had fallen asleep fully dressed and now she felt grubby and untidy. The thought of having to sit down at a dinner table with Andreas and Athena was not one she was looking forward to, but Pia was right about one thing: she *would* need to make an impact. Andreas would no doubt expect it of her. Still, with her suitcase full of the new clothes he had insisted on buying for her, she had no excuse *not* to do so.

'Maria's already unpacked your cases for you,' Pia informed her. 'I helped her,' she added. 'I love that little black number you've brought with you. It's to die for. Your clothes are gorgeous. Andreas kept coming in and telling me not to make so much noise in case I woke you up.' She pulled another face. 'He's so protective of you.

'Mama and I are so glad that he's met you,' she added more quietly, giving Saskia a look of warm confidence that immediately made her feel horribly guilty. 'We both love him to bits, of course,' she went on, 'and that hardly makes us impartial. But we were beginning to get so afraid that he might just give in to Grandfather and Athena for Grandfather's sake—and we both know he could *never* love her. I suppose he's told you about what she did when he was younger?'

Without waiting for Saskia to say anything Pia continued in a quick burst of flurried words, 'I'm not supposed to know about it really. Lydia, my sister, told me, and swore me to secrecy, but of course it's all right to discuss it with you because Andreas must have told you about it. He was only fifteen at the time—just a boy, really—and she was *so* much older and on the point of getting married. I know the actual age gap in terms of years would be nothing if it had been between two adults, but Andreas wasn't an adult. He was still at school and she... I think it was wonderfully brave and moral of Andreas to refuse to go to bed with her—and do you know something else? I think that although Athena *claims* to love him a part of her really wants to punish him for not letting her—well, you know!'

Athena had tried to *seduce* Andreas when he had still been a schoolboy! Saskia had to fight hard to control both her shock and the distaste Pia's revelations were causing her.

It was true that in terms of years—a mere seven or so—the age gap between them was not large. But for a woman in her twenties to attempt to seduce a boy of fifteen—surely that was almost sexual abuse? A cold shiver touched Saskia's skin, icy fingers spreading a chilling message through her.

Would a woman who was prepared to do something like that allow a mere bogus fiancée to come between her and the man she wanted? And Athena obviously did want Andreas very badly indeed— even if her motivation for doing so was shrouded in secrecy.

Andreas was such a very *male* man it was hard to imagine him in the role of hunted rather than hunter. If ever a man had been designed by nature to be proactive, arrogant and predatory that man was, in Saskia's opinion, Andreas. But there was something so alien to Saskia's own experience in Athena, a coldness, a greed, almost an obsessiveness that Saskia found it hard to relate to her or even think of her in terms of being a member of her own sex.

Her determination to marry Andreas was chillingly formidable.

'Of course, if it wasn't for Grandfather's health there wouldn't be any problem,' Pia was saying ruefully. 'We all know that. Grandfather likes to think that because he works for him Andreas is financially dependent on him, but...' She stopped, shaking her head.

'You are going to wear the black, aren't you? I'm dying to see you in it. You've got the colouring for it. I look so drab in black, although you can bet that Athena will wear it. Whoops!' She grimaced as they both heard male footsteps in the corridor outside the bedroom. 'That will be Andreas, and he'll scalp me if he thinks I'm being a pest.'

Saskia tensed as Andreas came into the room, watching as his glance went from the bed to where she was standing in the corner of the room.

'Pia,' he began ominously, 'I told you...'

'I was awake when she came,' Saskia intervened protectively. She liked Andreas's sister, and if she'd been genuinely in love with him and planning to marry him she knew she would have been delighted to have found a potential friend in this warm-hearted, impulsive woman.

Pia launched herself at Andreas, laughing up into his face as she hugged him and told him triumphantly, 'See? You are wrong, big brother, and you must not be so firm and bossy with me otherwise Saskia will not want to marry you. And now that I have met her I am determined that she will be my sister-in-law. We were just discussing what she is going to wear for dinner,' she added. 'I have warned her that Athena will be dressed to kill!'

'If you don't take yourself off to your own room so that we can *all* get ready, Athena is going to be the only one who is dressed for anything,' Andreas told her dryly.

Kissing his forehead, Pia released him and hurried

to the door, pausing as she opened it to give Saskia an impish grin and remind her, 'Wear the black!'

'I'm sorry,' Andreas apologised after the door had closed behind her. 'I asked her not to disturb you.'

So he hadn't been deceived by her fib, Saskia recognised.

'I don't mind; I like her,' Saskia responded, this time telling him the truth.

'Mmm... Pia's likeability is something I'm afraid she tends to trade on on occasion. As the baby of the family she's a past mistress at getting her own way,' he told Saskia in faint exasperation, before glancing at his watch and informing her, 'You've got half an hour to get ready.'

Saskia took a deep steadying breath. Something about the revelations Pia had made had activated the deep core of sympathy for others that was so much a part of her nature. Somewhere deep inside her a switch had been thrown, a sea change made, and without her knowing quite how it had happened Andreas had undergone a transformation, from her oppressor and a dictator whom she loathed and feared to someone who deserved her championship and help. She had a role which she was now determined she was going to play to the very best of her ability.

'Half an hour,' she repeated in as businesslike a manner as she could. 'Then in that case I should like to use the bathroom first.'

CHAPTER EIGHT

'So, SASKIA, how do you think you will adjust to being a Greek wife—if you and Andreas *do* actually get married?'

Saskia could hear Pia's indrawn gasp of indignation at the way Athena had framed her question, but she refused to allow herself to be intimidated by the other woman. Ever since they had all taken their places at the dinner table Saskia had recognised that Athena was determined to unnerve and upset her as much as she could. However, before she could say anything Andreas was answering the question for her.

'There is no "if" about it Athena,' he told her implacably. 'Saskia *will* become my wife.'

Now it was Saskia's turn to stifle her own potentially betraying gasp of shock, but she couldn't control her instinctive urge to look anxiously across the table at Andreas. What would he do when he ultimately had to back down and admit to Athena that their engagement was over? That was *his* problem and not hers, she tried to remind herself steadily.

Something odd had happened to her somehow; she was convinced of it. Andreas had walked out of the office adjoining 'their' bedroom earlier this evening and come to a standstill in front of her, saying quietly, 'I doubt that any man looking at you now could do anything other than wish that you were his, Saskia.'

She had certainly never had any desire to go on the stage—far from it—and yet from that moment she had felt as though somehow she had stepped into a new persona. Suddenly she had become Andreas's fiancée and, like any woman in love, not only was she proud to be with the man she loved, she also felt very femalely protective of him. The anxiety in her eyes now was *for* him and *because* of him. How would he feel when Athena tauntingly threw the comment he had just made back in his face? How must he have felt when he had first realised, as a boy, just what she wanted from him?

'Wives. I love wives.' Aristotle, Athena's accountant, grinned salaciously, leaning towards Saskia so that he could put his hand on her arm.

Immediately she turned away from him. Saskia fully shared Pia's view of Athena's accountant. Although he was quite tall, the heavy, weighty structure of his torso made him look almost squat. His thick black hair was heavily oiled and the white suit he was wearing over a black shirt, in Saskia's opinion at least, did him no favours. Andreas, on the other hand, looked sexily cool and relaxed in elegantly tailored trousers with a cool white cotton shirt.

If she had privately thought her black dress might be rather over the top she had swiftly realised how right Pia had been to suggest that she wore it once she had seen Athena's outfit.

Her slinky skintight white dress left nothing to the imagination.

'It was designed especially for me,' Saskia had heard her smirking to Andreas. 'And it is made to be worn exactly the way I most love—next to my skin,' she had added, loudly enough for Saskia to overhear. 'Which reminds me. I hope you have warned your fiancée that I like to share your morning swim so she won't be too shocked...' She had turned to Saskia. 'Andreas is like me, he likes to swim best in his skin,' she had told her purringly.

In his skin. Saskia hadn't been able to prevent herself from giving Andreas a brief shocked look which, fortunately, Athena had put down to Saskia's jealousy at the thought of another woman swimming nude with her fiancée.

Whilst Saskia had been digesting this stomach-churning disclosure she had heard Andreas himself replying brusquely, 'I can only recall one occasion on which you attempted to join me in my morning lap session, Athena, and I recall too that I told you then how little I appreciate having my morning peace interrupted.'

'Oh, dear.' Athena had pouted, unabashed. 'Are you afraid that I have said something you didn't want your fiancée to know? But surely, Andreas,' she had murmured huskily, reaching out to place her hand on his arm, 'she *must* realise that a man as attractive as you...as virile as you...will have had other lovers before her...'

Her brazenness had almost taken Saskia's breath away. She could imagine just how she would be feeling right now if Andreas *had* indeed been her fiancée. How jealous and insecure Athena's words would be making her feel. No woman wanted to be reminded of the other women who had shared an intimate relationship with her beloved before her.

But Andreas, it seemed, was completely unfazed

by Athena's revelations. He had simply removed her arm by the expedient of stepping back from her and putting his own arm around Saskia's shoulders. He had drawn her so close to his body that Saskia had known he must be able to feel the fine tremor of reaction she was unable to suppress. A tremor which had increased to a full-flooded convulsion when his lean fingers had started almost absently to caress the smooth ball of her bare shoulder.

'Saskia knows that she is the only woman I have ever loved—the woman I want to spend my life with.'

The more she listened to and watched Athena the more Saskia subscribed to Pia's belief that it wasn't love that was motivating the other woman. Sometimes she looked at Andreas as though she hated him and wanted to totally destroy him.

Aristotle, or 'Ari' as he had told Saskia he preferred to be called, was still trying to engage her attention, but she was deliberately trying to feign a lack of awareness of that fact. There was something about him she found so loathsome that the thought of even the hot damp touch of his hand on her arm made her shudder with distaste. However, good manners forced her to respond to his questions as politely as she could, even when she thought they were intolerable and intrusive. He had already told her that were he Andreas's accountant he would be insisting she sign a prenuptial contract to make sure that if the marriage ended Andreas's money would be safe.

Much to Saskia's surprise Andreas himself had thoroughly confounded her by joining in the conversation and telling Aristotle grimly that he would never ask the woman he loved to sign such an agreement.

'Money is nothing when compared with love,' he had told Aristotle firmly in a deep, implacable voice, his words so obviously genuine that Saskia had found she was holding her breath a little as she listened to him.

Then he had looked at her, and Saskia had remembered just how *they* had met and what he really thought of her, and suddenly she had felt the most bitter taste of despair in her mouth and she had longed to tell him how wrong he was.

At least she had the comfort of knowing that his mother and sister liked her, and Pia had assured her that their elder sister was equally pleased that Andreas had fallen in love, and was looking forward to meeting Saskia when she and her husband and their children came to the island later in the month.

'Lydia's husband is a diplomat, and they are in Brussels at the moment, but she is longing to meet you,' Pia had told her.

She would have hated it if Andreas's close family had *not* liked and welcomed her.

Abruptly Saskia felt her face start to burn. What on earth was she thinking? She was only *playing* the part of Andreas's fiancée. Their engagement was a fiction, a charade…a *lie* created simply to help him escape from the trap that Athena was trying to set for him. What she must not forget was that it was a lie he had tricked and blackmailed her into colluding with.

Aristotle was saying something to her about wanting to show her the villa's gardens. Automatically

Saskia shook her head, her face burning with fresh colour as she saw the way Andreas was watching her, a mixture of anger and warning in his eyes. He couldn't seriously think she would actually *accept* Aristotle's invitation?

'Saskia has had a long day. I think it's time we said our goodnights,' she heard him saying abruptly as he stood up.

Saskia looked quickly round the table. It was obvious from the expressions of everyone else just what interpretation they were putting on Andreas's decision, and Saskia knew that the heat washing her face and throat could only confirm their suspicions.

'Andreas...' she started to protest as he came round to her chair and stood behind her. 'I don't...'

'You're wasting your breath, Saskia.' Pia chuckled. 'Because my dear brother obviously *does*! Oh, you needn't put that lordly expression on for me, brother dear.' She laughed again, before adding mischievously, 'And I wouldn't mind betting that you won't be lapping the pool at dawn...'

'Pia!' her mother protested, pink-cheeked, whilst Athena gave Saskia a look of concentrated hatred.

Hastily Saskia stood up, and then froze as Aristotle did the same, insisting in a thick voice, 'I must claim the privilege of family friend and kiss the new addition to the family goodnight.'

Before Saskia could evade him he was reaching for her, but before he could put his words into action Andreas was standing between them, announcing grimly, 'There is only one man *my* fiancée kisses...'

'If you'll take my advice, you'll keep well away from Aristotle. He has a very unsavoury reputation with women. His ex-wife has accused him of being violent towards her and—'

Saskia turned as she stepped into the bedroom, her anger showing. 'You can't mean what I *think* you mean,' she demanded whilst Andreas closed the door. How could he possibly imagine that she would even contemplate being interested in a man like the accountant? It was an insult she was simply not prepared to tolerate.

'Can't I?' Andreas countered curtly. 'You're here for one reason and one reason only, Saskia. You're here to act as my fiancée. Whilst I can appreciate that, being the woman you are, the temptation to feather your nest a little and do what you so obviously do best must be a strong one, let me warn you now against giving in to it. If you do, in fact...'

If she *did*... Why, she would rather *die* than let a slimeball like Ari come anywhere near her, Saskia reflected furiously. And to think that back there in the dining room she had *actually* felt sympathetic towards Andreas, had actually wanted to *protect* him. Now, though, her anger shocked through her in a fierce, dangerous flood of pride.

'If you want the truth, I find Ari almost as repulsively loathsome as I do you,' she threw bitterly at him.

'You dare to speak of me in the same breath as that reptile? How dare you speak so of me...or to me...?' Andreas demanded, his anger surging to match hers as he reached out to grab hold of her. His eyes smouldered with an intensity of emotion that Saskia could see was threatening to get out of control.

'That man is an animal—worse than an animal. Only last year he narrowly escaped standing on a criminal charge. I cannot understand why Athena tolerates him and I have told her so.'

'Perhaps she wants to make you jealous.'

It was an off-the-cuff remark, full of bravado, but Saskia wished immediately she had not said it when she saw the way the smoulder suddenly became a savage flare of fury.

'*She* does? Or *you* do...? Oh, yes, I saw the way he was looking at you over dinner...touching you...'

'That was nothing to do with me,' Saskia protested, but she could sense that the words hadn't touched him, that something else was fuelling his anger and feeding it, something that was hidden from her but which Andreas himself obviously found intolerable.

'And as for you finding me *loathsome,*' Andreas said through gritted teeth. 'Perhaps it is unchivalrous, *ungentlemanly* of me to say so, but that wasn't loathing I could see in your eyes earlier on today. It wasn't *loathing* I could hear in your voice, *feel* in your body...was it? *Was it?*' he demanded sharply.

Saskia started to tremble.

'I don't know,' she fibbed wildly. 'I can't remember.'

It was, she recognised a few seconds later, the worst possible thing she could have said. Because immediately Andreas pounced, whispering with soft savagery, 'No? Then perhaps I should help you to remember...'

She heard herself starting to protest, but somehow the words were lost—not because Andreas was refusing to listen, but because her lips were refusing to speak.

'So when exactly *was* it that you found me so loathsome Saskia?' Andreas was demanding as he closed both his arms around her, forming them into a prison from which it was impossible for her to escape. 'When I did this…?' His mouth was feathering over hers, teasing and tantalising it, arousing a hot torrent of sensation she didn't want to experience. 'Or when I did *this*…?'

Now his tongue-tip was probing the lips she was trying so desperately to keep firmly closed, stroking them, tracing their soft curves, over and over again, until she could hear herself moaning helplessly as they parted softly for him. But still it seemed he hadn't extracted his pound of flesh, because even this victory wasn't enough for him.

'What? Still no answer…? I wonder why not,' he was taunting her, before adding bitingly, 'Or do I need to wonder at all? You are a woman who is used to giving her body to a man, Saskia, who is used to experiencing pleasure. And right now you want that pleasure from *me*.'

'No,' Saskia moaned in denial, trying to turn her face away from his and to break free of him.

'Yes,' he insisted rawly. '*Yes*. Admit it, Saskia… You *want* me… Your body wants *mine*. It wants the sexual satisfaction it's used to…it aches and craves for.'

A shudder of shock ripped through her as Saskia recognised the truth of what he was saying. She *did* want him, but not in the way he was suggesting. She wanted him as a woman wanted the man she loved, she realised shakily. She wanted him as her lover, not merely as her sexual partner, someone with whom she could find a release for a basic physical need, as he was so cruelly saying. But how could she love him? She *couldn't*... But she *did*.

She had fallen in love with him virtually the moment she had set eyes on him, Saskia acknowledged despairingly, but she had told herself that because of her loyalty to her friend he was out of bounds to her and that she could not, *must* not allow herself to have such feelings, just as she could not allow herself to have them now. Although for very different reasons. Megan was no longer a barrier to her loving Andreas, but Andreas himself and what he thought about her certainly was.

'Let me go, Andreas,' she demanded.

'Not until you have admitted that I am right and that you want me,' Andreas refused. 'Or are you trying to goad me into *proving* to you that I am right?'

Saskia flinched as she felt the suffocating, dangerously toxic mix of fear and excitement explode inside her.

She hesitated whilst she tried to formulate the right response, the only sane, sensible response she could give, and then she realised that she had waited too long as Andreas told her rawly, 'You've pushed me too far, Saskia. I want you, but you already know that, don't you? How could a woman like you *not* know it? You can feel it in my body, can't you?' he demanded. 'Here...'

Helplessly Saskia leaned against him whilst she tried to absorb the shock of having her hand taken and placed so explicitly against the hard, intimate throb of his maleness. If only she could find the strength to drag her hand away, to tell him that she didn't want the intimacy he was forcing on her. But despairingly she knew that she was too weak, that there was no way she could stop herself from aching to use the opportunity he had given her to touch and explore him, to know him…to know his maleness…to—

She gave a small moan as her body started to shake with tremors of desire. Andreas's heart was pounding so savagely that she could feel it almost inside her own body. Earlier in the evening, when he had almost absently caressed the ball of her shoulder—the touch of an established lover for his beloved—she had shuddered in mute delight, but that was nothing to what she was feeling now.

She ached for him, hungered for him, and when she closed her eyes she could see him as Athena had so tauntingly described him—proud and naked as his body sliced the water. She moaned again, a high, sharp sound this time that had Andreas covering her mouth with the hard, hot, demanding pressure of his, the words he was groaning against her lost as his passion sent a kick of shocking voluptuous pleasure searing through her.

Her mouth was properly open beneath his now, her tongue hungry for the sensual melding stroke of his, and the intensity of her own feelings was dizzying and dazzling her.

'You want me… You need me…'

She could feel him mouthing the words and she couldn't deny them, her body, her emotions were saturated with the intensity of a response to him so new to her that she had no defences against it.

Everything else was suddenly forgotten, unimportant. Everything else and every*one* else. All she needed... All she wanted... All she could ever want was here within her reach.

She moaned and trembled as she felt Andreas's hands on her body and over her dress, their touch hard, hungry...excitingly, *dangerously* male. The unfamiliar intimacy of his body against hers was depriving her of the ability to think or to reason properly. There was no place for reason to exist in this new world she was inhabiting anyway.

'I want to see you...watch you whilst I make love to you,' Andreas was saying thickly to her. 'I want *you* to see me... My God, but I can understand *now* just why all those other men fell victim to you. There's something about you, some witchery, some— What's wrong?' he demanded as he felt the abrupt way Saskia had tensed against him in rejection.

Saskia could not bear to look at him.

With those few contemptuous words he had destroyed everything, totally obliterated her wonderful new world and brought her crashing back to her old one. She felt sick to her soul from her own behaviour, her own folly.

'No, no, I don't want *this*,' she protested frantically, pushing Andreas away.

'What the...?' She could hear the anger in his voice, feel it almost, but still he released her.

'If this is some kind of game—' he began to warn her, and then stopped, shaking his head in disbelief.

'My God, I must have been out of my mind anyway, to even contemplate… I suppose that's what too many years of celibacy does for a man,' he threw at her unkindly. 'I never thought I'd be idiotic enough…'

He turned back to her, stopping when Saskia froze.

'You're quite safe,' he told her grimly. 'I'm not going to touch you. There's no way—' He broke off and shook his head again, and then walked abruptly away from her, telling her brusquely, 'I've got some work to do.'

The bedroom was in darkness when Saskia woke up, and at first she didn't know what had woken her. Then she heard it again, the rhythmic sound of someone swimming. The patio doors to the pool area were open, and as she turned her head to look towards them she could see the discreet lights which were illuminating it.

Andreas was swimming… She looked at her watch. It was three o'clock in the morning and Andreas was swimming…tirelessly up and down the pool. Warily she sat up in bed to get a closer look as his powerful crawl took him to the far side of the pool. As he executed his turn Saskia lay down again. She didn't want him to see her watching him.

Beneath the bedclothes she was naked, apart from a tiny pair of briefs. The one thing Andreas had apparently forgotten to buy for her had turned out to be any kind of nightwear. *That* discovery had caused her to remain for nearly fifteen minutes in the locked privacy of the bathroom, agonising over what she should do until she had finally found the courage to open the door and make an undignified bolt for the bed, her body hidden from view by the towel she had wrapped around it. Not that she need have been so concerned. Andreas had remained out of sight in his office.

But he wasn't in his office now. Now he was swimming in the pool.

Beneath the protective cover of the bedclothes Saskia's brain worked feverishly. Should he be swimming alone at night? Was it safe? What if…? Almost the very second that fear formed her ears registered the fact that she could no longer hear the sound of Andreas swimming. Quickly she lowered the bedclothes and looked anxiously towards the pool area. The water was still, calm—and empty of its sole swimmer.

Andreas! Where—? She gripped hold of the bedclothes as she saw him climbing out of the water—totally naked—totally! She tried to drag her recalcitrant gaze away from his body but it was no use; it was refusing to listen to her, refusing to obey her, remaining fixed in hungry female appreciation on the pagan male beauty of Andreas's nakedness.

Surely any woman would have found the sight of Andreas breathtaking, Saskia thought fervently, her gaze devouring the pure sensuality of his back view as he walked across the tiles. His skin shone sleekly, still damp from his swim, and beneath it the muscles moved in a way that had a shockingly disconcerting effect on her *own* body.

Naively Saskia had always previously assumed that there could be little difference in seeing a statue or a painting of a naked man and viewing the real thing, but now she knew how wrong she had been. Perhaps it was her love for him that made the difference, perhaps it was... She gasped as he suddenly turned round. He seemed to be looking right into the bedroom. Could he see her? Did he *know* that she was watching him? She lay perfectly still, praying that he could not do so, unable to bear the humiliation of his mockery if he were to come in to her now. If he were to...

She just managed to suppress the audible sound of her own longing. If he came to her now and held her, touched her, kissed her...*took* her as she was so aching for him to do, it wouldn't be in love but in lust. Was that really what she wanted? she asked herself sternly. No, of course it wasn't, was her helpless response. What she wanted was for Andreas to love her the way she did him.

He was turning away from her now, his body silhouetted by the light. Saskia sucked in her breath sharply, every feminine instinct and desire she possessed flagrantly ignoring her attempts to control them. He looked... He was... He was *perfect* she acknowledged, silently whispering the soft accolade beneath her breath as her eyes rounded and she saw that the male reality of him far, far outreached anything she had ever thought of in her innocent virginal imaginings.

Once again he looked towards the bedroom and Saskia held her breath, praying...hoping...*waiting*... She expelled it on a small rush of sound as he reached down and retrieved his robe, shrugging it on before walking not back to the bedroom and to her

but away from it. Where was he going? she wondered. Back to his office?

For what felt like a long time after he had gone
Saskia lay where she was, afraid to move, unable to
sleep and even more afraid to think. What was the
matter with her? How could she possibly love a man
who had treated her as Andreas had done, who had
blackmailed her, threatened her, refused to allow her
to tell him the truth about herself? A man who had
the lowest possible opinion of her and yet who, despite that, had still kissed her. How could she? Saskia
closed her eyes. She didn't know the answer to that
question. All she knew was that her emotions, her
heart, her deepest self were crying out—how could
she *not* love him?

'Sunbathing? I never thought I'd see the day when
you would just laze around,' Pia teased Andreas as
she came hurrying out of the villa in the tiniest little
bikini Saskia had ever seen and curled up on the
vacant sun bed next to where Saskia was lying.

'Saskia didn't have a good night. She needs to rest
and I didn't want her overdoing things or lying too
long in our strong sun,' Andreas lied unblushingly to
his sister.

'Oh, poor you,' Pia immediately sympathised with
Saskia as she studied her pale face.

Guiltily Saskia said nothing. After all, she could
hardly admit that the reason she was so jaded was
because she had spent so many of the night hours
when she should have been sleeping thinking about,
fantasising about the man lying right next to her. In
daylight Saskia dared not recall the very personal and
intimate nature of her fantasies. She knew that if she

did so her face would be as brightly coloured as it was now pale. Mercifully Andreas had put her huge eyes and pale face down to travel tiredness.

'Well, that's one improvement you've made on my brother's lifestyle already, Saskia,' Pia approved with a grin. 'Normally when he comes to the villa we can't get him out of the office. When did Grandfather say he is going to arrive?' she asked Andreas.

'I must say I'm surprised that your grandfather intends to come to the island at all at the moment,' Athena answered for Andreas as she and her accountant came out of the villa to join them.

Saskia's heart sank a little as she saw them. Over breakfast Ari had been so over-fulsome in his praise of her, and so obviously sexually motivated, that she had been glad to escape from him.

As Pia started to frown Athena added maliciously, 'He isn't very happy with you right now, Andreas...'

'My grandfather is never happy with anyone who takes a different view from his,' Andreas told her dryly. 'He has a quick temper and a short fuse and thankfully an even shorter memory—'

Andreas had insisted that Saskia was to lie beneath the protection of a sun umbrella because of her fair skin, but as she watched Athena untying the wrap she was wearing to reveal an even smaller bikini than Pia's, Saskia felt envious of her rich golden tan.

'How uncomfortable you must be lying in the shade,' Athena said, adding bitchily, 'I would *hate* to have such a pale skin. It always looks so...'

'Saskia's skin reminds *me* of the purest alabaster,' Andreas interrupted Athena smoothly.

'Alabaster—oh, but that is so cold.' Athena

smiled, giving Saskia an assessing look. 'Oh, now you are frowning and looking grumpy,' she told Andreas softly, 'and I know *just* the cure for that. Let me put some oil on for you, Andreas, and then…'

Saskia could hardly believe it when she heard herself saying firmly, 'I'll do that for you, darling.' Turning to look at Athena, she added boldly, 'A fiancée's privilege.' And then, ignoring both the frowning look Andreas was giving her and her own shaking hands, she got up off her sun lounger, took the bottle of oil Pia was offering her with an approving smile and walked over to where Andreas was lying.

Very carefully Saskia poured a little of the oil into her cupped hand and then, even more carefully, leaned over Andreas's prone body, making sure as she did so that she stood between his sun bed and the one Athena was reclining on in a pose carefully designed to flaunt to full effect her generous breasts.

Saskia's hair swung over her face as she nervously started to smooth the oil over Andreas shoulders. His skin felt warm and sleek beneath her touch. As sleek as it had looked last night. She paused as her hands began to tremble. Last night! She must *not* think about *that* now. But somehow she found herself doing so; somehow, too, her hands were moving sensually against his skin, stroking, smoothing, even kneading instinctively when she found that his muscles were bunching beneath her touch.

He had been lying on his stomach with his eyes closed, but suddenly they opened and he told her abruptly, 'That's enough. I was about to go for a swim anyway.'

Even so it was still several seconds before he actually got up and walked away from her to the end of the pool, diving in cleanly and then swimming virtually a full length beneath the water before resurfacing and starting to lap the pool with a hard, fast-paced crawl.

Andreas tried to concentrate on what he was doing, to empty his head of any thoughts as he always did when he was swimming. It was his favourite way of relaxing—or at least it had been. Right now the *last* thing he felt was relaxed. Even without closing his eyes he could still remember exactly how it had felt to have Saskia's hands moving over his body, soft, caressing…knowing…

He slid beneath the water, swimming under it as he tried to control his aching body. God, but he wanted her; ached for her; lusted for her. He had *never* felt like this about anyone before, never needed anyone with such an intensity, never been in a situation where he simply could not control himself either physically or emotionally. She *must* know what she was doing to him, a woman of *her* experience…a woman who prowled bars at night looking for a man. Of *course* she must; of course she *did*. And yet…

And yet he couldn't stop himself from contrasting what he knew cerebrally about her with the way she had felt in his arms, the soft, hot sweetness of her kiss, the desire hazing her eyes and the shock which had later replaced it. She had caught him off guard just now, when she had refused to allow Athena to touch him—caught him off guard and filled him with a certain hot male triumph and pride that she should feel so possessive about him. But of course she didn't—did she? She was simply acting, playing out the role he had forced her into.

Andreas frowned. His own mental use of the word 'forced' and the admission which it brought rasped against his conscience like sandpaper. It was wholly out of character for him, against his strongest held beliefs to force anyone to do anything, but he had begun to fear he could find no way out of the present situation without endangering his grandfather's health. What he was offering was an explanation, not an excuse, he warned himself sternly and if he had now discovered that he had merely exchanged one hazard for another which was even more potentially dangerous then he had no one but himself to blame.

Had Saskia seen that betraying surge of his body before he had turned away from her? Athena had. Athena... Andreas's mouth hardened.

At fifteen, and still a schoolboy, he had tried to convince himself that he was mature enough to take over his father's role, strong enough to support and protect his mother and his sisters. But a part of him had still been childish and he had often ended up crying alone at night in his bed, confused and angry and missing his father, wondering furiously why he had had to die.

That period had surely been the worst of his life: the loss of his father and then Athena's attempt to seduce him. Two events which together had propelled him into an adulthood and maturity he had in no way been prepared for.

Athena's desire for him had held none of the classic 'Mrs Robinson' allure. She had been coming on to him for weeks, ever since he had returned home from school for the summer holidays, but he had never dreamed that she was doing anything other than playing some mysterious adult female game that was beyond his ability to comprehend—until the day he had found her in his room—naked!

When she had handed him the vibrator she was stroking herself with, commanding him to use it on her, it had been all he could do not to turn on his heels and run. But boys ran, and he hadn't wanted to be a boy, but a man...the man his father would have wanted him to be, the man his mother and sisters needed him to be.

'I don't think you should be in here, do you?' he had asked her woodenly, avoiding looking at her naked body. 'You are engaged to be married.'

She had laughed at him then, but she hadn't been laughing later, when he had held open his bedroom door and commanded her to leave, warning her that if she didn't he would have no compunction in getting a couple of members of staff to physically remove her.

She had gone, but not immediately, not until she had tried to change his mind.

'You have a man's body,' she had told him angrily. 'But like a fool you have no knowledge of what to do with it. Why won't you let me show you?' she had coaxed. 'What is it you are so afraid of?'

'I'm not afraid,' he had responded stoically, and truthfully. It hadn't been fear that had stopped him from taking advantage of what she was offering but anger and loathing.

But Athena was a woman who couldn't endure to accept that he didn't want her. Tough! Her feelings, if she genuinely had any—which he personally doubted—were her problem. His grandfather was a very different matter, though, and even without the cloud currently hanging over his health, Andreas would have been reluctant to quarrel with him— though he felt that the old man was being both stubborn and difficult. How much of the blame for that lay with Athena and how much with his grandfather's fiercely guarded fear of growing old and the future Andreas could only hazard a guess at.

It was ironic, really, that the means he had adopted to help him overcome his problems should have resulted in causing him even more. An example, perhaps, of the modern-day ethos behind the ancient Greek mythology Saskia had expressed a love of. She might love Greek mythology but she most certainly did not love him. Andreas frowned, not wanting to pursue such a line of thought.

'That is a very pretty little ring you are wearing,' Athena commented disparagingly as she got up off the lounger and came to stand next to Saskia.

They were alone at the poolside, Athena's accountant having gone to make some telephone calls and Pia having left to help her mother, who was preparing for the arrival of her father.

'But an engagement ring is no guarantee of marriage,' Athena continued. 'You look like a sensible girl to me, Saskia. Andreas is a very wealthy and experienced man. Men like him get so easily bored. You must know that yourself. I suspect that the chances of you actually walking down the aisle and marrying Andreas are very limited indeed, and they will become even more slender once Andreas's grandfather arrives. He doesn't want Andreas to marry you. He is very old-fashioned and very Greek. He has other plans for his only grandson and for the future of the business he has built up.'

She paused, watching Saskia calculatingly, and Saskia knew what she was thinking. Athena too had other plans for Andreas's future.

'If you really loved Andreas then surely *he* would be far more important to you than your own feelings. Andreas is devoted to his grandfather. Oh, I know he may not show it, but I can promise you that he is. Think what it would do to him emotionally, not to mention financially, if there were to be a rift between them. Andreas's mother and his sisters are both financially dependent on their grandfather... If he were to banish Andreas from his life then Andreas would be banished from *their* lives as well.'

Athena gave a deep, theatrical sigh and then asked pseudo-gently, 'How long do you think he would continue to want *you* once that had happened? And I can *make* it happen, Saskia...you know that, don't you. His grandfather listens to me. It is because he wants my business to be joined to his, of course. That is the Greek way of doing things.' She bared her teeth and gave Saskia an unkind smile. 'It is *not* the Greek way of doing things for a millionaire to allow his heir to marry a penniless foreigner.

'But let's talk of something more pleasant. There is no reason why we shouldn't come to a mutually happy arrangement—you and I. I *could* sit back and wait for Andreas to leave you, but I will be honest with you. I am approaching the age when it may become less easy for me to give Andreas the sons he will want. So, to make it easy for us both, I have a proposition to put to you. I am willing to pay you *one million pounds* to remove you from Andreas's life—permanently.'

Saskia could feel the blood draining out of her face as shock hit her. Somehow she managed to drag herself into a sitting position on the sun lounger and then to stand up, so that she and Athena were face to face.

'Money can't buy love,' she told her fiercely. 'And it can't buy me. Not one million pounds, not one hundred million pounds! *No* amount.' Tears stung her eyes and she told herself that shock had put them there. 'If at any time Andreas wants to end our engagement then that is his prerogative, but—'

'You're a fool—do you know that?' Athena breathed, her whole face contorted with fury and malice. 'Do you really think Andreas meant what he said about not insisting on a prenuptial agreement? Ha! His grandfather will *make* him have you sign one, and when Andreas grows tired of you, as he undoubtedly will, you will get *nothing*...not even any child he may have given you. Greek men do not give up their children. Greek *families* do not give up their heirs.'

Saskia didn't want to hear any more. Without even bothering to pick up her wrap she started to walk towards the house, only just managing to prevent herself from breaking into a run.

As Saskia reached the house Pia was coming out of it through the open patio door.

'Saskia...' she began in concern, but Saskia shook

her head, knowing she was in no fit state to talk to her—to her or indeed to anyone. She felt degraded by what Athena had said to her, degraded and angry. How dared Athena believe that her love was for sale...that *money* mattered more to her than Andreas...that she would *ever*...? Abruptly Saskia stopped. What was she *thinking*? She turned round and went back outside, heading not for the pool area but beyond it...to the island and the pathway along the cliffs. She needed to be on her own.

The full irony of what had happened was only just beginning to sink in. She had agreed to come to the island only because Andreas had blackmailed her into doing so and because she couldn't afford to lose the income from her job. Yet when she was offered what amounted to financial security for life, not just for herself but more importantly for her beloved grandmother, as well as an immediate escape from her intolerable situation, she turned both down.

Angrily Pia started to hurry towards where Athena was lying sunning herself. After what she had just overheard there was no way she was not going to tell Athena what she thought of her. How dared she treat Saskia like that, trying to bribe her into leaving Andreas?

Andreas!

Pia came to an abrupt halt. Perhaps she ought to tell her brother what Athena had been up to and let him deal with her. Saskia had looked so dreadfully upset, and no wonder. Reluctantly Pia listened to the inner voice warning her that Andreas would not thank her for pre-empting his right to be the one to confront Athena. Turning on her heel, she walked back inside the villa in search of Andreas.

CHAPTER NINE

LESS than a third of the way along the path that circumnavigated the island Saskia stopped walking and turned round. She couldn't go on; she had had enough. Loving Andreas—being so close to him every day in one sense and yet with such an unbridgeable gap between them in all the senses that really mattered—was more than she could cope with. Her love for him, her longing for him, was tearing her apart.

Slowly she started to walk back to the villa. She had no idea what she was going to do—throw herself on Andreas's mercy and beg him to release her from their 'agreement'? There was no point in trying to tell him what Athena had done. He was hardly likely to believe her, not with his opinion of her, and besides, she didn't want him to know. If he did...once he did... Andreas was no fool, he was an astute, sharp-minded businessman, it wouldn't take him long to guess what had happened, how she felt, and that was something she could not endure.

Once she reached the villa Saskia went straight to 'her' room which, thankfully, was empty. The maid had been in and the bed was freshly made. Quickly removing her swimsuit, she went to have a shower.

'Andreas,' Athena purred seductively as she saw him coming out of his grandfather's office.

'Not now, Athena.' Andreas cut her short. He had spent the best part of the last couple of hours trying to come to terms with feelings he had never expected to have, never mind *wanted* to have, and now that he had come to a decision he was anxious to act on it without any delay, especially from Athena.

It was no use trying to hide the truth from himself any longer.

He had fallen in love with Saskia. How? Why? When? To his exasperation no amount of analytical self-probing on his part had been able to produce any kind of logical answers to such questions. All his heart, his body, his emotions, his very soul kept insisting over and over again was they wanted her; loved her; craved and needed her. If the logical-thinking part of him that was already fighting a desperate rearguard action should dare to argue, then his emotions would see to it that his life was no longer worth living.

But look at what she *is* he had tried to remind himself. But his emotions had refused to listen. He loved her as she was, past errors of judgement and all. Errors of *judgement*? Picking up men in bars...coming as near as dammit to selling herself to them—if not for money then certainly for the pseudo-love they had offered her.

It wasn't her fault, his heart had protested in loving defence. She had been deprived of her father's love as a child. She was simply trying to compensate for that. With love, *his* love, she could be made whole again. She would forget her past and so would he. What mattered was the here and now and the future they would share…a future which meant nothing to him without her in it.

And so it had continued, on and on, when he was supposed to be working. In the end he had had no option other than to give in, and now he was on his way to find Saskia to tell her…ask her…to beg her if necessary.

'Is Saskia still outside?' he asked Athena, impatient to tell Saskia how he felt.

Athena's eyes narrowed. She knew that look in a man's eyes, and to see it now, in the eyes of the only man she wanted, was not to be tolerated. If Saskia couldn't be induced to leave Andreas then *he* must reject her, and Athena knew exactly how to make *that* happen.

'Oh…' Immediately she faked a look of concern, 'Didn't you know? She's gone for a walk…with Ari. I know you won't like me saying this, Andreas, but—well, we all know how much Ari likes women, and Saskia *has* been making it rather obvious that she reciprocates… Not whilst you're around, of course…'

'Andreas—' Pia tried to stop him several minutes later but he refused to stop or listen.

'Not now Pia, whatever it is…' he said brusquely, before striding down the corridor towards his suite.

Goodness, but he looked angry, Pia reflected as she watched his departing back. Well, what she had to tell him wasn't going to lighten his bad mood, but he would have to be told. She knew that.

Andreas could hear the sound of the shower running as he walked into the bedroom and slammed the door behind him.

'Saskia?' he demanded, striding towards the bath-room and pulling open the door.

Saskia blanched as she saw him. She had just that second stepped out of the shower and wrapped a towel around her damp body—thank goodness.

'Why are you having a shower?' Andreas de-manded suspiciously.

Saskia stared at him nonplussed.

'I've just been for a walk and it was hot and...'

Andreas could feel the shock of his jealously jolt right through his body, exploding inside him, almost a physical pain. It furnished him with some very vivid and very sexual images of just why Saskia might want to cool down. Like any man in love, he couldn't bear the thought of his beloved in the arms of someone else, and he reacted predictably.

Taking hold of her, his fingers gripping painfully into the delicate flesh of her upper arms, he gritted jealously, 'You just couldn't wait, could you? Where did he take you?'

'He...?' Saskia started to protest, confused by both his words and his actions. 'What on earth...?'

But Andreas wasn't listening.

'Was it out in the open, where anyone could have seen you? Is *that* what you like, Saskia...demeaning yourself so completely that...? But of course you do. I already know that, don't I? You *want* to be treated badly, to be used and then discarded like a... Well, then, if that's the way you like it then let's see if *I* can come up to your expectations, shall we? If I can give you what you so obviously want.'

He was a man no longer in control of what he was doing, wanting passionately to stamp his possession on her—body and soul—to make her his and wipe from her memory all thoughts of any other man!

What on earth had happened to turn Andreas from the cool, remote man she was familiar with into the raw explosion of male fury and passion she was facing now? Saskia wondered in bemusement. It was passion she could sense most strongly, she recognised dizzily. It emanated from him like a heat haze, drawing her into its danger and excitement, melting, burning away her own protective caution.

Wasn't this secretly what a part of her had *wanted* to happen? For him to look at her as he was doing now, with the fierce, elemental need of a man no longer able to fight off his own desire.

Somehow, seeing Andreas so close to losing control allowed her to give full reign to her own feelings and longings.

'You're mine,' Andreas was telling her rawly as he pulled her hard against his body. 'Mine, Saskia… And what is mine I mean to have full measure of,' he added thickly.

Saskia could feel her skin starting to quiver responsively where he was touching it. He slid his hands oh, so deliberately up her bare arm and over her shoulder, his fingertips caressing the nape of her neck. Blissfully she arched her spine, offering herself up to his touch, feeling the quiver-raising goosebumps on her skin moving deeper, growing stronger, as they became a pulse that echoed and then drove her heartbeat.

'Kiss me, Andreas…'

Had she actually said that? Demanded it in that

unfamiliar husky little voice that sounded so sexy and made Andreas's eyes glitter even more hotly?

'Oh, I can promise you that I'm going to do far more than just kiss you,' Andreas assured her as his hands very deliberately removed the towel from her body. 'Far, far more,' he repeated sensually, before adding, 'But if a kiss is what you want…'

His hands were spread against her collarbone and her throat, his thumbs massaging her fragile bones, his lips brushing just the merest tantalising breath of heat against the pulse that raced so frantically beneath her skin.

'Where exactly is it you want me to kiss you, Saskia?' he was asking her. 'Here…? Here…? Here..?'

As his mouth moved tantalisingly over her throat and then her jaw, covering every inch of her face but her lips, Saskia heard herself start to moan softly with longing until, unable to endure any more of his delicious torment, she put her hand against his face and turned his mouth to hers, exhaling in a soft swoon of relief as she finally tasted the hard warmth she had been aching for.

'Andreas… Andreas…' She could hear herself whispering his name as she slid her fingers into his hair and clasped his head, probing the hard outline of his lips with small, frantic thrusts of her tonguetip.

Over her shoulder Andreas caught sight of their entwined reflections in the mirror. Saskia's naked back view was as perfectly sculpted as that of any classical statue, but her body was composed of living, breathing flesh, and just the feel of her sweetly

firm breasts pressing against him, never mind what
the dedicated assault of her honey tongue was doing
to him, totally obliterated everything but the way he
felt about her.

Against the delicate pallor of her Celtic skin his
hands looked shockingly male and dark as he caressed her, held her, moulded her so close to his body
that he could taste her small gasp of sensual pleasure
as she felt his arousal. His clothes were a hindrance
he no longer wanted, but he couldn't make the time
to remove them until he had punished that sexily
tormenting tongue of hers for the way it was destroying his self-control.

He felt the deep, racking shudder of pleasure that
ran right through her body as he opened his mouth
on hers, taking into his domain full control of their
kiss and of her.

Saskia gasped and trembled, yielding the sweet intimacy of her mouth and the soft-fleshed nakedness
of her body to Andreas's dominance. What was happening between them was surely the pinnacle of her
whole life, the reason she had been born. Here, in
Andreas's arms, love and desire were coming together for her in the most perfect way possible.

Saskia had forgotten what she had been going to
tell him, why it was so imperative for her to leave.
This was what she had wanted to happen from the
very first second she had set eyes on him.

Unable to bring himself to break the intoxicating
sensuality of their shared kiss, Andreas picked Saskia
up and carried her over to the bed. Whatever she had
been before no longer mattered. From now on she
would be his.

The heavy natural linen curtains Saskia had closed over the large windows before taking her shower diffused the strong sunlight outside, bathing the room in a softly muted glow that turned her fair skin almost ethereally translucent. As he laid her on the bed Andreas gave in to the temptation to caress the taut quivering peak of one breast with his lips, savouring it in a slow, careful exploration which made Saskia's whole body shake with sharply intense arousal.

'No, I don't want to rush this,' Andreas denied to her, his voice thick, almost cracking over the words as he refused the frantic pleas of her writhing body. 'I want to take my time and savour everything!' he emphasised as his hand caressed the breast he had just been suckling, his thumb tip etching unbearably erotic circles around the sensitively receptive nub of flesh.

'I want you so much,' Saskia whispered achingly. 'I want you…' She stopped, her eyes clouding with a mixture of anxiety and uncertainty as she heard her own voice and briefly recognised her own danger.

It was too late. Andreas had heard her. Pausing in the act of removing his clothes, he leaned over her, bracing himself so that the muscles in his arms corded tautly, capturing her awed gaze whilst he asked her rawly, 'Where do you want me, Saskia? Tell me… Show me…'

But he already knew the answer to his question because he had already lifted his hand from the bed and brushed his knuckles in the gentlest of touches the full length of the centre of her body, letting it come to rest palm-down against the soft swelling of her most intimate heart.

'You haven't answered my question, Saskia,' he reminded her softly, as his fingertips drew delicate circles of pleasure against her, so jaw-clenching desirable that Saskia thought she might actually faint from the heat and intensity of the longing they were arousing.

'Tell me...tell me what you want,' Andreas was insisting, spacing each word between kisses so ravishingly tender that Saskia felt as though she was melting.

In the cocoon of her own private world he had become for Saskia the lodestone that drew her, the focus of everything she was experiencing, of everything she was and ever wanted to be, the centre of her world.

'I want you,' she responded feverishly to him. 'I want you, Andreas. I...' She shuddered, unable to say any more because Andreas was kissing her, sealing her mouth with a kiss that was a hot, passionate brand of possession. As he wrapped his arms around her Saskia clung to him shyly, stroking the side of his face.

'Look at me,' he demanded.

Hesitatingly she did so, the melting, soft, languorous longing of her gaze entrapped by the hot, fierce glitter of his.

Very slowly and tenderly he began to caress her. Saskia felt as though her whole body was going to dissolve with her longing for him, her need of him.

She reached out to touch his bare shoulder, his arm, and made a helpless little sound of taut female need against his throat as she pressed her lips to it.

Beneath his hands her body softened and responded magically, welcomingly, as though his touch was a special key. But *he* was the key to what she was feeling, Saskia acknowledged hazily, lost fathoms—oceans—deep in her love for him.

'There isn't going to be much time...I want you too much,' he told her almost bluntly, softening the words with another hotly passionate kiss that made her hips lift achingly against him whilst her whole body writhed in longing for him.

'Next time we can take things more slowly,' Andreas gasped harshly against her breast, his voice and actions revealing his increasing need.

Next time... Saskia felt as though she might die from happiness. 'Next time' meant that he shared her feelings, that he felt the same way as she did.

It seemed to Saskia almost as though the air between them throbbed with the intensity of their shared passion, with the way their bodies synchronised together with a perfection surely only given to true lovers.

Each sigh, each gasp, each heartbeat served only to bind her closer to him, emotionally as well as physically, until she was captive to him and her desire, her love, was laid as bare to him as her quivering body.

When he finally whispered to her, 'Now, Saskia... Oh, God, now!' she knew her body had given him its most eager assent before her lips could even begin to frame the words she wanted to say. Automatically she was already wrapping the slim length of her legs around his waist, raising up to meet him, to feel him. She heard him cry out as he entered her, a sound of both torment and triumph, and then he was filling her with his own unique intimate, heavy warmth, and her body, pausing only to tense briefly in sweetly virginal shock, welcomed each ever deepening thrust of him within her.

Andreas felt her body's unexpected resistance, his brain and his emotions even registered their shock at what it meant, but his body refused to react to that knowledge. It loved the hot snug fit of her around him, holding and caressing him, urging him to forget what he had just experienced and to satisfy the age-old demand her femaleness was making on his maleness. Deeper, harder, stronger, until you reach the deepest heart of me, each delicately soft contraction of her flesh around his urged him. Deeper, stronger, surer, until you are *there*. Yes, there…*there*…

Andreas felt as though his heart and lungs might burst as he drove them both to the place where they could finally fly free.

Saskia cried out in softly sweet awe and relish as she experienced for herself what true completion was…what it truly meant to be a woman, completely fulfilled, elevated to a place, a state…an emotion so piercingly intense that it filled her eyes with hot, happy exhausted tears.

Someone was trembling… Was it her…or was it both of them? She had heard Andreas groan in those final unbelievable seconds before he had wrapped his arms securely around her and then sent them both hurtling into infinity, calling out her name in a way that had made her tingle with raw emotion.

As he fought to regain control of his breathing, and himself, Andreas looked down at Saskia.

She was crying, huge silent tears. Of pain? Because of *him*...because he had...?

Even now his thoughts skidded away from the reality, the truth that his brain was trying to impose on him. She couldn't have been a virgin... It was impossible.

But his self-anger and guilt told him that it wasn't, and she had been. Unforgivably, he had hurt her and made her cry, selfishly taking his pleasure from her at the price of her innocence, so unable to control what he felt for her that he had not been able to stop when he knew that he should have done.

Sickened by his own behaviour, he pulled away from her.

'Andreas...' Saskia reached out towards him uncertainly. Why was he withdrawing from her? Why wasn't he holding her, caressing her...*loving* and reassuring her?

'What is it...what is wrong?' she begged him.

'Do you really need to ask?' Andreas responded tersely. 'Why didn't you tell me...*stop* me...?'

The anger in his voice was driving away the sweet mist of her joy and replacing it with anxiety and despair. It was obvious to her now that what had been so wonderful, so perfect, so *unique* for her had been nowhere near the same kind of experience for Andreas.

Andreas was furious with himself for not somehow having had the insight to know. She had been a virgin, and he, damn him, had practically forced himself on her... He was disgusted with himself, his pride scorched not just by his actions but his complete misreading of her.

'You *should* have stopped me,' he repeated as he got off the bed and went into the bathroom, returning with a towel wrapped around his naked body and his robe, which he handed to Saskia, and sitting down on the bed, turning away from her as she tried to put it on.

What would he say if she were to tell him that the last thing she had wanted was for him to stop? Saskia wondered wretchedly. Her hands were shaking so much she could hardly pull the robe on, never mind fasten it, and when Andreas turned to look at her he gave an impatient, irritated sigh and pushed her hands out of the way, pulling it on properly for her.

'You aren't safe to be let out alone. You realise that, don't you?' he exploded savagely. 'Even if *I* hadn't, Aristotle—'

'Aristotle!' Saskia picked his name up with loathing in her voice and in her eyes. She shuddered, and told him fiercely, 'No—never... He's loathsome and...'

'But you went for a walk with him...'

'No, I didn't,' Saskia protested.

'Athena said you'd gone for a walk,' Andreas insisted, but Saskia wouldn't let him finish.

'Yes, I did...on my own. There were things I wanted...' She stopped, lowering her head and looking away from him. Then she told him in a tear-filled voice, 'I want to go home, Andreas. I can't...'

He knew what she was saying; of course he did, Andreas acknowledged—and why! Of *course* she wanted to get away from him after what he had done...the way he had...

'You should have told me.' He stopped her sharply. 'If I'd known that you were a virgin...'

He might be concerned about taking her virginity but he obviously had no compunction at all about breaking her heart, Saskia decided angrily. For her the loss of her emotional virginity was something that hurt far more—and would continue to hurt.

How could she have been stupid enough to think he felt the same way about her as she did about him? She must have been crazy...*had* been crazy, she recognised grimly. Crazy with love for him!

'I thought...' she heard him saying, but now it was her turn not to allow him to finish.

'I know what you thought,' she cut in with sharp asperity. 'You've already made it very plain *what* you thought of me, Andreas. You thought I was some cheap, silly woman throwing herself at you because of your money. And when I tried to explain you wouldn't let me. You *wanted* to believe the worst of me. I suppose that Greek male pride of yours wouldn't allow you to acknowledge that you might just possibly be wrong...'

Andreas looked at her. His jealousy had led to this...had led to his unforgivably appalling treatment of her. He ached to be able to take her in his arms, to kiss away the traces of tears still on her face, to hold her and whisper to her how much he loved her, how much he wanted to protect her and care for her...how much he wished he could wipe away the wrong he had done her, the pain he had caused her... He ached too, if he was honest, to lie her down on the bed beside him, to remove the robe she was wearing and to kiss every silky inch of her adorable body, to tell her how he felt about her, to show her too. But of course he could do no such thing...not now...

To keep his mind off what he was feeling...off the way he wanted her, he told her gruffly, 'Explain to me now.'

For a moment Saskia was tempted to refuse, but what was the point? She *would* tell him, and then she would tell him that she intended to leave—but she certainly wouldn't tell him why.

Just for an irrational silly female heartbeat of time she ached for him to reach for her, to stop hurting her with words she did not want to hear and to caress and kiss her until her poor deluded heart believed once again that he loved her as she did him.

But thankfully she had enough instinct for self-preservation left to stop herself from telling him so. Instead she began to explain about Megan and Mark and Lorraine.

'She made you do *what*?' Andreas demanded angrily.

She was hesitantly explaining about Lorraine, and her insistence that Saskia make herself look more sexy, when, after a brief rap on the door, Pia burst in and told them, 'Grandfather has arrived. He wants to see both of you.'

'I'd better get dressed,' Saskia mumbled self-consciously.

Pia seemed oblivious to her embarrassment, adding urgently, 'Oh, and Andreas, there's something I want to talk to you about...before you see Grandfather.'

'If you're going to ask for an advance on your

allowance,' Saskia heard Andreas saying hardily to Pia as he walked with her to the door, allowing Saskia to make her own escape to the bathroom, 'you haven't picked a very good time.'

CHAPTER TEN

SASKIA glared reprovingly at the reflection glowing back at her from the bedroom mirror. Her own reflection. The reflection of a woman whose body had enjoyed in full measure every nuance of sensual satisfaction and was proud to proclaim that fact to the world.

That was *not* how she wanted to look when she confronted Andreas's grandfather—the man who was ultimately responsible for her being here...the man who did not think she was good enough for his grandson...the man who preferred to see him marry Athena. Neither did she want *Andreas* to see her like this.

Why on earth couldn't her idiotic body see beyond the delicious fulfilment it was currently basking in and instead think ahead to the loneliness and pain her emotions already knew were lying in store?

Andreas had returned to their room very briefly after Pia's interruption, showering and dressing quickly and then informing her that, although his grandfather was insisting that he wanted to meet her as soon as possible, there were certain matters he needed to discuss with him in private first.

'It won't take very long,' he had told her grimly, before striding out of the room without giving her a chance to tell him that right now, for her own sanity and safety, she wanted to get as far away from him as fast as she could.

Soon, now, he would be coming back for her, to take her and introduce her formally to his grandfather.

Saskia pulled an angry face at her still glowing reflection. She looked, she admitted angrily, the perfect picture of a woman in love. Even her eyes had a new sparkle, a certain glint that said she was hugging to herself a wonderful, special secret.

She had tried over and over again to tell her love-crazed body just what the real situation was, but it simply refused to listen. And so now... She gave a nervous start as she heard the bedroom door opening...

Andreas took a deep breath before reaching out for the bedroom door handle and grasping it firmly.

Pia had been so incensed, so protective and angry on Saskia's behalf, that it had taken her several minutes to become calm enough to spill out in a way that made sense the conversation she had overheard between Athena and Saskia.

'Athena actually tried to bribe Saskia to leave you. She promised her a million pounds if she did. Of course Saskia refused, but I don't see why Athena should be allowed to get away with such insulting and...and offensive behaviour. Grandfather should be told what she's really like—and if you aren't prepared to tell him...' she had threatened darkly.

'Andreas?' she had demanded when he made no response, obviously puzzled at his lack of reaction, but Andreas had still been trying to come to terms with the 'insulting' and 'offensive' behaviour *he* had already inflicted on Saskia. Now, to learn what Athena had done and how nobly Saskia had behaved made him feel… How *could* he have been so wrong about her, so judgemental and…and biased?

A tiny inner voice told him that he already knew the answer. Right from the first second he had set eyes on her there had been something—a sharp warning thrill of sensation and, even more dangerously, of emotion—which he had instantly tried to suppress. His infernal pride had resented the fact that he could fall in love with a woman who was so obvious, and because he had listened to his pride, and not his heart, he had witlessly destroyed something that could have been the most wonderful, the most *precious* part of his life. Unless… Unless Saskia could be persuaded to give him a second chance…

But, whether or not she would allow him the chance to prove his love for her, there was something that *had* to be done, a reparation that *had* to be made. He was Greek enough to think that Saskia should bear his name well before there was any chance of the world knowing that she might bear his child. She had given him her innocence and in exchange he would give her his protection, whether or not she wanted it.

He had told his grandfather exactly what he planned to do, adding truthfully that Saskia was far more important to him than wealth and position and even the love and respect of his grandfather himself.

He had even been tempted to refuse to allow his grandfather to meet her, rather than subject Saskia to any possible hurt or upset, but there was no way he wanted his grandfather to think that he was hiding Saskia from him because he feared she would not be good enough for him. Not good enough! She was *too* good, *too* wonderful…*too* precious…

His final act before heading back to the bedroom had been to tell Athena to leave the island immediately.

'Don't bother to try and persuade my grandfather to allow you to stay. He won't,' he had warned her truthfully.

Now he hesitated before going into the bedroom. He could see Saskia standing waiting for him, and his heart rocked on a huge surge of longing and love for her.

She looked as radiant as a bride, her eyes sparkling, her mouth curved in a smile that was a cross between pure joy and a certain secret, newly discovered womanliness. She looked...

She looked like a woman who had just left the arms and the bed of the man she loved.

But the moment she saw him her expression changed; her eyes became shadowed, her body tense and wary.

Helplessly Andreas closed his eyes, swamped by a wave of love and guilt. He longed more than anything right now to close the door on the rest of the world, to take her in his arms and hold her there for ever whilst he begged for her forgiveness and for the opportunity to spend the rest of his life showing her how much he loved her.

But he had his responsibilities, and primarily, right now, he had to fulfil the promise he had just made to his grandfather that he would introduce Saskia to him.

For his grandfather's sake he trusted that the older man would remember the promise *he* had made that he would treat Saskia gently.

As Andreas crossed the room and took hold of her

hand Saskia shrank back from him, terrified of betraying her feelings, knowing that she was trembling from head to foot simply because of the warmth of his hand clasping hers.

She knew that he was bound to make some irritated, impatient comment about the role she was supposed to be playing, but instead he simply released her hand and told her in a low voice, 'I'm sorry to have put you through this my...Saskia...'

'It's what you brought me here for,' Saskia reminded him brutally, not daring to look at him. Surely she must be imagining that raw note of remorse in his voice.

As they left the room the pretty little maid who looked after it came in, and Andreas paused to say something to her in Greek before following Saskia into the corridor.

It was only natural in the circumstances, Saskia knew, that Andreas should take hold of her hand again and close the distance between them, so that when they walked into the cool, simply furnished room that gave out onto the main patio area they did so with every outward appearance of a couple deeply in love. But what was surely less natural, and almost certainly unwise, was the sense of warmth and security that she got from being so close to him.

To try and distract herself from the effect Andreas's proximity was having on her, Saskia looked to where his sister and mother were standing talking to an elderly white-haired man Saskia knew must be Andreas's grandfather.

As they walked towards him he started to turn round, and Saskia could hear Andreas saying formally, 'Grandfather, I'd like to introduce Saskia to you.'

But Saskia had stopped listening, her attention focused instead on the familiar features of the man now facing her. He was the same man she had seen in the street in Athens, the man who had seemed so unwell and whom she had been so concerned about. He didn't look ill now though. He was smiling broadly at them both, coming forward to clasp Saskia's free hand in both of his in a grip heart-rockingly similar to that of his grandson.

'There is no need to introduce her to me, 'Reas.' He laughed. 'Your beautiful fiancée and I have already met.'

Saskia could see how much he was enjoying the shocking effect of his announcement on his family. He was obviously a man who liked to feel he was in control of things...people...who liked to challenge and surprise them. But where that trait in Andreas had angered her, in his grandfather she found it almost endearing.

'You and Saskia have already met?' Andreas was repeating, frowning heavily as he looked from his grandfather to Saskia.

'Yes. In Athens,' his grandfather confirmed before Saskia could say anything. 'She was very kind to an old man, and very concerned for him too. My driver told me that you had expressed your concern for my health to him,' he told Saskia in a broadly smiling aside. 'And I have to confess I did find that walk in the heat plus the wait I had for you to return from the Acropolis a trifle...uncomfortable. But not, I suspect, as uncomfortable as Andreas was, arriving at my office to discover that I had cancelled our meeting,' he added with a chuckle.

'You didn't really think I'd allow my only grandson to marry a woman I knew nothing about, did you?' he asked Andreas with a little swagger that made her hide a small smile. He was so very Greek, so very macho. She knew she should be annoyed, but he was so pleased with himself that she didn't have the heart to be cross.

Andreas, though, as it soon became obvious, was not so easily appeased.

'You decided to check up on Saskia—?' he thundered, giving his grandfather a hard look.

'You have definitely made a good choice, Andreas,' his grandfather interrupted him. 'She is charming…and kind. Not many young women would have taken the time to look after an old man who was a stranger to them. I had to meet her for myself, Andreas. I know you, and—'

'What you have done is an insult to her,' Andreas cut him off coldly, whilst Saskia stared at him in astonishment. Andreas defending and protecting *her*? What was this? And then, abruptly, she remembered that he was simply acting out a role…the role of a loving protective fiancé.

'And let me tell you this, Grandfather,' Andreas was continuing. 'Whether you approve of Saskia or not makes no difference to me. I *love* her, and I always will, and there are no threats, no bribes, no blandishments you can offer that could in any way change that.'

There was a brief pause before the older man nodded his head.

'Good,' he announced. 'I'm glad to hear it. A woman like Saskia deserves to be the focus of her husband's heart and life. She reminds me very much of my Elisabeth,' he added, his eyes suddenly misty. 'She had that same kindness, that same concern for others.' Suddenly he started to frown as he caught sight of Saskia's ring.

'What is *that* she is wearing?' he demanded. 'It is not fit for a Demetrios bride. I'm surprised at you, Andreas...a paltry plain solitaire. She shall have my Elisabeth's ring, and—'

'No.' The harshness in Andreas's voice made Saskia tense. Was he going to tell his grandfather that it was all a lie? Was the thought of Saskia wearing something as sacred to their family as his dead grandmother's ring too much for him to endure?

'No,' he continued. 'If Saskia wants a different ring then she shall choose one herself. For now I want her to wear the one *I* chose for her. A diamond as pure and shiningly beautiful as she is herself.'

Saskia could see Andreas's mother's and sister's jaws dropping, as was her own at such an unexpectedly tender and almost poetic declaration.

Ridiculously tears blurred her eyes as she looked down at the solitaire. It *was* beautiful. She thought so every time she put it on. But for her to treasure such a ring it would have to be given with love. It was the commitment it was given with that made it of such value to a woman in love, not its financial worth.

But Andreas's grandfather was brushing aside such irrelevancies, and demanding jovially, 'Very well, but what I want to know now is when you plan to get married. I can't live for ever, Andreas, and if I am to see your sons…'

'Grandfather…' Andreas began warningly.

Later, after a celebratory lunch and rather more vintage champagne than had perhaps been wise, Saskia made her way with solemn concentration back to her room. Andreas was with her, as befitted a loving and protective fiancé.

Outside the room Andreas touched her lightly on her arm, so that she was forced to stop and look at him.

'I'm sorry about what happened in Athens,' he told her, his brusqueness giving way to anger as he added, 'My grandfather had no right to subject you to—'

'In his shoes you would have done exactly the same thing,' Saskia interrupted him quietly, immediately leaping to his grandfather's defence. 'It's a perfectly natural reaction. I can remember still the way my grandmother reacted the first time I went out on a date.' She laughed, and then stopped as she saw that Andreas was shaking his head.

'Of course she would be protective of you,' he agreed flatly. 'But didn't my grandfather realise the danger you could have been in? What if he had mistimed his ''accidental'' meeting with you? You were alone in an unfamiliar city. He had countermanded my instructions to your driver by telling him to keep out of sight until he saw him return to his own car.'

'It was broad daylight, Andreas,' Saskia pointed out calmly. But she could see that Andreas wasn't going to be appeased. 'Well, at least your grandfather won't be trying to convince you that you should marry Athena anymore,' she offered placatingly as they walked into the bedroom. She came to an abrupt halt as she saw the new cases Andreas had bought her for their trip in the middle of the bedroom floor. 'What…?' she began unsteadily but Andreas didn't let her finish.

'I told Maria to pack for both of us. We're booked onto the first flight in the morning for Heathrow.'

'We're leaving?'

Even as she spoke Saskia knew that showing her shock was a giveaway piece of folly. Of course they were leaving. After all, there was no need for Andreas to keep her here any more. His grandfather had made it very plain during lunch that Athena would no longer be welcome beneath his roof.

'We don't have any option,' Andreas replied flatly. 'You heard my grandfather. Now that he's been given a clean bill of health he's itching to find something to occupy him. Organising our wedding and turning it into something between a lavish extravaganza worthy of a glossy magazine and a chance to gather as many of his business cronies under one roof as he can isn't going to be an opportunity he'll want to miss out on. And my mother and sister will be just as bad.' He started to scowl. 'Designer outfits, a wedding dress that could take months to make, plans to extend the villa so that it can accommodate the children my mother and my grandfather are so determined we're going to have…'

Greedily Saskia drank in every word. The mental image he was creating for her, the blissful pictures he was painting were becoming more alluring with every word he said. Mistily she allowed herself to dream about what she knew to be impossible—and then Andreas's next words sent her into shocked freefall.

'We need to get married immediately. We just don't have the time for that kind of delay. Not after... If you are already carrying my child then...'

'What are you saying?' Saskia protested, white-faced. 'You can't be serious. We *can't* get married just because...'

'Just because what?' Andreas challenged her bitterly. 'Because you were a virgin, an innocent who had never known a man before? I...I am Greek, Saskia, and there is no way I would *ever* abandon any child I had fathered. Under the circumstances there is nothing else we *can* do.'

'You're only half-Greek,' Saskia heard herself reminding him dizzily, before adding, 'And anyway I may not even be pregnant. In fact I'm sure I'm not.'

Andreas gave her a dry, almost withering look.

'And you're an expert on such things, of course. You, a woman who hasn't even...'

'They say you don't always...not the first time...' Saskia told him lamely, but she could see from his face that he had as little faith in that particular old wives' tale as she did herself.

'I don't want this, Andreas,' she insisted, trying another tack. Her voice and her body had both begun to shake with shock at what Andreas intended.

'Even if I am to...to have a child...these days that doesn't mean... I could bring it up by myself...'

'What on?' he challenged her. 'Not the one million pounds you turned down from Athena, obviously.'

Saskia's eyes looked bewildered at the way he'd slipped the thrust up under her guard.

'A child needs more than money. Much, much more,' she defended herself quickly. How did he know about Athena's offer to her? Athena herself wouldn't have told him. 'A child needs love,' she continued.

'Do you think *I* don't know that?' Andreas shot back. 'After all, surely I am far better placed to know it than you, Saskia. I had the love of both my parents as a child, and I can promise you I would *never* allow a child of mine to grow up without my love.'

He stopped abruptly as he heard the quick indrawn gasp of pain she had given, his eyes darkening with remorse.

'Saskia, my beloved heart, I am so sorry. I didn't mean to hurt you, just to make you understand that I could no more walk away from our child than I can from you.'

Saskia stared at him, unable to speak, to move, to breathe as she listened to the raw fervency of his declaration. He was acting. He had to be. He *didn't* love her. She *knew* that. And somehow hearing him say to her the words she so much ached to hear whilst knowing they were lies filled her with more anguish than she could bear.

Tugging frantically at the ring he had given her, she started to pull it off, her eyes dark with anger, sparkling with tears of pride and pain whilst Andreas watched her as he had been watching her all through lunch, and then afterwards when the wine she had drunk had relaxed her.

'I felt so angry when Athena offered Saskia that money,' Pia had told him passionately. 'And so proud of her. She loves you so much. I used to think that no one could ever be good enough for you, my wonderful brother, but now I know I was wrong. She loves you every bit as much as you deserve to be loved, as I one day want to love the man I marry…'

'She is perfect for you, darling,' his mother had whispered to him.

'She is a beautiful young woman with an even more beautiful heart,' his grandfather had said emotionally.

There had been one unguarded moment after lunch, when his grandfather had been teasing her about something and she had turned to him, as though seeking his protection. The look in her eyes had made him ache to snatch her up and carry her away somewhere he could have her all to himself and create that look over and over again.

Finally she managed to pull the ring off, holding it out to him she told him, head held high, 'There is no way I would ever marry a man who does not love me.'

Andreas closed his eyes, replayed the words to make sure he hadn't misheard them, and then opened his eyes again and walked purposefully towards her. He was about to take the biggest gamble he had ever taken in his entire life. If he lost he would lose everything. If he won...

He took a deep breath and asked Saskia softly, 'Shouldn't that be you wouldn't ever marry a man you did not love?'

Saskia froze, her face going white and then a soft, deepening shade of pink.

'I...that was what I meant,' she began, and then stopped as panic overwhelmed her. 'I can't marry you, Andreas,' she protested as he closed the distance between them, masterfully sweeping her up into his arms.

'And I won't let you go, Saskia,' he told her in a low, throbbing voice.

'Because of what happened...because there might
be a baby?' she guessed, but the words had to be
mumbled because Andreas was holding her so
tightly, his lips brushing irresistibly tender kisses
against her throat and then her jaw, moving closer
and closer to her mouth.

'Because of that,' he agreed, whispering the words
against her lips. 'And this...and you...'

'Me?' Saskia started to squeak, but Andreas
wouldn't let her.

Cupping her face instead, he looked down into her
eyes, his own grave with pain, heavy with remorse,
hot with love and desire, as he begged her, 'Please
give me a chance to show you how things could be
between us, Saskia. To show you how good it could
be, how good it *will* be...'

'What are you trying to say?' Saskia demanded
dizzily.

Still cupping her face, Andreas told her, 'I'm trying to say with words what my emotions, my heart,
my soul and my body have already told you, my
beloved heart, my adored, precious love. Surely you
must have guessed, felt how it was for me when we
made love?'

Lifting her head so that she could look into his
eyes, search them to see if she actually dared believe
what she was hearing, Saskia felt her heart starting
to thud in a heady mixture of joy and excitement.
No man could possibly fake the way Andreas was
looking at her, and if that wasn't enough his body
was giving her a very distinct and intimate message
of its own. Unable to help herself Saskia started to
blush a little as she felt her own body respond to
Andreas's arousal.

'I...I thought that must just be sex,' she told him bravely.

'What have I said?' she demanded in bewilderment when Andreas started to laugh.

'My dearest love,' he told her, still laughing, 'if I hadn't already had incontrovertible proof of your innocence, that remark would have furnished me with it. *Any* woman who had experienced "just sex" would have known immediately that—' He stopped and smiled down at her, tenderly kissing her before telling her gruffly.

'No. Why should I bother to explain? After all, there's never going to be any way that you will know what it is to have "just sex". You and I, Saskia, will be making love, sharing love, giving one another love for all our lives.'

'Oh, Andreas,' Saskia whispered deliriously as he pulled her firmly into his arms.

'No, Andreas, we can't,' she protested five minutes later as he carried her towards the bed and started to undress her.

'All my clean clothes are packed...I won't have anything to wear...and...'

'Good,' Andreas informed her without the remotest hint of remorse. 'I can't think of anything I want more right now than to have you naked in my bed with no means of escape.'

'Mmm... That's funny,' Saskia told him impishly. 'I was thinking exactly the same thing myself!'

EPILOGUE

'WELL, your grandfather may not have got his own way over our wedding, but he certainly wasn't going to allow us to have a quiet family christening!' Saskia laughed with Andreas as they both surveyed the huge crowd of people filling the recently completed and refurbished 'special occasions' suite at the group's flagship British hotel.

'Mmm... Are you sure that Robert will be okay with him?' Andreas asked anxiously as he focused with fatherly concern on the other side of the room, where his grandfather was proudly showing off his three-month-old great-grandson to his friends and business cronies.

'Well, as your grandfather keeps on reminding us, he's held far more babies than you or I in his time,' Saskia said, laughing.

'Maybe, but none of them has been *our* son,' Andreas returned promptly, adding, 'I think I'd better go and retrieve him, Sas. He looks as though he might be starting to get fretful, and he never finished that last feed...'

'Talk about doting fathers,' Pia murmured to Saskia as they both watched Andreas hurrying proprietorially towards his son. 'I always knew that Andreas would be a good father, mind you...'

Saskia smiled at her as she watched her husband expertly holding their son—born nine months and one day exactly after their quiet wedding, tactfully arriving three weeks after his predicted birth date. But of course only she and Andreas knew *that*...just as only they knew as yet that by the time he reached his first birthday he would have a brother or a sister.

'Isn't that a bit too soon?' Andreas had protested when she had first told him her suspicions, and Saskia had blushed and then laughed, remembering, as she was sure Andreas was as well, that *she* had been the one to initiate their first lovemaking after Robert's birth.

Andreas was the most wonderful father, and an even more wonderful husband and lover. Saskia gave a small sigh, a look darkening her eyes that Andreas immediately recognised.

If his mother was surprised to be suddenly handed her grandson whilst Andreas insisted that there was something he needed to discuss with his wife in private, she gave no sign of it, going instead to join Saskia's grandmother, with whom she had already formed a close bond.

'Andreas! No, we *can't*,' Saskia protested as Andreas led her to the most luxurious of the hotel's refurbished bedrooms and locked the door.

'Why not?' he teased her. 'We own the hotel and we are married—and right now I want you so much.'

'Mmm... Andreas...' Saskia sighed as his lips found the exquisitely tender cord in her throat that always and unfailingly responded to the sweet torment of his lips.

'Mmm... Andreas...what?' he mouthed against her skin.

But Saskia didn't make any verbal response, instead pulling his head down towards her own, her mouth opening sweetly beneath his.

'I knew the first moment I set eyes on you that you were a wanton woman.' Andreas laughed tenderly. '*My* wanton woman...'

Marco's Convenient Wife

PENNY JORDAN

PROLOGUE

'GOOD luck with your interview. You're bound to get the job, though—no one could find a better nanny than you, Alice. Your only fault is that you love children too much!'

As she returned her elder sister's warm hug Alice tried to smile. Even though it was over a month since she had left her previous job she still missed her two young charges. She did not, however, miss their father, who had made her last few months in the employ of his wife so uncomfortable, with his sexual come-ons towards her.

Even without his unwanted attentions, Alice knew she would not have accepted his wife's invitation to work for them in New York, where she had been relocated.

Her former employer was in many ways typical of some career women, who whilst needing to employ a nanny to look after their children, often resented and even deliberately undermined their nanny's role within the household.

But that was the price one paid for the job she had chosen to do, and now she was about to fly to Florence to be interviewed for a new post, that of looking after a very young baby—a motherless six-month-old baby.

'And thanks for agreeing to take Louise with you,' her sister, Connie, was saying. 'I know she's going to love Florence, especially with her artistic talents. Life hasn't been very easy for her lately, so I'm hoping that this trip will help her.'

Privately Alice felt that Louise, her sister's stepdaughter, was determined to express her own misery and insecurity by making her new stepmother, Connie, and her father feel guilty about their marriage, and that she was determined that nothing they did was going to please her and that included the gift of a four-day trip to Florence. Alice had agreed to accompany her by flying out to Italy four days ahead of her interview with the awesomely patrician-sounding Conté di Vincenti, who had advertised for an Italian-speaking English nanny for 'a six-month-old child'.

It had been that 'a six-month-old child' that had not just caught Alice's eye, but more importantly had tugged at her all too vulnerable heartstrings. It had sounded so cold and distancing, as though somehow the imperious *conte* was devoid of any kind of emotional attachment to the baby, and that had immediately aroused all Alice's considerable protective instincts.

After children, languages were her second love; she was fluent in not just Italian but French and German as well— a considerable advantage in a nanny, as her agency had approvingly told her.

The last time she had visited Florence had been when she had been eight and her elder sister fifteen and she had very happy memories of that trip, so why was she feeling so apprehensive at the thought of going back?

Because she would be accompanying and be responsible for Louise, who was currently manifesting almost all of the traits of teenagedom that made her parents despair, or because there was something about the very sound of her potential new employer that sent a cold little trickle of atavistic antipathy down her spine?

Alice didn't know, but what she did know was that over and above her own feelings were the needs of a motherless six-month-old baby.

CHAPTER ONE

FLORENCE was having a heatwave and the weather was even hotter than Alice had been prepared for. Whilst Louise slept in her hotel bed, bad-temperedly refusing to join her, Alice had taken advantage of her solitude to explore the early morning city on her own. Having just seen an elegantly dressed young mother emerging from a shop with her children, all triumphantly carrying tubs of ice cream, Alice couldn't resist the temptation of indulging in the same treat herself.

After all, according to her guidebook Florence was famous for its ice cream.

Carefully she started to make her way across the busy street, not really paying much attention to the vehicle that was blocking the road, although she was aware of a bright red and very expensive-looking sports car that was bearing down on both her and the parked vehicle. Just beyond her, the street ended in a set of lights, and as they were on red she determinedly chose to ignore the angry blare of the car's horn.

However, she was conscious of its delayed and engine throbbing presence behind her at the traffic lights as she gave and received her order for a tiramisu ice cream—her favourite Italian sweet. The young male assistant serving her made a boldly flirtatious comment as he handed her her change—bold enough to make her face flush bright pink, and loud enough, she realised as she turned away, for the man behind the wheel of the scarlet open-topped mechanical monster still waiting for both the obstruction to be moved and the lights to change, to have heard.

To have heard and to be thoroughly contemptuous of,

7

she recognised as she saw the way he looked down the length of his aquiline nose at her, his mouth curling in open disdain.

Totally mortified, Alice could feel her face burning even hotter, her enjoyment of her ice cream completely destroyed by her recognition of his contempt of her. No doubt he thought she was some silly Northern European tourist looking for a cheap holiday fling, she fumed as she gave him a look intended to be as corrosive as the one he had just given her. Unfortunately, though, she had not allowed for the effect of the extremely hot sun on her ice cream and as she turned to glower at him, in what she had planned to be a rebuffing and ladylike manner, she realised that her ice was dripping onto her top.

And that of course was the reason why her nipples should suddenly choose that totally inauspicious moment to peak openly and flauntingly with maddening wilfulness. And all the while she had to stand there waiting to cross the road, with his gaze pinned with deliberate emphasis and insulting thoroughness on the swell of her breasts.

Horrible, horrid man, she designated him under her breath, but she knew as she did so that he was also just about the most sensually magnetic and dangerous man she had ever set eyes on.

Just the merest link between her own bemused, shocked eyes and the hooded, mesmeric topaz intensity of his would have been enough to melt a full glacier, never mind her ice cream, she reflected shakily once he had driven past her.

And that was without him trying. Heaven alone knew what he could do if he really tried to turn a deliberately sensual look on a woman! Not that she was ever likely to know or want to know. Of course not! No. Never. Definitely not!

And as for that open-topped car—in this heat—well, that was obviously a deliberate pose, meant to underline his macho masculinity. She despised men like that! Men who needed to reinforce their machismo. Not that he had looked as though his needed much reinforcing—and no doubt that thick head of dark, dark brown but not quite jet-black hair would ensure that his scalp would never need protecting from strong sunlight.

'Damn the woman, where is she?' Marco looked irritably at his watch, and then frowned as he studied the empty foyer of the exclusive and expensive hotel just outside Florence, where he had arranged to meet the English-woman he was supposed to be interviewing. He was stalking imperiously up and down its imposing length with a lean and predatory male animal stride that caused the female hotel guest crossing the foyer to give a small, unstoppable little hormonal shiver of appreciation.

Oblivious of his effect on her, Marco continued to frown.

The fact that his interviewee had neither the discipline to be on time for their meeting, nor the good manners to send a message apologising for her late appearance, was not in his opinion a good advertisement for her professional skills, despite the fact that she had come so highly recommended by her agency that it had virtually sung a paean of praise in her favour.

He had not been in the best of moods even before he'd reached the city. His car, the normally totally reliable saloon he drove, had developed some kind of electrical problem, which meant that it was currently being repaired, leaving him with no alternative but to drive the ridiculous and, to his mind, totally over the top bright red Ferrari, which had belonged to his cousin Aldo, but which since Aldo's death had remained at the *palazzo*.

Unlike his Mercedes, the Ferrari was certainly the kind of car that attracted a good deal of attention—and the wrong kind of attention in Marco's opinion. His eyes narrowed slightly as he remembered the blonde girl he had noticed when he had driven into the city earlier in the day on his way to meet a colleague.

Her body had certainly approved of the car, even if her eyes had flashed him a look of murderous, 'don't you dare look at me like that' rejection, he reflected wryly.

Personally, he would far rather have a woman be attracted to him for himself than his car! Aldo, though, had not shared his feelings!

Where was this wretched girl?

To be truthful it had irked him a little that she had refused to stay in this hotel as he had wished. Instead she'd insisted on staying, albeit at her own expense, in a far less convenient, so far as he was concerned, hotel in the centre of Florence itself. This was apparently because she wished to do some sightseeing and because she had been concerned that the hotel he had chosen was too far out of the city centre and too quiet. An ominous statement, so far as Marco was concerned! As a student at university in England, he had witnessed the way in which some English girls chose to demonstrate their dislike of anything 'too quiet'!

Perhaps it was old-fashioned of him to abhor promiscuity, and to believe that a person—of either sex—should have enough self-restraint and enough self-pride not to treat sex as an emotionless act of physical gratification on a par with eating a bar of chocolate, but that was how he felt.

Irritably he shot back the cuff of his immaculately tailored pale grey suit and frowned. Angelina, the baby for whom he was seeking the services of a nanny, would be awake and wondering where he was. The traumatic loss of her mother had left the baby clinging to the only other adult who was a constant in her life, and who she seemed to feel safe with, and that was himself. Marco was not impressed with the standard of care or commitment the girl who'd originally been hired by Angelina's late mother was currently giving to the baby.

Grimly Marco reminded himself that now Angelina was his child, and that she was totally dependent on him in every single way. Right now it was Angelina who needed to come first in his thoughts and his actions. That was why he was so determined not to find merely 'a nanny' for her, but the right nanny, the best nanny—a nanny who would be prepared to commit herself, her time and to some extent her future to being with Angelina.

And this was where a battle was being fought inside him. His frown changed from that of irritated, almost antagonistic male, to one of deeply concerned protective paternalism. He felt such a strong sense of family and emotional responsibility to Angelina, that the only woman he would entrust the baby with had to be someone who could supply her with the love and security her mother's death had deprived her of, someone warm and loving, reliable and responsible.

And as the baby's mother had been British, he had decided to advertise for an Italian speaking British nanny for Angelina, so that she would grow up learning both languages.

The girl he had eventually settled on had in many ways almost seemed to be too good to be true, she had been so highly recommended and praised by her agency. But then of course they would not necessarily be dispassionate about her!

Now it seemed that he had been right to be dubious. Grimly he rechecked his watch. His autocratic features were so arrogantly and blatantly those of a sensually mature adult Italian male that it was no wonder the pretty girl behind the reception desk was watching him with awed longing.

He positively exuded power and masculinity, laced with a dangerous hint of potent sexuality. Just as the lean animal grace of the way he walked failed to cloak that maleness, so too the elegant tailoring failed to cloak the fact that the body beneath it was all raw magnificence and muscle. He possessed that kind of bred-into-the-bone sensuality that no woman could fail to recognise and respond to, be it with longing or apprehension. The kind of sensuality that went much, much deeper than the mere good looks with which nature had so generously endowed him, the kind of sensuality that neither money nor power nor position could buy!

There was, though, a touch of grim determination about the hard line of his mouth that set him apart from most other men of his race, a certain cool hauteur and distance that challenged anyone who dared to come too close to him uninvited.

At thirty-five he had behind him over a decade of heading the vast and complicated tangled network of his extended family; aunts, uncles, and cousins.

His father and mother had been killed outright when his father's younger brother had crashed the private plane he had been flying. Marco, or, to give him his correct name, Semperius Marco Francisco Conte di Vincenti, had been twenty-five at the time, and freshly qualified as an architect, aware of the responsibility of the role that would ultimately be his, the guardian of his family's history and the guardian too of its future, but relieved to know that that responsibility would not truly be his for many years to come. And then his father's unexpected death had thrown him head first into shouldering what had then seemed to be an extraordinarily heavy burden.

But somehow he had carried it—because it had been his duty to do so, and if in doing so he had lost some of the spontaneity, the love of life and laughter and the ability to live for the moment alone that had so marked out his younger cousin, Aldo, like him left fatherless by the crash, then those around him had just had to accept that that had been so.

Some of the older members of the family considered that he had allowed Aldo to take advantage of him, he knew. But like him his cousin had lost his father in the tragedy, and, at only sixteen, it surely must have been a far harder burden for him to bear than it had been for Marco himself.

Marco's frown deepened as he thought about his younger cousin. He had been totally opposed to Aldo marrying Patti, the pretty English model. The wedding had taken place within weeks of Aldo meeting her, and it had not surprised him in the least to learn that they had fallen out of love with one another as quickly as they had fallen into it.

But there was no point in dwelling on that now. Aldo had married Patti, and baby Angelina had been conceived, even if both her parents had by that time been claiming that their marriage had been a mistake and that they bitterly regretted the legal commitment they had made to one another.

It had been in his role of head of the family that Marco had felt obliged to invite them both to visit them at his home in Tuscany, in the hope that he could somehow help them to find a way of making their marriage work. After all, whilst he might not have approved of it in the first place, they now had a child to consider, and in Marco's eyes the needs of their child far outweighed the selfish carnal desires of either of her parents.

But, once he had left them to their own devices, an argument had broken out between Aldo and Patti, which had resulted in Aldo driving Patti away from the villa in a furious temper.

They would probably never know just what had caused the fatal accident, which had claimed their lives and left their baby an orphan, Marco reflected sombrely, but he knew just how responsible he felt for having been the one to have brought them both to the *palazzo* in the first place.

As Aldo's next of kin he had naturally taken on full responsibility for the orphaned baby, and now three months later it was abundantly obvious that little Angelina had bonded strongly with Marco. Marco's strong paternalistic instincts had meant that he had decided that it was both his duty and in the baby's own interests for him to make proper arrangements for her care.

In order to cut down on wasting time unnecessarily on interviews that would not lead anywhere, he had painstakingly spent far more time than he could currently afford sifting through the applications he had received, to make sure that he only interviewed the candidate or candidates who met all his strict criteria, and in the end Alice Walsingham had been the only one to do so; which made it even more infuriating that she had not even taken the trouble to turn up for their interview. It was eleven o'clock, half an hour past the time of their appointment. His patience finally snapped. That was it! He had waited long enough. If Miss Walsingham did ever decide to turn up, she was most definitely not the person he wanted to leave in sole charge of his precious child. Not even to himself was Marco prepared to admit just how attached he had become to his cousin's baby, or how paternal he felt towards her.

As he stepped out of the hotel into the bright Florentine sunshine it glinted on the darkness of his thick, well-groomed hair, highlighting his chiselled, autocratic features, and the lean-muscled strength of his six-foot-two frame.

Automatically he shielded the fierceness of his topaz gaze from the harshness of the sun by putting on dark glasses that gave him a breath-catching air of predatory power and danger.

An actor studying for a role as a Mafiosi leader would have found him an ideal model. He looked lean, mean and dangerous. No one would dream of making a man who looked as he did any kind of offer he might be tempted to refuse!

Irritably he returned to where he had left Aldo's Ferrari, which was parked outside the hotel, and he had just climbed into it and put the keys in the ignition when he suddenly remembered that he had not left any message for his dilatory interviewee, just in case she should choose to turn up!

Leaving the keys in the ignition, he climbed out of the Ferrari and strode toward the hotel.

'Oh, for God's sake, will you stop nagging me? You aren't my mother, you aren't anything to me. Just because your sister has managed to trap my father into marriage that doesn't give you the right to tell me what to do.'

As she listened to Louise's deliberately hostile and inflammatory speech Alice mentally counted to ten.

It was now five minutes past eleven, and she was over half an hour late for her interview appointment, but it had been impossible for her to leave Louise to her own devices after the teenager's totally unacceptable behaviour during their trip.

The previous night, Louise had sneaked out of the hotel without her, returning in the early hours very much the worse for drink, refusing to tell Alice where she had been or who with. Alice had been beside herself with anxiety.

As luck would have it, Alice had now learned that her sister's stepdaughter had spent the evening with a group of young American students who were studying in the city, and who it seemed had thankfully kept a watchful eye on her whilst she had been with them.

However, as one of the students had a little anxiously explained to Alice, Louise had spent a large part of the evening in conversation with a rather unsavoury character who had attached himself to the group and now it seemed Louise had made arrangements to meet up with the man.

In order to ensure that she did not do so, Alice had insisted that Louise accompany her to her interview.

Forced to do so, Louise had left Alice in no doubt about her feelings of resentment and hostility, as well as deliberately making Alice late for her appointment, but now, thank goodness, they had finally reached the hotel. She paid off their taxi driver, primly ignoring the appreciative look he was giving them both—two slender, blonde English beauties. One of whom, with her face plastered with far too much make-up, looked far older than her seventeen years and the other, whose clear, soft skin was virtually free of any trace of cosmetics at all, her hair a natural, soft pale blonde unlike her charge's rebelliously dyed and streaked tousled mane, looked far, far younger than her much more mature twenty-six.

Although she herself was unaware of it, even the simple skirt and top outfit she had chosen to wear for the heat of the Florentine sunshine made Alice look young enough to be a teenager herself, whilst Louise's tight jeans and midriff-baring top were drawing the interested gaze of every red-blooded Italian male who saw them.

Sulkily Louise affected not to hear what Alice was saying as she urged her to hurry into the hotel.

Under other circumstances Alice knew that she would have enjoyed simply standing to gaze in admiration at her surroundings. According to her guidebook, this particular hotel, once the home of a Renaissance prince, had been converted into a hotel with such sensitivity and skill by the architect in charge of its conversion that to stay in it was a privilege all in itself.

Unable to resist pausing simply to fill her senses with its symmetry and beauty, Alice was only aware that Louise's attention was otherwise engaged when she heard her charge exclaiming excitedly.

'Wow, just look at that car! What I'd give to be able to drive something like that.'

Turning her head, Alice was startled to see parked there in front of them an open-topped scarlet sports car like the one she had seen earlier that morning. Like, or the same? Driven by that same darkly, dangerously, and wholly male man who had looked at her as though…as though… Dragging her thoughts away from such risky and uncomfortably self-illuminating channels, Alice realised with shock that Louise was darting across towards the driver's door of the car.

'Louise,' she cautioned her anxiously. 'Don't...'

But it was too late. Totally ignoring her objections, Louise was sliding into the driver's seat, telling her triumphantly, 'The keys are in it. I've always wanted to drive a car like this...'

To Alice's horror Louise was pulling open the obviously unlocked driver's door and sliding into the driving seat. Totally appalled, Alice protested in disbelief, 'Louise, no!' unable to accept that Louise could behave so irresponsibly. 'You mustn't! You can't...'

'Who says I can't?' Louise was challenging her as she turned the key in the ignition and Alice heard the engine roar into life.

She could see a look in Louise's eyes that was completely unmistakable and her heart missed a beat. Her sister had warned her that Louise could be headstrong, and that the trauma of the break-up of her parents' marriage had affected her badly, as had the fact that her mother's new husband had made no secret that he did not want an obstreperous teenage stepdaughter on the scene to cause him problems.

Even so!

'Louise, no,' Alice protested, pleadingly, instinctively hurrying round to the passenger door of the car and wrenching it open, not really knowing what she could do, just knowing that somehow she had to stop her charge from what she was doing. But before she could do anything Louise had put the car in gear and it was starting to move, the movement jolting Alice forward.

Somehow she found that she was in the passenger seat of the car, frantically wrestling to close the door as the car set off lurchingly toward the hotel's exit.

Her heart in her mouth, Alice pleaded with Louise to stop the car, but everything she said only seemed to goad the younger girl on. Alice could hear the gears crashing as

Louise manoeuvred the car clumsily onto the road. She had only just passed her driving test, and so far had only been allowed to drive her father's sedate saloon car under his strict supervision. Alice, who could drive herself and who had driven considerable distances with her former young charges, knew that she would never have had the confidence or the skill to drive a vehicle such as this.

She gasped in shock as Louise started to accelerate, and only just missed hitting a pair of scooters bent on overtaking them.

The road stretched ahead of them, unusually straight for an Italian road, and heavy with traffic, a wall, beyond which lay the river, on one side of it and a row of four-or-so-storey buildings and a narrow pavement full of shoppers on the other.

Alice felt sick and desperately afraid, but somehow she managed to quell her instinctive urge to wrest the steering wheel from Louise's obviously inexpert grip.

Up ahead of them she could see a car pull out to overtake; she cried out a warning to Louise but, instead of slowing down, the younger girl increased her speed.

Alice held her breath, tensing her body against the collision, which she knew to be inevitable.

CHAPTER TWO

IT WAS the unmistakable sound of Aldo's Ferrari's engine being inexpertly fired that first alerted Marco to what was going on.

Sprinting towards the main road, he reached it just in time to see the two blonde heads of the female thieves who had stolen the car, which was now being driven with teeth-clenching lack of expertise towards the Tuscan countryside.

However, it wasn't the lack of driving expertise they were displaying that brought a grim look of tension to Marco's mouth. No, what was concerning him was the fact that he feared an accident, and, having already lost a much-loved cousin as well as having had to identify both his and the destroyed body of what had originally been a very pretty young woman, he had no wish to see history repeating itself.

He was already reaching for his mobile to report the theft when he heard and saw the collision he had been dreading.

To his relief he realised immediately that the crash was not a serious one. The driver of the other car was already out of his vehicle and heading for the Ferrari, which Marco could see had barely been damaged by the impact at all.

Cancelling the call, he started to run towards the scene.

Above the sound of Louise's frantic screams, Alice could hear the sound of approaching Italian voices. Her head ached where she had banged it on the windscreen, and as she tried to blink the pain away she realised that Louise was already standing on the pavement, beside the car, whilst somehow she herself was lying across both seats, with her head now against the driver's headrest.

She knew she had to get out of the car. And she knew the easiest way to do that would be to slide her legs over to the driver's side of the car, but her thoughts would only assemble in slow and painful motion as they fought their way through the dizzying sickness of her shock.

Someone, predictably a man, was comforting Louise, who was crying hysterically, but no one, Alice noticed, was bothering to help her. Somehow, though, she managed to get herself out of the car, just as the crowd that was surrounding it parted to allow through the tall, dark-haired and even darker-browed man who was now talking with the driver of the car they'd crashed into, handing him his card.

Then as he turned to look at her she recognised him. Alice thought she was going to faint. She would have recognised that eagle-eyed, imperious topaz stare anywhere, and she could tell from the way his glance moved from her face down to her breasts that he remembered exactly who she was as well.

It was the man she had seen earlier that morning, the man who…. Her head was throbbing and instinctively Alice pressed her hand to her temple. She felt so dizzy and sick, so unable somehow to draw her own gaze away from that angry, burning hostility of pure male fury. The shock of what had happened seemed to have robbed her of her normal self-control and maturity. Feeling as though she was going to cry, she longed desperately to have someone to turn to, some sturdy, reliable, pro-Alice male presence there to support and protect her. Such unfamiliar and undermining thoughts increased her sense of alienation from her normal 'self'.

He of the angry eyes and hard, forbidding mouth was focusing on her so intently that she felt like a helpless specimen trapped beneath a microscope.

In the distance Alice could hear Louise sobbing frantically, 'It wasn't my fault. I didn't do anything. She was the one who was driving the car. Not me...'

But although she registered what Louise was saying it barely made any impact on her at all. And the reason for that was the man now standing in front of her, towering over her, all six-foot odd, furiously cold, dangerously angry and intensely male of him, addressing her in icily perfect and whiplash sharp English as he demanded, 'If you are the perpetrator of this...this atrocity, then let me tell you now I fully intend to see that you pay for it. Have you any idea what you have done? The danger...the risk... someone could have been killed.' His voice became acidly sharp and harsh. 'Have you ever seen a victim of a serious road accident? Do you have any idea what it can do to the human body?'

Fresh nausea overwhelmed Alice. He wasn't saying anything to her she hadn't already thought for herself, but Louise, who could hear him, was now silent and ashen-faced, and instinctively Alice felt her first duty was to protect her. And now that she could see both cars, she could see too that surely he was overreacting. Anxiously she looked towards his car. The passenger door was crushed, there was broken glass all over the road. The car they had hit had lost its bumper and sustained a large dent, although fortunately its driver seemed to be unhurt, and indeed he was very evidently comforting Louise, who was shaking uncontrollably, telling everyone who would listen to her that it had been Alice who had been driving the car and not her.

Alice opened her mouth to correct her and defend herself and then closed it again.

How could she? Louise was seventeen; she had only just passed her driving test. Last night she had been drinking so heavily that she probably still had a dangerously high level of alcohol in her bloodstream, and she was in Alice's charge... Alice had promised her sister that she would take care of her...

Unaware of what she was doing, she looked up at the man confronting her in helpless appeal.

Marco felt himself stiffen as he saw the look Alice was giving him. She looked more like a child than a woman, with the pale swathe of her cheeks and her huge bruised eyes and trembling mouth; her delicately slender body. But he of course already knew about the sensuality and the voluptuousness of the breasts that were now concealed by a much bulkier top than the little strappy one she had been wearing earlier in the day when he had seen her.

Disconcertingly and with unexpected force his body responded to that memory and to her. Immediately Marco quelled his swift surge of unwanted physical reaction, waiting for what he already knew she was going to say to him, the appeal she was going to make to him, on behalf of herself and her companion.

He had seen beautiful women using their beauty to get what they wanted so many many times before. And of course the first thing this beautiful woman was going to do was to tell him what he had already worked out for himself—that she had not been the one who'd been driving the car. Cynically he waited for her to say as much, and to implicate her friend whilst pleading her own innocence. It was obvious to him from the one assessing look with which he had taken in the whole of the scene in front of him that there was no way that this woman could have been the one driving his car; to anyone with even half a trained eye it was blindingly obvious that the other younger, over-made-up girl with her skimpy clothes and frightened, sullen face had been the driver. As he waited for the woman facing him to denounce her companion Marco fiercely reminded himself of all the reasons why he had been opposed to his cousin's marriage to his English model girlfriend.

Cross-cultural marriages were always, by the very necessity of their nature, bound to be more of a risk than those between people who shared the same background and upbringing. For those marriages to work both parties had to be dedicated to their love and to one another, to believe in it, to be one hundred and fifty per cent committed to it and to be mature and strong enough to make it work. That was a very tall order indeed in today's modern climate.

He himself had never been sexually promiscuous. He was too fastidious, too proud, too controlled to ever allow his appetites to control him, and it added to his already short temper to realise just how intense his physical reaction was to the woman standing in front of him.

'Are you the one who stole my car?' he demanded curtly, suddenly impatient to get the whole thing over and done with and the woman and her companion turned over to the police.

But, to his disbelief, instead of immediately denying that she was to blame and incriminating her friend, he heard her saying in a soft, shaky voice, 'Yes... Yes, I'm afraid... that...that it was me.'

As she heard herself confessing to a crime she most certainly had not committed Alice felt her heart lurch joltingly against her ribs. She still felt sick and dizzy and her heart was thumping erratically in panic. Panic because of the trouble she was going to be in, she quickly insisted to herself, and not in any way because of the effect the man standing watching her with that masklike, uninterpretable, assessing look was having on her.

Heavens, but he was formidable... Formidable and sexy... The sexiest man she had ever seen. So sexy in fact that he was making her feel...

'Yes?'

She could hear the fury in his voice as he repeated her admission. 'Yes?' he repeated as though he wanted to make sure he had heard her correctly. 'Yes, it was you?'

It was almost as though he wanted her to deny the crime, Alice thought dizzily. But why? So that he could indulge in the pleasure of berating her, accusing her of being a liar as well as a thief? Well, she wasn't going to give him that pleasure!

Bravely pushing to one side her own shock and fear, she told him firmly, 'Yes. It was I. I stole your car.'

She could hear Louise making a soft, moaning, hiccupping sound and instinctively Alice looked anxiously towards her.

The younger girl's tears had washed tracks of make-up from her face, giving her a clown-like appearance of vulnerable youthfulness, and as she saw the panic and fear in Louise's eyes Alice found her heart aching with compassion for her.

It must have given her a dreadful shock when they had crashed. No wonder she was looking so afraid. Instinctively, Alice felt protective towards her, overcoming her own feelings of shock and hostility towards the man confronting her and the feelings he was engendering within her to tell him quietly, 'I apologise for...what has happened and, of course, I will make good the damage to your car, but my...my...friend is very shocked. We are due to catch a flight home to England this afternoon, and we still have to collect our luggage from our hotel, so if there is some way in which we can expedite matters... I can give you all my details. My name is Alice Walsingham and...' She stopped as she saw the frown darkening his face as he listened to her.

'Your name is what?' he challenged her softly.

'Alice...Alice Walsingham,' Alice repeated, her voice starting to tremble a little as a feeling of foreboding rushed over her like a cold incoming tide.

Marco could hardly believe his ears. So this was the woman he had waited in vain to interview, this small scrap of female humanity with her slender body, her provocative breasts, her pale blonde hair, her far-too-pretty face, and her certainly far-too-dangerously potent effect on his hormones!

That such a thing should happen to him and with this

woman of all women! A woman who excited such interest in the street from his own sex that a member of it was unable to refrain from extolling the pleasure the sight of her body gave him. A woman who had been an accomplice to the theft of his car…a woman apparently so careless of human life that she could have been an accomplice to an accident of even more hideous and fatal proportions than the one he had already had to endure. A woman who had lied and implicated herself in a theft to protect the true thief, who Marco could now see when he looked at her properly was much younger than he had first thought. A teenager, in fact. Against the urgings of his own self-protective instincts, he found himself remembering certain incidents from his cousin Aldo's youth, certain irresponsible actions from which he, as Aldo's elder and family mentor, had been obliged to extricate the younger man.

After all, he reminded himself with reluctant fair-mindedness, he had seen the look of discomfort on Alice's face when she had heard the ice-cream seller's full-bodied compliment; and she had too looked shocked to the point of actual nausea after the accident. As for the effect she had on him!

The one thing about Alice that had caught his attention when he'd read through her application and the letters of recommendation that had accompanied it was the emotional input she put into caring for her charges. It was that degree of involvement that he wanted for Angelina! He had expected her to be an emotional woman, and one with a deeply protective instinct, but what he had not anticipated and what he most certainly did not want was her totally unexpected aura of sensuality! She wore it as lightly and easily as though she herself was totally unaware of it, which made it even more of a danger than if she had wantonly flaunted it, Marco recognised.

Grimly he turned to Louise. 'And you,' he questioned her. 'You are?'

'Louise is in my charge,' Alice answered for her, assuming a firmness and authority she was far from feeling. She had bumped her head on the impact of the crash and it was aching horridly still and making her feel very poorly, but she had Louise to protect and that had to come before her own discomfort.

'She is only young and, as you can see, very upset. Her parents are expecting her return on this afternoon's flight and…it is my duty…my responsibility to see that she is on that flight.'

'Your duty…and your responsibility,' Marco emphasised. 'Where were those undoubtedly admirable virtues, I wonder, when you stole my car, risking not only your own lives, but those of other people as well? Have you any idea what a car smash can do, what carnage, what…destruction it can cause?' Marco demanded harshly as the nightmare images of the crash scene he had been called upon to witness when Aldo had driven away from the *palazzo* in the temper that had killed both him and his wife resurfaced.

With no way of knowing what he was thinking, Alice could feel her face starting to burn.

'I… It…I couldn't help myself,' she started to fib desperately. 'I have always loved…' Helplessly she looked at the car for inspiration, unable to remember in her panic just what kind of car it actually was…

Against his will Marco found himself being both intrigued and impossibly almost even amused as he witnessed her confusion as she hunted wildly for a rational explanation to cover both her behaviour and her protective fib. Anyone with any remote pretence to being a car lover would not have had to look wildly at the bonnet to realise what make of car they'd been driving.

'Maseratis,' he supplied dryly for her, his voice drowning out Louise's frantically whispered, 'Ferrari!'

'Yes. Maseratis,' Alice agreed, gratefully seizing on the name he had given her. 'Well, I've always loved them and when I saw yours, just couldn't resist. It was so tempting.

And you had left the keys in the ignition,' she told him reprovingly.

'So in effect it was my fault that you stole the car,' Marco suggested dryly.

She had the most revealing eyes, he decided, their colour a clear blue-green that was almost turquoise.

'Have you any idea just what his car means to an Italian man?' he asked her, speaking swiftly in Italian.

Without the slightest pause, she responded in the same language, telling him simply, 'I shouldn't have done it, I know.'

So she hadn't lied about her ability to speak his language, Marco recognised, and despite all reasons he knew he should summon the police and set about finding himself another nanny for Angelina, he knew that he was going to do no such thing.

A woman who for whatever reason was prepared to implicate herself in a crime to protect a younger person in her charge must have a protective instinct that would keep any child entrusted to her care safe and loved. And, so far as Marco was concerned, what Angelina needed more than anything else was just that very kind of security, even if it came wrapped up in a tantalising package with 'danger' written all over it!

'By rights I should summon the police and hand you both over to them,' he told Alice sternly, waiting for a few seconds as the colour drained from her face and she made a small, instinctive sound of protest and distress.

'However…you say that you are both booked on an afternoon flight back to England…but you,' he told her smoothly, 'or so I thought, were supposed to be being interviewed for a post here in Italy…'

Alice gaped at him. 'How do you know that?' she began, and then stopped as the unwanted, impossible, appalling truth began to seep hideously into her shocked brain.

'No!' she whispered, her eyes huge with despair.

'No. You can't be!'

'I can't be who?' Marco challenged her grimly.

Nervously Alice flicked her tongue-tip over her suddenly nervously dry lips, a gesture which Marco's eyes monitored whilst his body registered her action in a way that made him glad of the strength of will-power! Glad that it was strong enough to prevent him from covering the softness of her full lips with his own mouth. Richly pink, free of make-up, they reminded him unwantedly of the taut thrust of her nipples against her top.

Angrily he pushed his wanton thoughts away. He had neither the time to waste on self-indulgent analysis of them, nor the inclination to do so. Some things were best left undisturbed, unexamined... Her skin would be delicately pale, her breasts crowned with rose-red nipples and when he touched them with his lips she would...

As Alice heard him curse beneath his breath she jumped nervously. The heat beating down on her uncovered head was beginning to affect her. She felt confused and muzzy, and she wanted badly to be able to lie down somewhere cool—somewhere cool that did not include this formidable, sexy, downright disturbing man, she corrected herself shakily.

'I... My interview was with... I was supposed to be seeing...' she began to protest.

'Me,' Marco supplied for her with a softness that belied the steel-hard look he was giving her. 'Only you did not keep our appointment, which makes you unreliable as well as untrustworthy—and yet according to your agency...'

'I-I'm sorry I was late,' Alice began to stammer with what she knew to be ludicrous consternation. He thought she had stolen his car, after all, and here she was apologising for being late.

'To be late is an offence against the laws of good manners, and thus punishable by one's own conscience,' he agreed urbanely. 'But theft is an offence against the laws of the land and as such it is punishable by a term in prison...'

The way he was looking at her, his eyes now almost the colour of obsidian and just as empty of any kind of humane emotion as a piece of unfeeling stone, made her blood quite literally run icily cold in her veins. Shock and then fear crept over her in a painful tide. Prison! She knew that her fear showed in her face, and only her pride stopped her from protesting out loud.

Out of the corner of her eye she could see Louise, silent now, her shock as obvious as Alice's own in her suddenly very youthful, drawn white face.

As she struggled to find something to say a mobile phone started to ring imperiously. Almost as though she were observing the whole scene at a distance, Alice saw the man she now realised must be her once-prospective employer, the aristocratically named Conte di Vincenti, reaching to his pocket and removing his phone, swiftly responding to the call.

With her excellent grasp of Italian, Alice easily translated what he was saying and a fresh surge of anxiety seized her body, not this time for herself, but on behalf of the baby, whose sudden inexplicable and frightening sickness was the cause of the telephone call.

Swiftly instructing that a doctor was to be called, Marco ended the call, his face drawn into lines of harsh anxiety.

The nursemaid Angelina's mother had hired to look after the baby was not in his opinion a suitable person to have charge of such a young child. Bored and slovenly, she had no proper training for such a job, and so far as he could see no real love for the baby, but she was, apart from himself, the only person who was truly familiar to her and for that reason, until he found a suitable replacement nanny, he had felt unable to terminate her employment and send her back to Rome where he knew she would feel much more at home than in the Tuscan countryside.

It had been left to his housekeeper to telephone him and

advise him of baby Angelina's sickness. The *palazzo* was over an hour's fast drive away, and Marco had no time now to waste on a mere car accident in which mercifully no one had been hurt.

On Alice's CV had been the fact that she had some nursing experience, having done voluntary work in a local hospital, both as teenager and later too, when her employment commitments had allowed. Had it not been for his own too stubborn wariness where Englishwomen were concerned, Marco knew that Alice's obvious dedication to others would have inclined him towards selecting her as Angelina's nanny even over more highly qualified applicants.

However, now a new complication had entered the equation. The one thing that Marco had not been prepared for when he had mentally reviewed and tabulated the pros and cons of hiring Alice was that he himself might find her desirable! His reaction to her had caught him off guard. He had believed that he was armoured against any woman who was made in the same mould as the free-living, free-loving girl students he had encountered in England. So what was he saying? he asked himself sardonically, whilst he worried about Angelina.

That he could not control his own libido? No way!

Quickly Marco came to a decision. He would normally have been averse to having his hand forced by events, but now he wasn't concerned about that. He did not *want* to examine his decision more analytically—because of his concern for Angelina, he told himself. After all, his physical reaction to Alice was something he could control; baby Angelina's sickness was not.

'What time did you say your flight left?' he demanded.

White-faced with contempt and disbelief, Alice stared at him. What kind of man...what kind of father was he to give something as minor as a small car accident precedence over the health of his baby daughter? In his shoes the last thing she would have done would be to stand here, worrying about a mere car! Instead she would have been making her way as fast as she could to her baby's side.

So much for the myth that Italian men were wonderful fathers, who adored and protected their children!

Instinctively she felt a surge of desire to protect the baby and to castigate her father for his lack of concern; to show him just how contemptuous she felt of him in every way; as a trained professional, as an innocent victim of a crime she had not committed, and most of all as a woman.

A woman who had foolishly allowed herself to react to him in a way she was determined not to repeat!

Ignoring her throbbing headache, she accused him wildly, 'That poor baby! How can you be more concerned about your wretched car than her health?' Emotional tears filled her eyes, which she proudly refused to hide. She was not ashamed to show that she had normal human feelings, no matter how contemptuously that fact made him regard her. 'I thought that Italian men were supposed to love children,' she threw at him scornfully, unable to stop herself. 'But in your case it seems that your love of your car means more to you than the health of the baby.'

Something flickered in his eyes, an expression Alice could not quite catch, almost as though in some way her outburst had pleased him, but then as she focused more closely on him his expression changed, his hooded gaze seeming to deliberately conceal his reaction.

Turning his back on her, he flicked on his mobile and started issuing instructions into it.

When he had finished he turned back to her, and told her coolly, 'You are coming with me to the *palazzo*. Your...friend will be escorted to the airport and put on her flight home...'

Alice stared at him, hardly able to credit that she had heard him correctly. He was making her stay here, in Italy, at his home. Why? Shock, panic, fear, and a sharp, breath-snatching feeling she didn't want to name, but that she was forced to acknowledge came pretty close to a form of dangerous excitement, swirled the blood to her head. Was the heat of the Italian sun somehow affecting her brain?

It must be surely; there was no other acceptable explanation for that sharp, shocking, piercingly wanton feeling burning hotly through her body.

This man possessed none of the virtues she could ever want in a man; none of them, she insisted firmly to herself.

'You can't make me stay in Italy.' she began warningly.

She had already made up her mind that she was glad that she had not had the opportunity to be interviewed by him because there was totally no way she could ever countenance working for him.

His arrogance both infuriated and antagonised her, arousing emotions within her that she was totally unfamiliar with, making her feel, giddy, dizzy, dangerously close to losing her head. It was making her feel very much like a child exposed to danger, immediately wanting to run from it back to safety. She didn't like him. Not one little bit, but what she had just learned about his attitude towards his baby had aroused within her not just a furious sense of disgust and distaste for him as a man, but also an intense surge of pity for the small baby who was so dependent on him.

All she had been told about her prospective employment had been that she would have virtually sole charge of a six-month-old baby girl whose mother had recently died, and who needed a constant and loving female presence in her life.

That alone had been enough to make her yearn to provide her potential charge with all the protection and love she could give her. Those feelings were still there, intensified if anything by the cold-hearted manner of the little Angelina's father.

'You can't force us to do anything,' she responded forcefully.

'No?' Marco overrode her grimly. 'You have two choices, Alice Walsingham. Either you come with me

now, or both you and your friend face the legal conse-
quences of your crime. And to be honest I should have
thought, having read your CV and the reports from your
agency, that the decision would have been an easy and an
automatic one for you. What was it they said about you?
That you possessed an extremely strong nurturing instinct
and a genuine love and concern for children? It seems to
me that somewhere along the line you must have deceived
them.'

Before she could speak in her own defence, Alice heard
Louise give a faint sob of terror.

'Please, Alice,' the younger girl was beseeching her.
'Please, please do what he wants. I can't bear the thought
of going to prison.'

As she listened to her Alice knew that in reality there
was no choice for her at all. Not really.

There was no point in her making the mistake of hoping
that the man in front of her was simply bluffing. She could
see that he wasn't...

A large four-wheel-drive vehicle suddenly pulled up behind the red sports car. Its driver jumped out and came
hurrying towards them.

Listening to the swift exchange of Italian between him
and her persecutor, Alice realised that the new arrival
worked for the *conte* and that the *conte* was instructing
him to take care of the sports car, and escort Louise to the
airport, whilst he, the *conte*, drove himself and Alice to
his estate.

'Your luggage will be brought to the *palazzo* from the
hotel,' he informed Alice, without bothering to ask her
what her decision was. But then of course why should he?
It must be as obvious to him as it was to her from Louise's
white shocked face that there was no way she could subject
the younger girl to the ordeal of police questioning and
potentially a spell in prison, even if for her pride's sake
she was prepared to inflict such traumas on herself.

There was barely time to do anything more than

exchange a swift hug with Louise, who was now sobbing woefully, full of contrition and guilt as she hugged Alice back with genuine appreciation and whispered, 'I'm so sorry. I never meant—'

'Shush, it's all right,' Alice whispered back to her, trying to reassure her, but still warning her gently, 'I don't think it would be a good idea to say anything about this to Connie.'

The last thing she wanted was for her sister to worry about her, especially since Connie had hinted to her that she and Steven were planning to try for a baby.

There was just time for them to exchange a final hug and then Alice was being firmly drawn away by her new employer. To an outsider she suspected that the hand he had placed around her upper arm looked as though he were merely guiding her. But she knew better. She could feel the sharp bite of those steely fingers against her flesh, she could tell too, from the closeness with which he held her to his side, that he was not in any way guiding her, but guarding her…as in imprisoning… She was his prisoner. He had total control over her, and she knew that he would not hesitate to exercise that control should he feel the need to do so.

Her whole body ached with shock. She felt slightly sick from the hot beat of the strong Florentine sunshine on her exposed head, and from what had happened. But there was no way she was going to show any sign of weakness in front of this man!

Had it not been for Louise and the plight of the baby she would certainly never have allowed him to dominate her like this. He was everything she hated in a man. Everything she despised and loathed.

Too arrogant, too sure of himself, too wrapped up in his own self-importance and too damn sexy by far. Oh, yes he was certainly that all right, she acknowledged, unable to resist the impulse to give him a quick sidelong look.

And then wishing she had not given in to such temptation as he caught her betraying glance, faultlessly returning it with a smooth, knowing response that made her face flame and her heart thud in denial of what she was feeling.

But even by turning away from him she wasn't able to escape; all she found was their reflections in the shop window. It seemed there was no way she could escape from him—nor from the shockingly intimate feelings he was making her experience.

Fiercely she tried to concentrate on realities, rather than feelings. He was much taller than her, imposingly so, his whole bearing proud and autocratic, his expression hardening the chiselled perfection of his features.

She in contrast looked small and pale, overwhelmed by him. He could have been a rapacious Roman centurion and she his captive. A long, dangerous shiver of an emotion she wasn't prepared to name shocked through her.

CHAPTER THREE

ALICE woke immediately at the first soft whimper of baby Angelina's cry despite the fact that it was almost three o'clock in the morning and she had had barely two hours' sleep.

They had arrived at the *palazzo* the previous afternoon, just as the full lazy heat of the June sunshine had been bathing the creamy walls of the huge Palladian building in hot golden light. Set as it was against a magnificent back-drop of the surrounding Tuscan countryside, the effect on Alice's finely tuned senses had almost overpowered her, affecting her as headily as too much indulgence in strong wine.

It was almost too perfect, had been her verdict as they had driven up the Lombardy-pine-guarded private road that led to the *palazzo*, and then in through the delicate high wrought-iron gates past imposingly formal gardens and finally into an enclosed courtyard at the rear of the *palazzo* which had immediately seemed to enclose her, shutting her off from the outside world and reality.

A small, gnarled man of about sixty had hurried out to the car, engaging in a low-voiced conversation with the *conte*, of which Alice could only hear the sharp, autocratic questions that her new employer was throwing at him.

'Yes, the doctor has been called,' Alice heard the older man replying in Italian. 'but there has been an emergency at the hospital and so he has not as yet arrived.'

'You have left the car in Florence?' Alice heard the older man asking the *conte*, in an incredulous tone that immediately raised Alice's hackles.

How typical of what she already knew of the *conte* that

even his employees should know that he would be more concerned about the future of his car than that of his baby!

'There was an accident,' she heard him replying grimly, shaking his head immediately as the other man instantly expressed concern for his health.

'No. It is all right, Pietro, I am fine,' the *conte* was assuring him.

Grittily, Alice watched him. At no point during their hair-raising drive to the *palazzo* had the *conte* expressed either interest or concern in whether or not she had been hurt in the accident, and she was certainly not going to tell him just how queasy and uncomfortable she had felt during the drive, she decided proudly.

She still felt rather weak, though, and she was relieved to be ushered into the cool interior of the *palazzo*, which was, as she had somehow known it would be, decorated in an elegant and very formal style, and furnished with what she suspected were priceless antiques.

How on earth could a young child ever feel at home in a place like this? she wondered ruefully, as she followed the *conte* and his housekeeper, Pietro's wife, Maddalena, who had now joined them, through several reception rooms and into a huge formal entrance hall from which a flight of gleaming marble stairs rose imposingly upward.

The baby's suite of rooms—there was in Alice's opinion no other way to describe the quarters that had been set aside for the little girl; certainly they were far too grand to qualify for the word 'nursery' as she understood it— was at one end of a long corridor, and furnished equally imposingly as the salons she had already seen.

A nervous and very flustered young girl who was quite plainly terrified of the *conte* appeared from one of the other rooms in response to the *conte*'s voice. She was inexpertly clutching the baby, who was quite plainly in discomfort and crying.

Immediately Alice's training and instincts took over, and without waiting for anyone's permission she stepped forward and firmly removed the baby from the girl's anxious grip.

The baby smelled of vomit and quite plainly needed a nappy change. Her face was red and blotchy from distress and as Alice gently brushed her cool fingers against her skin, whilst reassuringly comforting her, she suspected that she probably had a temperature.

Out of the corner of her eye she saw the move the *conte* made towards her as she took control and cradled the baby against her shoulder. Automatically she turned towards him, only just managing to suppress a small smile of grim contempt as she saw him glance from the baby to his own immaculate clothes.

A truly loving father seeing his motherless child in such distress should have instinctively placed the baby's need for the security of his arms above those of his immaculate suit, especially when she suspected that the *conte* was more than wealthy enough to buy a whole wardrobe of designer suits.

A baby, though, could never be replaced; nor, in Alice's opinion, could a baby ever be given too much love or security. And she immediately made a silent but vehement vow that, just so long as it was within her power to do so, she would ensure that little Angelina never, ever lacked for love.

As she and the baby made eye contact Alice felt a soft, small tug of emotion pulling on her heartstrings, her feelings reflecting openly in her eyes and quite plain for the man watching her to see and comprehend.

He had heard of love at first sight, Marco acknowledged wryly, and now had witnessed it taking place.

Quickly he veiled his own gaze to prevent Alice from seeing what he was thinking.

Almost as soon as she held her, little Angelina stopped crying as though she had instinctively recognised the sure, knowing touch of someone who knew what she was doing.

Alice could hear the *conte* speaking to the nursemaid in

Italian. Alice wondered why a man as wealthy as the *conte* might choose to employ an untrained nanny to look after his motherless child. The girl looked haggard and white-faced and she had started to wring her hands as she explained how the baby had started to be violently sick, shortly after she had fed her.

Alice had already made her own professional diagnosis of what she suspected was wrong. Quietly but determinedly she walked towards the communicating door through which the nursemaid had appeared.

The room beyond it, whilst as elegantly furnished as the one she had been in, was in total chaos, and Alice grimaced as she saw the pile of soiled baby things heaped up on the floor, and the general untidiness of the room. It was plain to her that the girl whom the *conte* had left in charge of his baby daughter had no professional skills and very probably very little experience with babies.

Carrying Angelina into the bathroom adjoining the bedroom, she quickly started to prepare a bath for her, all the time holding her securely in one arm, sensing her fear and need to be held.

It astonished her when the *conte* suddenly appeared at her side, instructing her, 'Give her to me.'

The baby started to cry again, a small, thin, grizzling cry of exhaustion, pain and misery. Dubiously Alice looked at her unwanted employer, but before she could say anything the baby turned her head and looked at the *conte* and suddenly she stopped crying, her eyes widening in recognition and delight as she held out her arms towards the man watching her.

To her own furious outrage, Alice actually felt sharp, emotional tears start to prick her eyes at this evidence of the baby's love for her father. But what really shocked her was the easy way in which the *conte* had held his small daughter; whilst she prepared a bath for her, cradling her lovingly in his arms, soothing her with soft murmurs of reassurance until Alice was ready to take Angelina off him and gently remove her soiled clothes.

'I think that she may only be suffering from a bad bout of colic,' she told the *conte* as she gently lowered the baby into the water, keeping her attention on her all the time to ensure that she was not becoming in any way distressed, 'but of course I would advise that she is checked over by a doctor.'

What she did not want to say was that she thought that it could be the inexpert handling of the baby by her nurse that was responsible for her agitated state. How could anyone leave such a young child with someone who was quite plainly not qualified to look after her?

Surely, having lost his wife, the *conte* would want to do everything he could to protect and nurture her child? A child who, it was already obvious to Alice, was looking helplessly to her father for love and security.

The arrival of the doctor interrupted her private thoughts, and whilst he was looking at the baby the *conte* had dismissed the nursemaid to go downstairs and have her supper, an act of apparent kindness, which for some reason only added to Alice's resentment of him. He had shown no concern at all for the fact that she had not eaten in hours. Not that she wanted to eat particularly; she still felt slightly nauseous and suspected that she might still be suffering from shock. But just whether that shock had been caused by the accident or by the *conte* himself, Alice was not prepared to consider.

The doctor quickly confirmed Alice's own diagnosis that the baby was suffering from colic and was probably also slightly dehydrated. Surprisingly he openly admonished the *conte* for allowing such an obviously inexperienced girl to have charge of Angelina.

'I understand what you are saying, Doctor,' the *conte* had accepted, 'but I have had no real choice in the matter. The girl was chosen to take charge of Angelina by her mother. She has been with her since the first weeks of her birth, and I have been reluctant to remove her from the care of someone so familiar, although I have now taken steps to rectify the situation since, like you, I have been concerned about the girl's ability to be responsible for the needs of such a small child.

'Miss Walsingham here has been employed by me to take over full charge of the nursery and of Angelina,' he told the doctor, turning to indicate Alice. 'She is English, as Angelina's mother was, and a fully qualified nanny.'

The doctor looked at Alice appraisingly, before turning to say with very Italian male appreciation, to Alice, 'May I say how fortunate I consider Angelina to be to have such a pretty companion.' The avuncular smile he gave her before turning back to the *conte*, along with the twinkle in his eye, reassured Alice that he was simply being gallant.

'You will have trouble on your hands, I'm afraid, my friend,' he continued to the *conte*.

'I do not know whether to commiserate with you or envy you for having so much distracting temptation beneath your roof.'

Alice felt her face starting to burn. What on earth was the doctor trying to imply…? That the *conte* might be tempted. By her?

However, before she was able to formulate her own thoughts, the *conte* himself responded to the doctor, telling him with razor-sharp crispness, 'I have employed Miss Walsingham for her professional qualities as a nanny, and not because of her looks, and as for her ability to tempt our sex… Miss Walsingham's contract with me precludes her from encouraging any hot-blooded and foolish young man to be tempted by her.'

The hard-eyed look he gave her scorched Alice's skin.

'And since she has already foolishly exhibited to me just how irresistible she finds temptation, I fully intend to ensure that her will-power gets all the support it might need, and in whatever form she might need it.'

Alice gasped. How dared he take such a high-handed

attitude with her, and in front of someone else? She was acutely aware of the interested way in which the doctor was now studying both of them, his dark eyes twinkling as though he found something amusing in the situation. Well, he might do so, but Alice most certainly did not.

However, before she was able to speak the *conte* continued almost brusquely, 'It is essential that Angelina has stability in her life. She has already lost far too much...' His voice had become so sober that immediately Alice felt unable to take issue with him regarding the statement he had just made.

'Ah, yes, that was a terrible tragedy indeed,' the doctor agreed gravely as he finished his examination of the baby and handed her back to Alice.

To her astonishment, as she reached out to take the baby the *conte* forestalled her, taking hold of his daughter himself and saying over Alice's head to the doctor, 'Miss Walsingham was involved in a thankfully minor accident earlier today, and I think it would be a good idea if you were to check her over...'

'No. There's no need. I'm fine,' Alice responded immediately, bridling at the *conte*'s inference that she was almost as incapable of making her own decisions as the baby he was cradling against his shoulder with fatherly expertise.

At some point he had removed his jacket, and the fine white cotton of his shirt did very little to conceal the dark muscularity of the torso that lay beneath it. Alice could even see the shadowing of his body hair. And she actually felt her muscles threaten to go weak. Fortunately she was able to tense them against such betrayal as she forced herself to focus on the waiting doctor and not her employer.

'I am perfectly all right,' she insisted.

And it was, after all, the truth. That nauseous headache she was still suffering had simply been caused by the heat and her own intense emotions. The minute bruise she had sustained was luckily concealed by her hair, and there really hadn't been any need for the *conte* to draw attention to her health!

Quite why she felt so resentful and hostile towards his apparent concern for her health, she didn't know. Perhaps it had something to do with the anger she felt towards him that he could actually employ a woman he considered to be guilty of attempted theft to look after his daughter— who surely should matter far, far more to him than any mere material possession!

Reflecting now in the middle of the night on what had been said then, Alice reminded herself that the agency had told her before she'd left London that her prospective employer was looking for her to make a long-term commitment to her charge, and that she would be asked to sign a contract to that effect, but she had overlooked that fact in the turmoil of the accident and its aftermath. Now, however...

Quickly she got out of her bed and walked across to Angelina's cot. She was the reason that Alice was now awake, her instincts alert to the baby's distress even in her sleep. Angelina was lying awake, whimpering softly. Gently Alice lifted her out, checking her temperature and her nappy.

Her skin felt reassuringly cool, but her nappy needed changing, and Alice decided this would be a good opportunity to give her a small extra feed.

She suspected that she was slightly underweight and maybe even a little malnourished. If she was a slow feeder, then her young nurse might have become impatient.

Holding her tenderly against her shoulder, she padded into the room adjacent to the nursery proper, which had been converted into a temporary but very well-equipped kitchen, with everything to meet the baby's needs.

She had already prepared some bottles of formula before going to bed, and as she removed one from the fridge and started to heat it she studied the baby's face.

Her mother might have been English but she looked completely Italian. She had her father's dark hair and eyes, and Alice suspected she had also inherited the *conte*'s determined chin.

For a baby of six months she was a little on the small side. As she looked at her with grave, worried eyes Alice couldn't resist dropping a tender kiss on her forehead as she smoothed her baby curls.

She was adorable, but so vulnerable. Alice ached to protect and care for her; so much so, in fact, that she could almost actually feel a soft tug on her own womb as she held her.

Poor baby. No mother and a father who couldn't possibly love her as she needed to be loved.

In his own bedroom, Marco frowned as he heard over the intercom the soft, cooing sounds of love and tenderness that Alice was making to the baby.

He, like her, had woken at the first sound of Angelina's distress. His concern over the nursemaid's ability to take proper care of the baby had led to him having a sophisticated baby-alarm system installed in the nursery suite so that he could hear if Angelina cried.

Indeed he had been halfway towards the bedroom door when he had realised that Alice had picked her up.

He'd employed Alice primarily so that Angelina would have someone else to bond with other than himself, but also to give himself the freedom to concentrate on his busy professional life, so now he was surprised to recognise that he actually felt almost a little put out at the speed with which the baby was responding to her.

Alice Walsingham!

What was it about this pale, infuriating Englishwoman that was making him feel such ridiculous and unwanted things? Showing him such intimate and dangerous images; images of her lying beneath him in the soft heat of a summer night, her blonde hair spread against his pillows as he threaded his fingers through it and held her so that he could kiss that tempting mouth of hers into reciprocal passion; images of her holding a dark-haired child in her arms, a boy child who was not Angelina, but his child!

Marco didn't know whether to laugh or cry at his own folly.

Alice was a young woman who was quite obviously not very good at hiding her feelings, and he had seen the wariness and hostility in her eyes when she looked at him!

Those were feelings he would be wise to allow her to indulge in—for both their sakes.

There was a considerable amount of discreet family pressure on him to marry. He was after all the head of the family, but as yet…

Marriage. Now why on earth had thinking about Alice Walsingham sent his thoughts in that direction?

He belonged to the modern century and there was no way he could ever feel comfortable in any kind of 'arranged' marriage, but, on the other hand, at thirty-five he had seen enough marriages and relationships go wrong to feel a certain cynical wariness about the permanence of what his contemporaries called 'love'.

Against his will he suddenly found himself thinking that his mother would have liked Alice.

He could hear the soft sucking noises Angelina was making as Alice fed her, and with shocking, nerve-wrenching immediacy he was suddenly once again visualising her holding a baby in her arms, her face soft with maternal love, her breasts bare…

Grimly he banished the image. That was not the way he wanted to see her, not even in the privacy of his own thoughts, and it was most certainly not the way he wanted or intended to think of her.

He was a man, he reminded himself, and it was a long time since he had had a sexual relationship with a woman. Maybe so, but that had not bothered him until now.

In fact, when presented with the opportunity to rectify

such an omission, as he had been on many, many occasions, he had not felt the slightest inclination to take it, so why was he now thinking about a woman whom he had only met a matter of hours ago in such an intimate and specific way?

Grimly Marco looked at his watch.

It was four o'clock in the morning. He had to be in Florence at ten for an important meeting; right now what he should be doing was sleeping and not giving in to the folly of turning his newest employee into some kind of fantasy madonna.

Alice waited until the baby was a heavy sleeping weight in her arms before returning her to her cot. Gently laying her in it, she watched her for several minutes.

Just looking at her made her heart ache so. She knew it was totally unprofessional of her to get so involved, but she just couldn't help herself. All babies needed and deserved to be loved, but this one especially so, she decided fiercely. After all, she had the double burden of having lost her mother and having as her father the most coldly autocratic and unemotional, dislikeable man Alice had ever met!

The baby was asleep and so should she be. She still felt muzzy and headachy but it was too much effort to bother taking anything. After checking on Angelina one more time, she made her way back to her own bed.

CHAPTER FOUR

ALICE watched in loving concern as Angelina opened her eyes and looked at her with bewilderment and confusion as she realised that she was a stranger to her.

It was seven o'clock in the morning and Maria the nursemaid was hovering behind her. Quietly Alice moved away from the cot so that Angelina could see her familiar face, but, instead of looking relieved when she saw her, the baby started to cry.

Immediately Alice picked her up, soothing her, feeling the panicky thud of her tiny heart start to ease as she accepted the loving reassurance of Alice's arms around her.

Sulkily Maria declared, 'The baby, she does not like me.' Tossing her head, she announced, 'She is not a good baby. I stay with her only because I need the money. And because of her poor mother.' She crossed herself as she spoke, watching as Alice heated Angelina's morning bottle of formula. 'She will not drink her milk. She is very difficult,' she warned Alice. 'I shall be glad to go back to Roma.'

'Rome!' Alice exclaimed.

'That is where I was working, as a…a housemaid when her mother told me that she needed someone to help her with her baby. She said that she could not look after her on her own and her father, he was no good. He did not care about the baby. They argued about it all the time. She wished that she had not married him. She told me so. He was very unkind to her.

'There were many arguments. She did not want to have the baby. She showed me many photographs of when she was in England, wearing pretty clothes.'

47

The picture her gossip was drawing for Alice was not a happy one, and Alice knew that she should stop her from speaking so openly about the marital problems of the *conte* and his late wife, but against her will she found that she was listening to her, her indignation darkening her eyes as she reflected on the selfishness of her charge's parents.

'It is tragic that Angelina's mother was killed,' was all she would allow herself to say.

'Tragic, yes,' the nursemaid agreed, giving a dismissive shrug as she told her, 'Before the accident they had quarrelled very badly. She had drunk much wine. She told me that she was going to leave him once they got back to Roma.'

Alice tried not to show how appalled she was by the maid's revelations. How could the *conte* have behaved in such a way to his wife, the mother of his child? A child that neither of them had wanted, according to the nursemaid, who seemed to know in very intimate detail about the lives of her employers.

'Poor baby,' Alice couldn't help murmuring as she started to feed Angelina. 'To have lost her mother and to have such an uncaring father.'

'Yes, he was uncaring, that one,' the nursemaid agreed.

As Alice had suspected, Angelina was a slow feeder, but Alice did not try to rush her, coaxing and praising her and feeling herself melt with pleasure when she finally rewarded her with an empty bottle and an unexpected smile.

She had sent Maria downstairs with the baby's dirty laundry—later in the day she would speak to the housekeeper about it herself, but right now she was enjoying having Angelina to herself. She was just in the middle of telling her joyfully what a clever, clever baby she was when the nursery door opened and the *conte* walked in.

The moment she saw him Alice could feel all her antagonism and hostility towards him surging through her. This was a man who had quarrelled so badly with his wife that she had driven to her death; a man who had apparently neither loved nor wanted his child.

She tensed as he came towards her, standing so close to her that she could feel the cool, silky brush of his shirt sleeve against her bare arm.

'How is she this morning?' he asked Alice as he frowned down at the baby in her arms.

'She is tired, but she has finished her feed,' she responded automatically.

'She slept through the night?'

The unexpectedness of the question caught her off guard.

'Well, no…she didn't…but then I didn't expect her to do so,' she told him almost defensively. 'I am a stranger to her. And she has not been well. She must be so confused, poor baby. She has had so many changes in her life already.'

'Which is why I stressed to your agency that I want you to make a long-term commitment to Angelina. That commitment, as I am sure they will have informed you, requires you to sign a contract that would bind you to being Angelina's nanny for the next five years. I have to say that I find it…unusual that a woman like you should be prepared to make such a commitment.' He paused and looked at her so slowly and deliberately that Alice knew that both her colour and her temper were rising. What did he mean 'a woman like you'? She itched to challenge him, but her training refused to allow her to do so. However, no amount of training could prevent her from giving an angry little hiss when he continued smoothly, 'After all, even if there is no man in your life right now…' He stopped and looked at her in a way that made Alice fume with indignation. 'Unfortunately,' he told her grimly, 'the Italian male has a weakness for women of your colouring, even though experience has shown me that relationships between people of different cultures are beset by difficult problems. And it does not help the situation that so many Northern

European women seem to view Italian men as hot-blooded, romantic lovers, who are ruled more by their emotions than by their brains.'

Alice couldn't control her outrage any longer. She was a professional woman, here in her professional capacity, not some silly girl looking for romance. And if that was what he thought of her, why had he ever chosen to consider her for the job in the first place? But before she could voice her indignation the *conte* was continuing coolly, 'I must admit I had assumed from the photograph your agency sent me that you were far less...sensual-looking than has proved to be the case.'

Sensual-looking? Her? Alice didn't know whether to be offended or bemused.

It was true that the photographs the agency had of her were two years out of date, and portrayed her with her hair neatly drawn back off her face, and that the first time the *conte* had seen her she had been wearing it loose. It was probably also true that the fortnight she had spent in Dubai in the spring with her previous employers had turned her beige-blonde hair several shades lighter, and that life and the effect of running after two energetic young boys had honed her body down a dress size, but that was hardly her fault; and nor, surely, was it likely to make her attractive to the average male who would surely prefer his women on the voluptuously curvaceous side?

'Five years is a long time for a woman of your age to—' the *conte* continued, but Alice refused to let him finish his sentence.

'To what?' she challenged him sharply. The conversation they were engaged in was a dangerous one. Her instincts told her that and they were telling her something else as well. Something she really did not want to acknowledge or hear. Something that was making her pulse race and beginning to fuel an unfamiliar and heady sense of excitement—like the frothiness of champagne laced with the dark allure of a highly intoxicating spirit—and she, as she warned herself sternly, had no head for such things.

Her body, though, didn't seem prepared to listen to the wise cautioning of her brain! The stark, brooding look he was giving her made her toes curl and her heart lurch dangerously against her ribs.

What was he trying to imply?

'You are not a nun who has taken vows of celibacy,' he told her pointedly, 'and it is only natural that you should want—'

Alice had heard enough!

'What I want,' she told him explicitly, 'is to be allowed to do the job I have been employed for, which, as I understand it, is to bring some measure of stability, love and security in the life of a six-month-old baby who has suffered the unimaginable trauma of losing her mother. And if you think for one moment that I have come to Italy for any other purpose—' She gave him a scornful, proud look, driven into the kind of frankness she would normally have felt far too inhibited and self-controlled to express.

'I am a modern woman, *Conte*, and I can assure you that the last thing on my mind is either idle flirtation, or trying to find myself a husband.'

'It said on your CV that you love children.'

His comment caught her off guard.

'Yes, I do,' she agreed, frowning. Maybe, for some reason he had changed his mind about employing her, perhaps because of what had happened the previous day. If his conscience was pricking him about the irresponsibility of entrusting his daughter to a woman who, so far as he knew, had stolen his car, then that was one thing, but if he thought she was going to allow him to question her dedication to her work, then...

The length of his silence and the way he was looking at her made tiny trickles of nerve-pricking sensation quiver through her body.

'Well, surely, that being the case, it is only natural that at some stage you should want to give birth to your own.'

Alice opened her mouth and then closed it again. Of course she hoped some day to have her own family, and to have it with a man she loved and who loved her, but that lay in the future!

It occurred to her that what he was saying to her might simply be an unorthodox way of testing her dedication to her job. If so, he was about to find out just how dedicated and committed she was! There was only one baby in her life at the moment and that baby was his!

Somewhere deep inside Alice a small, urgent voice tried to make itself heard, but Alice was too angrily indignant to heed it. Her professional pride was at stake now!

'I am perfectly prepared to sign the contract, and to commit myself to Angelina, legally, for the next five years,' she told him swiftly.

Prepared to sign it; she wanted to sign it; after all she was already committed emotionally to Angelina, and nothing—nothing—would tempt her into abandoning the baby into the sole care of her patently uncaring father!

Against his will Marco found that he was focusing on the indignant heaving of her breasts as she glared furiously at him. They made him ache to cup them in his hands and see if they felt as soft and sweetly rounded as they looked.

Determinedly he averted his gaze, but not before Alice's body had recognised his interest, and, as though somehow that knowledge had sent a secret message to her senses, to her chagrin she suddenly felt her nipples harden and peak, provocatively thrusting against the delicate fabric of her top, just as they had done on the first occasion on which she had seen him.

She could feel her face burning with shame and anger. How could this be happening to her? She simply wasn't the sort of person who…to…be like this!

To her relief Marco was turning away from her, demanding, 'Very well, then, we shall go straight down to my study where you can read and then sign the contract…'

However, as Alice made to follow him to the door he stopped her, asking coldly, 'Haven't you forgotten something?'

And then to her chagrin he strode back towards the cot where the sleeping baby lay, leaving Alice to hurry after him.

'Don't wake her,' she whispered as he leaned into the cot to look at the baby. 'She needs her sleep.'

'I wasn't going to wake her,' he whispered back reprovingly. 'I simply wished to check that she was all right.'

As he spoke his voice softened and to her amazement as she looked at him Alice realised that he was actually smiling at the sleeping baby. And then, even more amazingly given what she knew about him, he drew the gentlest of tender fingertips against the baby's soft cheek, before blowing her a kiss.

It was all done so unselfconsciously and so lovingly that Alice knew that if she hadn't known better and her only observation of his parenting skills had been that one she would have immediately assumed that he was a loving and caring father.

'Oh, by the way,' he instructed her as she followed him out of the nursery, 'the senior members of my household address me by my Christian name of Marco. I wish you to do the same.'

Marco. Alice could feel the shape of it filling her mouth, its sound, soft and yet hard at the same time, velvet cloaking steel, unlike the man himself who was quite unmistakably steel on steel with no softening covering at all!

It disturbed Alice to have to acknowledge the effect he was having on her.

Dislike, that was what it was, she assured herself hastily, but still a feeling she did not want to name coiled itself around her heart, as insidious and dangerous as a serpent waiting to strike a mortal bite.

'I have to go out this morning. If Angelina shows any signs of being poorly, please call the doctor immediately. My housekeeper, Maddalena, will give you his number.'

As she followed him along the corridor and then down the imposing flight of marble stairs Alice reminded herself that it was for Angelina's sake that she was staying here. The baby needed her, and there was no way that Alice could abandon her.

Not now!

Marco's study was reached through a series of breathtakingly beautifully furnished ante-rooms, but, to Alice's surprise, once he opened the door to it and ushered her inside she saw that the study itself was unexpectedly plainly furnished—plainly, but very stylishly and expensively, she guessed shrewdly as she caught sight of the Pollock paintings on one wall, and observed the clean lines of the room's furniture.

It was a man's room, and the room of a particular man, she recognised, a room which initially looked as though it were a designer's set piece but which on closer inspection proved to have many small personal details: a cast footprint, which she guessed must be Angelina's; the bust of a man whose features were somehow familiar, although she didn't realise why until she heard Marco saying, 'My father. He and my mother were killed in a plane accident. My uncle, his younger brother, was flying the machine at the time and he and my aunt were also killed.'

Alice could hear her own indrawn breath of shock.

What he had just told her made him so much more human...so...so vulnerable. But she didn't want to think of him like that; didn't want to feel her heartstrings pulled on his behalf.

'It was my father who encouraged me to train as an architect,' he continued, more as though he was talking to himself than to her. 'He said that although one day I would inherit from him, I needed to make a life for myself, and not simply sit around waiting for his shoes, especially since it would be a long wait.'

Alice could hear the pain in his voice.

'I wish that might have been so.'

He could talk about the loss of his parents, and show her the pain he obviously still felt at their loss, Alice reflected, but he seemed totally impervious to the loss of his wife. Not even when he was talking about Angelina, her baby, did he mention her. Because that wound was too raw, or because he felt guilty about her death?

She watched as he opened a desk drawer and removed some papers.

'This is your contract,' he informed her, his eyebrows snapping together as he saw that she was still standing several feet away from his desk.

'It will be easier for me to point out the more important clauses in it if you come and stand here,' he instructed her, gesturing to the space beside him.

Reluctantly Alice moved towards him.

The air in the room had felt fresh and pleasantly cool when she had first walked into it, but now all at once she felt hot, unable to breathe properly, suffocatingly aware when she did do so that she was breathing in air that held a dangerously intimate male scent.

She tensed as Marco moved closer to her, putting the typed document down on the desk between them, waiting until she had read it before saying, 'If you are satisfied you understand and accept everything the contract contains, then please sign it.'

Silently Alice did so, watching as he added his signature to hers.

'So,' he told her softly. 'You are now in my employ and committed to Angelina's future.'

She started to move away from him, stopping as she caught her hip on the corner of the desk to let out a small sound of pain. Immediately he was turning towards her, asking what was wrong. She started to assure him that it was nothing, but to her consternation he reached out and touched her hip, his fingertips cool and impersonal against her skirt-clad body.

His touch might be impersonal but her reaction to it, to him, most certainly wasn't, she thought, realising her face was flaming.

She felt him tense, and then suddenly curse beneath his breath before reaching for her, imprisoning her upper arms within the firm grip of his lean fingers as he turned her in towards his own body.

Alice knew immediately what was going to happen. After all, hadn't she shamingly imagined it already a dozen, no, a hundred, times in the deepest and most private recesses of her secret thoughts? She could feel the frantic racing of her own heartbeat, and she could feel too the heavy malely aroused thud of his.

She reached out to try to stop him but when her hands encountered the fine smoothness of his cotton shirt, somehow of their own volition they spread out against it. Beneath her splayed fingertips she could feel the hardness of the torso his shirt concealed. Flesh, muscle, bone and hair, that was all it was—he was... Dizzily she closed her eyes.

All... It was everything. He was everything!

Was she going totally insane?

Frantically she opened them again and looked up, her gaze immediately enmeshed in the hot, golden-eagle-eyed shimmer of his.

Like a bird of prey he was transfixing her. 'No,' she whispered as she saw him lowering his head towards her own, but it was already too late and his mouth caught hers on the soft open plea, stealing her breath, silencing her objection.

His lips felt cool and firm against her own, their touch sending darkly chaotic thoughts and desires tumbling

through her; their movement against her mouth was knowing and experienced, first subduing her desire to fight and
then luring, tantalising, tormenting her into giving him the
self-betraying response he wanted. Why was it that just
that mere brush of his mouth on hers could make her want
to move so much closer to him; make her want to cling to
him; make her want to hold onto him and keep his mouth
on hers for ever?

The hands that had been imprisoning her were no longer
doing so, instead one of them was curled behind her neck,
supporting it, whilst the fingers of the other were entwined
in her hair, holding her still in willing enthralment to the
mastery of his kiss.

Enthralment?

Her body was on fire…aching…longing…but somehow
she found her panic gave her the strength to drag herself
back from the brink of the precipice luring her.

Pulling herself free of Marco, she demanded with unguarded emotion, 'What…why did you do that?'

The look he was giving her made her shiver. It was
deep, dark, hooded and unfathomable.

As he looked at her Marco wondered what she would
do if he told her the truth, which was that he had kissed
her because he had simply had no option.

Feigning a coolness he was far from feeling, he told her,
'I did it because you and I both know that it's what you've
been waiting for me to do from the first moment I saw
you. It was inevitable that it would happen, and, that being
the case, it will make life simpler for both of us that we
have got it out of the way.'

Alice could scarcely believe her ears.

'No,' she rejected immediately, 'that isn't true. I
never…'

'Yes,' Marco overrode her. 'When I saw you in the
street eating your ice cream, you looked at my mouth as
though it was me you wanted to taste, and perhaps now
that I've satisfied your curiosity we can…'

Alice felt close to tears. How dared he suggest that she…?

'No.' She refused to back down, to be bullied into accepting the blame for what he had begun. 'You were the one who looked at me…at…at my breasts,' she accused him wildly.

She would never normally have been so forthright, but he was forcing her to do so in order to protect herself…

'Because I wanted to taste them?' he suggested softly. He gave a small shrug. 'Very well, then, perhaps I did. Your top fitted very snugly and your breasts…' Deliberately he allowed his voice to trail away meaningfully.

Alice went white. This just wasn't the kind of conversation she was used to. Her body felt hot…cold…her mind and her emotions in total turmoil. How could he stand there so coolly, when she felt so…so…?

She couldn't work for him now, no way. Her glance fell to the contract she had just signed and, as though he had read her mind, he told her softly, 'I'm afraid it's too late for second thoughts now, and for regrets… You are committed.'

CHAPTER FIVE

COMMITTED! She was that all right, Alice acknowledged a couple of hours later as she turned away from what she was doing to smile at the baby who lay kicking happily on the baby mat that Alice had spread on the floor for Angelina to play on whilst she set about bringing order to the untidy nursery.

Already Angelina was gripping her new nanny's heart in her small baby fist, and Alice knew there was no way she was going to prise those small, dependent, but oh-so-strong little fingers free...and no way she really wanted to. But when it came to Angelina's father...

She shuddered as she remembered that scene in his study. How could she have behaved like that? She didn't know. She didn't want to know. Far better to simply put the whole thing right out of her mind. Far, far better.

But could she do that? She must, she told herself frantically. She had to. For Angelina's sake and her own.

Alice had spent the morning keeping a careful check on her new charge, gently encouraging her to get used to her as she cuddled and talked to her, in between checking over the nursery's equipment.

The drawers full of new and exquisite baby clothes made her catch her breath—in dismay rather than admiration; lovely though everything was, these were what Alice privately called 'dress-up clothes'. The type that in a traditional aristocratic family a baby would be dressed in to be passed around from one elderly relative to another—there was nothing remotely practical. Nothing a baby could wear to stretch or play or grow or experience life in. What had also struck her as slightly odd was the

59

fact that the clothes virtually all appeared to be new; as though they had been purchased *en masse* and by someone who had no real hands-on experience of what a baby actually needed.

In fact it seemed to Alice that everything in the nursery was new. The expensive soft toys sitting neatly on top of one of the dressers looked beautiful, but they would do nothing to encourage a six-month-old to acquire and practise new skills. It seemed plain to Alice that whoever had chosen these clothes and toys did not really have an informed idea of what a baby needed. Beautiful hand-embroidered clothes and traditional long dresses were fine for high days and holidays, but where were the dungarees, the tee shirts, and the robust clothes that an active baby needed?

At lunchtime Marco's housekeeper, Maddalena, arrived to introduce herself and to inform Alice that she was having a light lunch sent up to the nursery for her since Marco had informed her that Alice would be dining with him later in the day.

Dining with him! Shakily Alice digested this nerve thrilling information before telling Maddalena, 'I haven't seen Maria since earlier this morning. Do you know where she is?'

'Probably in Roma by now,' the housekeeper replied grimly, adding, 'She came downstairs and telephoned her boyfriend there, and when she had finished she told me that she didn't want to stay here any longer.'

Alice was not really surprised that the girl had left. She had expressed to Alice her dislike of the quietness of the *palazzo*, and her preference for the city, and it had been obvious that she was not really attached to Angelina.

Maddalena continued, 'Not that she is any loss. Not really up to the job. But knowing the mother…' She stopped; her mouth pursing disapprovingly.

'The accident must have been a dreadful shock for all of you,' Alice said gently and tactfully.

The housekeeper shrugged.

'As to that, we hardly knew her. She didn't like the *palazzo*. She preferred Roma. And then when she did come here! Well, all I know is that she left here in a temper, screaming that she had never wanted the child and that she was ruining her life. What kind of mother is it that leaves her baby like that, I ask you?' the housekeeper demanded indignantly of Alice.

'Angelina has two parents,' Alice felt bound to point out. The housekeeper was certainly painting a very unflattering description of Marco's wife, but there were always two sides to every story, Alice reminded herself. Who could say without knowing her just what had driven her to behave so recklessly?

'Ppff... The father was as bad as the mother was.'

Alice could hardly believe her ears. The last thing she had expected was for the housekeeper to actually criticise Marco and to her, a new employee.

'It is just as well that you are here. The poor little one needs someone to take proper care of her. That maid...' The housekeeper gave a dismissive shake of her head. 'She is no loss to anyone, least of all little Angelina...'

The housekeeper had gone before Alice could question her about whether or not Angelina possessed any other clothes.

His meeting over, Marco opened his briefcase and removed a letter that had arrived before he had left for the city. He had already read it, but he felt the need to read it again.

It was from Pauline Levinsky, the woman who had been Alice's employer prior to her coming to work for him. Marco had approached her through Alice's agency, wanting to check out her opinion of Alice as a nanny.

Her letter began with an apology for not replying to him earlier, explaining that she had relocated to New York and that his letter had been redirected to her.

It went on to tell him that, whilst she had no wish to alarm him, she felt she ought to warn him that although Alice had cared for her two sons, diligently and carefully, she had discovered that Alice had been sleeping with her husband. She had written:

> Of course, to some of these modern girls having sex has no more meaning than exchanging handshakes. It's just a game they play. Notches on the bedpost. How many men they can seduce. Since Alice had already tendered her notice, there seemed little point in threatening her with dismissal, although with hindsight I suppose I should have reported her to the agency. I dare say my husband has not been the only one, and, whilst I cannot fault her care of my children, I would urge you to be on your guard.

It was too late for him to do anything now, of course. Angelina needed Alice too much for him to dismiss her.

Perhaps the relationship had meant more to Alice than Pauline Levinsky knew? Perhaps she had actually loved the other woman's husband? Angrily Marco wondered why on earth he was trying to find excuses for Alice.

Unlike his late cousin, Marco was not a city lover, which was why he had chosen to work from the *palazzo* rather than from a more centrally located office.

Thinking about Aldo made him frown. After his and Patti's death, Marco had driven to Rome in order to collect baby Angelina's things from the apartment where his cousin and his wife had lived.

The baby's cot had been crammed into a tiny room, her few clothes had all been in an untidy heap on the floor, whilst the wardrobes had been crammed with Patti's designer outfits.

Disgusted by what he had found and the apparent lack of concern for Angelina's welfare on the part of her parents he had felt it had revealed, he had gone straight to one of Rome's most exclusive shopping streets, to completely re-equip a nursery and wardrobe for her.

Aldo and Patti had been married less than six months when Aldo had admitted to Marco that Marco had been right to counsel him against marrying so quickly, and that he was now regretting his impulsive actions.

But by then Patti had been pregnant, and Marco had urged Aldo to at least try to make a go of his marriage for the baby's sake.

If he hadn't done so, would both his cousin and Patti still be alive now? Broodingly, Marco acknowledged his own sense of guilt. But no matter how guilty he might feel, there was one person who ought to feel even more so, and that was Angelina's grandmother, Patti's mother, Francine Bailey.

She had been furious when Aldo and Patti had married. Marco had met her for the first time at the party Aldo and Patti had given after their return from honeymoon, when she had told him in no uncertain terms that she wished they had not done so, informing Marco that she had been making plans for Patti to go to Los Angeles, where there had been a producer who had been prepared to offer Patti a part in one of his films.

The moment Marco had been introduced to Francine he had disliked her. In his view it had been a great pity that Francine had not removed her daughter to Los Angeles before she had met his impressionable cousin.

She had made it plain to him at the party that the only virtue she'd been able to see in her daughter's marriage to his cousin was the fact that Marco himself was extremely wealthy.

She was, in Marco's opinion, one of those women who was trying to rewrite the story of her own life through her unfortunate daughter. And Francine had been determined that Patti would fulfil for her her own thwarted dreams of stardom, even if that had meant hothousing her into a vacuous blonde bimbo of a girl who'd had 'second rate' written all over her.

Francine had done everything she could to persuade her daughter to have her pregnancy terminated, and in the end it had only been Marco's intervention and his promise to take on full financial responsibility for the little girl in every single way that had persuaded Patti to go through with the pregnancy, which was how he had come to be appointed her temporary guardian.

As he drove out of the city Marco resisted the temptation to ring the *palazzo* to check how Angelina was. Was that because he didn't want Alice Walsingham to think he was checking up on her or because he didn't want to expose himself to the dangerous pleasure of hearing her voice?

It was too late now for him to acknowledge that she was too dangerous; too tempting a complication in his life—he should have known better than to invite her into it.

Right now his prime concern, his only concern, had to be Angelina and her welfare. Nothing could be allowed to be more important to him than that, especially not his own adult desires.

Angelina needed the security of Alice's continued presence in her life in these all-important early years. There was no way he could allow himself to prejudice that.

And besides, even if he had been foolish enough to feel some sort of attraction towards her, the Levinsky woman's letter had surely killed those feelings?

So why was he returning home having cancelled an afternoon meeting he should have been attending?

Why? For Angelina's sake, that was why! Maddalena had already telephoned him to report Maria's defection—not that the maid was any real loss—and naturally, as Angelina's guardian it behoved him to ensure that she was in the best possible and most caring hands, he assured himself.

*   *   *

The gardens spread out below the nursery windows looked temptingly beautiful and Alice longed to explore them. Babies in her opinion needed to breathe in fresh air, although here in such a hot climate Angelina would need to be protected from the sun.

She had found a top-of-the-range baby stroller, clearly as yet unused, which had made her frown a little—Angelina was six months old!

Scooping Angelina up and cuddling her, she laughed in delight when Angelina smiled back at her spontaneously and held out her arms to her. Alice dressed her as comfortably as she could.

At least here was one good reason for not trying to get out of having dinner with Marco this evening. She could use the occasion to point out to him that Angelina's wardrobe was in serious need of remodelling. A rueful smile curled her mouth. In a dozen or so years, she doubted that Angelina would be willing to change her designer labels for sensible chain-store clothes! Alice liked timeless, well-designed things herself, but right now she was dressed in a comfortable tee shirt and a soft practical denim skirt. Her contract had specified that she was not to wear a uniform; Marco, it seemed, wanted someone who was more of a surrogate mother to his little girl than a mere nanny.

Having negotiated the stairs with the stroller and finally found her way outside, with albeit some willing help from Maddalena, Alice recognised ruefully that Angelina's head wasn't the only one that should have protection from the strong sun, but unfortunately she had forgotten to bring her own hat down, and there was no way she was going to either go back upstairs with the stroller, or leave Angelina outside on her own.

Protected from the strength of the sun Angelina gurgled happily in her stroller as Alice walked her through the breathtakingly beautiful formal gardens. As she pushed the

stroller Alice talked to Angelina, commenting on everything she could see.

'Look, Angelina,' she told her, positioning the stroller
so that Angelina could follow the direction in which she
was pointing. 'Roses…'

Lifting her out of the stroller, she held her carefully,
close to the rose, breathing in its scent herself, rich, musky,
sun drenched, laughing as the baby copied her, her eyes
opening wide in awe.

'Rose,' Alice repeated, hugging her tightly.

In the distance she could hear water tinkling. Turning
to put Angelina back into the stroller, she gave a startled
gasp as she realised that they were not on their own and
that the doctor had arrived unannounced and was standing
watching them.

'What a delightful picture,' he complimented her with
old-fashioned charm as he smiled at her. 'I apologise if I
startled you. I thought I would call and see how our little
one was doing, although I can now see that my visit was
unnecessary.'

A little uncomfortably Alice admitted to herself that,
whereas she would have instantly resented Marco's unexpected appearance, suspecting that he did not trust her
judgement, where the doctor was concerned she felt only
gratitude for his professionalism.

'She seems fine, her temperature is down and she's finished all her formula. I'd like to start her on something a
little bit more substantial, but I'm a firm believer in babies
having only the freshest, organically produced foods.'

'A view with which you will find Marco will concur,'
the doctor told her warmly.

'He is a far better father to the little one than—' He
broke off exclaiming, 'Ah, here he is himself, so you will
be able to address your concerns about Angelina's food to
him.'

To her consternation Alice felt her face starting to pinken whilst her heart was pounding so frantically and so erratically that it was no wonder she felt dizzy.

The heat of the garden, which five minutes ago had seemed reasonably bearable, now for some reason made her feel as though she could barely breathe.

Mercifully yesterday's vicious headache had eased, although she was conscious that it was still there, lurking threateningly, and that it was extremely foolish of her not to have covered her unprotected head from the strong heat of the sun.

'Ah, Marco,' the doctor hailed the *conte*, 'I have just been privileged to witness the most delightful scene. Your charming Alice was showing Angelina one of your roses.'

His charming Alice... The doctor was making it sound as though she was...they were...hurriedly, anxious to dismiss her own thoughts, Alice rushed into a husky explanation, 'I believe it is important for even the youngest baby to receive sensory stimulation, of a positive kind, and the perfume of these roses...'

'They were planted by my mother. She loved their scent.'

She really ought not to have come out into the garden without something to cover her head, Alice acknowledged dizzily. The sun was far too strong for her, she was beginning to feel sickly light-headed and she knew that had she been on her own with Angelina she would have sensibly and immediately sought out some shade, or gone back indoors, but her pride would not allow her in Marco's presence to either show any weakness or to admit that she had made even the smallest error of judgement.

Angelina had now seen Marco, and a broad smile had broken out across her small face. Kicking excitedly, she lifted her arms imperiously demanding to be picked up.

A little to Alice's surprise, Marco immediately did so, leaning into the stroller to remove her.

For some reason the way he cradled her against his

shoulder brought a distinct lump of emotion to Alice's throat. He looked the picture of devoted fatherhood.

'It is a real pleasure to see the little one starting to thrive after all she has been through,' the doctor was saying, shaking his head as he continued. 'It is a mercy that she was not in the car.' He stopped, putting his hand on Marco's arm as he exclaimed softly, 'I am sorry, my friend, if I am distressing you. I have not forgotten that you lost someone you loved very deeply in that tragedy.'

Alice could scarcely believe her ears. According to everything she had been told Marco and his wife had been on the point of divorcing, but now here was the doctor implying that Marco had loved her very much. Alice didn't want to dig deeper into the unpleasant feeling that realisation was giving her! It wasn't jealousy, was it? Jealousy of a dead woman because…because what? Don't go there! her instincts warned her protectively.

Suddenly sharply conscious that Marco was watching her, she turned quickly away, and then gasped as the unpleasant physical sensations she had been fighting to keep at bay for the last few minutes abruptly overwhelmed her.

The knowledge that she was about to faint panicked her, her first thought relief that she wasn't holding Angelina, and her second, and last, distress that Marco was going to witness her weakness.

When she came round she was sitting propped up against a tree, sheltered from the sun by its leaves. The doctor was crouching at her side smiling reassuringly at her, whilst Marco was standing grimly to one side watching them both.

Anxiously she looked for Angelina.

'The baby,' she began shakily.

'Safe in her stroller,' the doctor reassured her. 'Marco put her there before he carried you over here. How do you feel? You gave us both quite a shock…'

'I...I...fine,' Alice assured him. 'I think I must have stayed out in the sun too long...'

'I am sure you are right,' the doctor agreed. 'But...' He paused and looked towards Marco.

'I have just informed the doctor about yesterday's accident. It concerns me that you could be suffering from concussion...'

Concussion! Alice looked at him in disbelief.

'I worked in a hospital,' she reminded him. 'And I think I'd know if I had concussion. I'm sure it's nothing more than the heat.'

One dark eyebrow rose in ironic disbelief.

'And I should have thought that with your nursing experience, you would also have known that you were suffering from heatstroke or sunstroke and done something about it, such as wearing a hat,' he pointed out dryly. 'I think it best that you are checked over. The doctor is on his way to our local hospital now and he will drive you there.'

Hospital! Alice stared at them both.

'No, that isn't necessary,' she protested stubbornly. 'I can't go to hospital. Who will look after Angelina?'

'I will look after her,' Marco informed her. 'And as for you not going...as your employer, it is my right and my duty to insist that you do, even if I have to take you there myself,' he warned her with ominously quiet emphasis.

Concussion! This was ridiculous. Alice knew that she had no such thing, and that she was simply suffering from the heat, but she could see that neither of the two men was going to listen to her.

'Marco is right to be concerned,' the doctor told her gently, confirming her private thoughts.

'You may believe that the accident did no damage, but it is best that we check. Unfortunately the symptoms produced by concussion can be similar to those caused by heatstroke, at least in the early stages, and I would be doing less than my duty as a doctor if I did not insist that you allow me to put all our minds at rest.'

Put like that, how could she continue to refuse? Alice admitted. She really had no alternative other than to give in and go with the doctor.

'If you feel well enough to walk to my car,' he began courteously. Out of the corner of her eye Alice could see Marco watching her, frowning.

'Perfectly well enough,' she told him with faked breeziness and assurance. And it wasn't entirely a lie. She fully intended to make sure that she was well enough, even if she had to grit her teeth against a second bout of sickening dizziness when she made to stand up.

She could see Marco's eyes beginning to narrow, but mercifully, before he could make any comment, Angelina started to cry.

All three of them looked towards the stroller instinctively, but it was Alice who started to walk towards it first. However, Marco quickly overtook her, cursing under his breath as he ordered her, 'Keep still. Do you want to faint a second time? I will look after Angelina. Wait here, please, and then I shall escort you to his car, to make sure that you get there safely.'

His high-handedness infuriated Alice; she felt as though he was brushing her impatiently to one side, deriding her skills, questioning her judgement and her professionalism, and before she could stop herself she heard herself demanding scornfully, 'You mean the way you were looking after her before I arrived…leaving her to the mercy of an untrained and even less caring girl, who was virtually half starving her with her ignorance, never mind….'

Horrified, she closed her mouth. Whatever her private opinions might be, she had no right to publicise them. And normally she would not have done so, but there was something about her new employer that got under her skin in a way that no one else she had worked for had ever done.

She was breaking all the rules about keeping a formal

distance between them, behaving in a way that was totally
unprofessional, allowing her emotions to run riot and dictate her behaviour. Alice knew but somehow she couldn't
stop herself! A quick look over her shoulder reassured her
that the doctor was too far away to have heard her, thankfully—but Marco quite plainly had.

'If by that you mean what I think you mean,' he began
in a dangerously clipped and quiet voice, 'then let me assure you that I was very much aware of the inadequacy of
the care Angelina was receiving, which was why I hired
you,' he told her pointedly.

Alice knew that it would be politic for her to seize the
opportunity he had given her and back off, letting the subject drop, but to her own consternation she heard herself
blurting out almost aggressively, 'She needs more clothes.
Those she has are far too formal and impractical. They
look as though someone has just gone out and...'

She stopped as she saw the way he was looking at her.

Curtly he told her, 'I had no other option. The things
she already had...' He gave a small shrug of distaste. 'Patti
was not the best of housewives—or mothers. If in my in-
experience I have not provided Angelina with what she
needs, then that can soon be rectified. In the meantime, if
you will oblige me by going with the doctor.'

Pointedly he stood between Alice and the stroller, waiting until the doctor had come up with them and then telling
him, 'We have delayed you enough. Let us get Ms
Walsingham safely in your car, so that you can return to
the hospital. If you will telephone me once you have the
results of the necessary tests?'

It was on the tip of Alice's tongue to say that there was
no way she wanted or needed him to check on her health,
but caution prevented her from doing so. The last thing
she wanted to do right now was to sound even more like
a petulant, overwrought child than she no doubt already
did.

After they had walked slowly to the doctor's car, and

Alice was just about to get into it, she found herself wishing that she had been allowed to kiss Angelina goodbye, and then, to her astonishment, as though he had somehow guessed what she was thinking, Marco turned and lifted the baby out of the stroller, holding her out to Alice! He really was the most complex man, so arrogantly hard and controlled one minute, and the next seemingly almost to understand her every emotion as keenly as though he were her most intimate companion!

Determinedly ignoring the powerful male arms holding her charge, and the fact that she now smelled not just of baby powder but of expensive male cologne as well, Alice leaned forward and kissed her tenderly on her cheek, whispering lovingly to her as she did so, 'Don't worry, little one, I shall be back soon.'

She was worried, though, and her face crinkled into an anxious frown as she told Marco, 'Who will give her her formula? There is some made up in the fridge, but Maria has left and—'

'I am perfectly capable of giving her her bottle,' Marco assured her wryly. 'It won't be the first time I have done so, I can assure you.'

'You won't try to rush her, will you?' Alice couldn't help herself from asking anxiously. 'Only she does tend to take her time, and—'

'I won't rush her.'

Marco was already turning away from her. Unhappily Alice closed the car door. Marco was her employer and in this instance she had to do as he was demanding, little though she liked it or thought it necessary.

The last thing she thought as the doctor drove away was that at least now she would be spared the ordeal of having dinner with him!

CHAPTER SIX

IN THE solitude of her hospital room, Alice started to get dressed. Just as she had known would be the case, the hospital tests had proved that all she was suffering from was a little too much Italian sun. When the doctor had smilingly given her that news, she had itched for Marco to be there so that she could say, 'I told you so.' But even more than she wanted to do that had she wanted to be back at the *palazzo* with Angelina.

However, when she had suggested as much to the doctor he had informed her that Marco had insisted that she was to remain at the hospital overnight.

'It was just the heat,' Alice had protested, and the doctor had smiled in acknowledgement but had then reminded her, 'When you've witnessed the appalling devastation of a fatal car accident as Marco has done, it is perhaps understandable that he should be anxious to ensure that you have not been injured.'

His gentle reproof had left Alice with no option other than to settle herself ruefully into the private hospital room she had been shown to—at the *conte*'s insistence it was a private room.

And now here she was getting dressed and wondering just how she was going to get back to the *palazzo*. Would Marco send someone to collect her, or would she have to make her own way back? She could hardly expect the doctor, busy man as he obviously was, to drive her.

By some miraculous means she had woken to find that the clothes she had been wearing when she had arrived at the hospital had been laundered for her, and the *en suite*

73

bathroom to her private room had provided everything she could have needed in the way of toiletries.

It was eight o'clock. Had Angelina wondered where she was when she had woken up or had there been so many strangers in and out of her short life that she'd simply accepted her disappearance?

The previous evening Alice had been provided with a menu from which to choose her breakfast, and when she heard the brief rap on her door she assumed that it was now being delivered, but when she called out, 'Come in,' to her consternation and shock it was Marco who opened the door and walked into her room.

Thankful that she was actually dressed, Alice demanded anxiously, 'Where is Angelina? Who is looking after her?'

'She is here with me,' Marco astonished her by answering, going back to the door to wedge it open and wheel in Angelina in her stroller.

To Alice's joy the baby recognised her immediately and smiled at her.

Alice noticed he was dressed in immaculately clean clothes, and it seemed to Alice that she was already looking slightly plumper.

Immediately she went to her, laughing as Angelina held out her arms to her. Unfastening her from the stroller, she picked her up to cuddle her, unselfconsciously crooning lovingly to her, 'Who's a pretty, pretty girl, then? Did you have all your formula? Let me look and see that new tooth you've got coming.'

'You don't need to see it, I can give you a categoric assurance that it has come through,' Marco told her feelingly, indicating a tiny little tooth-mark on his finger.

Alice couldn't help herself, she started to laugh.

'It's no laughing matter,' Marco told her dryly. 'Those teeth are sharp.'

It was only now seeing the baby that Alice acknowledged just how worried she had been about her. She had woken several times during the night worrying about her, and now she couldn't stop herself from beaming her pleasure and relief at seeing her to Marco as she told him guilelessly, 'Thank you for bringing her. I've been so worried about her...'

The bitterness of the look that Marco gave her as she spoke shocked her into silence. What on earth was it she had said that was making him look so angry? Surely as Angelina's primary carer she had every right to be worried about her? Wasn't that after all why he was employing her? Or had his fatherly instinct certainly become activated, and was he perhaps jealous that Angelina might become too attached to her?

Angrily Marco wondered just what it was about Alice that made it so easy for her to tug on his heartstrings. Never in the admittedly brief time Patti had been alive had he ever once heard her express the slightest degree of concern about her baby, and yet here was Alice, who had barely known her a full twenty-four hours, exhibiting intense anxiety about her.

Which was why he'd employed her, he reminded himself, sternly. And the only reason why.

Just as the only reason he was here right now instead of sending someone to collect Alice was because of Angelina!

'You mentioned yesterday that Angelina needed some clothes, so I thought, since the good doctor has declared you to be fit and well, that we could go to Florence this morning and you could pick out yourself exactly what you think is needed.'

Had she actually been foolish enough to think he had come to collect her for some personal reason?

If so she had learned a painful lesson, Alice derided herself. And anyway, she challenged her emotions, why should she care? He meant nothing to her. She didn't even like him.

Who had mentioned anything as simple as 'liking him'? a taunting inner voice mocked her unkindly.

An hour later, shaking her head in rejection of yet another designer babywear shop, its windows decorated with the most beautiful and impractical of outfits, Alice felt her heart begin to sink—in more ways than one. All the other women shopping in the expensive street were obviously Italian and equally obviously stunningly well dressed, and she was beginning to feel acutely self-conscious in her clean but rather basic outfit. Marco, of course, was immaculately dressed, father and daughter very obviously a pair, whilst she, she suspected, must equally obviously look an outsider.

'We shall have to go back to the *palazzo* soon,' she informed Marco warningly. 'Angelina will be due for another feed.'

'I know. I brought a couple of bottles of her formula with me. They're here,' he told Alice, lightly tapping the bag attached to the stroller.

Alice tried not to look as uncomposed as she felt at this usurpation of her role. It was on the tip of her tongue to question just how he had made the formula, but somehow she managed to stop herself. Angelina was Marco's daughter, she reminded herself, and she ought to be pleased that he was being so responsible instead of feeling pushed out and unnecessary.

'I thought we'd give it another half an hour and then take a break,' Marco was saying. 'There's an excellent hotel not far from here—I know the owner.'

He would do, of course, Alice found herself thinking ruefully as they turned a corner and walked straight into a busy, bustling street market.

Her eyes shining with mischief she announced to Marco, tongue in cheek, 'Now, this is much better. I'm sure we can find the sort of things Angelina needs here.'

To her surprise, instead of immediately refusing to take

another step, Marco actually nodded and started to walk in the direction of the first stall.

The street was a seething mass of people, the stalls awash with 'factory price' leather goods, coats, shoes, and designer bags of spurious parentage and of course the ever-present tee-shirt stalls.

The crowds seething through the narrow street were a mixture of bargain-hunting tourists, guides trying to shepherd their distracted sightseeing flocks, and even a fair smattering of elegantly and expensively well-heeled dedicated shoppers, but as Alice made to join them she felt Marco's restraining hand on her arm.

Enquiringly she turned to look at him, expecting to hear him express disdain for the market and insist that they shop elsewhere, but instead and to her confusion he told her firmly, 'These places are fun, I know, but please stay close to me. There will be pickpockets around. And I should hate you to be the victim of a theft.'

He was concerned for her! As she listened to him Alice could feel the heat of his touch burning against her skin. It shocked her that she should feel so acutely aware of him...far too acutely aware and in far, far too dangerous a way. The surge of the crowds threw her slightly off balance so that she fell against him. Immediately alarmed by the reaction of her own body to him, she tried to pull back. But it was too late, She had already started to overbalance, and he had of course reacted instantly and reached out to steady her with both hands. The jostling of the crowd had brought her up so close to him that her breasts were flat against his chest. One of his hands had dropped to her hip. She could feel herself starting to tremble as she realised that her lower body was resting against the hard warmth of his thigh.

She was aware of him with every pore of her skin, every part of her sensory system; she was aware of him in a thousand unwanted and alarming ways. She was aware of him with an intensity that shocked her and was totally outside her experience.

'Angelina,' she managed to remind him as she pulled herself away from him. She knew that her face was flushed and hoped that he would put it down to the heat of the sun. And that open, urgent peaking of her nipples? Would he put that down to the heat of the sun as well, or would he guess that it was caused by a heat of a very, very different nature?

Quickly she started to walk down the street, only to have to stop when Marco called out, 'Wait.'

As his hand snaked out to grasp her upper arm Alice willed herself not to allow that deep, intense quiver that had begun low down in her body, and which was threatening to spread to every single one of her nerve endings, to betray her even further by causing her whole body to shiver in sensual overreaction.

'This way,' Marco commanded, drawing her towards one of the stalls.

At first Alice thought he must have seen a babywear stall, but to her astonishment the stall he was leading her to sold, not babywear, but the most exquisite and obviously handmade straw hats.

'You need one of these,' he told her firmly. 'Then you will be able to keep your head covered from the sun.'

'Yes, I do,' Alice agreed uncertainly. She had already given the hats a quick glance and had seen immediately from the price that these were no cheap holiday items.

As though she had guessed what she was thinking, the stallholder immediately began to tell Alice in English, 'These hats, they are from one of Italy's most famous designers. She has a factory not far from here, and these are...'

As she fought for the right word Alice supplied for her in English, 'Seconds,' and then translated the word into Italian for her, earning herself a wryly impressed look from the other woman.

'You speak Italian?' she questioned Alice.

'Yes,' Alice confirmed. 'And these hats, whilst they are lovely, are far too expensive for me, I'm afraid.'

'But, no, they are a bargain,' the woman insisted. 'Try this one. It will be perfect for you, and I promise you it will be worth its cost.'

Before Alice could stop her, she was firmly placing one of the hats on Alice's head. A soft, natural-coloured straw, it felt as soft and as supple as fabric, and as Alice peeped into the mirror she was holding up for her she was forced to admit that both the style and the colour did suit her.

'The hat is possible to be folded,' the woman began to explain, and then with a small shrug switched to Italian as she told Alice that the hat was designed to be folded away, and that it was virtually the last one she had of a very special range.

Alice began to shake her head, but suddenly to her consternation she heard Marco saying firmly, 'We will take it.'

He was already handing over the money, whilst the stall-holder, emboldened by her success, was attempting to persuade him that Angelina too needed a hat, 'To match her mama's,' she announced.

Her mama's! Alice looked away from her and then wished she hadn't as her gaze immediately meshed with Marco's.

What was it that was making her heart ache in that darkly dangerous way? A secret wish that Angelina, whom she had already come to love so deeply, was her child, or an even more secret wish that Marco had sired her baby? What on earth was she thinking? That heatstroke must have been far more potent than she had realised! There was no way she intended to allow such thoughts to flourish! No way!

As they left the stall Alice started to open her bag to find the money with which to repay Marco.

'What are you doing?' he demanded when he saw her.

When Alice told him, he stopped walking and frowned.

'The hat is a…a necessary item of your wardrobe whilst you are working for me and as such it is my desire to pay for it!' he told her coolly.

'No. I can't let you do that!' Alice protested.

'You can't stop me,' Marco informed her, touching her arm before she could say anything else to tell her, 'There is a shop over there that has baby clothes.'

Distracted, Alice turned to look in the direction he was pointing.

Five minutes later, standing inside the shop she was nodding in happy approval of the outfits its owner was showing her.

'These are exactly the sorts of things she needs,' she told Marco enthusiastically.

'Fine. Get whatever you think she needs,' he responded.

Carefully Alice chose several outfits, shaking her head when Marco picked up one item, and telling him determinedly, 'No, that colour does not suit her.'

The smile that curled his mouth along with the tender look that accompanied it caught her off guard. They were, she told herself forcefully, for Angelina and most certainly not for her. How could they be?

'Are you sure that's enough?' Marco questioned her when she had finished.

'She'll be growing out of them so quickly, it's silly to get too many,' Alice informed him.

Angelina, who had been asleep, had started to wake up, and experience told Alice that she would soon be feeling very hungry.

'If that hotel you mentioned isn't too far away,' she began as Marco paid for their purchases, 'I think it might be a good idea to make our way there.'

As soon as she heard Alice's voice, Angelina turned to look at her, grizzling to be picked up and cuddled.

Only too happy to respond, Alice removed her from the

stroller for a cuddle as she told her, 'Formula time soon, honeybun…'

She had spoken to her automatically in Italian and the shop owner laughed, and joined in the conversation, informing Alice that she had a grandson of Angelina's age.

Angelina, wide awake now, started to exercise her new tooth on the exposed curve of Alice's neck.

'Oh, no, you don't, young lady,' Marco informed Angelina firmly as he saw what she was doing, and reached out to lift her out of Alice's arms to put her back in the stroller.

As they left the shop Alice couldn't help wondering how they had looked to the shop owner. Had she guessed that Alice was simply Angelina's nanny or had she believed that she was her child; that she and Marco were a couple?

Aghast by the direction her thoughts were taking, Alice brought them to a frantic, skidding halt.

What she was doing was crazy, idiotic, self-destructive and downright foolish. It was bad enough that she had fallen in love with Angelina, without her falling in love with her father as well!

Falling in love with Marco? Her? No, that was totally impossible! When she fell in love it would be with a man she could feel comfortable and relaxed with, not a too-sexy, too-arrogant man with one apparently bad marriage behind him, and an attitude toward his baby that…

But what exactly was Marco's attitude towards Angelina? Right now he was interacting with her as though parenting came as naturally to him as breathing.

'It's this way.'

Realising that Marco was waiting for her to cross the road with him, she shook herself free of her unwanted and disturbing thoughts and feelings.

As they walked into the foyer of a breathtakingly elegant private hotel a few minutes later, she realised she was attracting more than one interested and approving look from the men they had walked past.

Without really realising what she was doing she instinctively moved a little bit closer to Marco and the stroller. She could see he was frowning. Because he didn't want her so close to him? He hadn't made any move away from her, though, and in fact he reached out to place his hand on her shoulder as he pointed out a secluded table to her where they could sit and have coffee and still look out onto the busy street, with its distant view of the river.

'We'll need to ask them to heat up Angelina's bottle,' she warned him. 'And I'd like to change her.'

Escorting her to the table he had indicated, Marco inclined his head.

'Leave everything to me,' he told her, before asking, 'Would you like to have a cup of coffee before we order lunch?'

'Coffee would be lovely,' Alice agreed, busying herself moving Angelina's stroller so that the baby was tucked safely between her own chair and the window.

Alice was talking softly to Angelina, the baby's eyes fixed adoringly on her face, when Marco returned. He paused for a second watching them, his mouth twisting in wry acknowledgement of what he could no longer hide from himself. It was a pity that their children would be unlikely to inherit her blonde hair, and he wasn't sure whether or not he wanted their daughters to inherit their mother's dangerously sexy soft pink mouth. If they did, they would no doubt grow up tormenting every man who saw them in exactly the same way their mother was tormenting him right now...

Alice turned her head and looked at him. His heart slammed heavily against his ribs as he looked back at her.

Alice felt her heart miss a beat and then flutter frantically against her chest. Why was Marco looking at her like that...as though...as though...?

'I've had a word with the hotel manager, and he has put a room at our disposal where you may take Angelina when you are ready.'

Alice tried not to look impressed.

'I've also ordered our coffee,' Marco told her, pulling out a chair to sit down next to her.

As he leaned over to smile at Angelina his thigh brushed against Alice's.

The minute shudder that ran through her was immediate and unstoppable. The images forming in her mind were so sensual and so explicit that they shocked her. Shocked her and excited her, she acknowledged shakily. She had never felt so sexually aware of any man, so sexually aware of him and so sexually hungry for him!

How on earth had it happened? One moment she had disliked and despised him and the next, or so it seemed now, her body was a tormenting ache of sensual female need for his touch, for his mouth, for him!

Their coffee arrived, but Alice was oblivious to the admiring look the young waiter gave her, her eyes darkening with the intensity of the painful inward delving of her thoughts. How could this unwanted transformation of her emotions have taken place? That she should virtually immediately have felt love for Angelina was, so far as she was concerned, perfectly understandable, the baby was after all crying out for her to give and receive human love, but where on earth had her foolish heart got the idea that her father either needed or would reciprocate her love?

'Your coffee's getting cold.'

The crisp, almost critical note in Marco's voice made her realise how quickly she had become sensitive to every changing timbre of it.

'Angelina will be wanting her bottle,' she informed him shakily.

'Give it to me,' Marco instructed her. He summoned a waiter, to whom he handed the bottle Alice had removed from the bag, asking him to arrange for it to be warmed, at the same time also asking him to bring them some lunch menus.

'Everything here is freshly prepared and cooked,' he

told Alice once they had their menus. 'The pasta with beef is a speciality of the restaurant and I can recommend it. Or if you would prefer fish...'

'No, the beef sounds delicious,' Alice assured him, turning to smile at the waiter as he returned with Angelina's bottle.

Lifting the baby out of her stroller, she settled her comfortably in her arm, smiling at her as she began to feed her.

'She's already eating much better,' she told Marco enthusiastically. 'Babies are so sensitive to the emotions of people around them—she must be missing her mother so dreadfully,' she added, her voice faltering as she realised that Marco too might be missing the woman who had been his wife and the mother of his child. It was all very well for Maddalena to say that the marriage had not been a happy one, but that did not mean....

'Missing her! I don't think so,' Marco countered Alice's comment immediately, his voice harshly grating and so full of suppressed anger that it made Alice want to flinch.

'Patti never wanted Angelina, and once she was born she spent as little time with her as she could. She even insisted on having her delivered by Caesarean section before her actual birth date because she didn't want to miss some shallow social event she wanted to attend!'

Alice could hear the disgust quite openly in his voice.

No, there was quite definitely no love there in his voice for his dead wife, Alice acknowledged.

For some reason her eyes had started to mist with emotional tears. Blinking them away, she brushed her fingertip gently over Angelina's rosebud cheek as the baby clung to her bottle.

'She is so lovely, so precious. I cannot...' she began, and then had to stop as her emotions suspended her voice. There were some things it was neither right nor fair for her to say, especially about a dead woman who was not there to defend herself. Marco, after all, was her employer and...so far as he knew Alice was the woman who had attempted to steal his car and drive off in it.

It still bemused her that he had actually wanted to employ her knowing that, although she could at least understand now just why he had been so desperate to get a proper nanny for Angelina.

Their lunch arrived just as Angelina finished her bottle.

Putting her back in her stroller, Alice saw the waiter filling her wineglass and her eyes widened.

She didn't normally drink at lunchtime, but it seemed churlish to make a fuss, and the wine was deliciously smooth on the palate, she acknowledged as she took a small, tentative sip.

Like the French, Italians knew how to enjoy their food and make even the simplest meal an occasion.

All the tables around them had filled up, some with business-suited men, others with smart middle-aged women carrying glossy shopping bags with discreet designer logos and others with family groups, and a cheerful, happy buzz of chatter filled the room.

A young mother at an adjacent table smiled conspiratorially towards Alice as she saw Angelina. Her own two toddlers were immaculately dressed and plainly at home in such an adult environment.

'No, really, I couldn't,' Alice protested, refusing a final cappuccino. She had already eaten a full plate of pasta and beef, plus a deliciously wicked tiramisu ice cream, plus a large glass of rich red wine, and it was no wonder that she was feeling so wonderfully relaxed.

Not so relaxed, though, that she had forgotten her responsibilities.

'I'd better take Angelina upstairs to change her now,' she told Marco.

'Very well.'

As she stood up so did he, helping her to manoeuvre

the stroller into a clear space, and then pushing it into the foyer and towards the bank of lifts.

'We're on the fourth floor,' he informed Alice as he pressed the button.

Nodding absently, Alice waited until the lift doors opened and then stepped out.

'This way,' Marco instructed her, pushing the stroller with one hand whilst he removed an old-fashioned room key from his pocket with the other.

'This hotel was originally a private home,' he explained to Alice as he paused outside one of the heavy doors and inserted the key into the lock.

'During the conversion as many of the original features as possible were retained.'

'It is very beautiful,' Alice agreed, casting an admiring look down the corridor with its frescoed walls and ornately plastered ceiling.

Pushing open the bedroom door, Marco waited for her to go inside.

The room was huge, dominated by an enormous king-sized bed. Through its balcony windows Alice could see the river.

'I'll take Angelina through to the bathroom,' she told Marco as she lifted her out of the stroller. For some reason she had not expected him to accompany them to the room, and now for no logical reason she could think of she felt thoroughly unnerved by his presence and acutely aware of it—and of him. For no logical reason maybe, but she certainly emotionally knew exactly why she was reacting to him the way she was. Exactly why!

The bathroom was as generously proportioned as the bedroom, and fitted with gleaming white sanitary-ware.

Through the half-open door Alice was aware of Marco making a call on his mobile as she deftly undressed Angelina and started to change her. She had brought the changing bag attached to the stroller into the bathroom with her, with everything that she needed.

Marco was speaking into his mobile, and Alice tensed as she heard him asking how long it was going to be before the Ferrari was ready for collection.

Kissing Angelina's clean, bare skin, she started to re-dress her.

'You are so delicious, I could eat you,' she cooed to the baby, tenderly.

Marco listened to her. What was it about this woman that made her so instinctively, and so damn sexily, mater-nal? The way she made him feel right now meant that just to hear her, never mind look at her, made him ache in an entirely male and driven way to ensure that it was his children she would be mothering.

The words he could hear her murmuring to Angelina were only a mild echo of his own far more elemental and tormenting longing to say the same thing to Alice, and not just to say it, he acknowledged grimly as he listened to the garage's service manager explaining to him that the Ferrari was almost ready for collection.

Marco tensed as he saw Alice coming out of the bath-room, carrying Angelina.

'I think she's ready to go back down now,' she told him as she walked towards the stroller.

As she reached him Angelina turned in her arms, nuz-zling toward Alice's breast. Marco knew it was an auto-matic baby reaction, and equally automatic was his own body's reaction to it, to them. Angelina might not be his child, but he felt as though she were. He loved her as though she were, and the sight of Alice gently giving her her finger to suck as she tenderly placed her in her stroller did things to his senses he would have sworn to be im-possible before she had come into his life.

Within seconds of her putting Angelina in her stroller, she was fast asleep. Smiling, Alice stepped back from her and then gave a small gasp of shock as she came up against something solid.

She hadn't realised that Marco was standing behind her. Automatically she started to turn round and then wished she hadn't as she realised that Marco hadn't moved and that now they were standing body to body, and that hers was resting on him in a way that meant it must be impossible for him not to realise just how physically aware of him she was!

She could feel the air in the room prickling against her skin, her nerve endings felt so sensitive. She wished she were anywhere but here; she wished he were a thousand miles away and at the same time she wished he were a thousand millimetres closer. She wanted....

'Why are you looking at me like that?' she demanded shakily, saying the first thing that came into her head. 'If it's because of your car, I can pay for the repairs,' she told him, her head lifting proudly.

'To hell with the Ferrari,' Marco responded to her forcefully, shocking her with the intensity of his reaction. 'This has nothing to do with any damned car.'

Emotions seemed to crackle like lightning between them, but stubbornly Alice refused to give in to them.

'Then what, why...?' Alice's voice cracked nervously as she tried to move away, but Marco had placed a restraining hand on her arm, and now its palm was cupping the ball of her shoulder, and not just cupping it but also actually massaging it...

Unable to stop herself, Alice closed her eyes, swaying giddily. This just could not be happening; that message of sexually charged urgency she was getting from his touch just couldn't be real.

Helplessly she looked up at him. Just the sight of his mouth made her feel weak and dizzy. She wanted to reach out and trace the shape of it, with her fingertip, her lips, her tongue.

She could feel her whole body reacting to him, aching for him!

As though it were happening in slow motion she

watched the downward descent of his head, his mouth coming towards her own, felt her heart slamming against her chest wall, her body shuddering from head to toe as he slid his hand beneath her hair, cupping the back of her neck, his thumb stroking the soft, sensitive skin behind her ear.

She could hear the soft, sighing half-moan, half-purr of pleasure she was making as though the sound were coming from somewhere else, her lips already parting in moist eagerness, her eyes heavy and sultry with longing as she semiswooned against him, her body drenched with sensual hunger.

The touch of his mouth on her own, instead of satisfying her need, only seemed to heighten and intensify it. Without knowing what she was doing she found that she was clinging to him, her body pressed tightly into his, desperately seeking its maleness as though it needed him to complete it; as though she needed him to complete her.

His tongue brushed her lips, rough, warm velvet mixed with pure, sensual silk, a thousand unbelievable sensations condensed into one tantalisingly brief touch. Immediately her mouth clung to his wanting more, her own tongue darting boldly against his seeking the intimacy she craved.

His hand touched her breast, and immediately she ached to be naked against him, to feel his touch against her bare skin.

As though he had read her mind, he pushed aside her top, his hand dark against the white fabric of her bra. Her whole body quivered as he pulled the fabric away from her breast, her flesh softly pale against the masculine darkness of his. Unable to stop herself Alice started to moan, gasping for breath as she did so.

His thumb rubbed slowly against the hard nub of her nipple and she cried out in helpless longing, desperate for the feel of his mouth where his thumb had been, ready to offer herself up to her desire for him. Marco was everything she wanted.

She cried out in shocked arousal as he dropped to his knees in front of her and started to kiss the exposed flesh above the waistband of her skirt, slowly moving upwards as he pushed up her tee shirt.

Her entire body was trembling with aching longing as his mouth moved closer to her breast... Another minute, another few seconds of the tormenting, achingly teasing, unbearable, erotic little kisses and his mouth would be on her breast and he would...

The sudden sharp cry that Angelina gave burst through the private bubble of their mutual desire, fracturing it, bringing them both into frozen stillness, even the previous sensual heaviness of their breathing suspended as they both looked towards the stroller.

It was Alice who broke away first, though, tugging down her tee shirt, her face hot with self-conscious embarrassment and disbelief at the way she had been behaving as she hurried over to the baby.

Picking her up, she walked over to the window with her, comforting her, and glad of the excuse not to have to turn round and face Marco. What was he thinking? Was he as shocked by what had happened as she now was, or was he cynically used to foolish young women throwing themselves at him...wanting him...?

Alice cringed as she realised what she had done. He was her employer, a newly bereaved man...a father...and if his sexual needs had overwhelmed him, well, no one would blame him for them having done so, but people would view her behaviour in a very different light. Unfair, but true nonetheless, Alice acknowledged as she tried to recover her composure, telling Marco without turning round, 'I'll take Angelina back downstairs...'

There was no point in her trying to pretend to herself any longer; somehow or other she had been idiotic enough to fall in love with Marco!

*   *   *

Grimly Marco watched as Alice put Angelina back into the stroller, carefully keeping her back to him.

How the hell had he managed to allow things to get so out of control? After all, it wasn't as though he didn't know exactly what she was under that damnably convincing mask of madonna-like innocent sensuality. She'd had an affair with a married man! Maybe more than one! That kind of behaviour was totally abhorrent to him! Well, there was no way it could be allowed to happen again! He was forced to concede that it had shocked him to discover just how strong his desire for Alice was. A sign that he had lived a celibate life for too long, no doubt! Was she perhaps thinking that he could fill the place left empty in her life by her ex-lover…the place left empty in her bed?

Before he shared his bed with a woman he needed to know his relationship with her was exclusive—and committed; emotionally as well as sexually.

No doubt to a woman like Alice such old-fashioned ideals would simply be amusing; something she simply could not comprehend!

What on earth was she doing? What was happening to her? Alice wondered wretchedly. She had heard of nannies falling into the trap of becoming emotionally and sexually involved with their male employers, but she had never imagined it could ever happen to her! She had always considered herself to be far too sensible.

CHAPTER SEVEN

'I'LL bring Angelina in.'

Nodding, Alice got out of Marco's car. They had travelled back from Florence virtually in silence, and despite the air-conditioning inside the car she had felt stifled and barely able to breathe, as though somehow the sheer weight and burden of her own emotions were sucking the energy and life-giving oxygen out of the air around her.

As she hurried towards the *palazzo*, she was acutely conscious of Marco striding ahead of her pushing the stroller, an action that in another man would no doubt have made him look as domesticated and safe as a big, soft, neutered cat, but that in Marco only had the unnerving effect of actually emphasising his sexuality. No sexually tamed fireside cat this one. Oh, no, he was all lean, dangerous, predatory, feral, hunting male.

The moment they stepped in the cool hallway of the *palazzo*, Maddalena came hurrying towards them, as though she had been anxiously awaiting their return.

'*Conte*, she began with unusual formality, 'there is someone—'

'So at last,' a harsh woman's voice began. 'I have been waiting virtually all day to see my granddaughter, and this…this creature has totally refused to so much as allow me even a glass of water. But then I suppose I should not have expected anything else. After all, like master like servant.'

Alice gasped, instinctively taking a step back from the woman who had erupted into the hallway.

She was tall and bone-thin, dressed in clothes that, whilst obviously expensively high fashion, were openly far too young for her. The skin of her face was pulled so tightly against her bones that Alice wondered that any surgeon with a reputation to worry about could have performed such easily detectable surgery. She fixed Marco with a fulminating glare, totally ignoring Alice's presence as she demanded theatrically, 'Where is my darling precious little girl's baby? Where is she? You have no right to withhold her from me—'

'Calm down, Francine.'

Alice could hear the icy distaste in Marco's voice as he interrupted her emotional tirade.

'Calm down! My daughter is dead, thanks to the dangerous driving of your precious cousin, and now you are trying to steal her child from me. I won't allow you to get away with it, Marco. I am sure the courts will support my claim that her place is with me. After all, I have a blood tie with her that is far stronger than yours. You are only her second cousin, whilst I am her grandmother,' she announced triumphantly, whilst Alice stared at her in bewilderment.

What on earth was she saying? Marco was Angelina's father, surely?

'You may, as you say, have a closer blood tie with Angelina than I do,' Marco was agreeing, totally confounding Alice, 'but her father Aldo appointed me as her guardian.'

'You make me sick,' the woman he had addressed as Francine threw furiously at him. 'Aldo never wanted the baby.'

'Maybe not,' Marco agreed coolly, 'but then neither did your daughter, and as I remember it you were the one who counselled her to have her pregnancy terminated, and even though Aldo had not planned to become a father, he refused to countenance a termination.'

'She had been offered a movie contract.'

Alice could see the grim compression informing Marco's expression as he listened to her bitter response, and she could hear too the suppressed anger in his voice as he told Francine savagely, 'If you think for one minute there is any way I would allow you to have any contact with or influence over Angelina after the way you controlled and ruined your own daughter's life for your own selfish reasons, then you are very, very wrong.'

'What are you saying?' Francine demanded in a high-pitched voice. 'I did everything for Patti. Everything! Sent her to dancing classes, went to auditions with her, paid for her breast implants. Everything. I was the one who helped and encouraged her, who—'

'Who helped and encouraged her to do what?' Marco interrupted her sharply. 'To model semi nude on the pages of a downmarket tabloid. If that is true mother love, then…. There is no way you are going to play any part in Angelina's life, Francine, and as for your coming here and pretending concern for her—don't think I haven't forgotten that you couldn't even be bothered to attend the funeral of the daughter you claim to have loved so much!'

'That was because I couldn't bear the thought of my beautiful baby being buried. Because I was too ill to be there…' She was everything to me. And now I want to bring up her daughter…my granddaughter,' she told him triumphantly. 'Angelina is a girl baby. She needs a mother's influence, a female presence in her life. You may be her guardian, but I am her closest next of kin. She needs me in her life,' she told him, with what to Alice seemed to be sickeningly false piety. 'Maria has already been in touch with me to tell me how concerned she has been for her. How you left her knowing she was ill, and refused to call a doctor until Maria begged you to do so. She says you've dismissed her, the very person her mother chose to look after her, and apparently now you've appointed a new nanny to look after her. It's obvious how little you care about her!'

'What? No way is that the truth…'

Marco had gone white with the intensity of his fury and

Alice couldn't blame him. She was still dizzily trying to come to terms with the fact that he was not Angelina's father. Not her father and yet his love for her was shiningly apparent.

'A man cannot bring up a little girl properly,' Francine went on, 'not when she is not his child, and I doubt that any court would actually allow you to do so. There are…' She paused delicately. 'There are certain potential moral issues to be considered…'

The look in Marco's eyes now was positively murderous, and Alice couldn't blame him.

'If you're trying to imply what I think you're trying to imply,' he began ominously, 'then let me tell you—'

'No, Marco, let me tell you that I want Angelina and I intend to have her. And there is no way that you can stop me.' She paused and then said softly, 'I must say I was rather surprised to learn just how wealthy a young man Aldo had been. After all, he kept my poor darling Patti very short of money. That's so very naughty of him when it now turns out that he was close to being a millionaire.'

'So that's it,' Marco commented grimly. 'I might have known! Well, for your information Aldo's inheritance was actually held in trust for him, and unavailable for him to break into it.'

'But it now belongs to Angelina?'

The greedy look in her eyes, which Francine was making no attempt to conceal, sickened Alice. No wonder Marco wanted to protect Angelina from her grandmother. In his shoes Alice would have felt exactly the same.

'In theory, yes, although she will not be able to draw on the capital until she is of age.'

The cool but still calmly good-mannered way in which Marco was answering Francine's questions made Alice marvel at his self-restraint.

'No, of course not. But as her grandmother no doubt I shall be able to make use of the income for necessary expenses for her,' Francine told him with open smugness.

Giving Marco a smile of triumph, she turned to Alice, eyeing her assessingly, with ice-cold, unfriendly eyes.

'You must be the new nanny. Poor Angelina.' She gave a theatrical sigh. 'She must be missing Maria dreadfully. I'm going up to my room now, Marco. Please have something light sent up to me, will you? I refuse to even try to talk to this appalling housekeeper of yours. And you, Nanny—you may bring my granddaughter to me…er… once she has been fed and changed.'

Turning on her heel, she headed towards the stairs, her exit almost as dramatic as her appearance.

Weakly Alice looked at Marco. Now she realised what Maddalena might have meant when she had told her that neither of Angelina's parents had been truly worthy of her.

'Angelina needs her feed,' she told Marco huskily.

Fortunately the baby had slept through the altercation and was only just waking up, her gaze fixed trustingly and lovingly on Alice's face.

'I'll come up with you,' Marco announced abruptly. 'There is something I wish to discuss with you.'

As she lifted Angelina out of the stroller Alice's heart sank. Please don't let him bring up what happened this afternoon! she begged silently as he followed her with the stroller.

The nursery felt welcoming safe and familiar. Alice went to put Angelina in her cot, but Marco stopped her, saying, 'No. Give her to me.'

She must have been blind to have ever believed that he did not love the baby, Alice acknowledged as she saw the look he gave her.

The innate honesty that was so strongly a part of her nature forced her to admit uncomfortably to him, 'I hadn't realised that you were not Angelina's father…'

'You thought she was my child?'

He looked astonished.

'She looks like you,' Alice defended herself, 'and whilst the agency had informed me that she had lost her mother in tragic circumstances they had not said that...' She bit her lip, her voice stumbling to a halt as she saw the look of naked anguish in his eyes.

'Aldo was my cousin, my younger cousin, and we were as close in many ways as though we were brothers. We both lost our parents in the same accident.' He paused, his expression so bleak that Alice ached to be able to say something to comfort him, but how could she? What right did she have to do so?

'I have to admit that Aldo was perhaps a rather spoiled young man. I counselled him not to marry Patti, they were too different!' He paused, his expression grim. 'But Aldo was a very headstrong young man. They had very different aspirations, but neither of them were prepared to listen to any voice of reason or caution; they had fallen in love... Or so they claimed.'

'But you did not consider that to be important,' Alice heard herself challenging him sharply.

She refused to be quelled by the frowning look he was giving her.

'I didn't say that. Love is always important...but their interpretation of love would not be mine, and if it was "love" then I regret to say it was a love of only a very short-lived duration, although it gave me no pleasure when Aldo confirmed that my prediction that this would be the case had proved to be correct. By then Angelina was on the way...'

At the mention of Angelina, Alice put her anger to one side.

'Did her mother really consider terminating her pregnancy?' she couldn't help asking in shock.

'Patti was very much influenced by her mother, and you can see what kind of woman Francine is,' Marco replied.

'What's going to happen? Will she be able to take Angelina away from you?' Alice asked him uncertainly.

'Not whilst I have breath left in my body to prevent it,' Marco assured her vehemently.

'But she does have a…a legitimate claim on her,' Alice pressed him anxiously.

Was she imagining that slight betraying pause before he answered her? That barely discernible hesitation and skilfully covered concern?

'In so far as she is her grandmother, where as I was never legally appointed Angelina's guardian, I'm afraid so, yes,' Marco acknowledged.

'I am a single man with no experience of bringing up a child, and there are those…' He paused, his eyes bleak. 'I am afraid that in the world we live in today, it is necessary for every caring adult to question the motivation of a man bringing up a child who is not his own in a way that it is not with a woman.'

Alice silently digested what he was saying. She knew, of course, what he didn't want to put into words. And she also knew who was the best person to protect Angelina.

'Francine is an instinctive actress and she is very adept at concealing her real personality when the occasion demands it. One hint from her that I might have hidden motives in keeping Angelina with me, and no right-thinking court or judge would want to take that kind of risk.'

Alice could feel her heart starting to beat faster with increasing dread.

'Surely there must be something you can do…some way…? Alice began, pausing and shaking her head as she told him huskily, 'You can't mean to let her take Angelina.'

There was no doubt in her mind just where Angelina's best interests lay and it certainly wasn't with her grandmother, whom Alice had immediately disliked and distrusted.

Although he was not betraying it, inwardly Marco was fighting the same emotional turmoil as Alice.

Agitatedly she waited for Marco's reply, but then Alice couldn't help saying her thoughts aloud. 'If only you were married. Then surely she couldn't do anything!'

Marco tensed and stared at her. She was right, of course. If he had a wife, then there was no way that Francine could try to claim that he might have some unspeakable ulterior motive in keeping Angelina with him.

'No,' he agreed softly, fixing his gaze on Alice. 'She couldn't.'

Something about the way Marco was looking at her made Alice's heart start to pound frantically fast.

'What…? What is it?' she asked him uncertainly.

'I think you have just given me the answer to my problem.' Marco applauded her. 'I should have seen it for myself,' he continued, more as though he was talking to himself than her, Alice reflected as she waited nervously.

'I thought that in providing Angelina with a nanny who would guarantee to stay with her for a specific length of time that I was doing the very best I could for her, but now I realise that my thinking was not far-sighted enough. What Angelina needs to protect her now is not a nanny, but a woman who would have far more authority in her life in the eyes of the world. What Angelina needs is a mother, a woman who loves her and who has a legal title to prove her right to play the role of mother in her life, and I can think of no one who could fill that role for her better than you, Alice.'

Alice felt as though she wanted to sit down. Her head was spinning, her legs felt weak, and her heart was thudding so heavily that she felt the shock waves of it reverberating right through her body.

Her lips had gone painfully dry, and she was forced to moisten them with the tip of her tongue before she could reply, her body shaking as she saw the way that Marco's gaze homed in on that tiny betraying gesture of nervousness.

'What…what are you trying to say?' she asked him, but she suspected that she already knew what his answer was going to be.

'In order to protect Angelina from Francine I need a

wife—you have said so yourself! Under the circumstances, who better to be that wife, than you?'

'What?' Even though she had been half expecting it, Alice was still gripped by shock. 'No,' she whispered. 'We can't. I can't.'

'Yes, we can. We have to,' Marco insisted fiercely. 'For Angelina's sake.'

If she had still harboured any fugitive thoughts about Marco's love for or commitment to Angelina, what she was hearing and seeing now would have totally put them to flight, Alice recognised.

Here was a man who was totally dedicated to protecting the child fate had placed in his care, even to the extent of marrying a woman he did not love, in order to do so.

She loved Angelina too; could she do any less?

'Think about it,' Marco demanded insistently. 'The more I do, the more sense it makes.'

'I know what you're saying,' Alice was forced to agree, 'but…but marriage?'

Her face had gone pale and Marco could guess what she was thinking.

'So far as you and I are concerned, it will simply be a business arrangement,' he told her calmly. 'A business arrangement, which can be ended after a period of, say, five years, whenever you choose, just as your existing contract can be. I suspect that by that time Francine will have lost interest and found someone else to fasten her greedy talons into, preferably a rich film producer who will keep her safely in Los Angeles,' he added wryly. 'And Angelina will be at school.'

'No, it…it's impossible,' Alice repeated weakly, but she knew that her voice lacked the conviction it should have held. The trouble was that there were issues here that had nothing to do with the 'business arrangement' he was discussing so calmly.

'Why?' Marco was challenging her. 'You have already signed a contract agreeing to remain with Angelina until she goes to school. In agreeing to marry me you would merely be adding another dimension to that agreement.'

Another dimension! Marriage! And to a man she already knew she was far too deeply and dangerously emotionally vulnerable to! Some dimension!

'But we are talking about marriage. And not…not a…a business contract,' Alice protested.

When he didn't reply, she turned away from him slightly, her voice muffled as she told him, 'For a man like you I expect that, historically in your family, marriage *is* usually a business arrangement, but in my family, for me…' She stopped and shook her head.

'I thought you loved Angelina,' Marco said softly.

Alice could feel herself weakening.

'I do,' she acknowledged, unable to resist looking at the baby as she did so, feeling her heart melt with love for her. Yes, it melted with love for Angelina, and it over-heated with the adult form of exactly the same emotion for Marco, she reflected grimly, although he quite plainly did not feel the same way about her!

'I don't think you've given enough thought to what you're suggesting,' she told Marco valiantly, fighting hard to stave off her own potential downfall. 'You know very little about me. I might not have the right…qualifications to be Angelina's mother.'

She struggled for some logical way to make him see that what he was suggesting was impossible and then re-minded him with relief, 'After all, I tried to steal your car.'

'No, you didn't,' Marco countered her admission coolly. 'The young lady who was with you was the thief, you simply took the blame to protect her.'

'You knew that!' Alice gaped at him, unable to conceal her astonishment.

'I knew it.' Marco confirmed.

'But you never said anything. You…'

'Do you really think I would have even entertained the thought of employing you to look after Angelina had I thought you had been the thief?' He shook his head, answering his own question as he told her, 'No way. The reason I was so determined to hire you was because I could see just how loyal and protective a person you were. And because I knew just how desperately Angelina needed someone like you. No, not someone *like* you. Only you,' he corrected himself softly. 'There is no one else like you, Alice, not for Angelina. Surely you can't desert her now, knowing how much she needs you. Knowing how attached to you she has already become? She has lost so much already in her short life. Her mother…her father…'

He was pulling all her emotional strings at once, and very powerfully so too, Alice acknowledged, but if she had any sense she would resist the pressure he was putting on her.

If she had any sense. Since when has anyone in love possessed that quality? she asked herself ruefully, and she was in love twice over…once with Angelina…and a second time with him!

'And as for you not having the right qualifications! You have the only qualification Angelina needs. Your love for her!'

'This is crazy,' she protested.

'No!' Marco corrected her. 'What would be crazy would be for Angelina to be handed over to Francine to have her life destroyed as she destroyed her poor, wretched daughter's life.'

Alice knew that he was speaking the truth. And as Marco had already stated, logically, there was really very little difference in working for him as Angelina's nanny for the next five years and remaining with her for the same period as his wife in name only.

How could she desert Angelina when she needed her in her life so much?

How could she agree to a business arrangement of a marriage with Marco when she loved and wanted him so much?

Hadn't this afternoon taught her anything at all?

'Yes!' That he was the most wonderful man to be kissed by, she found herself thinking recklessly.

Hastily she called her thoughts to order, reprimanding herself for her own foolishness.

There would be no more kisses between them, she reminded herself sternly. From now it was going to be strictly business between them!

Marco frowned as he heard the demanding knock on the door of his study. It was nearly midnight and he had been working for the last three hours, coming to his study immediately after dinner.

Tomorrow, before he firmly asked Francine to leave, he intended to make it clear to her that there was no way she could expect to take Angelina away from him.

Thinking of Angelina made him think of Alice, though, and thinking of Alice made him ache for the feel of her delicious body in his arms, and her equally delicious mouth against his own, just as it had been this afternoon.

'Marco, I know you're in there.'

His frown deepened as Francine walked in.

'I've been thinking...about Angelina,' she told him coolly. 'She is my granddaughter and that means the world to me, but I can see the situation from your point of view. Aldo was your closest relative and your heir and now that he is dead...' She gave a small shrug. 'I can make things easy for you, Marco, or I can make them difficult.'

He watched her, without saying anything, but then there was no need for him to do so; he had already guessed the real purpose of her visit to the *palazzo*!

'If you could, for instance, see your way to...putting a certain sum of money at my disposal, I am sure we can come to some mutually beneficial agreement over Angelina's future. I am thinking in terms of, say...' She paused and gave another small shrug.

'Well, let us say, for instance, one million dollars... That is hardly anything to you, Marco. You are a very, very wealthy man...'

'You want to sell me your granddaughter, is that what you are saying?' Marco asked her bluntly. 'I had heard that you had attempted to sell your daughter to the highest bidder—'

'How dare you say that?' she stopped him, her face an unpleasant shade of red.

'I dare say it because it is the truth. You put Patti into the meat market the minute she was old enough to be there.'

'She had a very wealthy boyfriend when she was modelling,' she interrupted him.

'A wealthy boyfriend...' Marco's mouth compressed angrily. 'The man was over three times her age and already married. You sold her to him.'

'She wanted to be with him.' She was almost screaming at him now. 'She enjoyed being with him a damn sight more than she enjoyed being with your tight-fisted cousin. When I think of the opportunities she lost because of him... She wanted to leave him. Did he tell you that? She was going to come to LA... He killed her.'

'No, if anyone killed both of them it was you, Francine. You were the one who destroyed their marriage with your greed, and your soulless craving for money. History repeats itself, doesn't it? You sold your daughter and now you want to sell her child to me. One million dollars, you say...'

Slowly Marco shook his head. He was tempted to give in and pay her, but he knew that if he did the matter wouldn't end there. Francine would come back wanting more money and then more.

Marco didn't trust Francine at all. He disliked her and he knew that she felt exactly the same way about him and that if she thought she could hurt or damage him in any way at all she would try to do so. Even if that meant damaging her own granddaughter.

She was starting to scream at him, telling him that she would make him pay for not acceding to her demands, that if he had really cared about Angelina, really wanted her, he would have been glad to pay her.

It was half an hour before she finally realised that he was not going to give in and left, hurling insults and threats at him as she did so.

Listening impassively to her, Marco made himself a silent promise that he would never, ever allow her to subject Angelina to the same kind of abuse she had subjected Patti to! Now if anything he felt it was even more imperative that he and Alice should marry.

CHAPTER EIGHT

ALICE had agreed to marry Marco! Marco was going to be her husband; she was going to be his wife. But in name only, Alice reminded herself quickly as she got shakily out of bed and went to see if Angelina had woken up.

The baby was still asleep, lying peacefully in her cot. Beyond the window of her room, the sky was a wonderful soft shade of blue, the morning sun shining on the gardens of the *palazzo*. Marco's home, her home for the next five years. But it would have been that anyway, Alice argued determinedly with herself. After all, her contract stipulated that she would work for Marco until Angelina was five.

Work for him, yes, but marry him!

She could always change her mind; walk away from him, and from Angelina! She could, but Alice knew that she wouldn't. It simply wasn't in her nature to abandon anyone who needed her, especially when that person was a helpless six-month-old baby.

And her own secret feelings for Marco? How was she going to cope with those for the next five years? How was she going to conceal them? They said that familiarity bred contempt—perhaps she would discover that playing the role of Marco's wife would banish those unwanted and dangerous feelings!

It was an argument that was so frail and full of potential minefields that Alice had no wish to pursue it.

She was going to marry Marco. Only to protect Angelina from Francine. Would Francine come to the nursery to see her granddaughter?

As she worked capably through her morning routine, Alice's head was full of anxious questions.

Angelina was awake now, and Alice, who had pulled a robe on when she had got up, picked her up and sat on the comfortable chair in front of the window, cuddling her and talking to her, enjoying the pleasure of their shared sleepy early-morning togetherness.

A couple of hours later when Alice's mobile started to ring, and she recognised that her sister was calling, she had no inner warning of what was to come as she answered the call.

'Alice?' her sister demanded excitedly, before Alice could even say hello. 'You dark horse, why on earth didn't you say anything? Not even a tiny hint! Mind you, Louise says that she isn't surprised and that it was obvious to her that the sparks were flying between you the first time you met.

'We couldn't believe it when Dad rang us first thing this morning to say that Marco had been on the phone to him to formally ask for your hand in marriage. Mum and Dad are both here now, by the way, and they want to talk to you. We're all really looking forward to coming over. Marco sounds wonderful, and we can't wait to meet him.

'It's really generous of him to want to fly us all out and put us up at the *palazzo*. It sounds so grand. Louise says that he is grand.'

Alice's head was reeling. Marco had telephoned her family and told them that they were going to be married— had formally asked for her hand in marriage—without a word of warning to her...without discussing what he planned to do with her?

Her sister was speaking to someone else, and Alice could hear her laughing.

'Louise is pretending not to be excited about being a bridesmaid, but of course she is. She says to tell you, though, that there's no way she is going to wear pink. Has Marco got a big family? I suppose he will have, being Italian... It's all so romantic... He obviously can't wait to marry you... Four weeks. It's no time at all. The parents want to have a word...'

Numbly Alice spoke to her parents, although after the call was over she couldn't honestly remember just what she had said to them or to her sister's husband, who had also wanted to congratulate her, and Louise, who had re-iterated her refusal to wear pink.

From her father she had learned that Marco had rung them first thing that morning to formally request her hand in marriage, and to invite her family over for the wedding, which he had informed him would take place in just under four weeks' time.

Picking up Angelina, Alice made her way downstairs. She needed to talk to Marco and right now!

In the main salon she bumped into Maddalena who beamed with pleasure when she saw her and came hurrying over to her.

'The *conte* has told us that you are to marry! You will make him a good wife and a loving mama for this little one,' she added as she stroked Angelina's face. 'Please God, in time there will be other little ones to keep her company.'

Other little ones! Alice digested her comment in silence, praying that the housekeeper wouldn't notice how hot her face had become! Of course it was only natural that she should assume that she and Marco would want to have children.

'I need to speak to Marco, Maddalena,' she told the housekeeper. 'Do you know where he is?'

'He is in the library,' Maddalena told her, giving her a roguish look that promptly made Alice's face burn even more hotly.

'And...er...Francine?' Alice asked hastily. She was surprised that the other woman had not been to the nursery to see Angelina.

Maddalena gave her a fulminating look and tossed her

head, saying contemptuously, 'That one. She has gone. She is no good. None of us like her.'

Her shocked disbelief drove out Alice's earlier self-conscious embarrassment. Francine had gone! Without making any attempt to see Angelina or to talk to her about her, to ask how she was, to check on her welfare, and to check Alice's suitability to have charge of her?

Alice tried to imagine anyone in her own family behaving in such a way and found that she couldn't.

Such behaviour appalled her and reinforced the dislike and distrust she had already felt towards Francine. So far as Alice was concerned Francine was totally unfit to have charge of a child. Her behaviour only confirmed Alice's belief that she had no real option other than to do whatever she could to protect Angelina.

Even if that meant marrying Marco?

Even if that meant marrying Marco, she told herself firmly.

She suspected that Marco had been right when he had told her that Francine's interest in Angelina had been totally mercenary, but it still hurt for the baby's sake to have her feelings so callously confirmed. No grandparent worthy of the name could surely have left without making at least some attempt to see her own flesh and blood?

She was halfway down the length of the huge formal salon, one of a series of interconnecting rooms of vast proportions and elegant architecture, when Marco suddenly appeared from the opposite direction.

'I was just on my way up to the nursery,' he said.

'I was looking for you.'

They both spoke together and then stopped, Marco's expression carefully watchful, whilst Alice was conscious that she was fumbling her words slightly and looking self-conscious.

'My sister has just telephoned me,' she told him when his silence told her that he was waiting for her to speak first. 'You had no right to speak to my family without telling me first,' she protested indignantly. 'They think now that…' She stopped and bit her lip.

'They think what?' Marco pressed her.

Angelina had fallen asleep against her shoulder and was a heavy weight in her arms, and, as though Marco sensed her discomfort, he commanded Alice, 'Give her to me. Are you all right now? Your heatstroke—?'

'I'm fine,' Alice assured him. 'Well, so far as my heatstroke goes. But I really wish you had spoken to me before telephoning my family. My parents. My sister. All of them now believe…they think…'

'They think what?' Marco encouraged her.

Alice could feel her face starting to burn a little with her own discomfort. He was the one who was responsible for the fact that her family thought their marriage was a love match, so why on earth should she be feeling self-conscious and guilty about explaining their misapprehension to him. And explain it she must, since he had taken the step of inviting them all to their 'wedding' because now they would assume…expect…

'They think that we…you… They think our marriage is going to be a…a normal one,' she managed to tell him, her face a soft pink with discomposure. 'Especially with you asking my father so formally, and…and inviting them all here for the wedding. Why did you do that?' she demanded accusingly.

'Because it was the right and proper thing to do,' Marco returned promptly. 'You are their daughter, I shall be their son-in-law.'

'But don't you see? Now they think…. They think that you and I…that we're in love,' Alice finally managed to burst out uncomfortably.

Marco shrugged dismissively. 'So…is that a problem?'

'Well, of course it is,' Alice told him forcefully. 'Now they will expect—' She stopped, her flush deepening as she unwantedly mentally visualised just what her family would be expecting when they arrived for the wedding. A

loving couple who couldn't keep their eyes or their hands
off one another. Who were eagerly exchanging whispers
and kisses, who openly showed their love for one another.
A couple, in short, deep in the throes of their new-found
love.

'Our marriage is just a business arrangement and—'

'You were going to tell them that?' Marco challenged
her in disbelief.

Alice grimaced. The truth was that she hadn't got as far
as thinking just what she was going to tell her family, and
in fact the craven thought had occurred to her that she
really didn't need to tell them anything, since they already
knew she would be asked to remain with Angelina until
she reached school age.

'I wasn't going to say anything to them,' she was forced
to admit when Marco continued to stand in front of her,
automatically rocking Angelina in his arms as he waited
for her reply.

'Not tell them anything!'

She could hear the reprimand and disbelief in his voice.

'I didn't want to complicate things,' Alice defended herself. 'After all our…our marriage is surely just a small
extension of my contract… My family wouldn't have understood, they're old-fashioned and my sister…' Her voice
trailed away unhappily.

'For this to work, for us to be able to convince a court
that Angelina is in the right environment, it is essential
that so far as everyone else is concerned this is a "normal"
marriage,' Marco told her grimly. 'How do you think
Francine would have reacted if she had found out that we
were keeping our "marriage" a secret? That so far as your
family were concerned you are merely working here? Do
you really think she wouldn't have pounced on something
like that with glee so that she could use it in court against
us?'

There was nothing that Alice could say. She knew what
he was saying made sense, and she knew too that it was

impossible for her to explain to him how she really felt, not without running the risk of betraying her love for him!

'Whilst we are on the subject of our marriage,' Marco was continuing, 'That was why I was on my way to see you. I have made arrangements that the ceremony will take place at our local church four weeks from now. There will be other legal formalities to be gone through, as well as the religious ones, but these will not be too complicated. However, there will be a great deal to do here at the *palazzo*. I have already instructed Maddalena to take on the extra staff she will need. My family comprises several distant branches, filled, I am afraid to say, with some rather eccentric and elderly individuals who will all expect to be invited here to witness our marriage and share in its celebrations. Don't worry,' he told Alice when she made a small sound of shock. 'They will all fall on your neck with tears of gratitude, as they have been informing me that I should marry for many years now. However, my three eldest great-aunts all share a keen rivalry with one another, and one would need the skills of a Solomon to please them all.'

'Then why haven't you married?' Alice couldn't help asking him.

The frowning look he was giving her suddenly made her remember her first sighting of him. Now once more he was looking at her with that thoroughly arrogant disdain that made her own nerve endings prickle so sharply.

'Until now it hasn't been necessary,' Marco told her curtly.

'Necessary?' Alice shook her head in disbelief.

'People don't get married because it's ''necessary'',' she protested emotionally. 'They get married because they're in love. Because they can't bear not to be together.'

'So Aldo informed me,' Marco agreed dryly.

'Are you saying that love doesn't matter?' Alice challenged him, unable to prevent herself from asking the question. She didn't know why they were having this con-

versation, or rather she did, but she wished that she were
not being such a fool as to persist with it.

'Marriage for me has to be about more than mere sexual
desire,' Marco told her loftily. 'It has to be about a true
sharing of ideals and goals, of backgrounds and beliefs. It
has to be based on something that will last for a shared
lifetime and not burn out in a blaze of over-satiated lust.
In my opinion far too many people seek to sanitise physical lust by misnaming it love.'

His scornful dismissal of the importance of love warned
her of the fate she could expect if he were ever to recognise just how she felt about him. Before she could stop
herself, she was bursting out, 'I don't agree with you. I
think that love matters more than anything else, and…and
I always will. I would hate to be the kind of person who
thinks that it doesn't matter. But I suppose to someone like
you…'

'What do you mean someone like me?' Marco demanded. He didn't like her criticism and what he liked
even less was his own fierce reaction to it.

A little uncomfortable now about her outburst, Alice
tried to placate him.

'Well, it's obvious that a man like you—a man in your
position, with your family background,' she amended hastily when she saw the ominous way he was frowning at
her, 'would think of marriage in different terms to someone like me. I expect that you are used to the kind of
marriages where it's more about…about position and
wealth, than two people who love one another…' she finished. 'I suppose it's all about having different values.'

From the look in her eyes it was obvious to Marco that
she considered her own values to be vastly superior to his.

Infuriated, he was tempted to tell her that his parents'
marriage had been a fairy-tale love match, but instead he
chose another means of retaliation.

'Indeed it is,' he agreed smoothly. 'And as I have on

good authority, your values, unlike mine, are very modern.'

Alice's forehead crinkled into a small frown of incomprehension.

'What are you trying to say?' she demanded warily.

Marco gave her a savage look.

'As you have just pointed out, we are two different people from two different cultures, and, whilst I know how totally and completely committed you are to the children in your care, your moral values are not the same as mine.'

'My moral values?' Alice interrupted him sharply.

Marco looked away from her briefly before telling her, 'I know about your…affair with your previous boss.'

Alice was totally unable to make any response. What on earth was he talking about?

No way would she ever, ever even contemplate having an 'affair' with any married man, or any man loosely attached to someone else! The very thought revolted her.

'It was mentioned in the letter I received from his wife, in response to my request for a reference. She said that you were the best nanny she had ever had, but that her husband had confessed to having sex with you! She also hinted that there might have been other employer's husbands…who had enjoyed your…favours.'

Alice had always suspected that Pauline Levinsky had harboured an irrational resentment against her because she'd felt that Alice had been closer to her children than she'd been herself. But for her to do something like this!

Alice could vividly remember the day she had gone to Pauline and tactfully explained to her that instead of relocating to New York with the Levinsky family she had decided that the time had come for her to leave. It had been Pauline herself who had brought up the subject of her husband, Clive, and who had directly asked Alice if Clive was the reason she wanted to leave. And it was Pauline as well who had apologised when Alice had finally reluctantly admitted that she was leaving because she felt

uncomfortable about Clive's increasingly possessive attitude towards her, coupled with his constant references to
his sexual frustration.

She could remember how grateful she had felt towards
Pauline when her boss had immediately offered her an
apology.

How could Pauline have done this to her? Alice felt
sickened, humiliated, too hurt to realise what Marco's real
opinion of her was to even attempt to explain or to defend
herself.

When she was finally able to speak all Alice could say
was, 'You believe something like that about me but you
want to marry me?'

Marco narrowed his eyes slightly as he heard the anger
trembling in her voice. Her reaction wasn't what he had
expected. He admired the fact that she had made no attempt to explain or deny anything, but the stark look in
her eyes surprised him.

'Angelina is my prime concern here,' Marco replied
coolly. 'My only concern,' he underlined pointedly. 'And
so far as our marriage is concerned, it is merely a business
arrangement,' he reminded her. 'Were I looking for a
proper wife...' He paused, but Alice knew immediately
what he was thinking.

'You would never choose me? Well, I would never want
you either,' she lied fiercely. 'When I get married, properly
married, I want it to be to someone I love so...so much
that I can't bear to live without him. Someone who believes in love and who cherishes and values it,' she told
him passionately.

What he had just said to her had hurt her very badly,
and instinctively she wanted to defend and protect herself.
His cynical misjudgement of her hadn't just hurt her, it
had also put a totally different slant on the fact that he had
kissed her. Did he think she was the kind of woman who
slept around? With married men?

She knew that if it hadn't been for Angelina she would

have turned on her heel and walked out, torn up her contract and booked herself a seat on the first flight home.

But she simply could not do that to the little girl.

A new and totally untenable hideous thought struck her; a question bubbling to her lips that she had to ask.

'If you thought…if you believed…that about me, why did you employ me?' she demanded huskily.

Marco studied her.

As much to punish himself as punish her, he told her silkily, 'Well, it wasn't because I wanted to share the favours you've been giving to others.'

The fury of the look she shot him made him grimace ruefully. Were all women naturally good actors?

'Originally, you were the only applicant who fulfilled all of my criteria. Had I received Pauline Levinsky's letter before you had begun working for me and before Angelina had so obviously bonded with you, then no doubt I would not have employed you. However,' he continued coolly, 'so far as your, er…predilection for other women's husbands goes, it is not an issue, since I do not have a wife. Fortunately, by the time Angelina is old enough to need a moral role model…'

'I will be out of her life,' Alice completed bitterly for him. What on earth had she got herself into?

'Now,' Marco was continuing, as though the bombshell he had just dropped meant nothing, 'to get back to the matter in hand. You will of course need to make a visit to Milan to appoint a designer to make your wedding gown, and those of your attendants. I understand my friend the young car thief will be one of them, and also that she most assuredly will not wear pink.'

Alice stared at him. How could he indulge in humour after what he had just said? If she had needed any proof that he felt no personal emotion for her whatsoever, she had just received it, Alice acknowledged.

To her chagrin, knowing that actually hurt her more than

knowing that he thought she was the kind of person who indulged in casual sex!

'I'm sure I can find something simple and off the peg here in Florence,' she told him dully. 'As you said yourself, our marriage is just a business arrangement, after all, and not a proper marriage. We don't love one another.'

Alice was proud of the way she had managed to deny her feelings. She just hoped that she would be able to go on denying them!

'It is still a marriage, and both our families will have expectations of it. Beliefs, which I do not intend to damage.'

Mercifully, before he could say anything else Angelina woke up and started to whimper. 'Maddalena told me that Francine has left,' Alice managed to steady her voice enough to say as she took Angelina from Marco, carefully making sure that she didn't accidentally come into physical contact with him as she did so, cuddling her until she had calmed down before laying her down.

After what he had just said to her, he must never, ever guess how she felt about him. Could he really not see that she was simply not the sort of person to indulge in the kind of behaviour he had accused her of? Theirs was a business relationship, entered into solely to protect the child they both loved, and from now on her pride must make sure that he never had any reason to suspect she had ever dreamed of it being anything else.

'Yes, she has,' Marco agreed.

'Do you think she will still try to take Angelina away?' Alice asked him, giving a small shiver of apprehension as she did so.

'What I think is that if she does, the fact that you and I will be married should ensure that Angelina stays where she belongs, with people who love her,' Marco told her firmly.

'Now, we have a great deal to discuss. We shall of course be hosting together a pre-wedding dinner for both our families, and a post-wedding party. It is a tradition in my family that when the heir marries, a large feast is held for the estate workers—but I shall make all the arrangements for that. I have invited your family to fly over to join us one week before the wedding; that should allow time for our little Ferrari thief to try on her bridesmaid's gown. Of course your sister will be your principal attendant. Since my great-aunts are extremely traditional, not to say old-fashioned in their outlook, they will as a matter of course expect us to be sleeping in separate rooms, so there should be no embarrassment on that score, although, whilst we are discussing such a delicate subject, I suspect that we shall be expected to indulge in the occasional display of mutual affection.'

'No!' Alice's face had gone paper-white, fear and anxiety sharpening her voice.

'No,' she repeated. Shaking her head vehemently, 'I won't. You can't expect me to do anything like that.'

The intensity and immediacy of her rejection brought a dark glitter of anger to Marco's eyes.

'You're overdoing the pseudo-virginal hysterics,' he warned her grittily. 'After all,' he continued unforgivably in a voice as smooth as honey, 'it isn't as though you're being asked to do anything you haven't done before, many, many times, and of course with far more intimacy.'

It was too much for Alice to bear. Blindly she retaliated, telling him fiercely, 'That was different. I didn't have to pretend, then. I wanted him…them…' she corrected herself recklessly as she saw the look in his eyes.

She gave a small, high-pitched cry of fear and panic as she was unceremoniously dragged into Marco's arms, and imprisoned there whilst his mouth savaged hers.

Innocent as she was, even Alice knew that it was a mistake to challenge a man sexually, and even more of one to imply that he was sexually inferior to another. That was no doubt why Marco was kissing her so passionately now, forcing her lips to part as his tongue thrust deeply into her mouth causing her whole body to shudder in tormented recognition of the sexual symbolism of his intimate kiss.

This was the kind of kiss a man gave to a sexually experienced woman, she realised, the kind of kiss that immediately propelled them both into a shockingly sensual place.

She felt his hand touching her body, boldly taking possession of her breast, expertly caressing its peak into a tormented nub of frantic longing. Dizzily Alice knew that ultimately she was going to hate herself for the way she was feeling, but she simply did not have the experience to fight back against such a sustained and erotic attack. Helplessly she swayed towards Marco, wanting to be even closer to him, her hand reaching up towards his jaw in her need to prolong the intimacy of his kiss, but as soon as she touched him he stepped back from her, manacling her wrists with his hands as he kept her at a distance, demanding, 'Now tell me that you were acting.'

There was nothing Alice could say. No way she could hide her shame.

'We can't do this,' she whispered in anguish.

'We can't not do,' Marco corrected her harshly. 'It's too late to change your mind now.'

His own behaviour had shocked him. He was behaving like a jealous lover!

CHAPTER NINE

MISERABLY Alice ducked her head as she and Marco came out of the renaissance church where, like them, so many of Marco's ancestors had been married.

Only she knew just how badly affected she was by this mockery of what should have been one of the most special and meaningful days of her life.

In a deliberate act of self-loathing, she had chosen not the pure white dress she was fully entitled to wear, but instead one that was a rich, warm cream.

'I thought it would cause too much comment if I wore scarlet,' she told Marco flippantly just as they left the church.

To her relief her family had fully understood and supported her determination to pay for her own dress and those of her attendants, although Marco had not been very pleased when she had told him of this decision.

'What's wrong? Are you afraid that it might not be good enough? You should have thought about that before you asked me to marry you,' she had thrown angrily at him. 'I am not letting you pay for my wedding dress.'

'We made a business arrangement,' Marco had reminded her grimly. 'And as part of that arrangement, naturally I am prepared to pay for any clothes you will need to support your new role.'

'I don't care what you say. You are not buying my wedding dress,' Alice had retorted.

And that had only been one of the fierce arguments they had had in the lead-up to their wedding day.

Unfortunately one of the most serious ones had been

one she had lost—and it had been over her engagement and wedding rings.

When Marco had produced the huge ring that he had told her was traditionally worn by the di Vincenti brides, she had blanched in horror at the thought of wearing something so patently irreplaceable, but Marco had been insistent.

'My family will expect to see you wearing it,' he had told her. And he had been right; the first thing his great-aunts had looked for when she had been formally presented to them had been the family ring.

Unexpectedly, Alice had rather taken to Marco's great-aunts. They made her laugh with their quaint, old-fashioned ways, but she could see beneath their bravado that they were three elderly ladies who felt apprehensive about the way the modern world was going. None of them had any children and so Marco, although both he and they would have immediately denied it, obviously had a very special place in their hearts.

From all of them she had learned about his childhood, and his teenage years; the courage with which he had taken on his father's mantle, the differences between him and Aldo, whom they had all denounced as a very spoiled and selfish young man, and from them she had learned too just how important it was to them as a family that Marco continued the family line with children, especially a son of his own.

She already knew, of course, just how strong his sense of duty was; far, far stronger than his own feelings!

As she'd listened to them her heart had grown heavier and heavier. No doubt one day Marco would have sons, but of course she would not be their mother!

As their wedding guests pressed close to them to offer them their congratulations, Alice looked towards her sister, who had happily taken charge of Angelina.

Like Louise, she was wearing a dress in soft, shifting layers of differently shaded lilac silk organza.

It suited her and Alice could tell her that her brother-in-law, Louise's father, thought so too.

As Louise picked up the train of her dress she rolled her eyes at Alice and told her in her newly acquired grown-up manner, 'Don't say anything, but I'm sure Dad is trying to persuade poor Connie to have a baby. Honestly, you'd think he'd have more sense.' She shook her head derisively. But Alice could see that she was far from averse to the idea of a stepsibling, and her heart lifted a little.

As she smiled at her Louise gave her an uncertain look and whispered gruffly, 'Thanks for not saying anything to them, about…you know what…'

The previous evening at dinner, the celebration family dinner, Marco had presented Louise with a beautiful gold charm bracelet and hanging from it had been a perfect miniature Ferrari.

The words of their so recently spoken vows were ringing still in Alice's head as she sat beside Marco as his wife for the lengthy formal dinner being given to celebrate their marriage. Over five hundred guests had been invited, despite the reservations and doubts Alice had raised when Marco had discussed his plans with her.

'It is expected. It would cause gossip if we didn't, and I don't intend to give Francine any ammunition to fire at us,' was all he had said when she had tried to protest that it surely made sense to keep their marriage low-key, especially in view of their inevitable ending of it.

The meal was over and the final toasts had been drunk. Angelina was lying fast asleep in her stroller at Alice's side.

Somehow, foolishly, perhaps, she had not realised just how she was going to feel when they exchanged their wedding vows, how momentous the occasion would be, how solemn and awesome; how portentous and binding the words were going to sound, and how both her senses and her body were going to react to them.

But it was too late now to feel that she had committed a sin against the sanctity of marriage and the sanctity of her love. She was Marco's wife.

In name only, she reminded herself shakily. It was a business arrangement, that was all.

In the ballroom, beyond the salon where they had eaten, they could see through the folded-back open double doors that the band was starting to play.

Alice frowned as she recognised that those people seated closest to them were all turning to look at them.

The speeches were over, surely?

'Alice...' she heard Marco saying formally as he pushed back his chair and stood up.

What was he expecting her to do? Confused, she looked at her sister, who laughed and told her softly, 'Everyone's waiting for you and Marco to begin the dancing. It's tradition that the bride and groom have the first dance, remember.'

Of course... Flushing, Alice pushed back her own chair, conscious of how warm and strong Marco's hand felt as he took hold of her. She saw him frown as he felt the icy coldness of her fingers.

Her eyes felt heavy with the tears she knew she must not shed; tears for all that this day should have meant and all that would now be denied to her for ever. She knew that, no matter what her future held, this day would cast its shadow over any happiness she might have had for ever.

They were on the dance floor now, with Marco drawing her closer, so close that she could feel the beat of his heart against her own body, fierce, thunderous. Dangerous. She missed a step and trembled as he held her closer, instinctively looking up at him and then wishing that she hadn't.

She could see the firm thrust of his chin, the full, warm curve of his bottom lip. Her trembling became more intense and she could feel his hand tightening around hers. He smelled faintly of the cologne he wore and a taunting, sensual Marco smell that made her ache to close her eyes and just stand there breathing it in. Breathing him in, and impressing on her mind for ever this heartbeat of time.

The slow strains of the old-fashioned romantic waltz filled her ears, the heat of Marco's body enveloping her. She felt as though they were enclosed in a small, private island of their own, an island where nothing else existed, only the way she felt about him and the way she longed for him to feel about her.

She missed another step and gasped as he held her, almost lifting her against his body.

'You're tired.' He made it sound like an accusation.

'No,' she denied.

The intimacy of dancing with him like this on the day of their wedding, their marriage, brought an emotional lump to her throat. Abruptly the music stopped, bringing her back to a reality she didn't want. In his arms she had been able to imagine…to pretend… She made to turn away from him but he restrained her.

'Our guests are waiting,' he told her.

Puzzled, she asked him, 'What for?'

'For this,' he responded, drawing her back against his body and slowly wrapping one arm around her before cupping the side of her face with his free hand, tilting her face up towards his own.

His kiss was slow and measured, savouring her mouth, an intimate act for a public audience, made all the more shocking and dangerous somehow by the fact that outwardly he made it look so tender whilst inwardly she knew it meant nothing at all. At least not to him.

When he finally released her their guests were clapping and laughing. Fiercely Alice blinked away her threatening tears.

Other couples were joining them on the dance floor now. Alice pulled away from Marco.

'I want to go and check on Angelina.'

'Your sister is with her,' he reminded her.

'She is my responsibility,' Alice insisted stubbornly. 'She is why you have married me, after all.'

'And why you have married me,' Marco responded.

'You must be disappointed that you aren't having a honeymoon.'

Alice shook her head as she listened to her sister. It was two o'clock in the morning and the festivities were finally over.

'No, I'm not,' she told her, truthfully.

They had reached the top of the stairs, and Alice turned automatically to head for the nursery.

Laughing, Connie stopped her. 'Where are you going?' she asked her. 'The master bedroom suite is that way…'

'Oh… Yes. But Angelina…'

'Maddalena and I have moved Angelina's things into the master suite for you,' Connie told her with a gentle smile. 'Marco explained that there hadn't been an opportunity yet for the two of you to redecorate the rooms he had been using, and that you planned to do that together. I don't suppose Angelina will mind sleeping in his dressing room for the time being, though. Not when she's got the two of you so close to her…'

Alice swallowed nervously as she listened to her sister. Foolishly perhaps, she had not really given any thought to where she would be sleeping once she and Marco were married. Somehow she had assumed that she would simply go on sleeping in her room in the nursery suite, but it seemed that she had been wrong.

As she hesitated outside Marco's bedroom door, it suddenly opened and Marco himself was standing there.

'One bride,' her sister told him mischievously before adding, 'Is Angelina okay? Maddalena and I checked on her an hour ago.'

'She's fine. Fast asleep,' Marco responded, standing back from the doorway, and somehow without knowing quite how it had happened Alice discovered that she had walked inside and that the door was being closed, shutting her in the room with Marco.

She had not been in his bedroom before, and she glanced round it quickly and nervously. Like all the rooms in the *palazzo* it was huge, and furnished in what she guessed were priceless antiques.

'I can't sleep in here,' she told him huskily, panic suddenly filling her.

'I'm afraid you not only can, but must!' Marco informed her coolly. 'After all, it's what everyone will expect. We are now man and wife.'

'Yes, but only because of Angelina…I… You said this was going to be a marriage in name only.'

'Which it is, but you can't sleep apart from me tonight, of all nights. Surely you must realise that?' Marco told her giving her, a grim look as he added derisively, 'You're off stage now, Alice. You can forget the wide-eyed virgin-bride look! And you can forget anything else as well. I shall spend the night in my dressing room. There is a bed in there. After our guests have left tomorrow we will have time to talk about the future properly.'

Alice felt too unhappy to argue with him or to protest at his high-handedness.

And besides, if she did she suspected he would only deride her.

'The bathroom is through there,' Marco told her, indicating one of the two doors opening off the bedroom.

'Your sister and Maddalena have brought some of your things from your own room, I believe…' he added before going into the dressing room and closing the door behind him.

Some of her things… Which of them? Alice wondered worriedly.

It was her habit to sleep in nothing other than her own skin, a sensual pleasure she especially enjoyed indulging in at the *palazzo* where the bed linen was cool, crisp cotton, smelling of fresh air and herbs. However, the thought of padding naked around a room with Marco in such close proximity was not one she felt in any way relaxed about.

Had her sister thought to bring her a robe, or had she assumed that, as a new bride, Alice would neither want nor need to wear any such thing?

Marco stared broodingly out of the dressing-room window into the soft darkness of the night, trying to come to terms with his feelings, and the simple truth he had had to confront.

From the moment Alice had come into his life she had unwittingly challenged his own beliefs, overturning things about himself he had thought were set in stone. He had tried to resist, telling himself that it was for Angelina's sake that he had been able to recognise how much she was able to give the baby in terms of love, and how much more important that was than the differences that existed between their sexual moral codes.

He had tried to dismiss his own desire for her as an unimportant irritation that could be ignored; he had even, shamefully, at one point, tried to find some way of convincing himself that Alice had deliberately incited it, but thankfully his conscience had refused to co-operate.

Instead he had tried to separate Alice into two different people: the Alice whose love for Angelina was unconditional and unquestionable, and whom he just had to watch with the baby and he was filled with the fiercest and purest emotions it was possible for him to feel, and the Alice who'd thought nothing of having sex with a married man.

Over the past few weeks, the Alice who gave herself so unstintingly to Angelina's care had touched his emotions more and more deeply. And as for the Alice who had apparently given herself equally unstintingly to her lovers— Marco closed his eyes, a muscle tensing in his jaw.

There was no point in lying to himself any longer—the emotion motivating him when he thought of that Alice was not self-righteous disapproval, but raw, male jealousy.

He might genuinely have been prompted to suggest a marriage between Alice and himself as a means of protecting Angelina, but today, standing in church beside her, he had known that he was marrying her because he loved her.

And the Alice he loved was the whole Alice; all of her; just as she was perfect. He had no right to judge her. It was his jealousy and his perhaps outdated beliefs that were at fault, and not Alice herself.

Earlier in the evening dancing with her, holding her in his arms, breathing in her perfume, he had ached so badly for her, but there was no way now that sex alone could ever be enough to appease his hunger for her.

Outside in the main bedroom Alice suddenly frowned. She had removed her veil and her headdress earlier in the evening but she was still wearing her wedding dress, and she now realised that unless she asked for Marco's help in removing it she was going to have to spend the night sleeping in it, since it fastened all the way down the back with a long row of tiny little buttons.

No doubt it would cause a stir if she appeared at breakfast in the morning still wearing her wedding gown!

Walking a little unsteadily to the closed dressing-room door, she knocked self-consciously on it, and called out hesitantly, 'Marco.'

Pausing in the act of unfastening his shirt buttons, Marco went to open the door.

Alice felt her heart starting to thud far too heavily as she looked at him, one hand lazily unfastening the buttons on his shirt whilst he stood there, his mouth slightly twisted in an expression she couldn't understand.

'I'm sorry to disturb you,' she began and then stopped. Did her voice sound as betrayingly nervous and self-conscious to Marco as it did to her?

She touched the side of her throat, her fingers playing

with her hair, and then tensed. There was something about the way Marco was watching her.

Had his expression changed, or was it simply the shadows that were giving him that hooded, dangerous look that was making her heart beat so fiercely fast?

Desperate to evade his gaze, Alice dragged her own away only to discover that it was now resting where his unfastened shirt was revealing a dark expanse of hard-muscled torso, finely covered in soft dark hair.

Marco was her husband; she was his wife; they had just been married.

A fine shudder of reaction skittered over her body as her emotions overwhelmed her. The intensity of her own longing, her own love made her feel dizzy. Alice swallowed. Hard. Very hard…and not because she felt nervous. No way did she feel nervous. No, what she felt was…

Her arm had actually lifted of its own volition, her fingertips aching to delve into that sexy, silky darkness, and explore that soft, silky evidence of his maleness, before she somehow managed to stop herself.

Her throat had gone dry, her tiredness forgotten. Desperately she tried to remind herself of just why she had gone to him.

'I…I need some help with my dress,' she managed to whisper. 'The buttons…' To show him what she meant she turned round.

'I can't unfasten them,' she explained.

'Yes, I can see what you mean.'

She had never heard Marco's voice sound so terse.

'I can't sleep in my dress.' Why wasn't he doing anything? She could feel the searing heat of his breath against the exposed nape of her neck. It made her ache to be closer to him, to turn round and demand, beg that he treat her as a woman and not as a business partner.

'I can't ask anyone else.' Her voice trembled and her face burned with the humiliation of knowing just how dangerously close she was to making a complete fool of herself.

Marco did not share her feelings; she already knew that.

'No,' she heard him agreeing, his voice deep and unfamiliarly strained. 'You can't.'

'Your dress makes your waist look tiny,' Marco told her, unexpectedly spanning it with his hands. His voice sounded different somehow, deeper, thicker, and Alice knew that there was a betraying tremble in her own as she responded automatically.

'It's the boning inside it.'

'Boning?' Marco sounded bemused. 'I thought that went out with the Victorians,' he commented as he began to carefully unfasten the tiny buttons.

Tensing her body against any betraying reaction to him, Alice gritted her teeth.

There was a tallboy with a mirror on it in front of her and in it she could see her own reflection and Marco's as he slid the tiny loops over the even smaller buttons, but it wasn't the sight of his dark hands busily unfastening her dress that suddenly caused her to draw in her breath. No, it was the realisation that once the dress was completely unfastened and unsupported it would slither from her shoulders, and all she was wearing underneath it was a tiny pair of briefs. No bra, no hose, just a minute pair of silk briefs.

Marco had reached the small of her back. Alice could feel the heavy weight of her dress starting to drag it downwards, another few buttons and it would... She started to panic, trying to pull away from him.

'Wait,' he instructed her, refusing to let go. 'I haven't unfastened them all yet.'

Not all of them maybe, but he had unfastened enough of them, Alice recognised as her dress slid to the floor with a whoosh before she could grab hold of it.

Frozen with self-consciousness, Alice couldn't move.

In the mirror her gaze met Marco's, her colour getting

higher with every breath she took. Marco looked as though he had been turned to stone, as immobile as she was herself apart from the fierce glitter darkening his eyes. She heard him breathe a harsh, ragged sound that brought her skin out in a rush of sensual goose-bumps, and galvanised her into protective action.

As though they had actually felt the heat of that breath on them, her nipples pouted and stiffened. Instinctively Alice tried to conceal what was happening to her from him; the urge to lift her hands and cover her breasts was automatic.

But shockingly Marco reacted faster, so that it was his hands that covered her nakedness, cupping their soft shape, concealing their flaunting arousal.

'Alice! Alice!' she heard him groan in a tone of voice she had never heard him use before, deep raw, hungry, making her shiver with excitement and longing.

He bent his head and kissed the side of her throat, causing a million zillion quivers of wild, frantic delight to soar through her.

'Have you any idea what you're doing to me?' he demanded thickly. 'Do you know how tempting this is? You are?' he whispered roughly. 'Far, far too tempting!' he answered his own question, his voice thick with desire. 'Do you know what you're doing to me? How much you are making me want you?'

Alice certainly knew what he was doing to her, and how very, very tempted, how shockingly, achingly tormented she was!

He was turning her round, so that her naked breasts were pressed tightly against his equally naked chest, his hands sliding down her back to pull her right into his body, and then cupping the soft, rounded shape of her buttocks.

She could feel how aroused he was. Knowing that he wanted her made her feel sensually powerful, increasing her longing for him.

Ruthlessly she ignored the tiny voice trying to remind

her that he did not love her, and that his sexual arousal was just an automatic male reaction to her nakedness.

She didn't want the truth.

No, what she wanted was the fantasy of believing that he loved her.

Without knowing she had done so, she breathed his name, exhaling it in a soft, enticing sound of intimate invitation and desire.

It ran over Marco's senses like a small electric current, heightening everything he was already feeling. It was impossible for him to resist her.

He could feel her body quivering beneath his touch; reality was being consumed in the fiercely burning fires of his desire.

He kissed her forehead and then her eyelids, her cheek and the shockingly responsive place just behind her ear, making Alice moan openly in aching pleasure.

Marco could feel his self-control slipping away. He kissed her mouth, slowly, carefully, trying to restrain himself. Her lips trembled beneath his and her hand gripped his shoulder, her fingers digging into his flesh as she shuddered against him.

She was irresistibly responsive, making him feel that she was powerless to control her reaction to him. It was a dangerously powerful aphrodisiac. For a second he hesitated, reminding himself that he was a man of honour and that their marriage was solely a business arrangement, at least so far as she was concerned, no matter how he might feel about her, but the feel of her against him was too much for his self-control.

'You want me?' he asked her, determined to let the decision be hers.

Alice tensed. Here was her chance to stop what was happening if she wanted to. She was poised on the brink of taking a step that once taken would change her life for ever. But hadn't her love for Marco already done that?

Wouldn't she regret it for the rest her life if she refused what he was offering her now?

Taking a deep breath, she nodded, and then just in case he hadn't understood she told him huskily, 'Yes, I want you.'

Such simple words, to make his heart ache with such heaviness and his body pulse with such longing, Marco acknowledged.

Cupping her face, he kissed her slowly, savouring every centimetre of her mouth with an intimacy that momentarily caught Alice off guard. His hands were caressing her body. Against her mouth he whispered, 'Aren't you going to undress me?'

Her undress him? Alice began to panic. She had forgotten that Marco believed her to be sexually experienced, and a seducer of married men!

Alice's stiffness and lack of response made Marco frown. Had she changed her mind?

He tried to look into her eyes, but she immediately dropped her lashes, veiling them from him.

'I think it might save time if you did that yourself.'

Alice didn't know how she had managed to find the courage to whisper the soft words. She felt as though her whole body were on fire with self-consciousness.

Save time! Marco was too engrossed in his own thoughts and feelings to register her discomfort. Picking her up, he carried her over to the bed, slowly lowering her onto it and leaning over her so that her breasts were pressed against the warm nakedness of his chest.

'You're right,' he told her thickly. 'We don't need to waste time on unnecessary preliminaries when what we both want is this!'

He was kissing her now in a way that shocked her nearly as much as it excited her. His hands shaped her naked breasts. As he ran the tip of his tongue round her softly swollen mouth he ran the pad of his thumb around her aching nipple.

Her whole body arched as though a bow had been drawn taut from her breasts to her sex. Unable to stop herself, Alice made a small pleading gasp of sound, which she tried to smother against Marco's shoulder, but instead of releasing her from her torment her reaction only caused him to increase it.

The way he was touching her nipples made her whole body shudder with desire. And the only way she could stifle the sounds of agonised need she was making was to bite sharply into the firm flesh against her lips, whilst her fingers clenched into the sheet, which the passionate thrashing of her body had ruckled.

The sensuality of her response to him was driving Marco out of his mind. Tugging at his clothes, he tore them off as quickly as he could without releasing her, knowing that he was simply not able to release her. The feel and taste of her, the scent and heat of her were like an immediately addictive drug.

The hand he had had to lift from her body to unfasten his trousers had left her breast exposed, its peak taut, tempting him, taunting him to respond to its erotic invitation. Dragging off the last of his clothes, he covered it with his lips, laving it fiercely with his tongue before drawing it deeply into his mouth and sweetly savaging it with the raw sensuality of his need.

His hand slid down her body, parting her legs, seeking her warm, female heat.

Deep shudders ripped through Alice's body. She had thought she knew all about sex, and that experiencing it would hold no surprises for her, but the raw sexuality of what was happening was showing her how wrong she had been.

Somehow, without knowing how, she had buried her fingers in Marco's hair, holding his head against her breast as she submitted to the ferocity of the sensation that swept her in wave after wave.

She could feel the wet heat of her sex, and feel, too, the

way it was responding to Marco's touch, expanding, opening. His fingertip stroked and searched and then circled, and the nub of flesh normally so innocently dormant swelled and pulsed with pleasure.

'Marco. Marco.'

Barely aware that she was even speaking, never mind what she was actually inciting, Alice kept on repeating Marco's name in a frenzied litany of uncontrollable need.

Marco hesitated. He could sense how close she was to her fulfilment, but this first time for them together he wanted that fulfilment to be part of his.

Still stroking her, he moved over her, kissing her passionately as he started to thrust into her.

Beneath his kiss Alice gasped, her eyes widening as she felt her body stretch to accommodate him. Oh, but it felt so good. He felt so good.

Helplessly she clung to Marco, overwhelmed by what she was feeling. All she knew was that the sharp pang of pain she was suddenly experiencing was somehow a part of the so much greater pleasure; that the feeling of being totally filled by him was one that she was enjoying too much to care about the pain.

Marco felt her body's tension, its tightness, he heard Alice's small cry but it was too late for him to stop what was happening. To withdraw now would be to risk hurting her even more. He tried to control his body's demand for completion, but it was too late.

Alice's fingers tightened into the hard muscle of Marco's arm as beyond the pain she could feel something else, somewhere else, a place so powerful and achingly sweet that tears filled her eyes at the thought of not reaching it. Desperately she pressed closer to Marco, silently willing him to take her there, and then miraculously that was what he did and the small, tiny waves of sensation moving with such wonderful pleasure inside her had become larger ones, thudding, rolling, curling, ocean-wide breakers of such pleasure that she could hardly bear to endure it.

In its aftermath her whole body felt as though it were humming with happiness. Drowsily she looked at Marco, trying to suppress her small, instinctive wince as he withdrew from her. She felt so tired. She could hardly keep her eyes open. She started to yawn.

Grimly Marco watched her.

CHAPTER TEN

'ALICE.'

Reluctantly Alice opened her eyes. Daylight was pouring in through the bedroom window and as Marco leaned over her, a towel draped round his hips, his body gleaming from the shower he had obviously just taken, she could see the scratch marks on his skin. Scratch marks she had inflicted last night at the height of her passion!

Miserably Alice tried to swallow. If she had been foolish enough to entertain some secret hope that last night's intimacy would somehow magically cause Marco to announce that he loved her, she knew now just how wrong she had been.

No words of love had passed his lips last night and, from the look she could see in his eyes, he certainly wasn't about to utter any now.

'Why didn't you tell me you were a virgin?' Marco asked her tersely.

He had been awake half the night mentally lashing himself for what he had done, for his crassness, his selfishness, his sheer male brutality in hurting her, but instead of telling her what he was actually feeling Marco heard himself sounding as angry as though she were the one at fault.

Marco's anger banished Alice's self-pity. Grabbing the sheet, she sat up in the bed and faced him. 'What was the point?' she challenged him. 'You had already decided that I was sexually experienced; a woman who seduced married men.'

She held her breath, waiting to see how Marco would react, willing him to tell her that he had never for a moment really doubted her. And then once he had done that

137

she wanted him to take her in his arms and tell her how much last night had meant to him and how it had made him realise that he loved her.

But of course he did no such thing. Instead he walked towards the window and stood there with his back to her.

'You do realise that this changes everything between us, don't you?' he told her.

She could hear from his voice just how seriously he was taking things.

'How could my virginity do that?' she asked him uncertainly.

She could hear his irritated indrawn breath.

'How could it not? Do you think I am the kind of man who goes around deflowering virgins?' He stopped and shook his head, swinging round to focus on her. 'Do you imagine that I like knowing that my...my desire was so out of control that I could not restrain myself? We will talk later about Mrs Levinsky's reasons for lying to me about you, but I think I guess what they were. Jealousy is a very dangerous weapon. I have no excuses to offer you for what...what happened. You are now my wife in every sense of the word. It is my duty, my responsibility...'

'No,' Alice protested, struggling to come to terms with what he was saying. 'We made a business arrangement, that is all.'

'Last night changed all that irrevocably,' Marco told her implacably. 'Do you realise that you could be carrying our child...my child?' he threw at her.

Alice gripped the sheet ever harder. A baby. Marco's baby... She could feel herself melting, yearning...and she had to fight to hold onto reality.

'We must both hope that you are not,' Marco said sternly.

He didn't want her to have his child?

'We have agreed that our marriage will end in five years' time,' Marco reminded her as though he sensed what she was thinking. 'I considered myself to be honour bound to stand by that arrangement. However, if you were to have my child, there is no way I could allow him or her to be brought up by anyone other than myself.' He paused and looked past her before continuing, 'And knowing what I do about you I know that you will feel the same way. You have very strong feelings about love. I know that. I cannot compound what I have already done by tying you to a loveless marriage.'

Alice's heart had started to thump far too heavily. There! He had told her now that he did not love her. How much more plainly did she need to hear it?

As though her silence exasperated him, he grated harshly, 'Why did you let it happen, Alice? To punish me for misjudging you? To make an irrevocable, unassailable point? Didn't you think…?'

No matter why she had done it, he was the one who was at fault. Marco knew that. But he also knew that the reality of starkly putting into words that she did not love him was tearing him apart.

This wasn't a pain he was going to have to endure for a matter of weeks or months, but for the rest of his life!

Dangerously close to tears, Alice glared at him.

'Didn't you think?' she challenged him.

'Think? In the state I was in?' Marco's expression was self-derisory.

He could see Alice starting to frown and he cursed himself inwardly. If he wasn't careful he was going to reveal to her how he felt about her, and that was a burden he was fiercely determined he was not going to place on her.

At least he hadn't guessed how she felt about him, Alice comforted herself. At least she was to be spared that humiliation.

'It seemed a good idea at the time,' she responded, giving a small toss of her head.

'A good idea?'

She could see the way Marco's throat constricted as the

words were ripped from it. He was looking at her as though he would like to strangle her.

'How could you behave so irresponsibly, throw yourself away so casually…? Especially when…'

He stopped, but Alice guessed what he had been about to say. Especially when he didn't love her and she meant nothing whatsoever to him.

Marco tried to calm himself down. He knew the demands pride and self-respect could make on a person, but for Alice to go to such dangerous lengths. Had she no sense of self-preservation?

'It wasn't really that important,' Alice told him with a bravado she was far from feeling. The truth was that it was only the most important thing she had ever done! 'At my age virginity can get to be something of an embarrassment, and, besides, I thought it was time I found out what all the fuss is about!'

She felt she ought to get that in, just to make sure she had made it plain to him that she was not foolish enough to be dreaming dreams of love.

Marco could scarcely believe his ears. He watched her through narrowed eyes. She sounded convincing enough, but something, some instinct, told him that she was lying to him. Why? Was she aware of the challenge she was issuing? And the way his own instincts were leaping to meet it, and to show her right here and now just how much pleasure her body was capable of?

Grimly he decided to teach her a small warning lesson, for her own sake as well as his!

'Indeed,' he responded silkily. 'Dare I hope that I came up to your expectations?'

Uneasily Alice rubbed her tongue-tip round her nervously dry lips. She knew she had been deliberately goading him.

Unable to risk looking directly at him, she told him as insouciantly as she could, 'It was… It was interesting, but not something I would want to repeat.'

Marco stared at her. He was tempted to let himself believe that she was deliberately trying to incite him. If he
thought for one minute that she actually wanted... But then
she turned her head and he saw the dark bruise on her
collar-bone—a bruise he himself must have inflicted at the
height of his passion—and guilt poured through him, filling him with self-contempt.

It was bad enough that he had taken her virginity. He
wasn't going to let himself be so weakened by his love
for her that he used it as an excuse to keep her in his bed.
In five years' time he wanted to be able to keep his promise to her to set her free. It was a matter of honour to do
so, but if she should conceive his child Marco knew there
was no way he would ever be able to let either of them
go.

'What happened between us last night must never happen again, Alice, and I intend to make sure that it does
not!'

Alice could feel her face starting to burn at the humiliation of the warning he was giving her. Did he really think
that she was so lacking in self-respect that she would try
to initiate sex between them?

'Good. I'm glad to hear it,' she replied in a high, brittle
voice.

For a second Marco had a dangerous impulse to take
hold of her and make her retract her words. To caress her,
kiss her, love her until she was crying out to him. For him.
For his love!

He felt as though he were sinking in quicksand; as fast
as he tried to control his feelings, they pulled him back
down!

She was so innocent; so inexperienced that she had no
idea just how special and rare what they had shared had
been. The pleasure she had given him! The way her body
had responded to him...welcomed him...clung to him...

Marco could feel the savage burn of his own renewed aching need.

He had to get away from her before he did something he would regret!

CHAPTER ELEVEN

GENTLY Alice removed the sample of fabric Angelina had picked up from her baby fingers.

Alice was trying to make a final choice for the new wallpaper and fabrics to decorate the new master bedroom suite.

The suite comprised two bedrooms, one of which was ostensibly going to be Angelina's room complete with a bed for 'emergencies' and a playroom off it, with another large room which supposedly would be Alice and Marco's.

In the meantime all three of them were still sharing Marco's existing suite, although Alice had managed to insist that Marco slept in his own bed whilst she slept in the smaller bed in the dressing room so that she could be closer to Angelina.

True to his word Marco had kept her at a distance, physically as well as emotionally. And that of course was exactly what she wanted! At least it was what her pride demanded she wanted! When he spoke to her his voice was terse, his desire to spend as little time with her as possible hurtfully obvious.

The new suite was also going to include two dressing rooms, a shower room, and a separate bathroom, as well as a small private sitting room, and it was Alice's responsibility to choose the décor for the entire suite, whilst Marco was naturally taking charge of all the architectural, design and building work.

Marco had been anxious to get the plans finalised because he was due to fly to Rome the following day for a series of business meetings about a major project he was involved in.

Tickling Angelina, who had now cleverly produced another new tooth, Alice glanced at her watch. It was virtually time for her to get changed for dinner—a formality that had bemused her a little at first, but that she had now grown accustomed to. And at least she had found a use for all those expensive little outfits of Angelina's!

Whilst she might have refused to allow Marco to provide her with a new wardrobe full of expensive designer clothes, there was no reason why Angelina shouldn't wear hers. As was customary with Italian families, Angelina, whilst too young as yet to join them at the table, was there with them whilst they ate their dinner, much to Alice's relief. At least with Angelina there she had someone to talk to, someone with whom she could behave naturally.

Somehow or other without ever discussing the subject she and Marco had evolved a system that allowed them both the privacy to use the bedroom and the bathroom without the other being present whilst at the same time maintaining the fiction of their newly married status.

Alice knew that logically speaking she ought to be grateful to Marco for his discretion and for the fact that he was adhering to the agreement they had made, but instead what she was actually feeling was a sense of rejection and loss; a feeling of being cheated of something that she as a woman should have been experiencing.

The truth was that her body ached far more now from the lack of Marco's possession than it ever had done before he had possessed it, humiliating though it was for her to have to admit as much.

Maddalena was a stickler for punctuality, and in exactly ten minutes' time dinner would be served in the small, at least by the *palazzo*'s standards, pretty dining room, which had originally been decorated by Marco's mother.

When Alice pushed the stroller into the room a few minutes later, she found that Marco was already there, standing with his back to her, and looking out of the

French windows that opened out onto a small, private, enclosed garden.

He had obviously opened the French windows because Alice could hear the sound of water splashing from the ornate stone fountain, which dominated the elegant courtyard.

Although he turned round when he heard them coming into the dining room, he didn't smile. He looked preoccupied and distant Alice recognised, a feeling that was intensified for her during the course of their meal, when he seemed to have retreated behind an invisible wall into a dark, brooding silence that she felt reluctant to break.

After they had finished eating and Alice made to take Angelina upstairs to put her to bed, Marco announced abruptly that he intended to go with them.

'I shall be leaving early tomorrow morning for Rome,' he told Alice tersely. 'You've got my mobile number—please don't hesitate to use it if you need to reach me for any reason.'

Nodding, Alice suspected that he was thinking back to Angelina's illness. Happily the little girl had gone from strength to strength since then, and was now rosily chubby, and eating well enough even to please Alice's exacting standards.

'Angelina is going to miss you,' she told him as he helped her upstairs with the stroller. 'She could really do with a high chair now,' she commented once they had reached the bedroom.

'She can't feed herself yet, of course, but the sooner she gets used to eating with us, the better... I was wondering if it would be all right for me to go into Florence and buy one whilst you're away...'

'What...? Oh, yes. Of course. Get whatever you need, Alice.'

Alice frowned as she heard the tension in his voice. Something was wrong. She could sense it. By the time she re-emerged into the main bedroom half an hour later, to confirm to Marco that she had finally made up her mind about which fabric she wanted for their bedroom curtains, Alice was feeling anxiously on edge. But abruptly her own anxiety evaporated as she saw that Marco, obviously unaware of her presence, was standing beside the tallboy, frowning down at the photograph of his cousin Aldo that he was holding.

Alice felt her heart contract in a bittersweet pain of sadness and compassion as she looked at him.

Only two photographs had decorated the tallboy on their marriage. One had been of Marco's parents together with him as a little boy and the other had been of his cousin.

Now there were three photographs there, the new addition being one of herself on their wedding day with Angelina.

She had been shocked at first to see it there, but then she had reasoned that it was perhaps there because Marco felt that the other members of his household would expect it to be there.

'Marco.'

She said his name quietly, and was not surprised when he did not immediately respond to her.

Slowly he replaced the photograph and then turned round.

'Today would have been his birthday,' he told her sombrely. 'He would have been twenty-seven…'

'For as long as I live I will never, ever forget the scene I witnessed when I was called to the accident,' he added grimly. 'Nor will I ever stop feeling that there was something I could have done to prevent it. Something I should have done.'

'No. You mustn't say that,' Alice protested immediately, forgetting her own feelings, as she was swamped by concern and compassion for him. Going over to him, she touched his arm as tenderly as she would have done had he been Angelina.

'He was an adult, Marco. A man. He made his own decisions…'

'Did he?' Marco asked her grimly. 'Or did Patti and I make them for him? It's true that I never wanted them to marry…but God knows I never wanted this.'

The feel of his flesh beneath her fingertips was distracting her, making her think. Making her want him. Hastily Alice moved back from him, unaware of the look he was giving her as she did so.

He stopped speaking and looked away from her. 'I used to chide him for his lifestyle, for living so…so…' He shook his head. 'But at least I can comfort myself—if indeed it is a comfort—that he enjoyed life to the full. That he lived it to the full. That he experienced love, shared it, even if it was in my eyes a shallow-rooted, ephemeral emotion and not what I myself would want. He conceived a child…the only way humans have of defying our mortality.'

Wisely Alice made no attempt to speak. She could sense that he needed to unburden himself, to vocalise his own feelings of bitterness and loss.

As he moved towards the desk in front of the bedroom window, Alice was surprised to see an open bottle of wine on it. Although Marco drank wine with his meals—as indeed she was now learning to do so herself—she had never before seen him touch alcohol at any other time, and yet here he was now filling his glass with the rich ruby liquid and lifting it to his lips, drinking deeply.

'He was the youngest member of my family, a brother to me almost. I never thought…'

He took another deep gulp of his wine. 'I felt protective towards him in the same way you do towards your charges, Alice, and the fact that he is dead makes me feel that I failed him. That there should have been some way I could sense what might happen, that I could have, should have done something to prevent it.'

And he took another deep swallow, virtually emptying his glass.

'How could you possibly have known?' Alice said gently, aching to comfort him.

'He only came here to the *palazzo* because he wanted me to hear his side of things, because he was concerned I would hear the gossip about the disintegration of his marriage from someone else. It was at my insistence that he brought Patti with him. I thought some time here together away from the distractions of Rome might help. But all it did was focus on the differences between them.

'When they left for the evening to go to Florence, I never dreamed that that would be the last time I would see them alive…'

He picked up the wine bottle, obviously intent on re-filling his glass, but instinctively Alice moved towards him, giving a small murmur of protest.

'No? No, you do not approve of me losing myself in drink…drowning out my pain in its embrace… But what alternative do I have?' Marco demanded harshly. 'You? My wife?' The bitterness of the brooding look he gave her shocked her. 'Would it disgust you to know that right now I ache so much that I could take you even without love?'

His words made Alice recoil with pain, but before she could say anything he was moving towards her, challenging her.

'I know already that you are woman enough to give your love to a needy child, but are you woman enough to let me lose myself in you, Alice? To drown out my pain in you; within you… To let me feel that I am alive, human…a man!'

She knew that it was the wine he had drunk and his pain that were making him say such things. And sex was a male anodyne, she knew that too!

Recklessly she made no attempt to move away from him, even though the voice of common sense within her was warning her that she should do so, and that if she stayed where she was Marco might quite legitimately take her presence as a tacit invitation.

That he might do exactly what he was doing, she recognised dizzily as he came towards her, and took hold of her, running his hands up and down her bare arms, his wine-scented breath dangerously seductive against her skin as he kissed her forehead and then the side of her throat.

'Let me... Let me lose myself in you, sweet Alice.'

The words of denial were on the tip of Alice's tongue. After all, she knew full well she ought to utter them, to put an end to this dangerous folly right now for both their sakes, but somehow they refused to be spoken as her body responded to Marco's words in its own special language, shuddering delicately beneath his hands, her breasts swelling and firming, her nipples clearly visible beneath the fine fabric of her dress, her eyes suddenly dark and heavy with her emotions as she stared up into the unreadable intensity of his.

'Sweet, loving Alice... How much you have tormented and tantalised me these last few weeks. The scent of your perfume in this room, the sound of your laughter when you are playing with Angelina, the shape of your body beneath your clothes when you move, and my memories of just how it looks without those clothes.

'I want you, Alice! I want to lose myself in your sweetness...forget the pain and the guilt and...'

Alice didn't know which of them it was who shuddered so deeply that both their bodies felt the sensation and she didn't even think she cared. Right now all that mattered was that Marco wanted her; that he needed her and everything that was her welled up inside her to meet that need.

Instinctively she moved closer to him, lifting her mouth generously to his.

He covered it immediately with his own, making her tremble. His kiss was hard and possessive. The kiss of a man driven by fierce passions, she recognised instinctively as he parted the softness of her lips with the swift thrust of his tongue.

His hands were cupping her face, holding her still beneath the elemental possession of his kiss. She could have broken away if she wanted to, Alice knew, but it was as though some force stronger than any desire she might have had to protect herself kept her where she was, her body just brushing against Marco's as slowly, breath by breath, he deepened his kiss.

She felt one of his hands slide from her jaw to her throat, slowly caressing her skin before moving down over her back to rest just below her waist, and then tighten around her so that now she was totally body to body with him.

'Can you feel how much I want you?' he whispered against her ear.

Alice shivered convulsively, her physical reaction betraying just how aware of his arousal she was—aware of it and aroused herself by it.

'You have the most beautiful breasts, just made to be kissed,' he told her thickly. 'What is it? Don't you believe me?' he asked her when she automatically started to shake her head, overwhelmed by the intimacy of what he was saying to her. 'Do you want me to prove to you just how beautiful I think they are?'

The dress Alice was wearing was an old favourite, a slip of black jersey that moved fluidly with her body and that zipped up the back. She tensed a little as she felt Marco reach for the zip, but, even though her eyes widened and filled with uncertainty, her body still trembled with excitement and desire as he unfastened the dress, and slowly slipped it from her shoulders. As it slid to the floor, Alice automatically closed her eyes, afraid not just of her own nakedness but also of what Marco might see in her eyes, the helpless, foolish, aching love she knew might be revealed there.

What she was doing was so reckless. So dangerous, so potentially self-destructive. She knew how he felt about her, or rather how he didn't! Did she really want to burden herself with the knowledge that she was using his present vulnerability to satisfy her own aching longing for him?

She felt him kissing the base of her throat whilst his hands cupped the balls of her shoulders.

The evening air felt softly cool against her naked skin, but Alice knew that it wasn't the air that was making her nipples peak so urgently.

Marco's hands were cupping her breasts, whilst his lips feathered tiny kisses against her closed eyes. She could feel her nipples pressing into the palms of his hands, aching with longing as he slowly caressed her breasts.

Tonight, just as she had been on the night of their wedding, all she had been wearing beneath her dress was a pair of briefs.

'Your skin is so soft. So tenderly pale,' Marco murmured. 'There is something about you, sweet Alice, that brings out the hunter in me, the desire to feast myself on the tender sweetness of your flesh, so very, very different from my own. Does it shock you to hear me say these things to you?' he asked her.

Alice couldn't speak, but had she been able to do so she would have told him that she suspected that he would not be saying them to her if it weren't for the combination of his grief for his dead cousin and the effect of the wine he had drunk. She sensed that together they had lifted the taut control he had been exercising over himself, allowing her to see once more the man who had filled her with such physical pleasure and satisfaction on the night of their wedding. He had wanted her then, and he wanted her again now. Wanted her, yes, but he did not love her, she tried to warn herself.

Her body, though, didn't want to hear her warnings; recklessly it was responding to Marco's touch with flagrant sensuality.

'Don't look at me like that,' he suddenly said thickly as his hand left her breast to cup the back of her neck. Instinctively she looked up at him and then wished she hadn't as she saw the blazing look of desire burning in his eyes.

'Not unless you mean what those huge eyes of yours are saying to me! Do you?' he asked her. 'Do you want me to take you to my bed, and keep you there, sweet Alice, to cover your nakedness with my own and touch you in all the ways that a lover touches a woman, pleasures her. Loves her.'

Alice was shaking so much she suspected that if he hadn't been holding her she wouldn't have been able to stand upright.

He was seducing her with his words just as thoroughly as he was with the slow, seductive caress of his hands on her virtually naked body. Soft, stroking caresses that warmed her flesh and tormented it, making her ache for more, so much, much more…

'You haven't answered me,' he reminded her, bending his head to place a soft kiss at either side of her mouth and then to circle her lips with the tip of his tongue, causing her to melt helplessly against him, her lips parting eagerly for the deep thrust of his tongue.

Instinctively she moved urgently against him, her hands clinging to the fabric of his shirt whilst deep within her body she felt the sharply piercing ache of her own need. Helplessly she returned his kiss with all the intensity burning inside her.

'But now you have,' Marco told her softly as he released her mouth, and swung her up into his arms to carry her over to the bed.

'Now you have told me that you want me as much as I want you.'

As he lowered her onto the bed he placed his lips against her breast, gently caressing her nipple.

Alice gasped and tensed, her whole body a bow of shocked delight as she trembled from head to foot with the intensity of her own pleasure.

That Marco knew what he was doing to her, how he was making her feel, was obvious by the way his own passion suddenly flared into hot, reciprocal hunger, his hand supporting her arched body whilst his mouth caressed her other breast, and not gently this time either, but Alice had gone beyond wanting gentleness. As her body responded to his passion she tried to silence the sharp, high cry of frantic need that rose in her throat and failed, but the sound she had made, so shocking to her, only seemed to incite Marco.

He caressed her breasts with his hands and his mouth until Alice felt she couldn't bear the pleasure any more. It stimulated and excited her, but at the same time it left her feeling empty, aching… Needing.

Frantically she gave in to her own need to respond, pressing small, moist kisses on Marco's throat, his exposed shoulder, where she realised she must have pulled so hard at his shirt she had torn off the button. She could hear the small keening noises she was making as she tried to articulate her need to have the same access to his naked body that he had to hers, but she hadn't realised she had actually stated that need out loud until Marco suddenly released her and sat up beside her, his gaze holding hers, his eyes brilliant with a mixture of male triumph and hot desire as he boldly finished quickly removing his shirt.

'Is this what you want?' he asked her thickly.

Alice couldn't help herself. Immediately she reached out and touched him, her eyes wide and dark. Totally engrossed in what she was doing, in the feel of the soft, silky dark hairs beneath her fingertips, the hot, male scent of his skin, and the way it felt and tasted beneath her lips as she placed them against it, she was oblivious to the fact that Marco was removing the rest of his clothes until the fingers she was blindly smoothing over the tautness of his muscles suddenly dipped low enough to touch the flat plane of his belly.

Immediately she froze, but it was too late, Marco was

urging her to touch him even more intimately, to touch and caress him in the same way, he whispered to her, as he was going to touch and caress her.

As he spoke he was gently teasing her briefs away from her body, his lips feathering delicate kisses against her skin.

'Do you know just what it does to me to know that I have awakened you to your desire, Alice?' he asked her rawly. 'The night of our wedding I hurt you, I know, but I think I gave you pleasure as well. Tell me,' he demanded. 'Tell me if I did?'

Alice moaned. Just listening to what he was saying to her was driving her need to a fever-pitch. Just remembering how she had felt that night...

Her body ached with need for him; it filled every single cell, every nerve ending, the feeling so intense that it was almost a physical pain.

'Tell me,' he was insisting.

Dizzily she thought that it must be a male pride thing that was making him so insistent, unaware of just how much his love for her made him ache to feel that she had some pleasure from his touch.

'It was...it was good,' she admitted unsteadily.

'Good,' Marco repeated. 'How good? So good that you will take the memory of its pleasure with you to the grave? Because if not, tonight it will be that good,' he promised her softly. 'Tonight I will give you all the pleasure there is. All the pleasure you need. Tonight you and I will celebrate life together.'

Alice knew he was thinking about his cousin and the shortness of his life.

Blindly, her own emotions acutely sensitive, she opened her mouth to his kiss.

'I want this to be as good for you as I know it's going to be for me.' She could hear Marco whispering to her, between the deep kisses he was giving her, taking her mouth with possessive passion as his touch became more and more intimate and her body relaxed against it and then began to clamour eagerly for it.

As she arched her hips and writhed helplessly against his hand Alice felt him lift his mouth from hers and groan against her throat whilst his body was convulsed by a long, deep shudder.

Just the feel of his body against hers was making her ache so much with longing for him. There was a need deep inside her, an emptiness that only he could fill, an urgency driving her, compelling her.

When Marco reached for her, Alice wrapped herself around him, her hands clinging to his shoulders, her legs wrapped high and tight around his body, welcoming the remembered sweet, fierce shock of his now careful thrust within her.

Her body seemed to have been made especially for this, especially for him, Alice thought dizzily as every sensi-tised nerve ending reacted to the feel of him thrusting deeper inside her, in a surge of hot, sweet, wet pleasure that defied description. She had thought it would be im-possible for her to feel more pleasure than she had done that first time, but now she knew she had been wrong! That the feeling of being totally filled by him was one that she was enjoying as much as she could sense that he was; that the need that drove him was exactly the same need that drove her to have him there as deep within her as it was possible for him to be, and, once there, to move in exactly the way he was doing, all male, savage, powerful heat and possession, all wonderful, loving pleasure.

Alice gasped as the contractions of her own fulfilment gripped her, more intense, more shocking, more everything that she had ever imagined they might be. She knew she cried out Marco's name and that he responded with a gut-tural sound of raw, male, agonised release of his own, but these were peripheral recognitions, her whole world, her whole being concentrated on the intimate intensity of the pleasure Marco had just shown her.

As she finally slid down from the heights tears glistened on her cheeks, her eyes dazed and luminous with the intensity of her experience.

Too exhausted to conceal them from him she simply lay there as he brushed them away. It would be so easy now to convince herself that she could see tenderness in his eyes, but she had to remember the realities of her situation. Just because Marco had made love to her, that did not mean that he loved her. He had felt vulnerable. He had needed someone and she had been there.

It would be extremely foolish of her to start imagining anything else.

Marco woke up with a jolt. The bedroom was in darkness, and there was absolutely no sound from the dressing room, which would have indicated that a wakeful Angelina had brought him out of his deep sleep. There was one unfamiliar sound in his room, though, in his bed. There was the soft whisper of Alice's breathing.

Alice! His heart missed a beat and then another before thudding heavily against his chest wall.

The wine he had drunk earlier was no longer intoxicating his bloodstream, and the sharpness of his grief for Aldo had softened to a dull ache, but neither of them was any real excuse for what he had done.

What had happened to the self-control he had always prided himself on having?

The last thing that Alice would want when she woke up, he told himself bitterly, was to find him in bed with her, a reminder of the way he had played on her compassion.

Very carefully Marco slid out of the bed, pausing only to equally carefully and gently tuck the covers protectively around Alice's sleeping body before straightening up. She looked so young, so tender, so desirable in her sleep. Unable to stop himself, Marco leaned down again and tenderly brushed a soft kiss against her lips before heading for the dressing room, and the small narrow bed in there in which Alice normally slept.

When Alice woke up Marco had already left for Rome. Alice told herself that she was glad and that she needed some breathing space without him to give her the strength to cope with her love for him.

She couldn't go on like this. But she couldn't leave either. Just as Marco was doing, she was committed to putting Angelina's needs before her own.

It was nearly a week since Alice had last seen Marco. He had rung her every day and sometimes twice a day during his absence, but only of course to check on Angelina. Tonight he would be home, although he'd informed Alice his flight was not due to arrive until the early hours as he had a final appointment in Rome that would last until after dinner.

The phone rang as she was crossing the salon on her way to the garden with Angelina.

Automatically she answered it, her stomach muscles clenching in nervous excitement as she anticipated hearing Marco's voice, but instead she discovered that her caller was Francine, Angelina's grandmother.

Immediately Francine demanded to speak to Marco.

'I'm afraid that isn't possible,' Alice told her as politely as she could. 'He's away on business at the moment.'

'Oh, it's you!' Francine responded unpleasantly. 'The little nanny, or, should I say, the new *contessa*... Don't think I haven't guessed just what this marriage is all about! Well, he isn't going to get away with it. He isn't going to stop me... I've taken legal advice... When will he be back? I want to see him,' she demanded abruptly.

'Er...'

When Alice hesitated, anxiously, not sure what kind of response Marco would want her to make, but knowing full well just what she would like to say to Francine given free choice, especially about her neglect of her granddaughter, Francine cut across her uncertainty with a contemptuous, 'Trying to protect him? How pathetic! I suppose you've fallen for him…you know he's just using you, don't you? I have every right to see my granddaughter and that is exactly what I intend to do. As of now…and if need be I shall remain at the *palazzo* until Marco does return…'

Alice's heart sank deeper with every word the other woman uttered, but she knew that there was nothing she could say that would prevent her from arriving at the *palazzo*. She just hoped that Marco would return before she did!

For the rest of the day Alice worried anxiously over Francine's threats.

Alice hadn't been sleeping properly since Marco had been away, with the result that by the time she had finished her evening meal she was already yawning.

There was no reason for her not to have an early night, she told herself. Marco was not due back until the early hours, and once he did return there was no reason why he should want to see her, was there?

Some women experienced tiredness in the early weeks of their pregnancy. Alice's heart gave a dizzying thump. By rights she ought to be praying that she was not pregnant, instead of secretly hoping that she was! Marco's baby! Was it wrong of her to long to have his child?

He had sworn that if she did conceive that he would not let him or her go! He had told her too that he knew she would never leave her baby, which meant… She couldn't spend the rest of her life living with him, loving him, knowing that he did not love her! But neither she suspected would she be able to find the strength to leave.

During Marco's absence she had taken to sleeping in the big bed in the main bedroom, not because it was any more comfortable than the smaller bed in the dressing room, but simply, she acknowledged guiltily, because it was Marco's bed. Because being there somehow eased the ache of longing for him that tormented her.

Tonight, though, she would be sleeping in her own bed!

Knowing that he would be arriving home so late, Marco had left his car at the airport. As he drove into the long private drive that led to the *palazzo* he acknowledged both how tired he was and how much he had missed Alice.

In Rome he had constantly been subconsciously looking for her, listening for her laughter, and the sound of her voice, low and loving as she spoke to Angelina.

If she should conceive his child, she would have to stay with him. Just the thought of watching her body grow with his child filled him with a gut-wrenching surge of raw longing. He must not allow himself to think so! Alice had a right to give her love as freely to the man of her choice as he had given his to her! If he tried to deny her that right, then he couldn't love her!

Alice shivered as she remembered her nightmare. In it Francine had been laughing as she'd told them that the courts had decided that Angelina should live with her. Alice's mouth felt dry, and her eyes gritty. Sliding out of her bed, she padded into the main bedroom through which she had to walk to reach the bathroom, and then stopped as the moonlight revealed Marco's sleeping form in the bed in front of her.

He was back! She hadn't even heard him arrive.

Impulsively she tiptoed across to the bed, unable to resist the temptation to look down into his sleeping face. In sleep his features looked gentler, his dark hair tousled, and the beginnings of a beard shadowing his jaw. Without thinking what she was doing, Alice reached out and touched it with her fingertips, wondering dizzily at the sensation of it against her own soft flesh. Even when he was asleep his maleness was a powerful aura that enraptured and held her. Her fingertips had reached his mouth. She started to tremble as she traced the shape of his lips. He was breathing deeply and softly.

She gave a shocked gasp as suddenly his eyes opened at exactly the same time as his mouth closed round her fingertips, and his hands fastened on her waist, jerking her onto the bed beside him.

'Marco,' she protested, but the sensation within her caused by the sensual way he was licking and sucking her fingers made the sound of his name more of a long, shaky moan of desire than any real, recognisable objection.

Her fingertips were released, but her hand was still held captive.

'There's no way I should be doing this,' he groaned. 'And no way that I can stop.'

And then he was kissing her properly, his mouth hungrily demanding on hers.

A fierce surge of pleasure filled her, knowing that he wanted her so much, a dangerous ache filling her womb this time, her body was so eagerly ready—so hungry for his touch that her own lips were parting, her tongue tangling sensually with his the moment she felt his mouth open.

The touch of his hands on her body was every pleasure she could ever want; he was all the pleasure she would ever want, and she couldn't stop herself from showing him how she felt as she pressed tiny, hungry kisses against his throat, his chest, his arms, whilst he pulled her even closer into him. She wanted all of him! Everything! Every sensation, every sense fulfilled and satisfied simply because it was with Marco.

She wasn't a novice bride now. Her body knew him, and it knew itself as well, it knew what desire and pleasure were and how to give and receive them. And he had shown her and taught her all of that, so he had no one but himself to blame, she reasoned passionately.

This time it was his turn to shudder and groan as her

passion surprised and overwhelmed him, her hands revelling in the sensation of touching him, the freedom to touch him wherever she wished, to learn and know him and to feel his response to her, against her hands, against her lips, within her body... She was possessed by a sense of urgency and fate, an inner knowledge, a need to seize this special moment.

To have him, most of all, deep, deep within her, where she wanted to hold him for eternity, whilst she revelled in the female triumph of having given him his pleasure in the same heartbeat as she had taken from him the seeds of eternity. As he spilled himself inside her, Marco cried out in desperation. This was not how it should be, not how he had intended it to be, but somehow he was powerless to deny himself! He started to reach for her, needing to hold her and then realised what he had done.

As Marco moved deliberately away from her, Alice was bitterly aware of his rejection.

CHAPTER TWELVE

'FOR the last time, Francine, no. There is no way I am going to pay you anything—for any reason...'

As he faced Francine's furious disbelief, watching as she paced the floor of the *palazzo*'s library, Marco acknowledged that he was tempted to give in and pay her what she wanted. If he had thought for one minute that in doing so he would remove her from Angelina's life for ever, he would willing have paid three times the amount she was asking him for, but he knew what would happen if he did.

Blackmail was an invidious, creeping thing. Sooner or later and probably sooner, Francine would be back for more money, and if he paid her off now all he would be doing would be creating a situation where she continued to demand blood money from him. If that happened Angelina would never be safe. No, risky though it was, going to court to establish who Angelina should be with was in Marco's opinion the right course of action to take.

'You'll regret this,' Francine warned him bitterly. 'You claim you love Angelina, and yet you won't even part with a measly million dollars to keep her,' she taunted him. 'Some love...'

'I could say the same thing to you,' Marco pointed out coldly to her, 'but then we both know, don't we, Francine, that where you are concerned love doesn't come into the equation, other than your own love for yourself? Has it occurred to you the damage you're doing to your own case by coming here like this and trying to blackmail me?'

'How are you going to prove it?' Francine sneered. 'By producing one of your paid lackeys. My brief will make sure everyone knows that they are dependent on you for

162

everything, and that your word is law here, Marco. And if you're thinking of your new wife...' Her sneer deepened. 'How much did you pay her to marry you? Or did she do it for free? Silly girl...a man always values so much more what he has to pay for. And the more he pays, the more he values it.'

'As I'm sure you have good cause to know, Francine,' Marco responded quietly. 'But if you ever dare again to mention Alice in the same breath as your own sordid set of values, let me warn you right now, I will make sure that you have good cause to regret it.'

'Don't you dare threaten me,' Francine warned him furiously. 'This is your last chance, Marco. If you don't take it, then I promise you I am going to take Angelina away from you. She is my flesh and blood; I am her closest living relative.'

'A mother who sold her own daughter to the highest bidder. No court in the world will give you so much as access to her once they know your history, Francine,' Marco told her coolly, with a confidence he was inwardly fighting to hold onto.

'You'll pay for this, Marco,' Francine threw at him as she turned on her heel. 'My God, I promise you, you are going to wish you had paid me when you had the opportunity because there's no way now I will ever let you have Angelina.'

'That decision doesn't rest with you,' Marco reminded her. However, as he watched her storm out of the *palazzo* and head for her car Marco knew that inwardly he was not as confident as he had pretended.

In a fair and just world he would gain custody of Angelina for her own sake, but...but Francine could be extremely plausible when she chose, and she was also both dangerous and manipulative.

Francine was shaking with fury as she drove away from the *palazzo*. She had been so sure that Marco would give in to her this time. She was desperate for the money she had asked him for…more desperate than he could possibly imagine. There was a dark and dangerous side to Francine's life that not even Patti had known about.

She had first visited the United States as a young woman searching for the GI father who had abandoned her mother without knowing she was pregnant. When she had finally found him Francine had been disappointed to discover that he was far from being the wealthy, successful man she had fantasised about him being, but was in fact a careworn accountant working in a factory in New Jersey.

He had been married with three children, Francine's younger half siblings…whom Francine had liked even less than she had liked her father, but there had been one thing he had done for her and that had been to give her her American nationality.

And it was because of that that she was in so much trouble now. Or at least that was how she perceived her situation.

She had started gambling when she had left her newly discovered father and made her way to Nevada, initially to work as a croupier and then more latterly to spend her earnings at the gaming tables.

It had been there that she had first met Jack. The man who for many years had been her lover, even while Francine had been married and living in England with her husband and Patti. Jack, it was rumoured, had connections with the Mafia. He had loaned Francine money, which over the years had built up into an horrendous amount; an amount that he was now demanding that she repay…either in cash or in another way—helping him with his illegal activities. And it was that other way that had sent Francine into a frantic frenzy to Marco, desperate to get from him the money to repay Jack.

Once she was dragged into his gangster lifestyle, she would never be able to break free. Her punishment if she were to be caught could mean that she might even lose her own American citizenship, and there was no way she wanted that to happen!

The wheels of her hire car spun on the gravel of the *palazzo*'s long driveway.

Alice, who had been walking Angelina in her stroller, saw the cloud of dust thrown up by the speed at which Francine was travelling.

She had been outside in the garden when she had seen the other woman arrive, and she was relieved to see that she was now leaving.

There had to be some way to make Marco pay her that money, Francine fumed frantically. She had been so sure that he would buy her off! That was the whole reason she had threatened to lay claim to Angelina. The last thing she wanted was a dependent child; she had never wanted Patti to have her and had counselled her daughter to have a termination. Marco, of course, being typically Italian, was besotted with the wretched child.

Francine's hands tightened on the steering wheel of the car as she saw Alice with the stroller... With a sudden flash of inspiration she knew that her prayers had been answered, and what she must do.

Pressing her foot to the car's brake, she brought it to a skidding halt.

Alice coughed on the dust Francine's screeching halt had thrown up, wafting it away with her hand, whilst she watched uneasily as Francine got out of the car and walked towards her.

'Give me my grandchild,' Francine demanded imperiously the moment she reached them, stationing herself strategically in front of Alice and reaching swiftly into the stroller, lifting Angelina out before Alice could stop her.

At being handled by a stranger whose touch lacked the loving tenderness she was used to, Angelina immediately started to cry, her distress adding to Alice's anxiety.

'You're frightening her,' she cautioned Francine protectively. 'She isn't used to being held like that. Look let me show you what she likes…'

'I don't give a damn what she does or doesn't like,' Francine retorted unpleasantly, breaking off to give a small angry scream and quickly hold Angelina at arm's length as the baby reacted to her roughness by sicking up some of her food. 'Don't you dare be sick on me, you little brat,' Francine told her furiously, shaking her so hard that Alice immediately tried to remonstrate with her.

'You don't like what I'm doing. Tough!' Francine told Alice contemptuously. 'She's my grandchild and she's coming with me.'

Alice couldn't believe what she was hearing… Francine couldn't possibly just walk off with Angelina like that. Francine was now turning round, still holding Angelina, without any concern for the baby's comfort, and heading for the car, opening the driver's door, and for the first time Alice realised that the engine was still running.

Panic filled her. One read about such things—children being abducted in custody wars—but she had never for one second imagined that it might happen to Angelina.

'You can't take her! Please…' she protested, her throat dry and raw with fear. 'She's just a baby! She doesn't know you… In half an hour she'll need a feed and…'

Frowningly Francine hesitated. What Alice was saying was true! She thought quickly, her eyes narrowing with concentration, and then told Alice, 'Well, if you're so concerned about her, you'd better get in the car as well. Who knows? Perhaps Marco will be prepared to pay double to get the pair of you back!'

Alice stared at her. Francine was kidnapping Angelina in order to make Marco pay to get her back? Frantically she searched the other woman's face. Everything she could see there confirmed all that Alice felt about her, and her fears for Angelina grew.

Francine was carelessly bundling Angelina into the back of her car, which didn't even have a baby seat—in another few seconds she would be gone. It would take Alice at least twenty minutes to get back to the house even if she ran, and by that time...

'Wait!' Alice demanded as Francine started to get into the car, ignoring Angelina's wails of protest. 'I'm coming with you. But we need to take the stroller...it turns into a car seat and—'

'No way! Either get in now or I'll leave,' Francine told her grimly.

What real options did she have? Alice asked herself. None! Shakily she got into the back of the car and tried to comfort Angelina as Francine proceeded to drive off at such a high speed that Alice was jolted back against the seat so heavily that the movement jarred her neck. Thank heavens she had Angelina wrapped protectively in her arms.

'Please,' she begged Francine. 'You are driving much too fast.'

'Poor little wifey. What are you trying to do? Make me slow down so that your wonderful macho husband can catch up with us? No way!' Francine laughed. 'No way do I stop until we're back in Rome and then, my dear, Angelina and I will be on the first flight to the USA where we will stay until your precious husband comes to his senses.'

Alice winced as she was thrown against the car door when Francine turned out of the drive and onto the main road.

There was no way Angelina could endure being driven even a few miles at such a break-neck speed without being sick, never mind all the way to Rome, and thanks to Francine all the baby had was the clothes she was wearing.

Alice had never in the whole of her life hated anyone as much as she loathed and detested Francine. How could she do this to any child, never mind her own grandchild? But Alice already knew there was no point in trying to reason with her. Angelina was snuggling as close as she

could to Alice, her baby eyes round with shock and distress.

'It's all right, little one,' Alice whispered tenderly to her.
'Don't worry...don't worry.'

As she rocked her Alice wished there were someone
there to tell her not to worry... Someone? Or Marco?

Out of the corner of her eye she watched in horrified
disbelief as Francine took a corner by driving in the middle
of the road, and only just missed being hit by the car coming the other way.

'Typical male driver!' Alice heard her mutter as she
increased her speed.

'God, I hate men! All of them, but none of them as
much as I hate your husband,' she told Alice bitterly. 'All
he had to do was to part with a mere million dollars. That
was all. He could have kept the bloody brat and you as
well, but, no...he claims to love the pair of you but he
obviously doesn't love you very much, does he?'

It was news to Alice that Marco had ever claimed to
love her, but wisely she kept her thoughts to herself.
Francine was already dangerously overwrought and frantically Alice tried to think of some way to calm her down
and get her to reduce her speed. If she didn't Alice was
desperately afraid that there could be an accident...

It was half an hour after Francine had driven off with
Angelina and Alice before Pietro, returning from the fields,
saw the abandoned stroller in the drive and rushed to report
what he had seen to Marco.

Marco, who had assumed that Alice was punishing him
for the previous night by keeping away from him, quickly
checked the bedroom and, on finding it empty, immediately hurried to his own car and drove to where Pietro had
found the stroller.

The tyre marks in the gravel told him everything he
needed to know. Francine! Francine was somehow respon-

sible for the abandoned stroller and the disappearance of both Alice and Angelina...

'Oh, my God,' he whispered to himself as he guessed what must have happened. 'Oh, my God!'

Once she got to Rome she would ring Marco from the airport. Just before she boarded her flight, Francine decided gleefully. And she would tell him that now the cost of getting custody of Angelina had doubled to two million dollars, with of course a further million thrown in for the safe return of his wife.

Quite how she was going to persuade Alice to board the plane with her, Francine hadn't worked out as yet, but she suspected that wherever she took Angelina, Alice would follow.

Surely Francine wouldn't simply be able to leave the country with Angelina, Alice fretted.

There would be legalities; formalities; the small matter of a passport, but she hesitated to say anything in case it drove Francine into an even greater frenzy than she was already in.

Angelina had been sick so often as they'd been thrown around the back of the small car that the poor little thing probably didn't have anything left in her tummy to be sick with, Alice recognised as she tried her best to comfort her.

The road from the *palazzo* was a narrow, twisting one as Alice had good cause to know. Even when Marco was driving she sometimes felt nervous, and Marco was a very careful driver.

Francine, on the other hand, was anything but, and Alice could have sworn that sometimes Francine forgot which side of the road she was actually supposed to be driving on!

The inevitable happened just when Alice had finally begun to relax and convince herself that Francine's driving was no worse than that of the drivers coming the other way. She had taken a corner far too fast, and had to swerve to avoid crashing head-on with the lorry coming the other way.

Alice felt the sickening lurch of the car as Francine lost control of it and looked up just in time to realise that they were skidding across the road right in the path of an on-coming car.

Reaching instinctively, she threw herself protectively on top of Angelina whilst the world turned into a hell of twisting, screeching, tearing metal, punctuated by a woman's screams and a series of bone-jarring thuds. She felt the pain in her legs, and then the numbness, but by then a blessed silence had fallen, a stillness in which she was at peace to let go of the pain tearing into her. Just as long as she didn't let go of Angelina...

Later Alice realised it could only have been a matter of minutes after the crash and her loss of consciousness before willing hands were pulling open the doors of the car, calling out to her in anxious voices that dragged her back from the abyss of her agonising pain.

'The baby! You must take the baby!' she heard herself insisting as she managed to twist her head to look into the eyes of the man bending anxiously over her.

Her back had stopped hurting now. She couldn't feel it at all, thank goodness. But she could smell petrol and sense the fear and anxiety of the men clustered around the doorway.

Her thoughts felt muddled and slow; she couldn't see Francine but she could feel Angelina's warm, squirming body lying protectively beneath her own.

'The baby!' she repeated to her would-be rescuers. It was an effort for her to talk, her lips felt numb, but she couldn't lift her hand to touch them because it felt as if the whole of her upper body was trapped beneath some heavy, crushing weight...

'Quick. There is a child in here,' she heard one of the

men say in Italian. And then another called out, 'We shall need to cut the woman free!'

Cut the woman free. What woman? Who were they talking about? Francine? Even though she disliked her, Alice hoped that she would be all right...

'The baby,' she repeated painfully...as the man leaning over her started to fade and recede in a sickening wave of dizziness... Angelina had managed to free one of her arms, and she reached out and touched Alice's face.

Alice could see the shock in the man's face, which irrationally annoyed her. Hadn't he listened to anything she had said?

'You must tell Marco, the *conte*, that Angelina is safe,' she told him slowly, as though she were talking to a child. 'He will be worried about her. You must contact the *palazzo*. Slowly and painstakingly she gave him the address and the telephone number, resisting the desire to cling onto Angelina as she was gently eased out from beneath her own body.

They had to hold her whilst someone put a huge wadding of cushions and what looked like discarded clothes beneath her where Angelina had been. Indignantly she tried to protest, but she could feel herself slipping into unconsciousness.

It took Marco less than half an hour after the police had informed him about the accident to reach the scene—he had driven there far faster than Francine, dreading with every kilometre what he'd been going to find.

Angelina, they had told him, was fine.

'And Alice? My wife?'

There had been a brief pause.

'She is trapped in the back of the car. She must have thrown herself over the baby to protect her and the force of the collision has pushed the whole of the passenger seat of the car into the back seat and over her,' he had been told sombrely.

When Marco reached the scene of the accident it was thronged with people.

'Your wife will have to be cut free,' he was told. 'We have had to send to Florence for the cutting gear...'

His heart buckled and twisted, tearing him apart. He had to be with Alice and nothing, no one was going to stop him.

'I must go to my wife,' he told the policeman grimly.

Even saying the simple words 'my wife' agonised him, bringing home to him just how much Alice meant to him, and how much he loved and needed her.

'She is unconscious at the moment.' The policeman frowned. 'There has been a spillage of fuel caused by the collision. And it isn't safe to allow anyone to get too close.'

Handing Angelina to Maddalena, whom he had brought with him, Marco demanded quietly, 'Let me see.'

Without waiting for the policeman's response, Marco pushed his way through the police cordon surrounding the accident and then stopped, his head spinning.

This was worse than the accident that had killed Aldo and Patti. The small car had virtually been crushed to nothing by the force of the impact with the much heavier vehicle it had skidded into. Ironically the driver's side of the vehicle was intact, but the passenger side...

'It is a miracle that your daughter is unhurt,' the policeman told Marco. 'Mother love is a wonderful thing. Your wife risked her own life to save her baby. She threw herself over the baby and her body protected her. Unfortunately—' gravely he looked at Marco '—unfortunately, she is now trapped beneath the front of the car and the passenger seat. We cannot move her, and we do not know just how badly hurt she is. The doctor has just arrived and he is trying to talk to her.'

His heart in his mouth, Marco strode over to the car. A man was crouched down beside the open passenger door, stroking Alice's hand.

'Can you feel anything…any pain—any sensation?' he was asking her quietly.

Alice was trying to concentrate on what she was being asked, but it was so very, very difficult! All she wanted to do was to close her eyes and go to sleep. Her body felt odd…heavy and yet somehow numb. There was a dreadful pain in her head and a metallic taste in her mouth. Her hand looked unfamiliar to her…limp and odd… At least Angelina was safe, she comforted herself hazily.

'No, you must stay awake,' the doctor was saying sternly to her. 'Don't close your eyes.'

Alice winced as he flicked his fingers painfully on the back of her hand. He was turning his head to speak to someone out of her line of vision, and she couldn't hear what he was saying.

Panic and fear swept through her as she tried to listen. She felt so alone!

An even greater depth of fear was surging through Marco as he reached the doctor and demanded to know what was happening.

'It is important that she remains conscious,' the doctor informed Marco, who had heard Alice's small gasp of fear and was reaching out protectively towards her.

'We don't know just what damage may have been caused as yet…and we won't know until we can cut her free. I shall need to stay here with her and talk to her. Keep her conscious,' the doctor explained patiently to Marco, recognising his feelings.

'Let me do that,' Marco demanded immediately. 'She is my wife.'

The doctor was frowning, but Marco was insistent.

Alice could hear Marco speaking to her; calling her name. Telling her that she must not go to sleep.

Hazily she tried to focus on his voice. How could he possibly be here?

Disbelievingly she forced her heavy eyelids to lift, her eyes widening in shock as she saw that she had not been imagining him, dreaming foolish dreams, he was here. Marco was here with her!

Joy filled her in an adrenalin, life-giving surge, quickly followed by guilt as she realised that he could not possibly be here for her, but because of Angelina.

'I tried to stop Francine,' she told him immediately, 'but she had Angelina. She said she was going to make you pay to get her back...'

Tears filled her eyes. And she gave a small gasp as Marco gently started to wipe them away.

There was blood on the cloth in his hand, she realised with a vague sense of shock.

'You must have cut yourself,' she told him in concern.

'It's nothing,' Marco told her. His voice sounded rough, as though something was stuck in his throat, as though he was somehow having trouble speaking. Because he was angry? With her?

Unaware of what Alice was thinking, Marco dipped his head so that Alice wouldn't see the tears in his eyes. The blood was hers from the cuts on her face, which the doctor had insisted were only superficial, but he didn't want to frighten her by telling her that.

It was hot inside the car, and his muscles were already aching from the crouched position he had adopted so that he could get as close to her as he could. Holding her free hand in his whilst he talked to her, telling her how brave she had been, reassuring her that Angelina was safe.

Alice felt as though she were in some kind of dream, lying there with Marco beside her, holding her hand tightly, smoothing the hair back off her face with his hand whilst he talked to her.

'How do you feel?' he was asking her. 'Are you in any pain?'

'My back really hurt when it first happened,' Alice told him confidingly, 'but the pain's gone now.'

'Has it? That's good,' Marco responded, whilst inwardly he made himself a vow that, no matter how badly injured she was, he would devote the rest of his life to taking care of her and loving her.

This was all his fault. All of it…

'Where's Francine?' Alice asked him.

'I don't know,' Marco answered her truthfully.

One of the witnesses had stated that they had seen a woman running away from the scene of the accident and he had assumed that she must have been Francine.

The truck with the cutting gear had arrived and the police were warning Marco that for his own safety he would have to move away.

Fiercely he refused.

'What a lot of noise,' Alice whispered as the machines were put to work.

'Mmm… You'll soon be free now,' Marco comforted her.

An ambulance was standing by and he could see the doctor watching and waiting.

From somewhere Alice was bleeding. He could see the red stickiness as they started to move the wreckage away from her.

'It hurts!' Alice whispered shakily. Her face was paper-white, her eyes huge and dazed with pain.

'Try to be brave just a little while longer,' Marco whispered to her, barely able to choke out the words.

The doctor was moving towards them, a hypodermic syringe in his hand…

'This is just going to relax you so that we can move you safely,' he told Alice.

She squeezed Marco's hand tightly as the needle slid into her vein.

*   *   *

'So today you are going home. What a pity,' the nurse teased Alice. 'We are going to miss seeing that handsome husband of yours.'

Alice gave her a brief smile. She had grown so used to her hospital bedroom these last four weeks. Felt so safe there that she felt reluctant to leave.

Everyone had been so kind to her; so protective of her. So ready to reassure her that she was very brave and very lucky.

Her worst injury had been the blood she had lost where the metal had pierced her flesh, but even the scar from that would fade in time, the doctor had assured her jovially.

Mercifully she had been spared any real awareness of those agonising hours when she had first been brought to the hospital and they had had to find out just how badly injured she might have been. Her back had been badly bruised. So badly that she had been black and blue, but by some miracle no permanent damage had been done apart from a small fracture to her collar-bone, which had now healed.

The scratches that had covered her face had also totally healed, and now the doctor had decided that she was well enough to leave. To go home... Home to Angelina and to Marco.

Marco! Was she strong enough to be with him and not betray her feelings to him?

And at least something good had come out of the accident. When the police had caught up with Francine at the airport she had been so terrified that she had willingly agreed to sign a document renouncing any claim on Angelina. As Marco had said to Alice, there was no way any court anywhere would grant her custody once they learned how narrowly she had escaped a prison sentence for dangerous driving and for putting at risk the life of the very child she claimed to love so much.

Tersely Marco had told Alice how much he regretted not simply handing Francine the money she had demanded, but, as Alice had told him, in her opinion all that would have done would have been to convince Francine that she could continue to blackmail him whenever she chose. And then Angelina would never have been safe.

But now Alice was afraid to return to normal life, and afraid too to return to the *palazzo*, because the reality was that now, with the threat of Francine fully removed from Angelina's life, Marco no longer needed her. At least not as a wife. And that meant...

Alice didn't want to think about what it meant.

'Ready, then?'

Nervously Alice nodded, watching as Marco picked her bag up off her bed and turned towards the door of her hospital room. At her own insistence, Alice was holding Angelina. Just as soon as Alice had been well enough she had pleaded with the nurses to allow her to have Angelina with her as much as possible, so that the little girl would not feel that she had abandoned her, which was of course why Marco had visited the hospital so much and stayed overnight—for Angelina's benefit, not for hers.

The one thing Alice had asked Marco to do for her had been not to inform her family about what had happened. Her sister had confided excitedly to her just before the accident that she was pregnant and Alice had not wanted her to worry.

Alice had been dreading the drive back to the *palazzo*, but, to her surprise, instead of driving her himself Marco got into the back of the car with her after he had strapped Angelina into her front baby seat, leaving Pietro to drive.

'It's all right, Alice,' he told her quietly, as though he had guessed how she was feeling. 'You'll be perfectly safe.'

And somehow Alice suddenly felt that she would be. But what surprised her even more than the fact that Marco was travelling in the back of the car with her was the way in which he calmly took hold of her hand and held it firmly within his own.

Alice stiffened as she tried to conceal her shock. Not once in all the time she had been in hospital had Marco ever touched her. In fact, she had gained the impression that he wanted to keep as much physical distance between them as he could, just as he had done at the *palazzo*, when she had known that he'd wanted to underline to her the fact that their sexual intimacy was just that and meant nothing emotional to him.

Just to sit there with her hand folded into the warm protection of his made her ache with emotional weakness. If only she could give her love full rein, and move closer to him, put her head on his shoulder and be drawn protectively into his arms. Desperately afraid that she might somehow betray to him just what her feelings for him were, she pulled her hand from his.

As he felt Alice withdraw her hand from his Marco stared out of the car window. Her rejection of his touch brought home to him the extent of his sins against her. He was facing a choice it was almost impossible for him to make.

On the one hand there was Angelina, who loved and needed Alice so much. Marco hardly dared let himself even begin to quantify the extent of the emotional damage it would do the little girl to lose Alice now. In the first hours of Alice's accident, when Angelina had been of necessity separated from her, she had cried unceasingly, and been inconsolable, until in desperation Marco had taken her to the hospital. The moment he had placed Angelina on the bed with Alice she had calmed down, and incredibly in her semi-conscious state, as though somehow she had known the baby had been there, Alice had reached out and placed her arm protectively around her.

No, Marco knew there could be no substitute in Angelina's life for Alice and Alice's mother love.

But on the other hand, there was Alice. Alice who had suffered so terribly because of him. Alice who surely had the right to love the man of her own choice, and to share his life with him, to bear his children. Marco tensed against the visceral savagery of his own pain at that thought.

What the hell should he do?

Knowing Alice, he suspected that she would insist on honouring her original contract to stay with Angelina for the early years of her life. And if she did, how the hell was he going to find the self-control to keep his distance from her?

Even if they ended their marriage, it wouldn't make any difference; he would still love her, still want her. It was his duty to protect her as it was to protect all those who worked for him—a feudal viewpoint perhaps, but one that was bred into him. But how could he protect her from himself?

Alice tensed as they reached a narrow hairpin bend. She needn't have worried, though; Pietro was a calm and careful driver.

Even so she was relieved when they finally reached the *palazzo*. Relieved and too tired to make any real demur when Marco announced that she was to go straight up to their room so that she could rest.

'They've started work on the new master suite,' he informed her.

'I would have liked to have had it finished in time for your return, but unfortunately that just wasn't possible. Mind you, that is perhaps as well, since I suspect you will want to oversee their decoration and refurbishment yourself. There's a firm I've used before who are experts at providing modern-day fittings such as wardrobes and the like, but fronted in such a way that they blend perfectly into the fabric of older buildings. As soon as you feel strong enough I'll set up a meeting with them, and with the two bathroom specialists whose stuff you liked.'

Alice almost missed one of the stairs. He was still planning to go ahead with the conversion?

Why?

She had had plenty of time to think whilst she had been

in hospital, and she had told herself that, with the threat of Francine permanently removed from Angelina's life, the first thing that Marco would want to do would be to end their marriage.

She had told herself that she ought to be pleased and that, with their marriage over, it would surely be far easier for her to conceal her love from him.

She couldn't possibly leave Angelina, of course, and if Marco should suggest that she did…

Weak tears filled her eyes at the thought of leaving the little girl. They were outside the bedroom door now, and as Marco opened it he told her brusquely, 'I'll leave you to get settled. Maddalena will be up shortly to see if you need anything.'

As he turned away from her Marco caught the silver shimmer of her tears, and stopped.

'What is it?' he demanded immediately. 'Why are you crying? Are you in pain? Where does it hurt? Tell me.'

Alice gave a small hiccupping sob. Trust Marco to think that the pain had a physical cause! But before she could say anything, to her bemusement Marco suddenly burst out, 'Alice. Alice, please don't cry. I can't bear it. I can't bear to think of how much you've suffered. Of how much I have caused you to suffer. I never meant it to happen, I swear to you.'

'No. No. Don't,' Alice heard him begging her as her tears fell even faster in reaction to her shock at realising that somehow he had discovered that she loved him.

'I didn't want it to happen either,' she wept, barely aware of the fact that they were now both inside the bedroom, and Marco was for some reason holding her in his arms.

'I didn't want to love you,' she told him. 'I…'

She could feel the tension in his body. The arms that had been holding her so comfortingly slackened and Marco stepped back from her. Alice shivered, missing their comfort.

'Alice, what are you saying?'

There was a shocked, almost warning note in his voice, but Alice ignored it.

What did it matter what she said now? After all, he had made it obvious that he knew she loved him.

'I'm saying that I love you, Marco. That I'll always love you and that I wish more than anything else in the world that I had conceived your child,' she told him recklessly. 'At least then I'd have something of you, to love. I know you don't want me. I know you'll want to end our business arrangement now, but please, for Angelina's sake, let me stay with her as you originally planned. She needs me, Marco, and I promise that I won't...'

As the words poured out of her Marco could only stare at her in disbelief.

'That you won't what?' he challenged her huskily when he realised that she had stopped speaking.

Alice shook her head, her face crimsoning as she refused to put into words just what she meant.

'That you won't allow me to do this,' Marco suggested, shocking her as he took her back in his arms, and bent his head to feather tiny little kisses against her lips...

'Or this,' he murmured softly against them as his tongue gently probed their closed line and helplessly it started to part.

Alice was shaking with anguish and longing. What was Marco trying to do to her?

Why was he tormenting her like this? And then to her disbelief she heard him telling her thickly, his voice raw with emotion. 'Alice, Alice, my little love, my dearest and only love. I hardly dare let myself believe that this is real. That you should love me when I have done so little to deserve your love.'

Marco was calling her his dearest love. His only love. Dizzily Alice tried to make sense of what was happening, but Marco was kissing her so passionately that it was impossible for her to think!

* * *

Several minutes later, having reluctantly released her mouth, Marco groaned.

'You should be resting...'

But as he looked at her there was a question, a fiery longing in his eyes that made Alice's heart beat very fast, and she couldn't stop the self-conscious colour warming her face as she instinctively looked from Marco to the familiar bed.

'Don't look at me like that,' Marco protested rawly. 'I am only a man, and the fear and despair I have gone through these last weeks!' He paused and shook his head. 'I thought I knew the full pain of loss, but I was wrong. I knew nothing. If I had lost you, my own life would no longer have been worth living.'

Alice fought to drag air into her lungs as her emotions reacted to what he was saying to her.

'But for me you would never have been in that car. If I had paid Francine instead of...'

Alice could hear the guilt in his voice. He had said that he loved her, but was that love merely a by-product of his guilt?

'You don't...you don't have to love me...' she told him, trying to find the right words for her thoughts.

'Yes. I do,' Marco contradicted her immediately. 'I have to love you, Alice, because that is my fate; my destiny... I think I probably knew that within hours of us meeting,' he added wryly.

Alice stared at him.

'Of course, I tried to deceive myself,' Marco continued grimly. 'After all, no man likes to admit that he is no longer in control of his own life. I had assumed that when I chose to marry it would be a calm, rational decision made for logical, sensible reasons. Of course I would respect and care for my wife, and of course...'

'She would not be British, and accused of sleeping around?' Alice supplied ruefully for him.

'You are right to remind me of my misjudgement of you,' Marco acknowledged bleakly. 'It does me no credit, and fills me with shame.'

'I can understand that a man in your position, with your family history, would have traditional values and traditional expectations,' Alice told him quietly, carefully searching for the words she needed. 'The fact that you believed that I was sexually promiscuous—'

'No.' Marco stopped her sharply. 'I admit I tried to think that of you as a means of self-defence, to protect myself from loving you when it seemed that you did not love me, but it didn't take very long in your company, Alice, for me to recognise and be humbled by the true, shining purity of your spirit. And once I had recognised that...' He paused.

'On the day of our wedding when we exchanged our vows, I knew that I loved you, and that I would always love you. I was even foolish enough to feel proud of the fact that my love was so strong and irrefutable. Unfortunately I was not strong enough to control my... feelings.'

There was a huge lump of emotion in Alice's throat. His quiet words meant so much to her.

'Unfortunately,' Marco continued wryly, 'I was not strong enough to control my...feelings, when faced by the temptation of knowing that you....'

'That you believed I was sexually available?' Alice supplied for him.

Immediately Marco shook his head.

'No. Certainly not. That was never in my thoughts,' he denied sternly. 'No, what I was going to say was knowing that you were my wife.'

'But it shocked you to discover that you were my first lover,' Alice reminded him. 'And when you were so distant with me and told me that it must never happen again, I realised you didn't love me.'

'On the contrary, it was very much because I did love you,' Marco corrected her ruefully.

'I had already misjudged you and now I had…abused the trust you had placed in me by agreeing to our marriage. I knew I couldn't trust myself; that I couldn't control myself; that once I touched you I wouldn't be able to stop. That was why I tried to distance myself from you—for your protection. If I had thought for one moment that you returned my love…'

Alice looked at him, her face pink.

'I should have thought that the way I responded to you…in…in bed must have given you some hint!'

'Perhaps it would have done,' Marco agreed, 'if I hadn't already convinced myself that your natural passion and innocence was responsible for the irresistibly sexy way you gave yourself to me. In fact that just gave me another reason to feel guilt and blame. And if you had conceived my child…'

Leaning her face against his chest, Alice whispered softly, 'I so much hoped that I would…'

'Alice…' She felt him shudder as he groaned her name, his arms tightening around her.

'If you had so much as given me a hint that you wanted that…'

A shyly mischievous look lightened Alice's eyes as she lifted her head and looked at him.

'I thought I'd given you much more than a hint,' she teased him gently, remembering how she had wantonly encouraged him to lose himself in her.

'Perhaps I wasn't concentrating,' Marco returned throatily, giving her a look that sent a thrill of pure longing right through her body.

'Perhaps you could hint to me again?'

'What, now?' Alice breathed recklessly.

Now, when there was no need for him to conceal it any more, the blaze of love and desire in his eyes was making her feel as if she were about to melt.

Daringly she reached up to kiss him, shivering with delight as she felt the shuddering reaction of his body to her intimacy. Her mouth brushed his, savouring its familiar shape and taste.

'Alice,' Marco warned her rawly.

Recklessly she ran the tip of her tongue along the outline of his lips, gasping in excited pleasure when his mouth covered hers, capturing her marauding tongue.

'Take me to bed, Marco,' she whispered throatily, when she was finally able to speak.

'Are you sure you're well enough for this?' Marco demanded solicitously a few minutes later as he gently pushed her hair back off her face and looked down at her where she lay against the pillows, her face flushed from the passion of the kisses they had just exchanged.

Her top was unfastened, revealing the creamy line of her throat and the soft swell of her breasts.

One of Marco's hands lay possessively against the full curve of one of them and Alice shuddered in wanton pleasure as he caressed it.

'I think it could be the best form of therapy I could possibly have,' she responded demurely, her own mouth curving into a tender little smile as she reached up to pull him closer to her.

'I don't know what I would have done if I had lost you,' Marco told her emotionally over an hour later as she lay sated and blissfully happy in the curve of his warmth, whilst the afternoon sun streaming in through the window played softly on their naked bodies.

'My life would have been over if you had been killed in that accident, Alice. Promise me you will never, ever doubt again that I love you.'

'I promise,' Alice assured him.

EPILOGUE

Five years later.

'DO YOU know what day it is today?' Marco asked Alice teasingly as he bent his head to kiss her upturned face.

She was in the small special courtyard at the back of the *palazzo* which they had turned into a safe play area for their children, and Marco had just returned from Florence where he had been overseeing some restoration work.

'Of course I do.' She laughed as she returned his kiss.

Out of the corner of her eye she could see their children: their four-year-old son Giancarlo, and the twin daughters who had been born eighteen months ago, and, of course, Alice's secret favourite, Angelina, who was firmly preventing the twins from fighting over their toys.

Like all children, theirs were individual and unique, and that was how she loved them, individually and uniquely, just as she could love the new baby who was due to make his or her arrival in another four months' time, but Angelina would always be extra special to her, just as the bond of love between them was extra special.

When she had risked her own life to protect Angelina's Alice had reacted as a mother, putting her child's safety before her own, and somehow in that split heartbeat of time a bond had been forged between the two of them that was just as strong as the umbilical cord that had bonded her to her birth children. Whenever strangers remarked on how alike she and Angelina were, they always shared knowing special smiles. No mother should have favourites, but sometimes a mother could just not help herself!

186

'So?' Marco demanded. 'What date is it?'

'The date you asked me to marry you,' Alice responded promptly, laughing as she added wickedly, 'For Angelina's sake.'

'For Angelina's sake and for my own sanity,' Marco agreed wryly, releasing her as Angelina left the twins to their own devices and ran across to join them, lovingly cuddling into Alice's side.

'I hope this isn't going to be more twins,' she told Alice feelingly as she patted her growing bump.

Alice laughed. Both she and Marco already knew that the baby she was carrying was another son, but that was going to be their secret.

'I think it's time to take the twins upstairs for their nap,' Alice told Marco ruefully as she hugged Angelina lovingly.

'Mmm,' Marco agreed, watching as Sibilla attempted to hit her twin with the doll she had wrested from her. 'I think I'll come with you.'

'Oh, you two aren't going to get all soppy, are you?' Angelina protested, rolling her eyes in five-year-old disgust.

'Mmm. Sounds like a good idea to me,' Marco murmured to Alice as they watched her run back to join Giancarlo.

'And to me,' Alice agreed softly.

If someone, anyone, had tried to tell her five years ago just how her life was going to turn out she would never have believed them, never have dared to believe she could be so loved or so happy...

But she was, and according to Marco he fully intended to make sure that she remained so for the rest of their lives together!

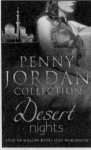
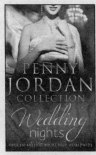

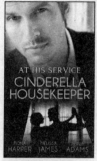

The World of Mills & Boon®

There's a Mills & Boon® series that's perfect for you. We publish ten series and, with new titles every month, you never have to wait long for your favourite to come along.

Blaze®

Scorching hot, sexy reads
4 new stories every month

By Request

Relive the romance with the best of the best
9 new stories every month

Cherish™

Romance to melt the heart every time
12 new stories every month

Desire™

Passionate and dramatic love stories
8 new stories every month

Have Your Say

You've just finished your book.
So what did you think?

We'd love to hear your thoughts on our
'Have your say' online panel
www.millsandboon.co.uk/haveyoursay

- Easy to use
- Short questionnaire
- Chance to win Mills & Boon® goodies

Visit us Online

Tell us what you thought of this book now at
www.millsandboon.co.uk/haveyoursay

YOUR_SAY